COOKIES, CANDLES, AND CUTE BUTTS FOR CHRISTMAS

Cameron D. James & Cali Kitsu

Winnipeg, Canada

Cookies, Candles, and Cute Butts for Christmas is our first co-written book. We are best friends who love Christmas, cookies, and our husbands' cute butts. We also love having fun together, which is exactly what we did when writing this book. The number of times that we laughed out loud during writing sprints, must be somewhere in the thousands.

This book is a high heat, super sweet, and very low angst MM romance.

If you don't like reading explicit sex between men, we can think of seventeen scenes that you might wanna skip, including a festive felching scene, but we'd recommend finding another book.

We hope that the story and characters we created make you feel happy, festive, warm, and maybe a little slutty, too.

As always, we would like to thank our husbands for their support of our endless shenanigans.

If you like this book, please check out our podcast *Cali & Craig Talk...* where we talk about cookies, butts, and writing.

<3, Cameron & Cali

Table of Contents

COOKIES, CANDLES, AND CUTE BUTTS FOR CHRISTMAS

CHAPTER ONE
UNEXPECTED MOTORBOATING

 BRADEN

This should be the last stop I need to make on my way to Frosty Bottoms. I pull into Speedy's gas station, stopping at the first pump on the driver's side. Before I can even get out to fill my tank, my phone rings; it's my nonna. "Hey, Nonna, I should be there in about forty-five minutes. Just stopping off for gas."

"Don't rush. I have Kellan here with me," she says. "I'll see you when you get here."

Kellan…my childhood best friend. Was he the one that got away? Or was it just a foolish one-sided crush, a love that never had a chance. I still have no idea. Either way, it appears he's at my nonna's, which is not a great surprise to me, but shit—I'm in my traveling clothes. Nothing but a pair of black gym shorts and a gray T-shirt, not exactly the outfit I would pick for when I was going to run into him for the first time in twelve years.

"Kellan is there? Now?" I check my watch. It's already past eight, why is he still there? He wasn't the doting type when we were young, so it's kind of odd sometimes to hear all that he does for my nonna. Don't get me wrong, it's nice, but it's just weird hearing that he spends so much time with her when we haven't spoken in twelve years. Not since that night. The night when everything changed. The night I was an idiot and kissed my best friend.

"Yes, dear, such a sweet man, always helping me," she says. "See you in a bit."

Aaand she hung up on me. Great. I step outside and start to fill my Jeep. I've thought about that night a lot over the past twelve years, and I'm still not sure what I did wrong. I can still feel my palm slipping on the swing chains, hand clammy and nervous as I stood in front of him and gripped the chains on his swing. I'd made up my mind that we'd sneak away from my going away party, and I'd tell him how I felt. We'd never talked about our feelings for one another, and honestly, I had no idea if he was into me, the way that I was into him. He was my best friend from the time we started kindergarten. As the years passed, the need to protect him began to feel more like protecting something I cherished, a responsibility that I was proud to have—he was mine, and I protected him because I wanted to, not because he was my best friend, who happened to be smaller than me, and was kind of a brat. Gosh, he drove me crazy sometimes. When he found out I was leaving for college, he became distant whenever I would bring it up. It didn't matter if it was after rugby practice, after working our shifts at the grocery store, or just hanging out— whenever I brought it up, or anyone else did, Kellan would shut down. He wouldn't even discuss it.

That night on the swings, I worked up the courage and lifted his chin, I had never been so close to his face before, never touched his face—and it was somehow soft. He looked at me confused; his baby blues held the slightest bit of tears from the awkward silence we'd shared until that moment. I brought my mouth close to his and inhaled, I was going to do it, and if I fucked everything up—well, I was leaving the next day anyway. He didn't look confused as I moved in closer, he looked hopeful, maybe? "Bray?" was all he said, it was all I needed to give me the courage to do it. I pressed my mouth to his and kissed him, afraid to push too fast, and unsure if what I was doing was even right, I touched my tongue to his, just barely brushing it. I can still remember how good it felt. This was *our* first kiss, the first time I kissed a guy, and not just any guy, it was Kellan. I was so fucking nervous, because as much as I was loving the way that he felt, I had no idea if he was into it, until he stood up, and held my face with both hands…never breaking from the kiss. He was kissing me back, and it was the best feeling I'd ever experienced; it was fucking euphoric. Which I can say at this point in my life, at thirty years old, I've not felt since then. Our tongues moved together like they were made for each other. I slid my hands down to his waist. Shit—his body was hot; I can still remember the way his waist felt in my hands. Sure, I'd seen him change clothes before, but I had no idea how good it would feel to hold him like this. I pulled him close and kissed him deeper, our bodies pressed so tightly that I could feel literally all of him pressed against me. I wanted more, our kiss became wild, and my hands moved on their own down to his firm round ass. I squeezed it and let out the lightest of moans, because fuck did I want him. He whimpered softly, while driving his tongue further in my mouth, pressing himself against me.

"Kellan, Braden! Are you guys out here? Everyone is looking for you!" Kellan's sister, Charlie's voice called, shocking the both of us. Instantly causing us to break apart.

Shit—not now. That stupid party.

Kellan was holding his mouth; he looked to be in shock. Whether that was from the kiss itself, or his sister, I still have no idea. "This—this shouldn't have happened," he said and started walking toward his house.

"Kellan, wait up, we need to talk. I want to—"

"No, I was fine," he said as I caught up to him. Tears streamed down his face. "You're leaving tomorrow, Braden, and now Charlie—I can't deal with this. Just tell my parents I wasn't feeling well."

"Kellan, don't just leave—don't just walk away."

But he did, and he never looked back. He never called, never reached out—nothing. Just silence. It sucked, but what could I do? He said he didn't want to talk to me. Was I supposed to keep pushing him? No. I couldn't do that. It hurt like hell, though…but Kellan was pretty stubborn, and if he'd set his mind on pretending nothing happened, then there was nothing I could do about it. But still that kiss—I've never forgotten it, and now, he's at my nonna's house. If only she hadn't fallen and hurt her ankle yesterday. All of this could have waited until I was ready to deal with it. God, how stupid does that sound? Deal with what? A kiss from when we were eighteen years old? He's probably forgotten all about it. I've seen him on his socials with Chad—ugh.

It's freezing outside. How can this part of the state be this much colder? It's only, like, four hours north. The screen on the pump displays a commercial for my hometown. "You're just sixty miles away from Frosty Bottoms, home of the largest Snowflake Festival in the state!" A montage of the businesses in town, along with Mr. and Mrs. Claus, plays along with the sounds of Christmas music.

The gas pump clicks off, and I get back into my Jeep and start the rest of my drive. At least it's warm in here. I rub my cat's nose through the gate on his carrier. "We don't like that Chad, do we, Mister Fluffykins?" He meows at me. He's always right. "Okay, well, we don't hate him, because technically we don't really know him. Never really had a conversation with him. But we just won't give him any free cookies from the new shop. What do you think, Fluffy?" He's so cute, brushing his orange fur against the carrier. "We'll be there soon, buddy," I say, poking my finger through the crate door and rubbing his head.

The shop—BJ's cookies. It's my shop now. Who would've thought a year ago that I'd be giving up my career as a veterinarian to go back home to Frosty Bottoms, to take over my nonna's cookie shop? Not me. But still, the timing couldn't have been better for my nonna to retire. A few months ago, I had a huge disagreement with my business partner, Molly. We'd started the practice fresh out of college, because we both had similar ideals. Unfortunately, with the rise of medical equipment and medications—things were getting too tight for her to continue offering discounted visits to clients and their furry patients, which was a problem for me, because I wasn't going to turn away any pet owner, regardless of their ability to pay. So, we disagreed on how we would move forward come the new year. She offered to buy me out of the partnership, and on the very same day, my nonna called to tell me she was going to retire after the busy holiday season. She wanted me to take over the shop. That had to be a sign, right? I mean, things like that just don't happen on the same day. I met with Molly, and we struck a deal. My only stipulation was that if there was ever a patient in need, and their owner couldn't pay—that she would notify me and give me the opportunity to help. I still feel bad about Ms. Finch, who lives on a fixed income and can barely afford anything outside of normal visits for her cat, Walter, who seems to constantly get in trouble. A four-hour drive would be worth it, if it means helping them both. Still, this timing is less than ideal, because my new house isn't built yet, it's expected to be ready by the second week in January, which is when I was going to start at the shop, but my nonna hurt her ankle yesterday at the tree lighting festival. Since the doctor ordered her to stay off it, I decided to push the timeline ahead and take over things as of tomorrow.

My hometown is a very Christmas-centered town. Everyone gets their Christmas cookies from BJ's, so it's not like my nonna could just close the shop for the season. Driving into Frosty Bottoms, everything looks exactly the same as I remember it from last time I was here. Christmas lights on the shops, and everyone in bed by 9:00

pm, except for the gay bar next door to the shop, that place seems to still be open. The streets are so narrow here. Makes the downtown area feel smaller, with everything right on top of each other.

My nonna's apartment is located directly above the cookie shop. Her lights are still on, but her blinds are closed tightly. Damn, I thought I might get lucky and catch a glimpse of him. I turn into the parking lot behind the building and pull into a parking spot beside my nonna's car. I look left to right, scanning for any car that looks like it could be Kellan's—of course, it would have to be something really obvious, like a personalized license plate, because I don't know anything about the adult version of him. How much do people change?

I lift my cat's crate onto my lap. "Well Fluffy, I don't think we're gonna get to see him tonight. Which is better, because I really should practice what I'm gonna say, when I finally see him." Because the truth is, that I want to talk to him…catch up and work toward reconnecting. I blocked out everything shortly after leaving for college. Once I knew he wasn't going to call or try to meet up, I just forced him out of my mind. But now, here I am, walking upstairs with my cat crate in one hand, suitcase in the other, just really hoping that I'll get the chance to talk to him soon, and preferably not make an ass out of myself while doing that.

KELLAN

"Do you remember the code for the keypad?" Leora asks.

"I've only been here like seven hundred times. Of course I remember the code," I say, rolling my eyes.

I have Leora cradled in my arms; it was the only way to get her safely up the flight of stairs to her second floor unit, just above her cookie shop. The keypad-secured door leads to a little foyer with two doors; one opens to an internal set of stairs to the cookie shop, and the other leads into Leora's unit.

The memory of yesterday is still vivid in my mind. I had accompanied Leora to the town's Christmas tree lighting. She had insisted on placing the star on top of the tree herself; she even had maintenance folks bring out a ladder for her. No matter how many times I told her that at eighty-something she shouldn't be doing this, she did it anyway. And when she placed the star on the tree and everyone gave her applause, she stepped back down and lost her footing. It wasn't a big fall, but it was still terrifying, and it still resulted in a fractured ankle. She spent the night in the hospital and was discharged today.

Once in the foyer, Leora slips a key into the lock on the door to her unit and we're soon inside, the crutches hooked over my shoulder clattering against the doorframe as we pass through. Her place is always warm and inviting and always smells like fresh-baked cookies, which is perhaps a side benefit of owning and running a cookie shop. As always, my stomach rumbles as soon as that scent hits me. Leora's cookies are wicked good, or whatever the kids today call them.

"On the couch?" I ask her as I carry her inside.

She swats my chest. "I'm not an infant. Now that I'm up the stairs, I'll be alright."

I give her my most patient sigh, the one I always give her when she is being feisty. "The doctor said to stay off it as much as possible."

"They always say that," she says.

Nevertheless, I set her down on the couch and place the crutches beside her. "Water? Coffee? Tea? Something to eat?"

She waves her hand dismissively. "Thank you, Kellan. Truly, thank you. But I can handle it from here."

I flit about her place, tidying things that need tidying. The magazines on the coffee table aren't perfectly piled. The mail on the kitchen table is scattered. There are dirty dishes in the sink. Oh God, the dishes.

I start filling the sink with hot water and add dish soap.

"Kellan…" she says.

I wave my hand dismissively at her. "Just let me help."

If I can be honest with myself, it isn't *just* the fact that Leora took a tumble and fractured her ankle. Yes, that was scary and, yes, that can be quite traumatic when you get older, but it's more about *him*.

She'd told me several months back that she was thinking of finally retiring. As long as I could remember, her cookie shop was *the place to be* on the town's main drag. I'd met many cute guys there over the years. When I later started up my own shop selling handmade candles, I landed a prime piece of real estate, right across the street from her. From our business relationship sprouted a friendship, which eventually evolved into me taking care of a number of things around her shop—moving heavy things, minor repairs, a backed-up sink, a broken window. I seemed to spend just as much time over at her shop as I did in my own.

With the sink full and bubbly, I grab the dishcloth and set to furiously scrubbing the plates from her breakfast, before the tumble. From what I remember, *he* is a neat freak. I can't have him come here and see the place looking messy. I can't have him look at me with annoyance.

In some ways, it would have been easier for her to close the shop upon retiring. But it's a family business, established over a hundred years ago. You don't just close up shop that easily.

Then she told me *he* was coming back.

Braden. Her grandson.

Braden and I had been best friends for most of our childhood. But things got weird around age eighteen, and there was that one kiss…and then he left the next day for college. It was a mess and shouldn't have happened, but I still remember it both clearly and fondly, even if we pretty much never spoke again.

We never talked about him leaving—I'd avoided it. There was no promise to call, no talks of visiting each other, no pinky promises. Pinky promises…we'd use those only when something really mattered to us. Dumb stuff to other people, probably to him, too, now that I think about it. I'm pretty sure I was the one who always initiated them. But, still, we'd link pinkies, and to this day, no pinky promise was ever broken, even the dumbest ones. Of course, maybe they were all dumb? We were just kids after all. But I didn't really need pinky promises to know Braden was going to keep his word, he'd always been reliable, truthful, protective. More importantly, he was always there—until he wasn't.

I occasionally stalk his Insta, but I'm not brave enough to follow him or reach out with a DM and strike up our old friendship. However, I'd made peace with the fact that Braden was coming back to town, coming back to my life. But I was prepared for it to happen in *January*. On the way home from the hospital, Leora had told me Braden had immediately piled everything into his car last night and hit the road this morning, determined to take care of her for these few weeks before she officially retired and he took over the business.

I told her that *I* could take care of her for these two weeks. But she didn't want to hear it.

I place the last dish in the dry rack, then drain the sink and give it all a quick wipe down. I circle the space one more time, looking for anything grimy or dusty and out of place.

"You're making me nervous with all that pacing," she says. "Go home."

"But, Leora, I should stay till Braden gets here." I really don't want to. No way in hell do I want to see him. I mean, I would eventually, especially since we'd be working across the street from each other, but, like I said, I was ready for that to start in *January*. For it to start now in early December is just a disaster, plain and simple.

"I'm fine. How many times do I have to tell you I'm fine?" She grabs the crutches and hooks them under her armpits. I watch as she struggles to stand, only to fall back onto the soft couch a moment later.

"You were saying?"

"Smartass."

I give her a smile. For all the banter we have, I really do care about her, and I know she truly appreciates all the help I give her.

I cross the room to her. "Come on," I say. I pick up the crutches. "If you want to *be* fine, let's get you used to crutches. I'm not leaving until you're able to get around safely."

She gives me a smile as she looks up at me. "Thank you, Kellan."

I hold out my hand, she takes it, and we get her standing on one foot. She then tucks the crutches under her arms. I slowly back up a step, holding my hands out to catch her if she falls in any direction other than the couch.

"How does that feel?"

She looks down at herself. "Like I'm old. But it's temporary."

I blow a raspberry. "You'll never be old. Now, try taking a step."

Cautiously and wobbly, she steps forward with her good foot, letting the crutches take her weight. When that foot lands solidly, she swings the crutches forward.

"Excellent!" I shout. I clap too.

She gives me serious side-eye. "I'm not five."

For that, I give her an encouraging whistle.

"Now," I say, "let's see you do a circle around the couch. That way if you tire or lose your balance, you can reach out to the couch for support."

She nods with determination, then sets about the task. She wobbles several times, especially when she turns the first corner of the couch, but she makes it all the way around. When she returns to the starting point, she looks up at me with a grin brighter than the star on the town's Christmas tree.

"I'll be hurrying around town before you know it," she says.

I give her a hug. "I'm so happy to see you do this."

"Maybe Braden won't worry so much about me," she says. "I don't need him doting on me."

At the mention of Braden's name, my anxiety ratchets back up to a thousand. My heart races, my breath comes shallow, and my mind plays through all the awkward conversations we'd be forced to have when we cross paths again.

My anxiety eats at me, makes me restless. "I should go since you're fine," I say.

"You have my key?" she asks.

I double-check my keyring. "Definitely do!" She'd given it to me a couple years back as a just-in-case. "But with…with Braden here, you likely won't need me."

She gives me the oddest of looks, and it lasts only the briefest of moments. "I'll be fine. I promise! Now go! You shouldn't be spending your one day off a week taking care of someone else's grandma."

"Call me if you need anything, Leora," I say as I head to the door. I quickly pull my boots on. I open the door and look back at her. "I mean it. Anything. Even if it's because you're bored and want to play cards."

I turn and leave—and collide face-first with *him*.

Muscled, gorgeous, strangely-smells-like-cookies-too, *him*.

BRADEN

I turn the doorknob, and the door opens from the other side—before I can react, there's a face pressed against my chest. "What the hell?" It's *him*…it's Kellan. Damn, he smells good, like cookies…or maybe that's the scent from my nonna's kitchen? Either way, it's been a few seconds, and Kellan's head remains pressed tightly in between my pecs. I'm frozen in place, and he is, too. There is, however, a certain part of me that is not frozen right now, and that would be thanks to his warm breath working its way through my shirt. Damn this thin shirt; I can almost feel his lips on my skin. He shakes his head side to side. Is he smelling me, or like motorboating me? "You…uh, see something you like?" I ask.

His voice is muffled as he replies against my chest, "I actually don't see anything. I'm sure this is a dream, I'm just gonna stay here until I wake up in the morning."

Same sense of humor that I remember. "Definitely not a dream, but you could stay until morning, if you want."

He quickly lifts his head. "What? Did you just ask me to stay the night?"

"What? No. I definitely didn't." I smile, and he smiles back, then shifts his gaze to the floor.

"It's, uh…good to see you, Kellan."

"Yeah, good to smell…you—see you, too, Braden. I gotta go. I'm really late for something. See you around."

Aaand there he goes, fumbling his way down the hall. He's just walking away; well, stumbling is probably more accurate. My mouth couldn't be open any wider.

"Braden dear, is that you?" My nonna's voice calls from inside.

"Yeah, I'm here, Nonna," I say, walking inside and closing the door behind me. I lean my suitcase against the wall and slip out of my shoes. "Come on out, buddy," I say, placing the crate down, and opening the gate for Fluffykins. I pick him up and give him a few kisses. He's craning his neck and wiggling in my arms. "Ahh, you don't care about me, you want to check out Nonna's." I place him down, and he happily trots around the apartment.

My nonna is sitting on her couch with the recliner out. Her foot is elevated; that's good. I walk over and give her a hug. I always forget how small she is, probably because she's got such a big personality. "How are you feeling, Nonna? Are you in any pain?"

She pats my back, squeezing me tightly. "No, of course I'm not in any pain! Oh, you look handsome, just like your father." She pinches my left cheek.

"Ahh, Nonna. I'm too old to have my face pinched," I say, standing up straight.

She gives me a false smile. "Awww, poor thing. Now, let's get a few things straight. Now that you're here, we're gonna lay down some ground rules, because it's too late to back out."

"Oh, here we go. I knew there would be something. What is it? Shop is falling apart? Roaches? You're on the brink of financial ruin?"

"You little shit," she says, swatting at me.

I take a few steps backward. "Can't reach me over here. Now spill it. What's wrong?"

"Oh, you worry too much!" she says. "Nothing is wrong! What do you take me for? All I want to say is, this is your home while you're here. I don't want you doting on me. Make yourself at home like that adorable little furball in the kitchen. Don't be fluttering around, making a fuss like Kellan."

"What do you mean, 'like Kellan'?"

"Oh, didn't you see him on your way in? Or did you two miss each other?"

Miss him? How could I have missed him? My dick is still tingling from his hot breath, while my brain is still about ten steps behind, currently in denial that his face was in my chest three minutes ago. I'm not gonna say that to my nonna, though.

"Yeah, I did. He seems the same. Face landed in my chest, and I think he might have been a little embarrassed. He left really fast, barely said a word to me."

"Kellan? That chatterbox? Hmm, maybe he *was* embarrassed if he didn't say much. Or he was just tired. Was running around here all day like a twink on parade."

"Pftt…what? Did you just say like a twink on parade?"

"Yes, he is a twink. That's what he tells me all the time! I can say that!"

"Nonna, Kellan is thirty-years old; he is not a twink. And that's not even—what a clown. Calling himself a twink." I can't help but laugh.

"Can't he be a twink and be thirty?"

"I don't know if there are any hard rules about it. I just wouldn't have called him that. Twink business aside, what was he parading around for?"

"Oh, he was just all over the place. I've never seen him so interested in cleaning, but today he was cleaning like it was the most important thing in the world. Then, he insisted on having warm cookies ready for you. Don't know what he was going on about. Swore you would want the caramel chocolate chip ones and was determined to have them ready. I said to him, Kellan—don't you think I know my Bobola's favorite cookies? Mint chocolate chip, get out of here with those caramel ones! But he wouldn't listen. By the way, the mint chocolate chips are downstairs if you want some. I can't get down the stairs, or I would've brought them up myself."

He remembered my favorite cookies.

"Anyway, I wouldn't think much of it. He was just trying to help. You're gonna need him a lot at the shop for the next few days. That's something I may have forgotten to mention."

"What do you mean? Why will I need him?"

"Well, because I can't show you how things run, or where anything is, and Kellan is always helping me. I did have Lucas helping out, but once I knew I was retiring, I got him a job at the bar. Now Lucas, oof, Lucas is a twunk. Gotta keep that one away from Kellan. Although, I don't know if they really get along. Anyway, these are things we can deal with tomorrow. For now, why don't you go grab a shower and get settled in? Have a cookie first, so I don't have to lie to Kellan when he asks if you did."

I don't even know how to process half of what she just said. All I can do is laugh at this point. "Well, you already have twinks and twunks, I don't know what you need me for. Never thought I'd hear those things come out of your mouth, that's for sure."

Walking into the kitchen, the scent of the recently cooked caramel, is freaking amazing. My smile is out of control right now. There are twelve caramel chocolate chip cookies, placed neatly on a green Christmas tree shaped tray on the counter. I can't believe he made these for me. Why would he do that, and just run away? I really wanted to talk to him. Damn, he looked good. Even as he was tripping over his own two feet, he still looked good.

I have to try one. They all look perfect, but this one looks like it has a few more chocolate chips than the others. Ooh, they're still warm. I take a large bite of the cookie. Oh, sweet mother—this is the best thing I've had in my mouth in a long time. Kellan made these for me. But why? Why would he do that? Gah…his face was in my chest, and I didn't even have time to react.

My nonna shouts from the living room, "The guest room is all set up for you and Fluffykins has a brand-new litter box ready. How are the cookies, dear?"

I finish the last bite of this amazing cookie, which may be the best cookie I've ever had, and walk into the living room. "They're really great. But why did he bake them for me?"

"Who knows?" she says, shrugging her shoulders.

"Maybe he figured you would have made them if you were able to, so he wanted to help you out." That makes sense. It was less about me, and more about helping my nonna.

"Uhhh…I'd say that's the least likely reason, Bobola. If he was doing it for me, he would've made the mint chocolate chip ones."

I exhale loud and long. He's already got my head a mess, and I've barely spoken to him. "I think I'm gonna grab that shower now, is that alright? Should I help you get to bed first?"

"Oh, come on now, I told you I can do it. No doting. If it makes you feel better, watch me use the stupid crutches."

I'm definitely not getting in the shower until I know she can get around. I lean against the wall and gesture toward the door. "Go right ahead. Pretend I'm not even here. If you can get to your bedroom, I won't bother you again."

She grabs the crutches from beside the couch and stands. "You boys are so ridiculous. I can do it," she says, making her way carefully toward her bedroom with the crutches. She turns to look at me as she enters her room. "See? I told you I could do it."

"Wow, look at that, you're still pretty spry, even on crutches."

"Of course I am. Now, it's about two hours past my bedtime," she says. "I'm going to pop a painkiller and go to bed. Do you have everything you need? The keys to the shop are on the counter if you want to check things out downstairs."

I grab my suitcase from beside the couch and smile. "I'm fine, Nonna. Thanks. If you need anything, just text me. After my shower,

I'll probably check the shop out." I head toward the second guest room on the opposite side of the apartment.

"You're gonna love the shower! It's so much better in that bathroom. There's a new shower head in there. The last time you came it was different. Kellan installed it for me. It's one of those waterfall ones. I got it so I could impress your mom this year when she comes over. She's always complaining about the water pressure in there. Not anymore, she's gonna love it."

"I can't wait to try it out! Goodnight."

I lift my suitcase onto the bed, beside my adorable cat. "Look at you, already settled!" I say to Mister Fluffykins, who has made himself quite cozy on one of the pillows. Ah, I don't blame him. The comforter and pillows are so fluffy, I want to lie down, but I need a shower before calling it a night. I give him a little kiss on the head and open my suitcase.

As I pull my things out, I find myself still confused over what just happened. So, he was here all day, cleaning and baking my favorite cookies, then he lands face first in my chest—says basically nothing, and leaves. Oh my God…wait, did I actually tell him he could stay the night? I can't believe that's what I said. He definitely left his face there on purpose. His breath was so warm—I really wanted to squeeze him, once I realized it was him. But why did he leave so suddenly? Was he really not happy to see me? I wasn't expecting that to be what happened when we saw each other. I was expecting something much more romantic, or at least sexy. He looked hot, even though he was fumbling his way down the hall. What a weird feeling to be so close to him after all this time. I rub the spot on my chest where his mouth was. I can still feel his breath, and the outline of his lips.

Damn it, how the hell am I turned on right now? That was the first thing I've said to him in twelve years, and I sounded like a schmuck. My dick is the real idiot here, though. It's getting hard for no reason. I look down and speak directly to it, "What are you excited about? He doesn't care about you; he doesn't care about anything. He said he was busy, probably off to get railed by his boyfriend, Chad. That lucky bastard."

I grab my clothes out of the suitcase, zip it back up, and head for the bathroom. This is gonna take some getting used to, almost all of my stuff is in storage.

This is such a nice bathroom. It feels like a spa in here, and it smells really good, too. What *is* that smell? I notice a candle on the counter. It's not lit, but somehow it smells amazing. *Dip Your Wick, Luscious Lavender* the label says. I laugh out loud seeing it. That's Kellan's shop, I love the name. Never thought he'd be making candles, but then again, I never thought I'd be making cookies.

I slide the glass door open to check out the shower head. Ooh, that is nice. He did a good job. I exhale staring into the shower. I am a ridiculous human. Thinking of him in this shower, installing the showerhead, is making me feel things. I pull my shirt off in front of the mirror. His face was squarely in between my pecs. I'm pretty solid after years of working out every day. I poke my chest a few times to see what his face would have felt. Well, I said something stupid, but he definitely felt how solid I am.

I don't know what the gym is like here, but I'll need to find out quickly. Until then, I'll just have to run in the mornings—oh wait, that's when I'll be getting the shop ready to open. Taking care of my body has always been a priority for me, and now I'll be working around cookies non-stop. I definitely need to come up with a routine, fast.

I really want to thank him for the cookies, maybe he'll let me take him out for dinner. Then I can eat his ass for dessert and fuck the hell out of him for not talking to me for twelve years. I run a hand down my face. Holy hell. What is wrong with me? I went from just wanting to talk to him, to wanting to fucking wreck him.

I wasn't expecting to want him this bad. I step into the shower and turn the water on cold. I need to cool off. I grab the bath pouf and wash myself quickly, because I know my brain all too well—any extra time in here is going to bring my mind right back to him, and I should really go downstairs and check out the shop.

I step outside of the shower and jump into a pair of gray sweatpants and my comfy sweatshirt. I really wish the shop wasn't going to be open tomorrow. A day to get acclimatized would have been nice. I dry my hair quickly with a towel, stepping into the bedroom. Ahh, Fluffykins is out like a light. "I'll be back soon," I say, and kiss him on his adorable little head.

The whole place still smells like caramel; it's amazing. I think that might be my favorite food smell. Walking past the kitchen, I see the cookies that Kellan made. The cookies that Kellan made for *me*. I wonder what he was thinking about while he was making these? Damn it, now I'm thinking about him, again. I grab the shop keys off the counter and shake my head at myself, then lock my nonna's apartment door and head downstairs.

I slip my ass off the barstool and stand. I've been fidgety since seeing Braden—hell, since before seeing Braden—and while the gin and Cokes were helping, they weren't the cure-all I'd hoped they'd be.

I'm still recovering from running into him—*literally running into him*. My hand still quivers, and my heart still skips a beat now and then.

It helps that the gay bar, Bottoms Up, is literally next door to BJ's Cookies, AKA Leora's place, AKA Braden's place for the next couple of weeks before he moves into his eventual new house in January, though he'll be in the shop every work day.

I drain the last of my third gin and Coke and gently place the glass on the bar top.

"Third time's the charm?" Chad asks. He's the bartender, and a close friend.

I give him a nod, but I know my facial expression will likely reveal the truth. I was never good at schooling my expressions.

"You'll get used to him being back," Chad says.

I rub my hands over my face. "I told myself I was ready and I firmly believed I was ready, but seeing him in person…"

"Running face first into him," Chad teases, "motorboating him."

"I'm never telling you embarrassing stories again," I say. I turn away from Chad, spinning on the stool. I then realize the place is empty. The only other person here, besides Chad and I, is Lucas, the twunk twenty-something who used to work at BJ's and is now Chad's apprentice bartender. He's sweeping the floor. "Closing time?"

"It *is* midnight."

I pull out my phone and check the time, as if the bar literally closing around me wasn't concrete enough proof of the time. And while I have my phone in my hand, I pop into Grindr to check the local profiles, nearly all of which are anonymous and headless, of course, except for Chad and Lucas, who are at the top of my results. Grunting to myself, I close the app and shove the phone back in my pocket.

"Need some help?" I ask them. I should go home. I need to go home. Senator Tunacan is patiently waiting for his dinner of, well, tuna, but if I go home and it's just me and Tunacan and my rambling anxious thoughts…well, it wouldn't be a good thing.

"Wanna stack some chairs?" Chad asks.

I nod once as I step away from the bar. I cross the dance floor to the far side of the room where the tables and chairs stand. I'd helped close down the bar several times before, so I'm familiar with the drill. The chairs get stacked in piles of five, right against the wall.

I do the task, and I'm happy for the mindlessness of it. It helps get my mind off a certain someone. But then the task is over far too soon. When I look up, Lucas is putting on his coat, and Chad seems ready to go, too.

"Done?" I ask as I cross the room to them.

Chad nods and hands me my coat. "Time to call it a night, mister."

I know that tone, know what Chad is after. He only calls me "mister" when he wants to take me home with him.

A good dicking would do me good. It usually helps.

But something doesn't feel right, so I don't give Chad the return flirting that signals I'm down for fun. "I should get to bed."

Chad gives me a little frown, but it disappears from his face almost as soon as it had appeared. "Sleep off the gin," Chad agrees, "leave your ex best friend in the past."

What he says leaves a weird feeling in my gut. Like I'm not sure if I'm ready to do what he suggests. Braden is back and will be part of my daily life; I can't just leave him in the past. Not anymore.

I slip into my coat and follow Lucas out the door. Chad comes through behind me, setting the alarm and locking up.

"Goodnight, Kellan," Lucas says. Then he glances at Chad with a look I know all too well. He has a crush. "Goodnight, Chad. See you tomorrow?"

Chad nods at the twunk. "See you tomorrow."

Lucas disappears around the corner, heading into the alley.

"Does he live in the dumpster?" I ask.

Chad laughs. "He rides a motorcycle, one of those souped up, colorful, Japanese kind. He parks it in the back."

I chuckle and lean against the brick wall behind me; the cold of the brick seeps through my coat and chills my back. I'm right at the edge of the bar; BJ's Cookies is just over my shoulder.

BRADEN

It's dark as I step inside the shop. The storefront windows are huge, so the streetlights give me just enough light to make my way around as I search for a light switch. Why the hell isn't the switch by the door?

Before I can find the switch, a laugh from outside draws my attention. I may not have heard that sound for the past twelve years, and the tone may be deeper, but I'd know it anywhere. It's Kellan. He's right outside the shop window standing very close to someone else. I have no idea who, because their back is facing the window.

But I can see Kellan, and he really is the perfect mix of adorable and sexy. I feel so strange looking at him. There's a part of me that wants to just go out there and insert myself into their conversation, because damn, this other guy is standing really close to him. Oh, I see—it's Chad he's talking to. I guess they *are* together, but based on Kellan's body language, and the way he's backing up, I'm not so sure.

I haven't seen Chad since our teams played against one another in college. I could play it cool and just go say hi, but we've really never even spoken. Ahh, I really shouldn't, Kellan obviously didn't want to see me. Not with the way he flew out of the door earlier. Then again, why did he bake the cookies for me? He must have wanted to see me. Damn, this shouldn't be so hard. I have to do something. I can't just sit here staring at him. He's shaking his head no at Chad; it looks like he's not interested in whatever he's offering. So, are they together or not? I should just ask my nonna. I drop my head back at my own stupidity. Why didn't I do that earlier? I really don't wanna watch them talking to each other, feels weird looking at him through the window. Maybe I should just turn the shop lights on? Damn it, where is the effing switch?

KELLAN

As we linger outside the bar, Chad steps closer to me, so close I can feel his heat. It feels good. Comforting. He leans in close like he wants to steal a kiss, but I don't move my mouth forward. He gets the hint.

"Do you want to come home with me?" Chad asks. "It's always so effing hot when we hook up. It would help get your mind off things, help you leave a certain someone in the past."

Part of me wants to take Chad up on his offer; my cock is so very hard right now. But the larger part of me makes me shake my head no, even though I don't quite understand why.

"Not tonight," I say. "I'm not in the right frame of mind."

Chad leans even closer, brushing his fingertips along my jaw. "We don't need your mind. We just need your body."

My mind is firm. "Sorry. Maybe another night."

There's a sadness in Chad's features, but he smothers it quickly. Chad steps back, putting space between us again. A silence soon settles between us, a silence in which I wonder if I should change my mind.

But I don't.

The throaty roar of a motorcycle echoes from the alleyway on the other side of Bottoms Up. The noise grows louder as Lucas drives up the alley and then emerges, pulling to a stop in front of us.

Lucas flips the visor of his helmet up. "You two boys going home together?" Lucas asks, a tightness to his voice.

"Not tonight," Chad says. "It's a date with my toys tonight."

Lucas's gaze settles on me for a moment. I know the look; he's assessing what existed between me and Chad, and he's wondering if he has a shot at what he wants. I give him the subtlest of nods. While Chad and I hooked up a handful of times, it was just that, a hookup. I have no ownership over the man.

His eyes sparkle as his gaze shifts back to Chad. "Looking to burn off a bit of energy before bed?"

Chad steps toward Lucas and his bike. "That thing capable of carrying both of us?"

"Of course. You just have to snuggle up close."

Chad looks back at me. "You okay getting home on your own?"

I wave my hand. "I live three blocks away and I've barely had anything to drink. I'm fine."

Chad smiles. "See you tomorrow, Kellan." He then hitches a leg up and over Lucas's bike and does just as Lucas had suggested—he snuggles in *close*. Like grinding-against-his-ass close. Like almost-already-having-sex close. He wraps his arms tight around Lucas's fit body and slim-fit coat. "Can I hold on tight like this?"

"Safety first," Lucas says. It might've been my imagination, but I could've sworn I'd heard a tremor in Lucas's voice, like he's a little overwhelmed at his luck tonight.

"Goodnight, gentlemen," I say.

A moment later, with another throaty roar, Lucas and Chad speed off into the night. I shove my hands in my pockets and hunch my shoulders to provide some semblance of warmth to my ears and then set off on the walk home.

 **BRADEN**

Can't say I'm upset at the way that ended. Glad I didn't have to see him leave with Chad…I really don't want to see him with anyone—except for me. Preferably bent over…what is *wrong* with me? Why am I feeling this way? It's so strong…it's as if my brain has forgotten that we haven't spoken in twelve years, like we're still best friends, and my dick is just interested in pounding him.

I really don't have time to dive into what I feel for Kellan, or why I feel the way I feel. I need to check out the shop. Now that the lights are on, the shop looks exactly the same as I remember it. Some of this equipment seems new. It can't be too hard to use. I'm sure there are manuals in one of these drawers. I open a drawer at the far end of the counter. Sifting through the folders inside, I find one that contains some equipment manuals. This is exactly what I was looking for. I pull the folder out and carry it toward my nonna's office—well, I guess it's my office now.

I like that the office is in the back of the shop, keeps me further away from angry customers. I open the door to the office and flip the light switch on as I step inside. Oh wow, there's a loveseat in here. This is amazing. I can take a nap on my lunch break, if I need to. Speaking of naps, that couch looks pretty damn comfy. I am so exhausted from driving, I stretch my arms up high, and yawn. There are a few papers scattered across her desk. Nothing is set up for me, due to the fact that my nonna got hurt unexpectedly. I glance at the papers strewn against the mahogany, unsure if it's okay for me to look at them. I better just ask my nonna tomorrow. I don't want to catch a glimpse of something private. I flip the light off and head back into the kitchen area.

I suddenly feel slightly panicked about running things here with zero help. But, it's okay, I can do this; I can definitely do this. I am absolutely not worried that the shop will be open tomorrow, and I won't have any time to get acclimated.

You know, I don't need to bring this file up to bed with me. I'll be back early in the morning, and I can look at it then. I put the file back in the drawer, then head upstairs.

I walk into my nonna's apartment, trying to be as quiet as possible. I head for the guest room, quickly step into the bathroom, and brush my teeth. I can't wait to get into bed. I slide into the nice warm bed, beside Mister Fluffykins. He stands up, then rubs against my face. "Yes buddy, I know. I'm a mess, right? He's got my head all confused, and it hasn't even been twenty-four hours." I sigh loudly, rubbing my cat's head. "Well, what do you think happened today, Fluffykins? Do you think he even cared that he saw me? Am I stupid for thinking that our friendship all those years ago could have still meant something? I need to talk to him. His place is right across the street. I'll try to talk to him after I close the shop tomorrow. I don't think he's dating Chad, just based on body language, but I could be wrong. Either way, I just want to talk to him." Fluffykins purrs loudly and rolls onto his back. "Yeah, I know, Nonna said he helps at the shop, but I don't plan on asking him for any help."

 **KELLAN**

No more than ten minutes later, I step into my darkened condo. Senator Tunacan charges through the house and skids to a halt at my feet, meowing like he hasn't been fed in years.

"Did you miss me?" I ask him as I lead him through the house and into the kitchen. I pop open a can of food and fork it out onto a plate, then put the plate on the floor. I watch as my fluffy orange friend scarfs down his food.

When the plate is clean, I let out a sigh. "Maybe a shower will help," I tell The Senator. He meows in response.

Heading to the washroom, I strip and step into the steamy shower. It rinses away the dirt and sweat of the day. Leora had a small frame and a tidy apartment, but carrying her up the stairs and doing a frantic clean-up of her place took a lot out of me.

Inevitably, my hand finds my cock and gives it a few tugs. And when I do, my mind goes to one place and one place only—the center point between Braden's pecs. He had smelled so good.

I yank my hand away. "I will *not* jerk off to him."

Instead, I think of a porn video I'd jerked off to last night, and it does the job.

With the shower done and the bathroom full of steam, I turn off the tap and pull on my bathrobe. I cinch it at the waist and wander through the darkened condo to the bedroom, where I find Senator Tunacan already in bed and waiting for me.

I pull on a fresh pair of briefs from the dresser, then ditch the robe and climb into bed. He climbs on top of me and starts making biscuits against my chest.

"You're such a pretty boy," I tell him. He gives me a meow in return. "I ran into another pretty boy today. Did you know that?"

Again, he gives me a meow. "Yeah, he's the one I was telling you about."

Done making biscuits, Senator Tunacan snuggles into the crevice between my body and the pillows piled next to me. I lay my hand on him, my fingers stroking the soft fur, and soon we both fall asleep.

Chapter Two
Bottoms Up

 **Braden**

"I got it, I got it!" Kellan shouts from the back end of the shop. My face, apron, and the walls are covered in sugar cookie dough, compliments of the mixer. I stand over the sink, splashing my face with water. So freaking embarrassing. I can't believe this is happening. At least there are no customers in the store. I wash my hands in the sink and look at Kellan, who I'm pretty sure is trying really hard not to laugh at me. "What the hell is wrong with that thing?" I ask him. "It just started spinning like crazy."

Kellan reaches into a cabinet and pulls a cleaning rag out. He's wiping the cookie dough off the walls. "Well, there's nothing wrong with the mixer—we call that human error."

I laugh at myself, because what else can I do at this point? I'm covered in cookie dough, and it's not even noon yet. "Yeah, I guess that would be the second error I've made today. I thought I knew what I was doing. The schedule says to start the sugar cookies around this time, and the instructions seemed pretty clear when I read them this morning. What did I do wrong?"

I watch as Kellan moves comfortably around the kitchen. He looks extra cute today, in his plaid blue shirt. The color complements his eyes perfectly.

"Well, the first thing you did wrong, was reading these instructions," he says. He removes the manual from inside the file.

"So, these are not for this mixer; these are for the old mixer. This mixer is new-ish." He places the instruction manual back inside the file and pulls out another one, then slides it across the counter toward me. "This is the one you want, but you really don't need it."

I pick up the manual, dropping an eyebrow at him. "Why don't I need it?"

"Because it's like two buttons," he says, pointing at the side of the mixer. "You turn it on and pick the speed. It's not rocket science. You just used the wrong adjuster. Basically, you told the mixer you wanted two hundred cookies made in five minutes, so the mixer was trying to mix faster than it's capable of."

"Ah, I see." I fold my arms across my chest, and ask, "What was the second thing that I did wrong?"

"Well, I was expecting a call for help this morning, and you didn't call me once. I'm over here a lot helping Leora, and she said she told you I'd be around to help." He looks down at the floor, then back to me. "So…why didn't you call me?"

"That's a loaded question, if ever I heard one."

"No, not loaded. Just asking," he says, folding his arms and leaning his ass against the edge of the counter.

What the hell does he mean this isn't loaded? There are a million reasons why I didn't call him. Which one does he want? I don't want to even think about the hurt that led to me not calling him. I just want to look at him. He really is the most gorgeous man I've ever seen. His ass is pressed against that counter, too. It's strange that I can still feel his waist in my hands after all these years. I wonder how it feels now?

His hand waving close to my face pulls me back to the present.

"Hello? Braden? Where did you go? I asked why you didn't call me?"

"Oh, sorry. I think the drive from yesterday finally just hit me. I zoned out for a minute. I didn't call you because I didn't think you'd want me to. You could have called me…phone works both ways."

He looks confused. He's tilting his head at me, and has a bit of a scowl. "What? Why would I call you to see *if* you needed help? You should have called me *when* you needed help this morning."

Oh my God. I am an idiot. I thought he was asking why I hadn't called him for the past twelve years. He just meant today. That's a much easier answer.

"Well, it's not like my nonna pays you. Seems unfair for me to ask you for help. Besides, I had the instruction manual. Everything was obviously under control," I say, gesturing to the mess on my apron and the walls.

He's staring at me so intensely, it's like he's trying to figure something out. "Clearly under control," he says. "You…uh, got a little in your hair, too."

"Ah damn." I pull my phone out of my pocket, using the camera as a mirror to find the cookie dough. My hair is in a tight top-knot, so I easily spot the small ball that wedged itself near my hair tie. As I'm trying to carefully pick the dough out, I catch a glimpse of Kellan, and he's looking at my ass.

The door to the shop opens, and the large silver bells attached to the handle jingle.

"Oh, here we go," Kellan mutters at the sight of the woman who enters. "She's gonna try and sleep with you. She isn't here for cookies," he says.

I raise my eyebrows at him, then glance toward the woman in the brightly-colored Christmas sweater. She's carrying a tray of something and waving at us with her free-hand.

I still have to help her, because she's a customer, even if what Kellan said is true. "Not interested in *that*," I tell him. "I'm more interested in why you ran away so fast yesterday."

The woman is looking me up and down as she walks toward the counter. Oh, I guess Kellan is going to help, too. He's following behind me, walking toward the register. He seems really bothered by her presence. I wonder why.

Her eyes widen exaggeratively. "You must be Braden! Oh, you are hot! All the ladies are talking about you!" She extends a tray of baked goods toward me. "I whipped these up this morning. It's not much, but I figured I'd introduce myself, I'm Rachel. I own the cake shop a few doors down. Now, don't think of me as competition, because I don't do cookies, just cakes, cupcakes, and specialty coffees."

Kellan stands beside me. "Why would he think of you as competition?"

She turns her attention to him. "Oh, I didn't see you there! How are you, Kellan?"

"Oh, I'm good. Gotta get back to the shop," he says, walking toward the door.

Damn it, no. I don't want him to leave. We were so close to having a conversation. I have to focus on this woman now, so I can't go chase after him. I don't even know if she really wants to buy anything.

"Thanks for your help, Kellan," I say. I smile at him, hoping he gives me a smile back.

He stops for a second before reaching the door, looks at Rachel, gives me a little nod, and leaves.

"Oh, now where were we?" she asks me.

I—why did he leave? He didn't even say anything, he just left. That sucked.

She's still holding the tray of baked goods toward me. I take the tray and force a smile. "It's nice to meet you. Thank you. I'm not big on sweets, but my nonna will love these."

She's talking about something, I honestly can't even focus on her right now. Kellan looked upset or confused—I have no idea why. What was he even feeling? I thought we were gonna talk and then this woman came in. I don't even remember what she said her name was.

She cackles loudly at herself. "Anyway, that's not for you to worry about. I shouldn't be surprised that you don't like sweets, just look at you," she says, eyeing my chest.

Thankfully the door opens, and several customers walk in.

"I'd better get going so you can deal with your customers. It was nice meeting you. Come down to the shop if you need *anything*," she says.

Among the group that enters are some familiar old faces. I haven't seen some of these people in years. Something about being here in this moment, catching up with people, feels like I'm part of the community again, it feels warm and happy. It's such a cozy feeling, this feeling of acceptance—and yet, there's a part of me that feels somewhat cold as I glance toward Kellan's shop.

"Thanks so much, I'll have the cookies ready for you on December twenty-second," I say, passing the customer their receipt.

I wish I could feel some sort of relief after that big rush, but there are around thirty orders here for the next few days. I should ask Kellan what my nonna's system was for managing all this.

KELLAN

I step out of BJ's Cookies and turn around to look at the shop. The last thing I want to do is watch Rachel throw herself at Braden, even if he's not interested. I take a deep breath and clear that from my mind and focus only on him.

Despite cleaning up, Braden still has bits of cookie dough all over his apron, so much so that it's visible from here on the street. I can't help but smile at the memory of him yelping and then turning around, splattered from chest upward with a whole bowl's worth of cookie dough. He even had a little bit on his nose that I wanted to lick off.

For all the weird feelings I'm having and for all the ways I want to avoid being around this man, seeing him decked out in dough was worth it.

He's going to be alright, I tell myself. I'd initially been uncertain about Braden taking over Leora's cookie shop, because veterinary skills aren't exactly transferrable to baking, but something about this afternoon had set my mind at ease...despite it being one big chaotic disaster.

Maybe it was the determination I saw in his eyes. When we were kids, if Braden set his mind on something, he made it happen. Whether it was joining the rugby team or winning the science fair, he didn't let anything stop him.

When an older couple pass by me and enter the shop, I turn and cross the street, the early December slush splashing beneath my booted feet. I enter my candle store—Dip Your Wick—and stomp my boots to shed off the excess snow.

"All calmed down at the cookie shop?" a friendly voice says.

I look up and find Riley, my cousin and casual employee. With the Christmas rush and the prospect of helping out across the street more than normal, I'd brought on a little extra help.

"It was messy," I say with a smile, "but he'll be alright now."

Riley comes around from behind the counter and approaches

the shop window, looking across the street to BJ's. "Have you talked to Braden much?"

I feel my cheeks warm with a blush, which I attempt to hide by rubbing the tip of my nose and keeping my cheeks behind my palms. I don't think it's working. "Briefly."

Riley turns on her heel and looks at me. "Your best friend for most of your childhood comes back to town and sets up shop across the street from you…and you talk *briefly?*"

I shrug out of my coat and walk to the back room to hang it up. "That was, like, twelve years ago, Riley," I say. "A lot has changed in over a decade. I've changed. *He's changed.*"

I'd run face-first into one of those changes last night. Braden had always been the bigger of the two of us and always had a bit more muscle, but *that* was unexpected. And unexpectedly pleasant. I can still smell him.

When I return to the counter area, Riley asks, "Did he ever find anyone? Settle down?"

I shake my head. "Not that I can tell. His socials are pretty sparse, and there seems to be no indication of a long-term relationship, at least not anything recently."

"Huh," Riley says.

"He's into guys, though, I'm pretty sure." I wish I could take those words back. As soon as they spilled from my mouth, I knew they were a mistake.

Riley spins around to face me. "Does he know you're gay, too?"

While we hadn't officially had that conversation…*does* Braden know I'm gay? It'd be pretty fucking hard to miss with the clues I've given him, with the biggest one being a kiss when we were eighteen.

While I hadn't said anything out loud, Riley's eyes go wide with excitement. I roll my eyes and say, "Just because we're both gay doesn't mean anything's going to happen. We're old friends, nothing more."

"They don't call it friends-to-lovers for nothing," Riley says. She settles in on the stool next to me. We both watch the view out the window. BJ's is a hopping place today.

"This isn't one of your fan-fiction stories, Riley. Braden and I aren't a trope."

"Every good love story has tropes, Kellan," she says. "They make the reader happy."

Our conversation is mercifully cut off when a nervous young man bursts into the store. He looks around with a wide-eyed look and when he sees it's just us here, he hurries up to the counter.

"Thank goodness, I'm the only one here," he says. "I have to buy a candle for my mother-in-law; she's coming for the holidays and always complains that our house doesn't smell like Christmas because we use a fake tree." He throws his hands out at his side to emphasize his frustration. His pitch rises as he rattles through his story, his anxiety clearly eating at him. "I have no idea how a candle would help, but my wife sent me here and told me to find something that will fix it. She shoved me out of the house and told me not to come back without the smell of Christmas—whatever the heck that means."

I glance at Riley, and we make eye contact. Normally, I'd leap at the chance to help a customer like this, but today I'm just... distracted.

"I've got this one," Riley whispers. Then she comes around the counter and approaches him, introducing herself and starting on what she does best—matching people to candles.

My attention, though, is pulled yet again to the window and the view of BJ's. The rush he'd had ten minutes ago had lulled, and I can only see Braden there. He dumps some flour in a bowl and a plume of it goes up high, dusting over him, and he throws up his hands in defeat.

"Riley," I say, interrupting her sales pitch for the young man. She's in the midst of pulling out the scented oil samplers. "Do you want a coffee? I'm gonna grab one."

Before she can answer, I'm already out the door. A blast of cold December wind comes barreling down the street and runs into me at full force, making me instantly regret not throwing on my coat. I hug myself and hurry to the opposite sidewalk and into the cookie shop.

"Kellan?" Braden says. He's trying to wipe off the flour that had exploded in his face, but his sideburns are still ghostly white. "Did you forget something?"

I fumble for words under the heat of Braden's gaze. Even after all these years, he still has that effect on me. His eyes have always looked deep, but as he's gotten older, they look deeper. Now that some of the initial franticness of him being back has started to fade, I take in the sight of this man who was once my best friend and who I'd once had some feelings for…who I'd once kissed.

He's filled out nicely, and it's clear he still works out, even if his competitive rugby days are behind him. He's dressed smartly, even for a day of baking cookies, and the top button of his shirt is open, revealing just a light smattering of chest hair, which matches the scruff on his face.

"Yeah," I say, still fumbling and searching for words. "Coffee. I would like some?"

He gives me a smirk. "Complete sentences. I would like some?"

I chuckle. Some of the tension is finally broken, though not completely gone. "Smartass."

He leaves the work table behind and comes to the espresso machine. Since he's focused on it, that gives my eyes plenty of seconds to linger on him. And now that he's closer, I can see some of his finer features. Features like the slight wrinkles at the corners of his eyes that came from smiling all the time, and the way he keeps his nails neatly manicured.

"I know how to work this," Braden says. "I know how to work this. I can do this."

I try to stifle a laugh. "I'm sure we can pull some college kid off the street to give you a lesson."

Braden rolls his eyes. "I worked at Starbucks for a month, I know my way around the espresso machine."

"A month? Only a month?"

Braden's cheeks darken, and he glances away. "Yeah, I got fired."

"You? You got fired?" I throw my head back and laugh. "For what?"

He puts his fists on his hips and glares at me with tight lips. There's something defiant in that stance, almost defensive. Eventually, he hangs his head, and his shoulders sag as he mumbles, "I kept breaking the espresso machine."

Don't laugh, I tell myself. For the love of God, don't laugh. I manage to redirect my mind past the laugh and say, "Would you like a tour of how it's done? I've helped out a handful of times when Leora's baristas had exams and stuff."

Braden steps back and waves his hands in a *be-my-guest* motion. I come around the counter and set to showing him how it works. "You take this and fill it with fresh ground espresso. Then tamp it down like this." I demonstrate each step. "Then hook it in here on the machine, prop a cup underneath, and then hit this button." I point to the button, but don't press it. When Braden doesn't move, I look at him over my shoulder. "If you don't press it, I'm not paying for this coffee."

"I wasn't going to charge you anyway," Braden says, but he steps closer and reaches past me to push the button. And in that small moment, his body brushes against mine.

There's heat and electricity in that touch, enough to make my cock go hard and my knees go weak. My eyes flutter closed as I take a deep inhale to steady myself. But since Braden is so close, I just get a big whiff of this man and his damned cookie scent.

Eventually, I bring my attention back to the espresso machine.

"I like an Americano," I say. I'm fully aware that Braden is still standing close to me, his body just a mere inch—at most—from mine. He's so close I can feel the heat radiating off him. I want to have him closer, to have his body pressed up tight against mine. "So, we top it off with hot water from this tap here on the side." I take my coffee in both hands and turn around, leaning back against the counter. "And that's how you make an Americano with Leora's espresso machine."

God, I hope my bulge isn't showing too much right now. I can't look down and check because that would make it too obvious. Though a tiny part of me wants him to see my bulge and be impressed by it.

I want to shake my head and let those dirty thoughts fall out. Braden is a friend and nothing more. Just a friend. I might've felt something for him at one point, and we might have kissed, but that was far in the past. There's no way he's holding on to it, too, so I just need to move on.

"No, uh…*cream* in your coffee?" Braden asks.

I swallow. "Um…I like it strong." My gaze trails along his thick biceps. "Strong…"

It might be my imagination, but I could swear Braden is flexing his biceps a little.

I clear my throat, hoping to clear my mind, too. I need to get off this lust train. This is *Braden*, my *friend*. Or, at least, my former friend. This is not some Grindr hookup.

I look around for anything to distract us in this moment, to get him to step back and for my libido to subside. My gaze lands on the basket of baked goods. I look at Braden and smirk. "How was Rachel?" I ask in a singsong voice. "Did you get her number?"

Braden rolls his eyes and waves his hand dismissively. "Not interested."

"She's single. Hot to trot."

"Hot to trot?" Braden says through laughter. "Not. Interested." He sighs. "She's not what I'm looking for."

I swallow and a cold sweat gathers at the small of my back. "And what are you looking for?"

"Someone with a deep voice, an Adam's apple,"—he eyes my shirt—"and wears the color blue, preferably."

Gay. I was right. This is doing nothing to help my raging hormones, though, and the mixed up mess of feelings tumbling through my head.

"If I didn't know better, I'd think the whole Rachel thing made you jealous," he says in a voice that's both sexy and low.

"Jealous? I've never been jealous a day in my life."

Braden rolls his eyes. "Please, Kellan. You were always jealous, even when I went to play with other friends when we were kids."

"Agree to disagree, I guess," I say. Silence settles between us. And tension. Lots of tension.

Thankfully, Braden finally backs up a step, putting some space between us. He leans so his ass is against the work table behind him, and he crosses his arms over his chest. There's a shift in his demeanor; he's no longer flirtatious and playful.

"So, about last night," he says, "why did you leave in such a hurry? You didn't answer me before."

I shrug my shoulders. How do I tell him he makes me nervous? Even now there are butterflies in my stomach.

"It was a long day," I lie. "I wanted to get home and get to bed."

"Mmhmm," Braden says. He looks at me expectantly, waiting for a more fuller answer. Instead, I take a sip of coffee. "You're sure that's all it was?"

I shrug. "It was yesterday. Let's put it behind us."

Braden nods his head in acquiescence.

"Last night aside," Braden says, "it's good to see you again, Kellan."

"You too, Braden." I take a sip of coffee, if only to just stop myself from babbling. That seems to settle the last of the quivers in my stomach, though I still feel a little bit unsettled. It'll take me a while to get used to having Braden back and getting past our history and seeing where our present takes us, even if it's just friends.

I had wanted to see Braden over the years—badly—but now isn't the time to dredge that up. Instead, I file that discussion away for later.

"Do you want to grab a drink after work?" I ask. "Bottoms Up is next door. We could catch up, work on drifting back together."

Braden arches an eyebrow. "Your boyfriend would be okay with that? With hanging out with another gay guy at a gay bar?"

I laugh out loud. "Boyfriend? I haven't had a boyfriend since college. Relationships aren't my thing, Braden. Too restricting, too confining."

"So, you're single?" His eyes seem to be searching mine, as if seeking out any sign I'm being untruthful.

"Don't knock it till you try it," I say. I give him a look. "And you are…"

Braden looks away. "Also single."

Noted.

"Anyway. Drink? At seven?"

He nods. "I'll see you there."

Shortly after that, I finish my coffee and retreat back across the street. While I'd been gone, Riley sold a large gift basket of Christmas-scented candles and oils to the nervous young man. The last few hours of the workday pass quickly.

At five, when BJ's Cookies closes, my gaze automatically seeks out the window across the street. I would always make sure Leora was okay, but I didn't have to do that with Braden. While it's not necessary, it doesn't mean I'm going to stop. I'm going to keep an eye on him. In the dim shop, I can see him doing the last of his clean-up and shut-down and eventually he retreats upstairs to his nonna's suite.

Riley left around five as well, leaving me to do all the final clean-up for the night.

When it reaches six o'clock, I lock the shop door and hurry home. I give Senator Tunacan a heaping pile of shredded chicken in gravy, then strip and hop in the shower. I scrub myself extra hard, making sure every crack and crevice is clean and smelling fresh. We're both single, after all, and we have that kiss in our past. While I'm not sure if we're truly headed that way now, you never know.

Then I shake my head. We're old friends, and he stopped talking to me after the kiss. He's not interested.

After the shower, I pull half the clothes out of the closet and toss them on the bed as I search for the perfect outfit. I settle on dark jeans and a tight-fitting polo that hangs on my frame in all the right ways.

The Senator comes into the bedroom, licking his lips and looking satisfied. I give his head some scritches.

"Daddy is going to go out for a bit tonight, but I promise to come home at a reasonable hour. Maybe we can watch that nature show you love so much, the one with all the birds."

The Senator meows in response and brushes against my shins.

No more than five minutes later, I'm hurrying out the door and back downtown. I want to get to Bottoms Up before Braden so I can watch the man enter. While there is likely not going to be anything between us, that doesn't mean I can't appreciate the view. Plus, I don't want to be late; Braden never appreciated tardiness.

The bar is semi-crowded tonight. It never gets super busy on a Tuesday night, but it's still busier than usual. I take a seat at the bar, and Chad comes up to me.

"I'll start with a Coke for now," I tell Chad.

As Chad puts the glass on the counter and fills it, he says, "How are things going with Braden? I saw you cross the street a few times."

"It's good," I say, taking a sip of the Coke. "He should be here soon. We're going to do some catching-up."

"He's coming to see you?" Chad whistles. "You got over that awkwardness real quick. Back into your full-on crush on him, I see."

"What? I don't have a crush on him. I never did."

Chad laughs. "Everyone saw it," he says. "It was a known fact. And when he fucked off after graduation, your little heart broke." A man down the bar waves Chad over, and he goes to serve him.

At precisely seven o'clock, the door opens, and Braden steps in. He'd clearly showered—his hair is clean and slicked-back—and with his jacket open, I can see Braden also changed his clothes, putting on something that hugs his muscular frame. When his gaze settles on me, his features brighten with a smile.

Braden comes and sits at the stool next to me.

"I'm glad you came," I say.

"Me too. You look great." He runs his finger along my thigh.

I can barely suppress a shudder from the electricity of his touch. So much for being just friends. Though this still doesn't mean all that much; gay men tend to be handsy. "Thank you. You too."

Braden turns on his stool and takes in the place. "It's nice in here. I've never been."

"Yeah, you should see it during Pride. It's like wall-to-wall sausage."

He makes an awkward cough and turns back around.

"What? You don't appreciate a good sausage fest? The take-home selection is easy to pick up."

Braden's cheeks redden. "I'm more of a relationship guy. Not so much into hookups. When I'm into someone, I'm *into* them."

"You don't get dick unless you date them? Seems like a lot of extra work just to get your rocks off." I'm having trouble wrapping my mind around that.

"I've had hookups," Braden says. His voice goes to a near whisper, like he doesn't want to talk sex in the middle of a gay bar where all people talk about is sex. "Just to, you know, let off steam. But relationships are what I want. Plus, relationship sex is *so much hotter*."

I chuckle as I lift my Coke to take a sip. "I'll take your word on it."

"I could show you relationship sex if you date me," Braden says, almost off hand, casually, easily.

I choke on my Coke, almost snorting it through my nose. I grab a napkin and wipe my face. "What did you say?" I need him to confirm what I'd heard; it seems too forward for this man I thought I knew so well.

Instead, Braden tries to flag Chad over, but he isn't coming his way. "Poor service," Braden says.

I look at what has Chad's attention so thoroughly. Chad is watching a customer get too handsy with Lucas. Though they'd only first hooked up last night, apparently that's enough to spark these feelings in Chad. I explain all this to Braden, who eyes up Chad and Lucas, as if assessing what he sees.

"I get it," Braden says. "I'm jealous too. Very jealous. When I date a man, he's mine and not to be shared."

I arch an eyebrow. "Like I said this afternoon, I'm not jealous."

"And like I said this afternoon, I don't believe you."

Finally, Chad comes over. "Can I get a rum and Coke, please?" Braden asks.

"Of course," Chad says. He places a glass on the bar and pours in the rum, then tops it off with Coke. "Good to see you, Braden."

Braden pulls out his wallet. "You too, uh…Chris?"

I know Braden knows who Chad is. He's up to something.

Chad leans his elbows on the counter, getting close to Braden. "Close enough. It's Chad. We went to school together, though we didn't share classes, but we did play on the rugby team together." His gaze rakes over Braden's form, sparking something deep in my gut that I don't like. "You must still play. You've got the body of an athlete."

Braden grins and looks down at himself. "Thanks. I don't play competitively anymore, but I've been known to play informally now and then." He gives Chad a wink. A fucking wink.

Chad slides a leaflet across the bar to set it beside Braden's drink. "Our annual Christmas masquerade party is coming up on Sunday. You should…*come*." Chad put too much emphasis on that word. That angry feeling in the pit of my stomach burbles.

"A masquerade?" Braden says. "Doesn't sound very Christmassy."

Chad shrugs. "You can wear reindeer antlers if you want." He nods at me. "Your boy comes every year and always has a stunning mask."

I tell Braden, "Your grandma makes my mask."

Braden quirks his eyebrows. "*My grandma* makes masks for you for a party at a gay club every year?"

"Allies doing the hard ally work," I say with a grin. "Leora is amazing."

Braden picks up the flyer and shoves it in his pocket.

Chad reaches across the bar, fidgeting with the buttons on Braden's shirt. "You should really leave these top buttons open," he says. When he undoes the buttons, he tugs on Braden's shirt. "Helps show off your pecs." The burbling feeling in my gut turns into a furious boil.

Braden puts his elbows on the bar like Chad, squeezing his pecs together, making more man cleavage. "Do you like the view?"

Chad trails his fingertip along the exposed patch of skin on Braden's chest. "I'd love an even better view later. I get off at midnight. Want to help me get off after that?"

Braden chuckles and stands up. He pulls out and opens his wallet. "What do I owe you?"

Chad nudges the glass forward. "For you? First one's on the house."

Now that boil is accompanied by a nuclear alarm in my head. Chad had once offered me a free drink and that night had ended with me naked and on all fours. I shove the drink back toward Chad, earning weird looks from both of them. Chad moves it forward several inches. I push it back again.

Chad gives me a look that I can't quite read, but it pushes me into action, fueled by that furious boil and nuclear alarm.

I leap to my feet, my stool scraping loudly against the floor as it's shoved backward. I grab Braden's bicep—holy eff it's huge and hard—and pull him closer, our chests crashing together.

Before Braden can protest, I kiss him hard and deep and passionately. Braden lets out the softest of whimpers, and the man's knees seem to weaken a bit. It's hot, it's urgent, and it's having the desired effect—it's marking Braden as off-limits. Chad smirks and walks away.

"You don't get jealous, eh?" Braden says, sounding breathless.

"Eh? What are you, Canadian?"

I grab that huge, hard bicep again and drag him across the room to the tables.

What the hell just happened? Holy shit. My heart is beating so fast…I can't believe he just kissed me. His mouth was on my mouth, and I barely had time to react. I should be enjoying the fact that I just tasted him, for the first time in twelve years, but damn it, why did he do that? He was obviously jealous. I don't even know what to say to him, my head is a mess, and he's just pulling me across the room. I sit down across from him at a small two-person table. The music blaring from the DJ is barely audible above the noise in my head right now. My hand is covering my mouth, my lips are still tingling. I don't even know what to say, meanwhile he's just sitting casually in his seat across from me. He looks completely unaffected. I'm staring straight at him, and he still hasn't looked at me.

Okay, we're gonna talk now, whether he likes it or not.

"Kellan," I say, holding my palms open on the table.

His eyes meet mine for a fraction of a second. "What's up?"

"What's up? What do you mean what's up? You just…you just kissed me and dragged me over here, that's what's up."

I can barely get the words out. Gah, the only part of me that's happy right now, is my stupid dick. I need answers from him. If he was jealous, he needs to just say it.

"I kissed you; it was just a kiss. It's no big deal," he replies.

No big deal? He's still the same bratty little Kellan. Only cares about what he wants.

He's calling the server over. Unbelievable. A young blond-haired guy quickly saunters over and gives him a smile. Oh, that's the motorcycle guy from last night.

"Lucas," Kellan says to the server, "can you get me a gin and Coke and he'll have"—he points to me—"Braden, what do you want to drink?"

"I don't want anything to drink. Thank you."

"Sounds good," Lucas says. He walks toward the bar, but is quickly stopped by a group at another table.

I have no idea what is going on inside Kellan's head right now. But I can't just sit here like this.

"Kellan, what the hell? You can't just kiss me and then pretend that nothing happened."

He shakes his head and finally makes eye contact with me. "Braden, I already told you, it's not a big deal. Do you know how many people I've slept with in this bar?"

"No, I don't and I'm not sure that I want to, but I'm guessing that *Lucas* is one of them judging by the way you stared at him when he came over."

"Lucas? No. Haven't slept with Lucas, but I'd be alright with that. Love getting railed by a twunk. I can point them out to you, if you want," he says with a chuckle.

"Point them out to me? What? No. I don't want you to do that. Is sex like a game to you or something?"

Kellan laughs. "It's not a game, but it's fun. I like having fun, there's nothing wrong with that. Last time I checked, I wasn't married or in a relationship with anyone, so I'm free to do whatever I want. Guys our age are either married, or if they're single have way more emotional baggage than I want. So, sex is the best thing for both guys involved."

Oh wow. I don't even—what the fuck does that mean? I have too much emotional baggage because I'm single? Is he serious? The only emotional baggage I've ever carried has been because of him. I scoff. "That kiss—it meant nothing to you? You're telling me that you felt nothing from that kiss?"

"I didn't say I felt nothing. I'm still hard for fuck's sake. Your mouth is fantastic…but if you mean emotionally—I'm not interested in that."

Alright. He's made it a point a few times now to tell me he doesn't want a relationship. If this is how he wants it…he thinks it's just sex…I'll fucking give it to him. I'll be damned if the thought of him getting railed by someone else keeps me up tonight.

Before I can chicken out, I stand up quickly and approach him. While gripping his forearm, I whisper in his ear, "You're not interested in baggage? I'm not interested in talking. What I *am* interested in is fucking that pretty little mouth of yours, and seeing your ass wrapped around my cock. Let's go."

He stands quickly, and I take him by the hand, pulling him toward the exit. Lucas bumps into me, holding a tray with a few drinks on it. I'm not gonna stop, because if I do, I may wuss out. I shout over my shoulder, "He doesn't need the drink!" I push the door open with one hand, ushering Kellan outside, still holding his hand.

Shit, it's really cold outside. I'm sure he's fine, he has a jacket on, and BJ's is only ten feet away. Why didn't either of us take our jackets off at the bar? Doesn't matter.

There's only one thing that matters right now—I'm going to fuck Kellan. And he's not going to forget it.

I take the shop key out of my pocket and lead him inside. Neither of us have said a word since the bar. I leave the lights off and pull him into the baking area, then lift him by his waist onto the counter. Fuck—this waist. It's the perfect size for gripping. My cock may blow before I even get started. The memory of when we were younger threatens to pull me in. The feeling of his waist makes my mood shift briefly to something softer, but no. Kellan doesn't want that. No emotions. He wants to be fucked. That's all this is. I yank his jacket off his shoulders and slide it down the long granite countertop. I quickly pull mine off and toss it in the same direction. I'm standing in between his legs, as he sits on the edge of the countertop. I grip his sides and pull him closer, so my dick is pressed against his. I'm so fucking hard, and I can feel that he is, too.

"Braden, I—" he says softly.

I lift his chin with two fingers. "Don't say my name. You want my cock? Yes or no?"

He looks to the side, almost shyly. "I do, but—"

"Show me." I rub my thumb across his smooth warm lips, and he parts them, allowing my pointer finger inside, welcoming it with his tongue. He's gently sucking it. Oh fuck—his tongue, it's so hot.

I tilt my head watching him. Our eyes meet in an intense sexual staredown. He licks the sides of my finger, then flicks his tongue up and down the sides, lapping up his own saliva, while maintaining eye contact. I feel my cock begin to leak, as he takes my entire finger back into his mouth.

I grip his hair with my free hand. "You're a sloppy little bitch…I like that."

He looks up at me, nodding his head slowly, still sucking. "God, I love dirty talk," he mumbles around my finger.

I pull my finger out and press my lips against his, pushing forward with my tongue. His tongue rolls against mine, while I hold the back of his head, deepening our kiss. He tastes so sweet, and his tongue is the perfect size. I desperately want to shove my cock in his mouth. He must look so pretty when he sucks dick.

He's grabbing at my shirt, trying to unbutton it, while our tongues are moving in ways I hadn't thought possible. What am I doing? This is Kellan. He's my—I back up, separating from the kiss, we're both panting, out of breath. I can't focus, my head feels all fuzzy. I can't do this.

Kellan grabs my waist, almost as if he can feel the conflict within me. He tugs on my belt buckle. "You can. I want you to," he says.

I watch as he unfastens my belt and scoots closer to me. He's sliding his fingertips inside my pants, attempting to unbutton them, but he looks frustrated with his position; he shifts his hips, trying to get closer. I watch as he tries to stand up from the counter. Placing a hand on his chest, I shake my head no at him. He moves closer and whines, "Braden. I want to suck your cock. Let me get up."

Damn that's fucking hot, but no, I'm not gonna do that. He needs to know who's in charge here.

I grab him by the waist, pulling his bottom half tighter against me, his body jerks from the forceful motion. I press on his chest, urging him to lie down. His body relaxes back onto the counter, and I remove his belt, unbutton his jeans and slide his pants off. Damn, he's beautiful. The smallest bit of moonlight combined with the faint glow of the streetlamps illuminates the small amount of skin peeking out from under his shirt, showing off the tiny trail of hair that leads into his tight black briefs. I rub my palm across his cock through his underwear. "What a good boy…I haven't even touched you yet, and you're so hard for me."

"Fuck—" he groans, covering his own mouth.

I slowly massage his cock through the soft black fabric, alternating between the front and backside of my hand. It's taking every ounce of willpower I have not to fuck him right now.

With every light stroke, he squirms, and it makes me harder. It makes me want him even more. He groans and reaches down to free his own cock from the slow and steady torment of my hand.

I grab his hand, stopping him before he can reach inside of his underwear.

"Braden, please—" he whimpers.

I smirk at him, moving my face in between his thighs, keeping a hold on his hand.

I want to taste him. His hips rise, as I bring my tongue to his base, licking him slowly up to the tip through the fabric. He squirms again.

"Holy shit. Please—why are you teasing me? I want you to fuck me, Braden."

I stand up straight and shake my head at him. "See, this is the problem with you bratty little bottoms. You think you have all the power, but you don't."

I softly flick his balls. "Don't tell me what you want. All I've heard from you all night is what you want. You'll get what I give you…" I drag my finger up his length. "I like to play with my food before I eat it. If you're gonna rush me—we can stop."

I can't believe I just said that to him. I mean, I tend to get a little rough in bed, but something about his attitude at the bar is still really bothering me. I want to fuck him, but am I really okay with this just being a hook up? No. I'm determined to make a mark on him.

His cock twitches under my finger, as I stroke him lightly up and down, feeling every inch of him. I raise my eyebrows and lean down, placing my hands flat on the counter, beside his face. I bring my mouth near his ear, rubbing his earlobe with my nose. "Mmm— you like that? Your cock jumped when I reminded you who was in charge. At least one part of you is obedient."

He nods silently and turns his face toward me. He's lifting his head, moving in for a kiss. "Good Boy," I say, capturing his mouth with mine. Kissing him is fucking mind blowing. He's holding my face tightly with his hands, while ramming his wet little tongue deeper into my mouth. He whimpers a bit whenever our mouths have the slightest separation. He's so thirsty, he's kissing me like the last fucking drop of water in the world is in my mouth, and he's desperate to lap it up. His hands move rapidly down my neck, gripping my shoulders, then slide down to my biceps, finally settling on my pecs. He separates from the kiss and reaches for the buttons on my shirt. "Can I?" he asks, holding the second button in between his fingers.

When he looks at me, it draws my soul in, and I can't have that right now. This is just sex—it means nothing to him. I dive back into his mouth, which he clearly understands as permission. His hands feel shaky as he fumbles with my buttons. Is he nervous? No. Come on, not after all that stuff he said at the bar. But, if he's nervous, I'll help him out. I stand up straight and take my shirt off, maintaining eye contact.

His mouth opens, and his breath hitches, while he looks my chest over. "So—fucking—hot."

I push his shirt up and lean down, hovering my face over his cock. He takes his shirt off then aggressively grips the bun in my hair. I look up while dragging my tongue along the skin just above his waistband. Licking the light brown hairs leading from his navel to his cock. "Mmm—your skin tastes sweet. How about your hole, is that sweet, too?"

He squeezes my bun tighter, lifting his hips. "Fuck me—please, Braden. Please—let me touch myself, if you're not gonna do it. I can't take it anymore."

He's so impatient. Always has been. I tug his underwear down and drop them on the floor. I part his legs wider, staring down at his fully naked body. His dick is on full display, wet with precum, and impressively hard, with far more girth than I expected. It's absolutely perfect, and it makes me thirsty.

He exhales and reaches for his own cock, quickly stroking it. Damn, I could get off watching this. My balls are fucking thumping inside my pants, my cock is painfully hard at this point.

Kellan is jerking himself so hard, he's panting, and I can't take my eyes off him. I feel my cock twitch, urging me to let it out. I need to be the one to make him come, or all this teasing will have been for nothing. I pull his hand off his cock and lick the inside of his palm, tasting him. The slightly salty taste drives me fucking wild, it sets off something primal in me. I want more. I wrap my hand around his cock and lick the tip, tasting more of him, it's like a drug to me somehow, and I can't fight how badly I want it, how badly I need it right now. I take all of him into my mouth, moving up and down, up and down, just trying to get another taste.

"Oh my God…Braden. Ffuck yes—hah—nnn—"

His breaths are heavy while his grip tightens on my bun, which will probably fall out soon. He's shoving his cock deeper into my throat, while I suck him. I use my hand to pump him along with my mouth, while he squirms beneath me. He's close—I'm gonna make him come. A dreadful realization is sweeping over me, ripping me from my trance. Once we finish, he's gonna leave…I don't want him to finish yet. I want to fuck him; I want to keep him here with me longer.

I need to be inside of him. I shake my head out of his grip, while taking my mouth off his cock.

He whimpers desperately, "Unnn—shit—no, please don't stop. I'm so close."

"I know you're close," I say, massaging his balls, which I purposely neglected until now. "What do you want, Kellan?" I tug them gently. "You want to come from my cock, or do you want me to play with you?"

"I—want your—"

I lick my index finger, then slide it in between his cheeks, pressing on his asshole. "Mmm—tight…I want you, but I can't fuck you on this counter."

"What? But—I want—"

I pull him into a sitting position, then hoist his naked body over my shoulder, like a sack of fucking presents. His hard, wet dick is pressed against my shoulder, it's so hot. His ass is right next to my face. I give it a crisp slap that echoes through the shop.

KELLAN

As I revel in the sexual rush of being spanked, I stare down at that amazing bubble ass as Braden carries me over his shoulder. I've never been manhandled quite like I'm experiencing now, and it's blowing my mind just how much I love it. Plus, I feel entirely safe and comfortable in Braden's hands because, well, it's Braden. Despite the distance in the past dozen years, I trust him with my life.

Even now, the manhandling continues. The hand that isn't holding me tight over his shoulder is pawing at my bare ass, grabbing my ass cheeks and squeezing them, the stretch tugging at my hole, already making me long for more attention there.

Braden kicks the door open to Leora's back office. I'd only been in here once before to repair a broken shelf. He doesn't turn on a light; the only illumination in the room comes from the security light in the hallway, casting a dim glow into the room.

Braden lowers me from his shoulder, setting me down on the

fabric-covered loveseat. I look up at him expectantly. My heart is racing in my chest, uncertain of what this all means, but I know what's going to happen. We're going to connect in ways we've never connected before, with closeness I've been dreaming of for more years than I can count. Still, this whole thing is unreal, like some sort of erotic dream come true.

For a moment, I wonder if it's real. But the ravenous look Braden gives me confirms that, yes, this is very real.

"Get down on your knees," he orders through gritted teeth.

I slide off the edge of the loveseat and fall to my knees. Braden's thick bulge is right in front of my face; I can feel the heat radiating off it, even through his jeans. Time seems to slow for a just a moment as this all sinks in, as it comes to me that my eighteen-year-old self's fantasies are finally coming to life.

Time resumes its normal pace, and he grabs my head, shoving my face into that bulge. His hard, girthy length presses against my cheek.

I let out a whimper of need.

"You like that, boy?" Braden says. His voice is tight with restraint.

I look up at him while mouthing his denimed shaft. My words come out mumbled as I say, "I need it. Fuck, I need it bad."

"Tell me how much you want it."

"I want it so bad," I say. "So bad. I need it right now."

Slowly, teasingly, Braden lowers his fly. I reach up to yank his pants down, but Braden swats my hands away. "I'm in charge here."

I let my hands rest on his lower thighs as I resume nuzzling his cock. He finally shoves his pants down to mid-thigh, and with them, thankfully, out of the way, there's now only a thin layer of cotton between my mouth and his hot shaft. It seems even bigger now with less fabric between us.

Then, finally, he lowers his underwear, shoving them to mid-thigh as well. I dive face-first toward his cock—but he stops me.

"Look up at me," he orders. I look up. "Who's in charge?"

"You are," I say.

"Good boy. Now open that pretty little mouth of yours."

Obediently, I do as told, letting my mouth fall open. He grabs his cock, resting his hand at the base of the shaft, and waves it around in front of my face. It strikes my cheek several times, making me whimper with desperate need.

"Ready for it?" Braden asks.

"Please," I beg. "Please let me suck it."

With Braden's hand gripping my hair and holding me in place, he shifts his hips forward, finally sliding that juicy cock into my eager mouth. I close my lips around his girth and run my tongue up and down his shaft.

He lets out a rattly breath. I know I'm an excellent cocksucker, and his contented sigh was confirmation of my superior skills. When he loosens his grip on my hair, I take over the rhythm, sliding my mouth back and forth from the tip to the base, shoving my face hard into his pelvis.

Braden lets out a pleasurable sigh and a small burst of salty precum drizzles onto my tongue. Fuck, this man tastes so good.

I reach a hand up and stroke and tug Braden's balls as I continue sucking him. And with my other hand, I finally grab my own cock and stroke in time with the deep oral dives.

I could keep sucking for hours, but eventually Braden grips my hair again and pulls me off his dick. My mouth suddenly feels so empty, like a piece of me is missing. I look up at him and find him looking down at me with eyes half-lidded. But there's still a sharpness of desire under those heavy lids.

"What do you think about me getting in that tight little ass of yours?" he asks.

I don't have to be asked twice. "Where do you want me?"

"Bend over the desk," Braden says, pointing to the side.

I do as I'm told and spread my legs, planting my hands on the desk, and stick my ass out behind me. I look over my shoulder at Braden. Fuck, the man is incredibly hot. He's even more amazing naked than my wildest dreams last night had conjured up.

I let my head fall forward and wait for Braden to claim my ass as his. Even now, I'm still overwhelmed by this whole thing, almost disbelieving it's even happening. Sure, I'd had my fantasies over the years and, yes, I've jerked to his Instagram more than once…but for this to be happening here and now? Un-fucking-real. Better than a dream come true.

There is a crinkle as Braden opens the condom and tosses the wrapper aside and then rolls it down his lengthy shaft. A moment later, rather than the sheathed cock at my entrance, my world is rocked by Braden's hot, velvety tongue.

He puts a hand on each of my ass cheeks and spreads me wide, pressing his face harder and shoving his tongue in deeper. He circles the rim and prods at the center and strokes up and down.

"Oh…fuck…" I moan. "Fuck me…" My cock pulses with precum, a long dewy strand dangling from the tip and threatening to fall to the floor.

My world is rocked again when Braden pulls his tongue out, but then slips in a spit-slicked finger. He slides it in and out, finger-fucking me, teasing my prostate with every deep thrust. Then he slides in two fingers, then eases in a third.

"Are you ready for my huge cock, boy?" Braden says.

I whimper. "Please fill me, sir."

"That's what I like to hear." He pulls those fingers out, leaving me feeling empty and needy again. "I'll fill you real good." His fat cockhead presses at my entrance.

I rest my head on the desk and relax every muscle in my body. I reach behind myself and pull my ass cheeks apart, trying to help accommodate his massive cock.

And it slides in. Easily. Like my body is made for it.

I'm a good bottom, but it isn't normally this easy. Perhaps this just indicates how badly I need him.

Braden's thick, strong hands grab at my waist, holding me in place. With his cock buried to full depth, Braden eases out three-quarters of the way, then slides back in. He does this over and over again, picking up speed with each repetition, until he's slamming into me at full force and full speed. The *slap-slap-slap* of our bodies echoes all around us.

His thrusts get harder, faster, sharper. I grip the sides of the desk, holding myself in place. But this makes the desk jerk back and forth with each powerful thrust. Papers shuffle, pencils roll and drop off the edge, and the desk noisily scrapes the floor. I wonder if it can be heard upstairs. But I don't want Braden to stop, don't want to put that worry in his head, because if I do, we might never get to this point again.

Each deep thrust runs Braden's cock full-force into my prostate, sending extra jolts of overwhelming pleasure through my body. My cock is so hard and so close to bursting, all without either of us touching it. Braden's fucking is just *that good*. I'm so fucking close to an orgasm just from bottoming, something I'd never had before.

He grunts as his thrusts pick up even more speed and urgency, pounding into me relentlessly.

My orgasm starts to build in me—that tight bundle of energy gathering at my taint, expanding into my balls, threatening to overwhelm me and bring my body screaming into ecstasy. But I hold back. I have to hold back. I have to hold on until Braden climaxes and fills the condom with his hot load.

"Fucking take it," Braden grunts. "Take my fat cock."

"Give it to me," I beg.

"Fuck, Kellan. God, your ass is so tight and hot." He grunts again. "You're gonna make me—"

Before he can finish that sentence, his hands grip tighter on my hips, and he shoves his body further into mine, collapsing on top of me. His body goes rigid and twitches and pulses as he shoots his load into me.

And I finally let go. I let that bundle of erotic energy encompass and overwhelm me. My cock bounces as jet after jet of cum rockets out, splattering loudly against the front of the desk and dripping to the floor below. It feels like my balls are emptying everything they have, even my very life energy.

I don't black out, but it almost feels like I do. Time seems to stop. I'm laying my chest across the desk, and Braden is on top of me. I struggle to catch my breath as my body slowly rolls back from that brink of orgasm.

I become aware of the tightness in my body, the soreness in my muscles. Braden's now-soft cock slips out of my ass with a wet pop sound. He pants in my ear, struggling to regain his breath. Sweat drips from him onto me, coolly splashing against my overheated skin.

"That…" Braden says, pausing to gulp in air, "was incredible."

I struggle to find words that adequately describe how in awe I feel. Eventually, I say, "That was utterly mind blowing. I don't care if we ever have sex again because that was just tip-top primo pounding. No other man has ever fucked me like that."

Braden's body goes stiff against mine again, but this time there's a coolness to it, like there was some sudden distance. He stands up, taking his weight off me.

"We should get dressed. I have to clean up."

I run to where we'd scattered my clothes and quickly dress. When I return to the office, I find Braden sitting bare-assed on the edge of the desk.

"Do you need any help?" I ask. "I can give things a good wipe down."

"No," Braden says, waving his hand dismissively. "I got it. Just go." There's a hardness to his voice that definitely wasn't there before. There had to be something I just wasn't getting—I'd given the biggest compliment I'd ever given a hookup, and he was reacting like he was offended.

"Is everything okay?" I ask.

"Yeah, it was just sex," Braden says. He gets up and pulls up his underwear and pants, then goes to find where he'd left his shirt.

I step out into the cold night and turn to say goodnight, but he closes the door to BJ's before I can do so. I give him a little wave, and he gives me a tight smile and a slight raise of the eyebrows as acknowledgement.

I turn on my heel, feeling awkward, and walk to the end of the block and turn the corner, heading toward home.

That was…confusing.

Undeniably, without a doubt, absolutely the best sex I've ever had in my entire fucking life.

But…

With how it ended, with him almost deflating and then rushing me out and not even saying goodbye…something was off. I run through everything we did and everything I said, and I keep coming up empty. I complimented him on his mastery over his dick skills, and I'm sure he had as mind-blowing an orgasm as I did, so…what's his deal?

Even though I blew the hardest load I could remember, I'm already growing hard again as I think about his body pressed against mine, his dick sliding into my ass, and the sheer immense pleasure he filled me with. And then there was—

"Oh…" My steps slow. "I kissed him. Multiple times."

I reach my condo and let myself in, shaking off the chill and stepping out of my boots and coat. Senator Tunacan wanders into the hallway and flops on the floor in my way.

I get down on the floor with him, lying next to him. "How was your night?"

His tail flicks, and he looks at me briefly, as if to acknowledge I'd spoken, but not dignify me with a response. I love this little guy so effing much.

I stroke him from head to tail, several times, eliciting a deep purr.

"Life is much more simple when you're a cat, isn't it? No rules about kissing, no accidentally pissing a cute guy off, no awkward social encounters." I pat his butt. When he doesn't respond with even a dismissive meow, I push myself to my knees. "You want to eat? Are you hungry?"

He immediately jumps to his feet and runs into the kitchen. I swear he knows whatever I say, but chooses to only acknowledge this fact when it personally benefits him. Thankfully, though, if he does fully understand English, he keeps what I say confidential.

Chapter Three
Snowflake Princess

 Kellan

I was out of sorts all day.

I was still recovering from that intense bang sesh last night. Even now, at the end of the workday, my legs are stiff and sore, and I'm almost walking bowlegged. Still. Almost a whole day later. Man, he knows how to fuck.

But beyond the physical discomfort is the weird emotional wall that went up between us almost immediately after the fucking was over. It was something I said. It had to be. But I didn't know what it was that had set him off, because I was complimenting him on his topping skills. Or maybe it was something else…

Whatever it was, it made the distance between our two shops feel insurmountable all day. I'd look out and across to BJ's Cookies, but I couldn't force myself out the door to actually cross the street. Whatever wall of ice that had gone up between us prevented me from entering the cookie shop.

It also seemed to prevent Braden from reaching out to me. From what I could see, day two of baking cookies for a living was going easier than day one, but it was still an unmitigated disaster. I could read lips well enough to get a sense of how much Braden was swearing when there were no customers in the store, especially when he seemed to have trouble with the mixer *again*. Yet, for all the difficulty he was having, he never once reached out to me for assistance.

"Do we have the last of the ballots in the basket?" a voice asks, bringing me back to the here and now.

Right. Chamber of Commerce meeting.

We're voting on who will be this year's Snowflake Princess, the host of the annual Snowflake Festival in downtown Frosty Bottoms. It was always Leora's task; they didn't even vote on it in a normal year, because she was simply the best at it and relished the role. But with her being out of commission this year and officially retiring after the month was over, the town needed a new Snowflake Princess.

The duties aren't all that difficult, but in the rush of the Christmas season, they feel like they'd be just a little overwhelming. Each business holds events in the days leading up to the festival; at Dip Your Wick, I'll be having a make-your-own-candle day. And on the day of the festival—the day before Christmas Eve—there's a bit of a celebration downtown and Santa comes to visit all the kids. It's a whole thing, and it's quite fun…but it sounds like a pain in the ass to organize. The Snowflake Princess is the town's point person for anything and everything about the festival and associated events; they're the problem solver, the festival host, and emergency backup for all things.

Rachel from the bakeshop and Tammy from the pottery studio had both nominated themselves for Snowflake Princess and were in the running. And then Robert from the glassware shop nominated me. At first, I shook my head and tried to turn down the nomination…until several others chimed in that I should do it. I couldn't turn them all down, so I let my name stand.

I really hope Rachel or Tammy get it, because I sure as hell don't want it.

The three elderly people at the front of the room—the president, treasurer, and secretary of the Chamber—silently tally the votes. While they do that, I look over my shoulder again, glancing at Braden at the back of the room. With him now running BJ's, he'll be participating in the Chamber's activities.

Braden is still avoiding eye contact with me, and I'm sure he knows he's being watched. He just wants to pretend he doesn't see me staring right at him. I give up, sigh, and turn my head forward again.

I'd thought about going up to him when he arrived at the Chamber meeting, but my hesitations made me stop. I was never really good with talking about feelings, and I wasn't prepared for that conversation with him, partly because this is a whole complicated mess of feelings that even I know I'm avoiding acknowledging. After all, last night's hot and sweaty fun hadn't exactly come out of nowhere, but I wasn't ready to think too deep on why that was and what that might mean.

"The votes were nearly unanimous," the president says. "There was one vote for Rachel."

"Oh no," I mutter. I had voted for Rachel. That means even Tammy and Rachel had—

"And the rest of the votes are for Kellan."

The room breaks into applause. Several hands pat me on the back. I'm stunned, to say the least.

That also means Braden voted for me. I sneak a look over my shoulder. Braden is still carefully avoiding eye contact, but there seems to be a ghost of a smile on his face.

I push myself to my feet and walk to the front of the room, turning around to address the small crowd. They applaud, and there are even a couple cheers. When my eyes find Braden, I see a woman stroking his bicep and whispering in his ear. He seems disinterested, but the woman doesn't seem to be catching on. He has to shrug his shoulder to get her off him.

"Thank you," I say, when the applause dies down. "Being a Snowflake, uh, *Princess* is a big responsibility. And while I can't be Leora—and no one but Leora can be Leora—I'm going to do my darndest to be the best Princess I can be."

"Put on the sweater!" someone shouts. I don't see who it is, but the voice sounds suspiciously like Braden.

"The sweater?" I ask.

I turn around to find Anna, the president, holding up the Snowflake Princess sweater. The sweater that Leora had designed and bedazzled and only she could pull off. The sweater that is at least a full two sizes too small for me.

"Put it on!" another voice shouts.

I take the sweater from Anna and turn to face the crowd again. "Well, *it is* tradition, after all."

I slip the sweater over my head and struggle to tug it down. Leora has a much smaller frame than me, and even though this sweater is baggy on her, it's like a compression vest on me. Finally, I manage to tug the hem all the way down.

Several people hold up their phones to take photos. True to theme, I give them a little princess wave, which earns a round of applause and laughter and several more raised phones for photos.

When I do a slow spin to turn and face the crowd on all sides of me, my gaze lands on Braden again. Another woman is hanging off him and clearly trying to make moves on him. This has to be maybe the fourth since the meeting started; with him being the hot bachelor in town, word has clearly spread among the local single girls.

If they only knew the truth. I'm still reeling from last night—mentally and physically—and also reeling from the very awkward ending of it.

I sit down to allow the meeting to continue and approach its end. When it's over, I stand and turn, wanting to gauge what Braden is thinking or feeling, maybe suss out what I'd done wrong. But he's already gone.

I'm so glad that's over. Now, I just have to hurry out of here, before someone stops me. I head out of the center quickly, slipping past the crowd of people gathered around Kellan. It's really nice to see that the community appreciates him and recognizes his talent. I don't know much about him as an adult, but after seeing the way that people support him, I feel the strangest sort of happiness.

Even though I'm still pissed at him, I'm happy he was elected, and I know my nonna will be ecstatic. She really loves him. But why *am* I so mad? I stole so many looks at him throughout the day from my shop window. I should have just talked to him. But no—I'm mad and whether it's a holdover from all the stuff when we were younger, or more so that he said *that* after sex…

I stop walking before entering my nonna's building. I don't want her to notice my frustration, or disappointment—whatever the hell I'm feeling. But damn, did he really mean that he wouldn't care if we never slept together again? I know I should talk to him, but I don't want to. Besides, he didn't try to talk to me today either.

I take a deep breath and unlock the door to my nonna's apartment. It's nice and warm in here. Fluffykins walks over to greet me, while I slide my shoes off at the door. "Oh, hello, did you have a good day?" I ask him, as I pick him up. He gives me an affectionate headbutt, and I kiss his forehead. "Tomorrow is your spa day. Are you excited?" He meows loudly. He's such a talker. "Yes, Nonna is sending you to the spa for Christmas. It's a new spa, not Geri's spa."

My nonna sounds like she's talking to someone, but not me. She must be on the phone.

"Braden's not here yet," she says.

I cuddle Fluffykins tightly in my arms. Whenever I used to come home from a long day at the clinic, we'd spend time talking about my day. I should go say hi to my nonna, though.

Is that…Kellan's voice? It is, and it sounds like he's on speaker phone. "Well, he was at the meeting. He stayed in the back; didn't say a word to me. Women were swooning."

"Didn't talk to you? Hmmm. That doesn't sound like Braden," my nonna says. "Maybe he didn't see you."

"Leora, are you serious?" Kellan asks. "Even if he didn't see me at the beginning of the meeting, he definitely saw me when they announced that I'd won. He was ignoring me on purpose. I saw him through the window a few times today. Looked like chaos over there."

Wow. He was just watching me while I struggled to make it through the day. That's embarrassing. I only messed half the things up because my head was such a damn mess. I can't be too mad, though, I was watching him for a good chunk of the day, too.

"Kellan, wait a minute," my nonna says. "This is serious. Let's talk about the masquerade party. Now, I assumed you two would be going together…"

"What? Why would you think that?" Kellan asks. "I didn't tell you I was going with him. Did—did Braden say that?"

That question sounded almost hopeful. Like he wanted me to have said it. But no, I can't go down that road. He doesn't care. He's probably just annoyed or something because my nonna is prying into his business.

"Well of course he didn't," she says. "I barely spoke to him this morning before he left for the shop. Seemed to be in a mood. I'm not used to seeing him like that. He wasn't exactly grumpy, but just seemed off. So naturally, I called Lucas to ask how your date with Braden went last night."

"That was not a—wait, Lucas? You called Lucas and asked him what happened between Braden and me last night? Some friend you are," he says with a laugh. "Why didn't you ask me?"

"Come on now, you're my best little twink. I'm not stepping out on you with Lucas. Don't get jealous," she says.

I feel kind of uncomfortable overhearing them. I want to just ignore everything that's happening in there, but I'm gonna let her know that I'm home. Wait, he was about to say it wasn't a date, and then he stopped. I wonder if he thought it was a date when he asked me? Eh, it doesn't matter. He doesn't sound interested. I'm just gonna talk loudly so he knows I can hear him.

Kellan scoffs. "Jealous? I am not jealous. If he wants to go sleep with what's her face from the cake place or Kelly from the flower shop, or Chad, that's his business."

Walking toward my nonna's room, I can see that she's in bed, sewing some kind of brown fabric onto what looks like maybe a mask? I'm not good with crafts, I have no idea what she's making. Oh, wait, it's probably for that masquerade party. Bar boy did say that my nonna makes Kellan a mask every year. Her cell phone is beside her on her nightstand.

I stand in the open doorway of my nonna's room and clear my throat loudly. I'm being extra loud, so Kellan knows I'm here, before he says anything else.

"Ahem. Hi, Nonna, can you please tell Kellan that I am not interested in sleeping with any of those people?"

My nonna tilts her head in confusion, but smiles, gesturing for me to come inside her room. "Come in, Bobola. Kellan's on speaker phone you could just—"

Kellan's voice interjects, "Ahem, Leora; Could you please tell Braden that I am also not interested in sleeping with any of those people."

My nonna looks more than confused. She takes her reading glasses off her forehead and points them at me. "What's going on here? Why are you telling me to—"

"Nonna, please tell Kellan that sex is merely a fun, non-committal activity, and since he is single, not married, last I checked, he is free to sleep with whoever he wants. Maybe the person he thinks about the most, especially when things are really good. If there's a person he thinks about during those times, he should sleep with them. Could be one of tho—"

"Now wait a minute—" my nonna says.

"Leora, can you please ask Braden what the hell he is talking about? I have never been so confused in all my life. Can you also tell him that everything he said made no sense. Just like him flirting with all the women in town earlier."

No, he did not just say that. He knows damn well that I wasn't flirting with any women.

My nonna picks her phone up from her nightstand then looks at me. "Okay. Braden, Kellan, What is going—"

"What? Flirting? Who was flirting?" I ask. "You know…I thought you didn't get jealous, Kellan. You sound jealous."

"Oh, he's right, Kellan dear, you do sound a bit—"

"I am not jealous! I'm confused, Leora!"

"Right, he's just confused," I say, facetiously. I give my nonna a false smile. "I need to exercise. I'm gonna go for a run. But you can tell *Mr. Not Jealous,* that kissing someone, when another person offers them a drink, sounds a lot like jealousy."

"Oh, now I'm really confused," my nonna says. "Who kissed who? You can't be talking about Kellan. Kellan doesn't kiss anyone. It's one of his rules, so who are we talking about? Lucas? Or Chad? Or is it someone else?"

I cover my mouth, trying to process what she just said. Wait, he doesn't kiss anyone? One of his rules? He kissed me last night…a lot. I doubt they talk about sex, so maybe he just said that to her at one point to get her off his back or something. The kiss at the bar wasn't clumsy at all, it was confident, delicious, and fucking hot…the kisses after that were even hotter. The way his tongue moved in my mouth—there's no way that's true.

Kellan hasn't said a word. He hasn't corrected her or said anything to me. He's just silent.

I need air. I—don't know what to make of what she just said.

"Sorry, Nonna," I say. "I'm going to get changed then head out for a quick run to let off some steam."

"Alright, be safe. You could just go to the gym, Bobola. It's open twenty-four hours," she says.

"That's a good idea. But for tonight I'm gonna stick with the run. I'll be back," I say, walking toward the guest room.

I hit the *END* button on my phone and let it fall to the couch cushion beside me.

"That was all kinds of awkward," I mutter to myself. I can't believe Leora told him about the kissing.

This burbling discontent between Braden and myself shouldn't have spilled over and involved her. And what was he even talking about? He seems to have some weird hang-up over who I sleep with. He could've had some say in that matter if he didn't leave me for twelve years.

Senator Tunacan apparently believes my words are aimed at him because he responds with a warbly meow.

"I don't know either," I tell the cat. When he meows again, I add, "And how, exactly, am I supposed to make things better? Especially after that?"

I sigh and rub my eyes; this is partly why I've avoided relationships my whole life. They're too messy and dramatic.

"Want a snack?" I ask The Senator.

My boy knows the word "snack." He leaps to his feet and launches across the condo to the kitchen. I pull out a few cat treats and toss them down the hall, making The Senator burn off some calories before consuming them.

Not long after that, he and I are settling into bed, with him curled up under my armpit. I roll onto my side so I'm hugging him.

"Boys are so confusing," I tell Tunacan. "But they drive me wild. Especially that one."

The Senator lets out a soft snore, and I soon join him.

Chapter Four
Kellan the Catnapper

 Kellan

"They're going to treat you like the handsome prince you are, aren't they?" I stick my finger through the cage front of the kennel and Senator Tunacan gives it a sniff and then looks away in disgust. "Don't be like that, mister. This cat spa day was a gift from your great-grandma Leora."

The Senator meows at Leora's name. I'm pretty sure he knows it. Leora and treats. Does he know my name? Of course not. Or at least he likes to make me think that. He also doesn't understand "get off the counter." Then again, Leora always has treats in her pocket for him, so he's motivated to learn her name.

I sigh and sit back in my seat, looking across the parking lot to the front door of Pussyfootin', the cat spa on the other side of downtown. The Senator has never been here, so I'm a little nervous to drop him off and abandon him for the day.

"We'll be okay," I tell The Senator. "We'll make it through the day and then we'll celebrate with a can of salmon."

Senator Tunacan meows impatiently.

I put my hand on the door handle. "Let's do this thing."

Before I could even open the car door, sunlight reflects off Pussyfootin's door as someone opens it and comes out. My heart just about stops when I see it's Braden.

"Crap," I say. I try to slide down in my seat, pushing my knees under the console, but I can still see through the windshield, which means Braden would be able to see me if he looks this way. And chances of that are high, since Braden is walking toward this stretch of the parking lot. "Damn it. Shit," I mutter. I let my upper body fall to the side, lying beside The Senator's kennel. "Fucking fucks."

I lie here for a while. I have no idea how long and if Braden has passed or turned out of sight or left the parking lot.

"Did he go?" I ask The Senator.

The cat looks at me through one of the holes on the side of the kennel and all I see in those large pupils is disappointment.

"If you weren't neutered, you'd understand," I tell him. He looks away with a huff.

When enough time has passed that I'm sure he's gone, I pull myself up. I look all around, searching for the man, but he seems to be nowhere in sight.

Part of me wants to turn around and take The Senator home, but it's too late to cancel his appointment. Plus, if I take him back home, I'd probably never bring him back here again. And I also have to be at work in three minutes, which means there isn't even enough time to go home.

"We can do this," I say. I take a deep, steadying breath, then pick up the kennel, exit the car, and cross the parking lot.

Bells on the door jingle as I enter.

"Ahh, this must be Senator Tunacan," the receptionist says. The nameplate on her desk says Susan. She's an older woman; it takes me a moment to place her, but I recall her from her multiple visits to the store. She likes to buy specialty imported candles that smell like pine for when she reads gay lumberjack erotica books.

"It is," I say, placing the kennel on the ledge and turning it so we can both look in on the cat. "And he's very nervous for his first time here."

She smiles at me knowingly; she's heard that line before. "Being nervous for the first spa visit is completely normal, but we will take care of this handsome fella for you. When you pick him up at the end of the day, he'll be so relaxed and content and clean and gorgeous."

I lean forward, bringing my face close to the cage door. "You'll be okay, mister. If you need to go home early, you just let Susan know, okay?"

Senator Tunacan's only response is a nice slow blink.

After putting on my bravest face for my cat, I leave and return to my car. I pull out of the parking spot, and no more than two minutes later, I'm pulling into the parking spot behind Dip Your Wick.

Mornings are my favorite time in the shop. There are few customers this early and Riley doesn't start work till the afternoon, giving me lots of peace and quiet. This is when I usually get some candles made or test some new fragrances.

Today is different, though, today I have to start working on the plans for the Snowflake Festival, of which I am the Princess.

It might have been the right choice for me to be Princess; it was always Leora, but over the years I'd been helping her more and more, and I pretty much know everything inside and out. Plus, it really is a well-oiled machine already, with most of the events planned and ready to go. I'm just the public face of it.

"I'll have to get the sweater let out a bit," I mumble. I'd never considered myself chubby by any means, but that sweater was *tight*. It also sparkled continuously because of all the bedazzling.

I open the folder that has the event applications from the other businesses in town, all set to take place over the next ten days or so, including my own make-your-own-candle event. *Come dip your wick at Dip Your Wick* was printed across the top of my application form.

The door opens unexpectedly, letting in a burst of chilly air. I look up to see the courier with a small stack of boxes which he places on the floor just inside the door. If I shift my gaze, I can see across the street to where Braden is in BJ's Cookies, serving a customer at the espresso bar.

"Hey, Louie," I call out to the courier as he's leaving. "You don't have to leave Leora's stuff with me anymore. Her grandson runs the shop now; you can deliver straight to him."

A couple years ago, Leora, Louie, and I had agreed that all her packages would be delivered to my store, and I would take them over to her. She claimed it was so that she wouldn't have to move boxes herself, but I'm pretty sure it was all a ruse to get me over there for visits more often.

Louie looks at his watch. "I'm really running late, man. My kid's class is doing this Breakfast With Santa thing and I gotta get over to the school."

I wave my hand. "Fine, go, go. Have a great time," I say. Louie thanks me and quickly leaves.

I sigh as I approach the boxes. I don't want to tell Louie the real reason why I don't want packages for BJ's delivered here—that it's because I want to avoid Braden.

I shuffle through the boxes stacked by the door. Indeed, a few of them are for Leora.

I look across the street again. Braden's customers appear to have left, leaving the man by himself.

"Time to put on my big boy pants." I pick up the boxes that are for BJ's Cookies, and head out the door. I'm planning to be back in less than two minutes, so I don't lock up or bother with a "back soon" note on the door.

The weather outside is even more frigid than when I'd dropped The Senator off at the spa.

I had intended to dart across the street, but found my pace slowed as I approached. This would be the first real face-to-face conversation since the fucking. Oh God, the fucking…I watch Braden roll some dough on the counter that had my bare ass planted on it just two days ago. I hope he sanitized it. Wait, it's Braden, I know he sanitized.

God, that fucking was amazing though. It still blows my mind just how hard Braden made me blow my load. I haven't even thought of jerking off since because I was still riding the sexual high of Braden's cock in my ass. Never in my entire life had I been so thoroughly dicked.

And that was it, though…I'd been *thoroughly* dicked. Not just physically, but emotionally and all sorts of other ways. Braden is fucking great at topping, and he has an amazing cock, but, really, if that's all it was, I wouldn't be as all-consumed by it like I am now. No, this is partly due to his dick skills, but partly due to our past and our connection. It's twelve years of unfulfilled need getting satiated.

An icy gust barrels down the street, slamming into me. I hunch my shoulders and try to warm my ears as I hug the packages tighter to my chest. Then I finally cross the last stretch of sidewalk to BJ's front door.

Braden looks up with a smile, but when he sees it's me, that smile falters.

"Good morning," he says. I don't feel warmth in those words, but they're also not frigid or dismissive.

"Hey," I say. I hold up the two boxes I'd brought. "I got some of your mail."

Braden furrows his brow as he dries his hands on a towel. He then walks over and takes the boxes from me. "Why didn't he bring these straight to me?"

I shrug a shoulder. "Leora used to get her packages delivered to my place. I think she used it as an excuse for me to come over and visit."

Braden puts the boxes down on the counter. "You've been helping my grandma quite a bit, haven't you?" That attempt at frostiness in his greeting melted away; now he sounds warm again.

Still, I can't quite read his intentions, especially under the intensity of his stare. The way those hot eyes bore into me make me weak in the knees. "I do what I can. Did. Did what I could…I guess. She probably doesn't need my help anymore."

"I appreciate it, Kellan, I do. Thank you." Now that warmth has spread to his eyes; I no longer feel like I'm being examined.

I nod awkwardly, then turn to go, but instead turn around again to face Braden.

"Can I ask…what I did wrong? We had amazing, mind-blowing sex"—at this, Braden's eyes shoot up at the ceiling, as if he's worried Leora will hear it, but I just charge forward—"and then you give me the cold shoulder and act like I'm some bad-breathed hookup."

Braden crosses his arms and leans a hip against the counter. "That's what it was, though, wasn't it? A hookup? It's just sex, after all."

I want to say yes, but something holds me back. Somehow, I know that's the wrong answer. It might've been a hookup in the traditional sense, but it had somehow meant much more to me in the moment than a hookup does—and still means much more to me now—but I don't understand these feelings and can't put them into words.

"Maybe," I say, finally. This earns a quirked eyebrow from Braden. "Did I do something wrong?"

"I think that much is clear," Braden says. Despite the words, his tone is still soft.

"Are you mad?" I ask.

Braden shrugs. "I'll get over it."

I don't know what to say. I know I have to figure out what I did wrong, and I have to do it *before* apologizing, otherwise the apology would be meaningless.

After a long pause between us, I say, "Well…I better get back to the shop."

Braden nods with a tight smile on his face. "It was nice to see you, Kellan."

This brings a smile to my face and a flush of warmth to my body. "I'll see you later," I say. I exit the shop and hurry across the street to Dip Your Wick.

When I enter, I let out a long shudder that has nothing to do with the cold. That man makes my body tingle in ways I've never tingled before. And, God, am I ever hard right now. Maybe now would be a good time to finally jerk off. After all, I have plenty of mental images to fuel my horny imagination—all of which feature Braden and his broad chest and heavy dick.

I can't jerk off at work, I realize, even if I do own the place.

I sigh and adjust myself so my boner isn't so obvious and isn't so aching, and then sit on the stool behind the counter. "Calm down, Kellan, calm down." I tell myself.

Alright, let's see what's in the box. I'm not sure what my nonna would have ordered that feels as heavy as this. The box isn't cold, so it can't be cookie dough. Looking at the counter space, my cock instantly tingles thinking of the last thing I lifted onto the counter—Kellan's ass.

Damn. I want to do it again; I want to taste him again. I've eaten at least five meals since then, and I can still taste him on my lips. I thought the cookie he made was the most delicious thing I'd put in my mouth—his ass was better. So fucking sweet. Damn. His ass felt like it was made for my cock…I know he felt it, too.

Why did he have to say that he didn't care if we never had sex again? How do I tell him that what he said bothered me? I had an opening a few minutes ago, and I should have taken it, but I didn't. Am I really overreacting here? I hate this. I feel like I'm being so damn immature right now, but what the hell am I supposed to do? He doesn't even realize what he said wrong. Now I have the whole kiss thing stuck in my head. It's—this whole thing is so confusing.

I place the box on the counter and get back to the task at hand, quickly grabbing the box cutter from my new junk drawer, and slice through the clear packing tape. Wait—what is that smell? It smells like freshly cut pine trees coming straight from the box. Well, if this is anything cookie related, I'm sending it back. Let's see what the packing slip says. Yep, that's what I thought. Peeking through the bubble wrap are the sides of green glass candles.

Perfect. How did he not realize this was his package? It's not even addressed to the shop. I sigh; I'm really not sure if I'm frustrated or flattered. Did he want to see me so badly that he pretended this package was for me? No. I'm sure there's a box over there for me, he must have just grabbed the wrong one.

I close the flaps on the box and head for Kellan's. Ooh, I get to use the little sign on the door. It's a cute little sign, that says, "Be Back Soon." My nonna told me that if I ever needed a break, and Kellan wasn't around to help out, I could just flip the sign. I feel a bit uncomfortable leaving the shop unlocked, but I'm sure it's fine. I'll be back quickly.

I stop before reaching the door and take in the sight through the shop window. "Dip Your Wick," that really is such a great name for a candle shop. Kellan looks busy talking to a customer near the register. I open the door, which has bells on it like mine. They jingle quite nicely, but the sound, or maybe just the sight of me, draws Kellan's attention.

The inside of the shop is so cozy. The farmhouse style Christmas décor and the lighting, not to mention the fantastic smells—the entire place is just mesmerizing. It feels like I've been wrapped in a warm blanket. I don't know what I expected it to be like in here, but I wasn't expecting this. It looks like something out of a magazine. I couldn't smile any bigger seeing what he's built. It makes me incredibly happy for some reason.

Kellan is walking toward me, giving me a confused look. He points at the box. "What uh—what have you got there? Something wrong with the order?"

I glance around the shop again, still completely in awe of it. "This is a really nice shop. It smells really good in here, too."

"Thanks, I appreciate that. Your nonna helped me with a lot of the decorating when I set up a few years ago. So…what's with the box? Something wrong with the cookie dough?"

I laugh a little, and place the box on the floor, squatting down to open it, and pull out a large green candle. "This cookie dough looks a lot like candles."

"Oh shit!" Kellan says. "Be right back." He heads for what looks like a back room.

I want to check things out. I haven't bought gifts for anyone yet, maybe there's some stuff here that could work. I walk around the store looking at all of the cute Christmas displays set up in the midst of all the candles. Oooh, this red and white candle looks promising, let's see how it smells. Mmm, peppermint candy cane. I love peppermint. This candle smells delicious. It's amazing that it's not edible, because it sure smells like it is.

Everything is so neatly organized. Kellan was always so messy when we were younger. I wonder when that changed. Damn, I really don't know anything about him anymore. I want to talk to him—really talk. But no, I can't do that, he's already made his stance on relationships clear. It wouldn't be fair of me to try and push him to do something that he's already stated he doesn't want. But damn, I want him. I want him so bad…in more ways than one…

I glance at my shop across the street. There's no one waiting outside, so it's fine, but what the hell is taking him so long? What is he even doing?

I don't want to rush him, but I have no idea when he's coming back. I walk toward the door that he went into and give it two quick knocks. "Kellan, I gotta get back to my shop. Everything okay? Do you have another box of mine?"

The door opens, and Kellen emerges, standing in front of me with his cell phone pressed in between his ear and neck, while carrying a big box in his hands. He speaks to the person on his cellphone, "Can you hang on one second, Frank?"

He smiles at me and passes me the large box. "Here you go, sorry that I mixed them up. I'm having the worst time keeping things straight. I'm all over the place today. I have my first meeting tomorrow as Snowflake Princess with the whole town, I gotta pick my cat up from the spa later, and it sounds like the guy who supplies the gingerbread scented oil for my candles has a shortage. Everything is such a mess right now."

I feel a little bad seeing how stressed-out he is. I wanted to talk to him about the other night, but this isn't the right time for that. How can I put this on him, right now? I know he asked me what he did wrong earlier, but the truth is that he didn't *do* anything wrong.

I'm just being overly sensitive. Besides, he did compliment me. It's not like he said that—

The door opens, letting in a blast of frigid air. "Yow! It's cold out there," Chad says, while stepping into the candle shop. He blows air in his hands and rubs them together, seemingly trying to warm them.

Fuck—not him. Not now. I still don't understand their relationship, or friendship—I know they aren't together, but he still makes me uncomfortable for some reason.

Kellan lifts his chin at Chad, pointing toward the back door that he came out of just a few minutes ago, then returns to his conversation on the phone, "Yes, Frank, I'm back."

Chad laughs and elbows me. This guy is way too comfortable touching people. "I'm going in the back room, because I've been a naughty boy," he says, with a playful wink.

I scoff loudly, trying hard not to roll my eyes like a teenager. I'm not interested in hearing about what he and Kellan are going to do together. I for damn sure don't want to think about Kellan calling him a naughty boy.

"Yeah, I gotta go," I say. "I left the shop open, and I've already been here too long."

Kellan turns and looks at me, then drops an eyebrow at Chad. "Hey," he says snapping his fingers at him. "You. Back room, go now." He covers the phone with his hand. "Sorry again, Braden. Next time I'll make sure I bring the— Yes, Frank, I'm still here," he says, speaking into his cell phone, giving me an apologetic smile.

Damn, I don't want to leave him here with Chad. But I also don't want to stay and see how things play out between them.

Chad playfully rubs his shoulder against mine. "Have you been to the gym yet? I haven't seen you there. Tonight is guys night. You should join us. All the guys from our old school go there on

Wednesdays. I think you were friends with everyone that will be there."

I shrug my shoulders. "How should I know? I have no idea who you're talking about. I've never heard of guys night at the gym. Do you all just go and work out together, or is there more to it than that?"

He moves directly in front of me, and whispers in my ear, "There are a lot of things I can show you at the gym. Or you can come into the back room with me, and we'll be naughty boys together." He grabs my biceps, and his eyes widen. "Damn, you must be hella strong," he says.

I really don't like him touching me. I know some guys are just flirty by nature, but I am not a fan of the way he acts. I back up a few steps, still holding the box in my hands.

He chuckles and looks me over. "Oh, playing hard to get…old school. No wonder Kel is so stuck on you. Guys that play hard to get are so much hotter than easy lays."

Kellan's been paying close attention during this whole exchange. Not sure what that's about. Although, if I had to guess, he doesn't like Chad talking to me. His side eye, combined with the kiss the other night, which was definitely triggered by Chad's flirting; makes me think he might be feeling some of the same things that I am.

Kellan shouts across the shop to Chad. "Hey! I told you to go into the back room. I need your help. Braden's trying to leave, just let him go."

Chad smiles and looks at Kellan. "Braden said he doesn't want to play with us in the back room, I'm trying to get him to come out for guys night." He turns and gives me a playful wink. "Offer is still on the table for tonight. We all meet up around seven, maybe we'll see you there."

"No, I don't think so," I say. "Thanks for the offer." I shift the box to my left hand and push on the handle. I quickly steal one more look at Kellan before leaving. His voice just changed into a high-pitched sort of squeal. It sounds like whatever he's dealing with just went from bad to worse.

"Later, Chad." I say, stepping outside of the shop.

"Wait," Chad says, placing a hand on my shoulder. "Kellan will be there tonight. You know that, right?"

What the hell is his angle here. Obviously, I know that Kellan will be there. "Why are you telling me this? You said it was guys night, so why wouldn't he be there—he is a guy."

Chad looks left to right, then whispers. "I'm telling you that it's guys night at the gym. Kellan is a guy, yes, but there are lots of other guys there, too. Guys that *like* Kellan…"

"Guys like you?" I ask.

"Mmm, worse than me. But yep, I'll be there, too. Anyway, I gotta get in the back room, he actually needs me for something. Later."

I nod, while giving him a forced smile, then head for my shop. Quickly, I flip the sign back to "Open" and walk inside. Thankfully, there are no customers in sight. I'm so annoyed. "Fuck! He's such an asshole…" I take the container out of the Styrofoam packaging inside the box and place the peppermint-sugar dough into the refrigerator.

Why was he there? I don't think he was there for sex, but he kept making it sound like he was. I do need to go to the gym, but I don't know if I wanna go with a bunch of guys from high school. Maybe it would be fun to catch up with everyone. Nah…I probably won't be able to talk to Kellan while we're there anyway. Besides, it's not like Kellan invited me, Chad did. Damn it, I didn't even get to talk to him.

I exhale leaning over the counter, resting my head on my arms. I've never felt so conflicted over anyone or anything. The only thing

I know is that I want Kellan all for myself. I can't even think of him having sex with someone else.

I'm gonna just call him really quick. If they're having sex, he won't answer. Wait, no—this is stupid, how could they be having sex at the store?

My cock tingles, reminding me that two nights ago, we had sex in this store, right inside the back office. Yeah, I'm gonna call him.

I walk toward the front window of the store and look at Kellan's shop. I don't see anyone walking around inside. I pull my cell phone out and press Kellan's name. Shit. The phone didn't even ring yet, and about five customers just walked inside. I tuck my phone back inside my pocket. This will have to wait.

The store is suddenly flooded with people. What the hell? Did the entire town just realize they need cookies?

After four straight hours of work, the rush has finally stopped. I am absolutely exhausted, and I still need to start several batches of cookies, clean, and pick up Fluffykins from the day spa. Ugh, there's also the whole gym thing to deal with. I should go—not using weights for a few days is already making me feel out of shape.

I'm calling him before I do anything else. I pull my phone out of my pocket, just as Chad and Kellan walk outside of the shop together.

God. He's been over there for like four hours. What was he doing over there? Kellan turns to lock the door, and Chad is grabbing his waist from behind. Don't like that. I watch as Kellan squirms out of his grip, then playfully pushes Chad backward.

Ugh, I hate seeing them together. Chad is so handsy…I'm gonna call Kellan and ask if he wants to meet up and talk later. Hopefully that will distract him from whatever he's thinking about doing with Chad.

I press his name in my contacts and watch him pull the phone from his pocket and look at the screen. He quickly shoves the phone back in his pants, then smiles at Chad. Voicemail…he sent me to voicemail. Now they're just walking down the street. They're not holding hands or exceptionally close, but still—I cannot believe that he sent me to voicemail. Wow. Here I am thinking that I would talk to him and explain how I was feeling, and he's just way more interested in Chad. That guy isn't even that cute. Besides owning the bar, what else does he have going for him? Doesn't matter. I have to finish like a million things before I leave anyway.

KELLAN

This day needs to be fucking over. It's one crisis after another, and it just isn't stopping.

Just as I was having a chat with Braden, I got a call from the mayor. He was letting me know that the permit requests for the whole Snowflake Festival hadn't been filed and if it wasn't sorted then the festival would have to be cancelled. And how would that look? I take over and kill the festival in a week flat.

Then, while I was on hold with him, my candle oil supplier called with yet another crisis. To make matters even worse, Riley called out for the day, and that's when Chad came over for all the projects I needed his help with, but instead of helping, he was busy flirting with Braden. God, I needed him to focus.

Now that Braden has left, and it's just Chad and me, I lead him into the back room. He'd promised to help me fix my payment processing software. There's a glitch in how it's set up that I can't root out and multiple people have been charged incorrect amounts.

As I set him up on the computer and log in, Mayor Dick comes back from putting me on hold and says, "I don't know what I can do for you. You have to file the paperwork or there's no festival."

"You don't know what you can do for me?" I ask him. "You're the freaking mayor, pull some strings! Declare a municipal emergency! I don't care—give me my permits!" There are other things I really want to scream at him, but I manage to hold back.

"Let me transfer you to Jennifer over in the permits department," Mayor Dick says. "If anyone can help, it's her."

I let out a heavy sigh of exasperation. "And why didn't you transfer me to Jennifer right at the start of this call? Or just have Jennifer call me? Or just ask Jennifer to make sure all the permits are in place?"

I can almost *hear* him shrug. He is the most useless mayor Frosty Bottoms has ever had. "I dunno. I'll transfer you over now."

Before I can tear into him, tinny hold music blares in my ear.

"All good?" Chad asks me. He's rooting around in the system settings on the payment processor.

"Yeah. Great. Real great."

Chad rolls his eyes. "That bad?"

"Jennifer in permits speaking, how can I help you?" a soft voice says in my ear.

"This is Kellan—Snowflake Princess Kellan—and Mayor Dick just told me that I don't have *any* permits in place for the Snowflake Festival?"

"One moment, please," she says. I hear the clatter of her typing on her keyboard. "Yeah, I'm seeing no permits here. You should have filed them three months ago."

"A day," I say. "I've been Snowflake Princess a day."

"Yes, I heard," she said, not sounding the least bit sympathetic. "Still, permits should have been handed in three months ago. We could rush them, but—"

"Rush them! Let's rush them!"

"—but my supervisor, who would need to approve them, is on holiday until the new year."

I've never wanted to smash my phone so hard. "In your supervisor's absence, who has authority to approve permit requests."

"That would be Mayor Dick."

In the most cold voice I've ever used, I say, "Please transfer me to Mayor Dick."

Chad looks up at me. "Sounds like you're having a blast. Offer Mayor Dick a free drink at Bottoms Up and see if that makes him approve it all."

"Thanks, man." When Mayor Dick answers, I use a voice that is calm and steady, but has such an edge to it that even Chad is uncomfortable listening to it. He's shifting in his seat awkwardly. I explain the whole thing to Mayor Dick and offer him a free drink at Bottoms Up.

"Oh, well, if it's that easy," Mayor Dick says, "permits approved."

I end the call a few moments later, and I am seeing red.

Chad motions for me to come over. He points out something on the screen and says something about the wrong tax code being applied when people use certain payment methods. I don't quite get it, but he apparently knows how to fix the problem.

He stands from his chair. "Now, what else you got? Lucas is handling the bar for the afternoon; I told him it's crisis central over here."

Perhaps in an effort to distance myself from everything going on, I ask, "How are things going with you and Lucas? You seem pretty close…"

He smiles broadly. "It's going *really* good. I don't…I don't get it. It's more than a hookup somehow. It means more, you know?"

"Wow," I say, feeling genuinely happy for my friend.

"So, what else ya got?" Chad says.

"Well…you know how you were telling me a while back that your aunt taught you how to crochet when you were a kid and you've always stuck with it as a hobby?"

Chad grins and tugs on the beanie on his head. "Crocheted this myself last weekend."

I lead Chad to the far end of the work room to where I've got a handful of Snowflake Festival items piled up. They were handed over to me yesterday after the meeting.

"This is the blanket that Santa and Mrs. Claus put on their laps at the festival and it looks like a moth or a mouse or something got into it." I pick up the blanket and stick my finger in a chewed-through gap in the crochet work. "Do you have the skills to fix it?"

Chad takes the blanket from me and eyes it up. "Yeah, I think I can do this. I'll just have to grab my stuff from the bar."

"You keep crochet supplies at the bar?"

"It gets real slow sometimes."

Chad hurries across to Bottoms Up and comes back with a fabric bag full of crochet hooks and yarn. I leave him to do his thing, but our moment of peace is interrupted by another phone call. I almost wish I had chosen not to answer it when I learn it's a different department at the city calling about the food trucks and all this paperwork I should have filed long ago.

The afternoon passes with Chad diligently repairing the blanket and me on phone call after phone call after phone call. Thankfully, it's a quiet day in the shop, and I only have a few customers to help, and they're the ones that know the shop well and really just need me to ring them through.

When five o'clock comes and Chad is just putting his hooks away—the blanket looks perfect—we head out the door. I lock up, and Chad grabs me from behind.

"Come here, Princess," he says. He's giving me his Bowser impersonation; I recognize it well from when we play Mario Kart. "I'll keep you safe from pesky plumbers."

I laugh and shove him away. "I'm a princess that takes care of herself, thank you very much." After we both laugh, I say, "Seriously, though, thank you for all your help today."

"You're very welcome, of course."

My phone buzzes in my pocket, and I pull it out. It's Braden. Seeing his name makes my heart race a little bit. God, I want to talk to him, but I want to do it when I have the ability to give him my whole attention and unlimited time. I don't want to rush him because I'm in the middle of things. Regretfully, I send the call to voicemail and put the phone back in my pocket. I'll call him as soon as I'm finished.

Chad gives me a reluctant look, but then says, "Can I ask for a favor in return? I think my car battery is dead. I realized at lunch that I left my lights on this morning and, well, they drained the battery."

"Of course, lead the way," I say. We head and grab my car and park next to his and jump start his battery.

From there, I head off to Pussyfootin' to pick up Senator Tunacan. When I get to the spa, they ring me through and go to get Tunacan's crate. When they do that, my phone rings again.

I sigh heavily when I read the name.

"What can I do for you, Mayor Dick?" I ask when I answer.

The receptionist places Tunacan's kennel on the counter. I take a peek in to see how handsome my little boy is, but he's turned around and all I can see is his butt. I mouth *thanks* to the receptionist, then pick up the crate and head out the door.

"Do you have a parade permit?" Mayor Dick asks.

I've never wanted to scream so hard in my life. "Why do I need a parade permit?"

"Santa is being led through town to the festival grounds. That sounds like a parade."

I get into my car and start it up. I look at Tunacan again, but he's still turned around. I stick my finger through one of the holes on the side, and I feel his whiskers as he turns to sniff my finger, but he doesn't lick it or nuzzle against it. Taking my hand back, I start the car, put the phone on the dash, and head toward home.

"I repeat what I said earlier today," I tell Mayor Dick, "I've been Snowflake Princess for a day."

He puts me on hold as he goes and talks to someone, and I start swearing under my breath. I pull into my parking spot and take Tunacan into the condo. I put the crate on the counter right as Mayor Dick comes back on the line.

"We might not need a parade permit if it's under fifty people in the parade."

"It's not a parade," I tell him. "It'll be under fifty, but let's call it a procession. They're going to the grounds, but people aren't lining the sidewalks to watch him arrive."

"But traffic will still have to be stopped, right?"

"I would rather Santa's sleigh not be in a car accident, so yes."

"Hmm," Mayor Dick says. "I think I can make this work."

"I remind you that you are the mayor and you have the power to do whatever you want."

He laughs once—only once—and then hangs up.

"Good God, what a useless mayor we have." I open Tunacan's crate. "And how is my pretty boy? Is he extra pretty now?"

Tunacan turns around.

"Oh fuck."

This is not Senator Tunacan. I recognize this cat from Instagram. This is Mister Fluffykins. Braden's cat.

I close the cage door before he can come out. "We have to get you back before your daddy tears me a new one. I thought my day was bad, but it's gonna get a million times worse if I don't get you back to the spa before he gets there. Plus, I gotta pick up my own boy!"

I yank my boots back on and reach for the door. Someone knocks. Loudly.

I freeze, not sure what to do. Then they knock again. "I'm coming, I'm coming!" I shout.

I open the door. Braden is standing there. And he's furious.

BRADEN

After finishing up all my tasks, it's finally time to get my little guy back from the kitty spa. Walking inside, I see Mister Fluffykins's crate. There's some kind of sticker on the side that I didn't put there. Why would they put a sticker on his crate without asking? That's weird.

The staff member at the counter smiles brightly at me and walks toward the cat crates. "Hello there! Oh, we loved having Mister Fluffykins here with us today!" She grabs the crate from behind and passes it to me. I can feel from the weight alone that this is not my cat. Looking through the front gate, I can see that it definitely isn't.

No…what the hell?

"This is not my cat," I say.

The employee laughs. "Oh, you're so funny! Mister Fluffykins was an absolute delight. Please thank Ms. Leora for sending him here," she says with a smile.

I am not in the mood for games. I look at the spot where only two other cats remain in a crate. I am absolutely livid, but I have to try and remain calm. Never once in all of my years of being a vet, did I ever mix up someone's animal.

I read her name tag and start again. "Susan, this is not my cat. Look at his collar and look at his crate, neither of these says my cat's na—"

I stop speaking at the sight of Kellan's name on the side of the kennel. Susan appears to have noticed it at the same time. "Oh, I see what happened! This is Senator Tunacan, this isn't Fluffykins. I think Kellan must've grabbed the wrong kitty. Here, I can try and call him," she says.

How the hell? How did he even leave and not realize he had the wrong cat?

"It's fine, I'll go drop his cat off," I say. "What is his address? I could just ask my nonna for it if you're not comfortable giving it to me. I gotta get my cat back."

Susan waves me off. "Yes, yes, I can get you that!" She smiles nervously while writing, then passes me a piece of paper with Kellan's address on it.

"How often do cats get mixed up here?" I ask.

"Never, with the exception of today," she says, sounding in disbelief herself. "We're just so sorry for the mixup."

I give her a nod and head outside.

I cannot believe this is happening. I sit inside my car, and place Kellan's cat; Senator Tunacan, on the passenger seat beside me. I like his name, and he's a very gorgeous cat. He's an orange tabby, just like mine. He's probably so frightened. I should introduce myself.

"Hi there, I'm Dr. Bray. It's nice to meet you, Senator."

The Senator turns his body around inside the kennel, refusing to look at me.

"Well now, I'm not the one who mixed you up. But I can

understand how you feel. I'm gonna bring you back home." I pat the top of his crate softly. Poor little guy.

I start the car and begin my drive to Kellan's. I should call him and let him know that I have his cat. Wait, that little shit hung up on me earlier. Yeah, I'm not gonna get sent to voicemail again. Damn it. How did he even take the wrong cat home? How could he not notice?

Chad. Fucking Chad. He left with Chad earlier…damn it, not only does he send me to voicemail, but then he takes my cat home because he's in such a rush to get back to Chad? Oh, my poor cat is there…who knows what Mister Fluffykins is seeing right now.

I pull into the condo complex, and park in front of Kellan's unit. I have to stay cool; I have to stay calm. I cannot yell. Even if Chad answers the door naked, I'm only here to get my cat. That's all that matters right now.

I lift Senator Tunacan's crate, and step outside of my Jeep. "Alright, we're here, you're home, Senator. Now, are any of these cars, Chad's car?"

He still hasn't changed his position inside the crate. "Alright, you don't have to answer me. I'll be cool no matter what happens."

I knock twice on the door. Admittedly, I'm a bit nervous. As much as I've told myself to stay calm, I really don't want to see a naked version of Chad answer the door.

"I'm coming, I'm coming!" Kellan shouts through the door.

Oh God. Anything but that. I can't stand thinking that he may have said that to someone else today.

The door opens, and I'm faced with Kellan, holding Fluffykins crate in his right hand.

"Oh, um, hi, Braden. I uh, they…the people at the spa mixed the cats up. I was going to bring him back to the spa, but I needed to finish up something real quick. I was just on my way out."

I take Fluffykins from him and pass The Senator over, then place the crate on the ground and squat down. "Awwww, hi, baby! Are you okay?" I stick my finger through the front of the crate. "Were you traumatized by this stranger taking you? Daddy is so sorry that this happened. I would never let anyone hurt you. Sometimes people are careless. They're too busy worried about getting la—"

I should stop. As mad as I am, I really don't want to be mean to him. But I am really pissed, not to mention disappointed.

"You know, I can't believe that you took my cat home and didn't even have the common courtesy to call me. Weren't you worried about your own cat? Did you even consider how I felt? How your cat felt? Cats are sensitive, Kellan…"

He's just standing there dumbfounded. He hasn't even talked to his own cat, who is still currently turned around in his crate.

"Braden, I…I was just headed out the door. I'm sorry you're mad, but you have no idea what this day has been like for me."

I refuse to feel sorry for him. If only I hadn't seen him flirting with Chad and purposely ignore my call—then I would feel bad, but not now, now I'm just mad.

"Oh my God, Kellan, I don't care about your sex life, having someone else's cat and not letting them know, was a shitty thing to do. No matter what you were doing…or who you were doing, you could've called me."

He somehow looks even more confused than before. He runs a hand down his face. "What the hell are you talking about? I don't even know what half of that was about. Yeah, I should have called, but I didn't, because I was busy, that's all that's to it." He gives me a light shrug then puts The Senator's crate down, letting him out inside of the condo.

"Tch. Unbelievable. You have such disregard for other people's emotions. Anyway, I gotta go. I'm not gonna stand here and force you to talk to me. You didn't want to talk to me earlier when I called and you sent me to voicemail, you didn't bother calling me about my cat, and I'm sure you don't want to stand here and talk to me now"— I raise my chin toward the inside of Kellan's condo—"so go finish up with bar boy and I'll be on my way."

I pick my cat up and leave before he can reply. Too mean, that was too mean. I didn't want to be an asshole to him. But damn it, he didn't even call me? Who wouldn't be mad about that? I sit inside my Jeep, and place Fluffykins on the seat beside me. "I'm sorry, buddy. I really am."

KELLAN

I close the front door and lean against it. Good God, can I ever do anything right with that man? I keep getting him on edge or angry at me and if there's one thing in this world I don't want, it's having Braden angry at me.

But…I finally understand when people say someone looks cute when they're angry. I might not say "cute" for angry Braden, but I'd certainly say "smoldering" or "so hot I might jizz my pants." And why does he always smell so amazing?

Still, despite how hard that whole encounter made me, I really didn't want him angry at me again.

The Senator sits in front of me and meows impatiently. He's home, and he's mad at me because he knows I took another cat home.

I try to apologize to him, but he weaves between my legs, brushing up against me and seems to indicate an apology might not be necessary.

"I'm sorry, pretty boy," I tell him anyway. "I'm so, so sorry. You're my number one boy. You'll always be my number one boy, no matter what."

The Senator meows aggressively.

"Yes, sir," I tell him. "I'll get your dinner now, sir. And you'll get extra to make up for the stress I caused you."

I walk into the kitchen, and he follows hot on my heels. When I put his dish on the counter, he gets extra excited.

"So…" I say to the cat as I scoop food onto the dish, "did you see him naked?"

The cat meows, but it doesn't sound like a yes to me. It sounds more like a "feed me already, human."

I put the dish on the floor. "Of course, you wouldn't see him naked. You didn't go home with him. Though…you don't have to be in his bedroom to see him naked, apparently."

My cock firms as I think of that night and how vigorously Braden had taken care of my needs. In addition to just being a fantastic top, Braden also has a nicely muscled body, made that way from a life of physical activity more than hardcore gym days. And that cock…that cock is a work of art.

When Senator Tunacan gobbles down his food, I pick up the dish and put it in the sink. "Are you going to behave tonight if I go out? I need to work out some tension at the gym. A certain someone has gotten me all worked up."

As if somehow understanding that I don't want to hang out, he wanders off by himself to sit in the dark in the bathroom.

I set about packing my gym bag with everything I'll need for a good workout. When I'm satisfied I have everything, I go out the door and drive halfway across town to Pump 'n' Go, the twenty-four hour gym run by an old classmate of mine.

As soon as I step through the door, I can already feel the tension of the day melting away from my body. My shoulders sit a little lower, and my breath comes a little freer. I'll feel even better once I've done my workout and given my body a good pump.

After changing, I set out into the machine area, intent on starting with some leg presses and leaving the memories of angry Braden behind me. When I navigate through the sea of machines, I see a couple familiar faces.

"You made it," Chad says.

"Good to see you," Geoff says. Geoff inherited this place from his uncle and is now the owner and operator.

"Hey, fellas," I greet them.

"Steam in thirty minutes?" Chad asks.

"I'll be there," I reply.

Chad likes to end every workout with a good sweat in the sauna, and I like to join him and the guys in there. It's partly because it is an opportunity to just connect with the guys, but also partly because the heat just feels so good when it melts through my muscles.

"I'll be there, too," a voice says behind me. I turn around and find Lucas. He looks at Chad with cock-hungry eyes. And the outfit he's wearing, a midriff crop top with *Submissive and Breedable* emblazoned across it, and a pair of sweat shorts that hide nothing and drape perfectly over his bubble ass, scream "bottom in heat."

I shake my head and set out to do my routine, sitting at the leg press and setting the weight at my previous record. I grunt as I push the weight with my legs. Time to push Braden out of my mind.

Geoff sits down at the machine next to me. "I hear Braden is back in town," he says.

I nod. "I just saw him, actually. I've seen him a few times this week." I've also been torn a new one by him, in more ways than one. Both the cookie shop rutting and Braden berating me about the cat mix-up competed for eternal replays in my mind.

"Chad says Braden is really built now, like, even more so than when we were younger. He says he's looking super hot nowadays."

I glare across the gym at the back of Chad's head, trying to telepathically warn him off. "He looks good," I say, finally, to Geoff. I push through a set, counting reps to twelve and then gritting my teeth as the final few become harder and harder.

"How do *you* feel having him back?" Geoff asks.

I furrow my brow. "What do you mean? He's an old friend, he's back, we'll see how things go."

"Mmhmm…" Geoff says.

"What does mmhmm mean?"

"It means mmhmm," Geoff says. "Your crush on Braden back in our teen years was a well-known fact. And now he's back and looking all hunky, and he's single and you're single, and while I failed high school math, I think I can put two and two together here."

That competition in my mind of the cookie shop fucking or him yelling at me vying for attention finally results with the cookie shop fucking winning the battle. I'm immediately immersed in a vivid memory of Braden ramming full-force into me and my cock erupting in pure pleasure, spraying cum all over the place.

"We're just friends," I tell him. When I push my twelfth rep, I go back to resting position and eye the huge clock on the wall to keep track of my rest between sets.

"I heard about the kiss," Geoff says. "It was like you were making a statement to Chad."

"It wasn't a statement," I say. Before I can stop myself, I add, "It was a warning to Chad to stay away."

With my one minute rest over, I set about doing another set of twelve reps.

When I finish, Geoff says, "Speak of the devil…"

Braden walks out of the changeroom wearing a spandex shirt

that stretches across his pecs and highlights the points of his nipples. And he's wearing a pair of running shorts that have to be illegal in several states.

It's like the outfit was picked perfectly to highlight just how damn good Braden's body looks. His body not only attracts my attention, but it attracts the attention of at least half the men in the facility, as well as a handful of women that like to guy-watch on Men's Night.

I avoid his eyes; I don't want to see that anger again. I'd apologized to Braden and Mister Fluffykins, but he was still steamed about it. A little more cooling off time would do us both good.

And he still hasn't told me what I did wrong after we fucked. I'd tried to get an answer out of him today, but the best I could get was Braden saying I didn't really do anything wrong…which I knew to be bullshit given the abrupt and tense silence that had immediately formed between us.

I push hard on the machines, determined to push him out of my mind.

But the more I work out, the more I find my eyes straying to Braden. Especially when he bends down to adjust the weights on the tricep press, giving me the perfect view of that firm, round ass. God, he's such a perfect man in every way. But when he stands again, I quickly look away.

I swear I feel the heat of his eyes on me. It's that almost supernatural sense some people feel when they're certain they're being watched. I'm certain I'm the sole focus of Braden's attention.

I only hope it's for a good reason and not still simmering rage over the cat swap fiasco. I still feel terrible about it. The cats are fine—Senator Tunacan is over it, and I'm sure Mister Fluffykins is too. But it's Braden I feel most terrible about. I'd lose my shit if my cat was missing, and I'd accidentally gone and put him in that exact position.

But while I understand his feelings and reactions, that doesn't mean I'm ready to make eye contact with him.

Twenty minutes later or so, when I've pushed through most of my workout, I see Chad heading toward the change room, with lost puppy dog Lucas hot on his heels. I chuckle to myself, hopeful that this unexpected Chad/Lucas matchup will continue to be fun for both of them. Or maybe even lead to more, if that's what they want.

Along with Geoff and a few other guys, I follow Chad and Lucas. As we pass Braden, he pops an earbud out and asks Geoff, "What's going on?"

Geoff stops to explain to him, but I keep staring straight ahead and keep on walking. I hear Geoff's answer, though. "We're all headed to the sauna for a sweat. It's a Men's Night tradition, you should join us!"

I leave them behind and catch up with the guys by the lockers. Stripping to naked, I grab my towel and follow the men into the sauna. I lay my towel on the bench and sit down bare-assed. The guys around me chat away about various things, mostly sports and celebrities, but I just close my eyes, tune everyone out, and enjoy the heat seeping into my muscles and thoroughly warming me up.

The conversation stills for a moment, and I pop an eye open. Geoff and Braden have entered. Geoff quickly snags a seat in the upper corner; it's his favorite seat, and the men had left it open for him.

Braden looks around kind of helplessly. He looks nervous and has his towel clutched securely in his hand, holding it tight around his waist. I glance over my shoulder and understand his predicament. The only seat left is next to me.

I shuffle over a couple inches to make room and invite him to sit. As much as I don't want to be around the grumpy, sexy man, I don't want to make him feel unwelcome here. And when I make my offer, our eyes meet for the first time since we were at my door arguing about cats. I don't see anger there. I don't see complete trust, but I don't see anger.

Braden eventually takes the seat, unwrapping and laying down his towel. He's wearing his gym shorts still.

"While shorts are allowed," Chad says from two seats above me, "you're looking a little overdressed for the venue."

I look up at Braden. "You can keep them on if you want. Don't listen to him."

Braden keeps his gaze locked on me as he shoves his shorts down to his ankles, steps out of them, and picks them up. "I'm good for nudity." There's a wolf whistle somewhere behind me—likely Chad—as Braden's heavy cock flops around with every movement.

Braden sits down beside me, and I close my eyes again. The sauna suddenly feels *very warm*, like someone has jacked up the temperature twenty degrees or so. But it feels like all that intense heat is just hitting me on the left side. Braden, I realize. Braden is on my left side. This is the closest—and the nakedest—he has been to me since being inside me. Immediately, that memory pops into my head again of him claiming my hole as his. Of him laying a blazing trail of kisses on my skin. Of him fulfilling every fantasy of him that I'd harbored for twelve years.

Don't pop a boner, I tell myself. Don't fucking pop a boner. Although boners were common during Men's Night saunas, as was the occasional blowjob or circle jerk, this is the wrong night to get one.

"So, Braden," someone says. It sounds like Geoff. "What have you been up to the last twelve years?"

The group chuckles, but Braden rattles through a Cliff's Notes version of his life, all of which I know through Leora's stories or from stalking his Instagram. Yeah, we lived our lives, and we had a good time doing it, but I can't help but feel a little resentment that I was not part of those twelve years for him. He kissed me, left, and went incommunicado for twelve years. That still hurts.

"And you guys?" Braden asks. The group—at least the ones who knew Braden back then—fill in the gaps. After all the stories are told, Braden asks, "Do you guys still play rugby?"

My eyes shoot wide open, and I turn around to look at Chad. Don't invite him, I silently and wordlessly plead. But Chad is ignoring me; he's too busy chatting up Braden to pay attention to me. Plus, given where Lucas's hand is, I'm pretty sure Chad is getting a subtle hand job from the younger man.

"We do!" Chad says. "Every second Monday we meet at Lancaster Park and toss around the ball. We're not as rough as we used to be now that we're all pushing thirty."

I turn back around and stare straight ahead at the blank wall in front of me. Tell them you're busy and you can't come, I telepathically plead with Braden, while watching him out of the corner of my eye.

"That sounds fun," Braden says. "This Monday, right?" He pauses for what I assume are nods from some of the other guys. "I can do this Monday."

Sounds of appreciation—even a soft cheer—come from the other guys. Braden is fitting back into the old crew very easily, almost like he belongs here, like they are welcoming him back home to the place where he belongs.

I close my eyes again, trying to focus on enjoying the heat once more, but all I can think about is Braden and how I can't escape the man. And how he is both infuriating and undeniably sexy at the same time.

Don't pop a boner, I remind myself.

BRADEN

Well, that was something. Didn't think this morning that we'd be naked together again today. Even though the sauna wasn't sexual—at least for Kellan and me, there was still something really hot about being completely naked next to him again. Thank goodness there were other guys there—any time I thought about the fact that his tight little ass was just an arm's length away, I just looked at literally anyone else until the feeling passed.

It's quiet inside my nonna's apartment as I step inside. My nonna is definitely asleep, and Fluffykins is probably sleeping, too. Oh, never mind, he's walking toward me from the kitchen.

"You're not asleep?" I ask, while lifting him up. "Were you waiting for me to get home?" He purrs loudly, rubbing his face against my cheek. "We won't tell Nonna, but you're not going back to that place ever again. Do you want a late-night snack? I bet you do."

I carry him into the kitchen and grab a can of cat food from the cabinet, quickly filling his dish. He leaps down from my arms and dives into his bowl. I feel like I could cry for some reason. Watching him eat his food and thinking that there was a point today that I didn't know where he was, just hurts me. I love my little guy so much. I feel like a bad parent for bringing him there—but that's stupid. Maybe it's not just the fact that he was missing earlier, I think it's a little bit of Kellan, too. Well, a lot of Kellan. So many feelings have been pushed down for so long, and they just crash over me sometimes. I shouldn't have gotten so upset with him. He's so stressed out; I should be offering to make things better for him. That's what he needs. Maybe that's why I feel so bad? The deepest part of my soul aches for him. I want to be the one to take care of him again. I want to hold his hand. I don't want to think about anyone else doing that.

I guess Fluffykins has decided he's had enough to eat, since he just walked away. Cats are so funny. He was so happy to see me and now he couldn't care less since he has a full belly.

I'm mentally and physically exhausted from this day. I just want to go to sleep. After a quick shower and my nighttime routine, I hop into my sweatpants and lie in bed. The down comforter feels so nice on cold nights like this. Although I miss my own bed, this one is just as comfortable.

Fluffy snuggles up beside me. "Why did I do that, buddy? Was I really too mean to him earlier? He looked so damn good at the gym. I should have apologized…no, he should have apologized. Shit, I don't know, I just know that I want him, but I'm still kinda mad." He meows loudly and rubs his face against my arm to comfort me. "I know, I know. But he's got me all confused. I can't understand these feelings I have for him and knowing that he doesn't feel the same frustrates me. And what the hell? He has sex with Chad midday, then Chad's already banging the other guy a few hours later. I can't— I just can't make sense of it. I saw him ignore my call; you don't ignore the call of someone you care about. No one would do that."

Chapter Five
Banging in the Closet

I cannot wait for Christmas to be over.

From the moment I woke up, I'd been inundated with messages about the Snowflake Festival—and every message had a problem that needed solving or a question that needed answering. If it wasn't the Chamber of Commerce's "marketing diva", a retired kindergarten teacher that never had to use a computer before she retired, sending me mock-ups of posters made in Microsoft Paint, then it was the mayor needing a full schedule of events to publish a leaflet with his smarmy face all over it. Everyone needed something from me, and they couldn't seem to do a thing without me.

I answer what messages I can before hastily downing a coffee and calling it "breakfast" then head out the door. I'm late for opening the shop, not that there are any customers at this hour, which I'm thankful for since a dozen new texts and emails pop up on my phone.

"How the fuck does Leora do it every year?" I mutter out loud as I read a text from the movie theater imploring me to get the city to somehow prevent a blizzard from storming in and forcing a cancellation of the movie night. "Even she can't control the weather."

After I send out a reminder email about social media branding guidelines, I want to scream in frustration when ten minutes later, I see the logo pop up on Instagram in all the wrong colors and stretched out of proportion. I turn off my phone and slam it face-down on the counter.

"Breathe, Kellan," I tell myself.

I feel frazzled. I *am* frazzled. I wonder if I look how I feel.

The door dings as Louie comes in with the couriered boxes. He eyes me up and down and says, "Whoa…what's up with you?"

I sigh. "Nothing." I point at the boxes in his hands. "Those better all be for me and none for BJ's."

Louie shrugs as he puts the boxes down. "Close enough."

"Louie…things have changed at the cookie shop. I don't take their packages anymore."

He lifts the top box and shows me the label. "BJ's Cookies, care of Dip Your Wick," he reads aloud. "And that's your address."

"I don't care," I growl. "Take it across the street."

He holds a hand up defensively. "Alright, alright, alright. I'll take it. Geez, what's got up your butt?" he said. Then he eyes me again. "Or maybe the problem is you *haven't* had anything up your butt for a while."

"Louie…" I warn.

"I'm going, I'm going," he says, taking the box with him.

I walk over to the stack of boxes Louie left and carry them over to the counter by the register. Thankfully, each of the remaining boxes was indeed for Dip Your Wick, and I didn't have to make that trek across the street. Thank God for small mercies.

The door burst open and a gust of cold wind comes rushing in. I'm about to shout that I wasn't going to change my mind about Louie taking the deliveries to the cookie shop, but then stop when I see it isn't Louie that has come in. It's Chad.

"Have you seen this?" he asks, waving his phone at me. His voice is filled with frustration.

I rub the center of my forehead. The headache that had been

threatening me all morning had finally rolled in like a dark thunderstorm. "Seen what?"

"Mayor Dick posted about the Snowflake Festival. He named *every single event,* except the masquerade party!" He scoffs. "Mayor Dick. More like major dick. Everyone knows he parties at the bar and ends up on his knees in the men's room every single weekend and the one event he *forgets* to put on his post is the one at the bar." He glares at me. "Do you think it's internalized homophobia? Is he ashamed of himself and chose to leave it off?"

I hold out my hand. "Calm down, Chad. Let's take this back a step. Can I see the post?"

Chad hands me the phone. That blossoming headache strengthens like a tropical storm evolving into a hurricane. I groan in frustration.

"What?" Chad asks.

"Yeah, he forgot the masquerade, but he's also using a logo from several years ago. Look, it even has the wrong year on it."

Chad crosses his arms and lets out a huff. "So, it's not internalized homophobia?"

I roll my eyes. "Considering Mayor Dick led June's Pride Parade in a leopard print speedo and nothing else, I'm going to assume he doesn't experience much internalized homophobia." I hand his phone back to him. "It's probably some unpaid intern who doesn't know what they're doing."

Chad glares at the phone for a moment more and then shoves it in his pocket. "You have more patience than me."

I sigh. "I'm about to lose that cool, though."

Chad's body language relaxes and a goofy grin appears on his face. "Boy trouble?"

"No. Well, yes. But, not." I rattle off all the things that have gone wrong so far today with the Snowflake Festival. "I've watched Leora do it for years now and I still don't know how she managed it all."

"Interesting, interesting…so this mood of yours has nothing to do with your boy sitting naked next to you last night and it was like there was this impenetrable wall between you two? Or the fact that we invited him to rugby?"

"What?" I scoff. "Don't be ridiculous."

"It has nothing to do with how you were all open and happy at the gym *before* Braden showed up, and then you were closed off and grumpy?"

I walk behind the counter. "It has entirely everything to do with this." I pick up the Snowflake Princess sweater in an angry fist and throw it down on the counter. "It has to do with everyone not being able to sort out their own problems, and it has to do with me stepping into a role I'm not ready for."

"Whoa," Chad says, stepping forward and holding his hands out in a "calm down" gesture. "We both know you can handle this."

I sit on my stool and slump my shoulders. "I know…" I say. "And I know I can ask Leora for help at any time, but she needs to rest and enjoy retirement." I put my elbows on the counter and lean forward. My gaze crosses my shop and then the street, finding Braden through the shop window of BJ's Cookies. "Things are weird between Braden and I."

Chad turns to face the window and leans his ass against the edge of the counter. "Uh-huh. Called it." After a moment, he says, "And what, exactly, is going on between you two?"

"That's just it. Nothing is going on between us." I let out an exhale. "We fucked a couple days ago—and, God, it was hot—and I did or said something wrong and it's been frosty between us ever since. He barely talks to me."

"Hold up." Chad spins around. "You had sex with Braden?"

"Maybe?"

"You said 'fucked'."

"I might've."

"Oh my God! How is he?" Chad rests his elbows on the counter, too, now in full gossip mode. "Is he good?" He whispers, "I saw how big he is when he was floppy at the sauna. When he's hard, is he extra-hung?"

I stick my tongue out at Chad. "I don't kiss and tell."

"I think what you're looking for is that you don't bottom and tell—but we both know you do, so give me all the deets!"

I shake my head. "Not this time, sorry." I gaze across the street again. Braden seems to finally be getting things under control over there. "This isn't some random hookup, *this is Braden*. Besides, I...I don't want to accidentally ruin it. I wouldn't want us to melt this ice and then have it circle back that I gossiped about his giant—uh, never mind."

Chad's eyes light up. "His giant what?"

I cross my arms and lean back. "Giant heart."

"Sure," Chad says, "whatever."

"And then there's his cat..." I say, covering my face with my hands.

"His cat is hung?"

"No!" I shout, balling my fists. I explain the cat mix-up and the reaming I got for it.

"Oh, yikes," he says. "If you were in a relationship I'd say you're in the doghouse. But if you're *not* in a relationship, I don't know what that makes you...maybe still in the doghouse."

"Helpful," I say. "Helpful."

My phone rings, and Leora's face pops up on the display. "Oh, geez, I better take this."

"If you're the Snowflake Princess now," Chad says, "does that make her the Snowflake Queen?"

I shoo him away and answer the call. "Hi, Leora!"

"Kellan! My favorite twink! How is the Snowflake Festival planning going?" she asks. Her voice seems as strong as ever. Apparently even a fractured ankle doesn't keep Leora down.

"It's, uh, it's okay," I say.

"Did Morris at the theater ask you to shoo away the snowstorms yet?"

"Uh…"

"It started as a joke," Leora explains, "but now he's going senile and I'm starting to think he believes we can do that."

I sigh and pinch the bridge of my nose. "That's helpful, Leora, I guess. I've had like a million other complaints and crises today, too. And a meeting at the Chamber of Commerce tonight at, I think, seven. Plus, there's apparently trouble with the church choir for the festival; they might back out last minute. And no one is listening to what I'm telling them and they're all just doing their own thing." When there's a chuckle from Leora, I ask, "How did you manage all the chaos?"

"With a dash of Christmas magic," she says. When I make a bit of an annoyed sound, she continues, "I don't mean some hokey bullshit Santa thing, Kellan, I mean just giving into the good feelings for the season. Everything will work out, if you just believe in magic."

"You're starting to sound like a Hallmark movie," I say. "Are you sure it's Morris that's going senile and not you?" From the corner of my eye, I see Chad cover his mouth in a gasp. He doesn't know that Leora and I have a good bantering relationship that includes the occasional lovingly hurled insult.

"So, if I'm senile, does that make you my imaginary friend?" she asks. "If so, I always thought I'd imagine more attractive friends."

I laugh, the humor breaking the tension and clearing my headache, if only for a moment. "Thank you, Leora."

"Always remember that it's okay to ask for help," she says.

A few moments later, the call ends, and I'm left smiling. But that smile only lasts a few seconds; Samantha from the deli three doors down barges into the shop.

"Jennifer from the café says *she* has the official sandwich of the Snowflake Festival, but it's always been my cranberry and turkey melt sandwich!" she shouts. "Tell that trash to smarten up and step off!"

That feeling in my chest that the weight of the world is on me suddenly returns.

"I'll leave you to it," Chad says, walking out and giving Samantha a wide berth. When he's past Samantha, he turns around and mouths *good luck* to me.

And so it continues for my entire afternoon, one complaint or crisis after another. There's that old expression that it was like herding cats, but I would much rather have that task than this nonsense the business community has thrown at me.

When the day is finally, mercifully, blessedly over, I lock the door and let out a long sigh of relief. I sag against the door and slide down to the floor. I close my eyes, wishing I could just fall asleep right here, right now.

Then a notification buzzes on my phone. "God fucking damn it," I mutter. I'd forgotten, yet again, about the Chamber of Commerce meeting at the community center. It's to finalize the Snowflake Festival plans. *Don't forget your Princess sweater!* the note attached to the calendar event reads. That had been typed in by the secretary of the board, not by me. I'd never willingly wear that too-tight jeweled nightmare.

I push myself to my feet, don the sweater, and then head out the door to the community center.

BRADEN

The sign on the community center door says: *Snowflake Festival Committee Meeting 7:00 pm.*

I check my watch, knowing full well that my nonna said it was starting at six. Ah…damn it. Now I'm an hour early. I'm not gonna sit in there for an hour and wait for this thing to get started. I can find something to do at the shop. As I turn to leave, I hear a loud crash from inside the building. Looking through the glass door, I see Kellan standing on the opposite side of the large room, surrounded by roughly four chairs that have fallen at his feet.

"Shit! What else can go wrong today?" Kellan shouts.

I open the door and step inside. I have to help him. Kellan is bent over picking up one of the black chairs, I don't think he even heard me come in. "You okay?" I ask.

He stands up straight and lifts the chair into its proper position, avoiding eye contact. "Tch. Of course, you would come in at this exact moment. I—what are you doing here so early? Meeting doesn't start for another hour."

He hasn't even looked up at me. "I can help if you need me to. I got the time wrong."

"Ha!" Kellan says. "*You* made a mistake? No…how can that be?" he asks facetiously, while lifting another chair.

That was funny. Reminds me of the banter we had when we were younger, before I ruined everything by kissing him. When he was just my sarcastic, smartass best friend. I laugh, because as much as he seems to like thinking that I made a mistake, I have to correct him. Mostly just because it's funny. "Yeah, well technically my nonna made the mistake. She told me it was starting at six."

Kellan shakes his head. "Oh, wow. I'd expect nothing less from her. She knew the time of the meeting"—he places a chair down—"she was just being a bit meddlesome, I suspect. She doesn't like that we aren't talking. Which isn't really my fault, or it is. I don't even know anymore," he says.

His phone rings loudly, and his posture drops. He picks up the last toppled chair and places it upright. Giving a loud sigh, he reaches into the pocket of his tight, slim-fit jeans and pulls his phone out. "Hi, Benji, I assume you're calling because something is wrong. What is it?"

I'm still standing in the entranceway, deciding if I should leave and give him privacy while he's on this phone call, or maybe I should try and help with the chairs? He looks so frustrated; he's just rolling his head in circles, with his hand on his hip. "Unnngh," Kellan whines, while laying his head on the counter.

Oh God, anything but that whine. He was so whimpery and needy the other night when we fucked. It was so hot.

Kellan turns to the side, facing away from me, and leans over the counter. His shirt lifts while he reaches for a pen, giving me a perfect view of his slutty little waist. His skin is so soft, I can still feel him in my hands, the soft smooth curve of his hips, and the way he quivered when he came. I want him…I want to hear him scream my name. I want to fuck his pretty little mouth again.

No, no. I have to calm down. I should probably just leave and come back at seven. I'm not gonna do anyone any good by being here like this. My dick is feeling way too strained right now.

"Well, that's great! Just fucking great!" Kellan shouts, then ends his call.

I watch as he walks toward a stack of chairs leaning against the wall.

Is he gonna try to pick all those up? Now I see how the chairs had fallen earlier. He must have tried to lift four at a time, and they toppled over.

"Are you sure you don't want my help?" I ask him.

"No, I don't. I got it." Kellan lifts the four chairs and when he turns to place them, his phone rings loudly again. "This day could not get any worse," he says. He puts the stack of chairs down and reaches into his pocket for his phone. He looks at the screen and finally makes eye contact with me.

I don't know why, but I feel like it's Chad that's calling. I can't really put it into words, there was just something similar in the way he just looked at me, and the way he looked at me yesterday, whenever Chad spoke to me.

I really need to make a decision here. Do I help him with the chairs even though he refused my help? Or should I just leave and come back later? I sigh inwardly. I feel so incredibly protective over him. It's probably just a holdover from our younger days, but still, I hate hearing his voice so stressed out and seeing him on edge like this. The stress is just pouring out of him. I want to make him feel better.

I need to start by apologizing. I can't do that right now, though. I'll just stress him out even more. Besides, he doesn't want a relationship…he doesn't like them. I want a relationship with him. I can't think of him as just a tool for sex…something to be used. I really hate that he sees sex that way. But fuck—I want to use him right now. Maybe I just need to get used to his way of thinking…things would probably be easier that way. After all, I am 100% certain that sex would make us both feel better.

"What's up?" Kellan asks, answering his phone. "The machine down again?"

I can't exactly block out his conversation. I'm constantly finding myself in these situations with him. Overhearing stuff that I don't really want to. I take my phone out and check my emails. As much as I try, I can't ignore the sound of his voice.

"What do you mean it's worse?" he asks. "No… No… Well, what the hell am I supposed to do, Chad? I am so stressed out right now. I don't have time to deal with every single thing that is going wrong. I don't know… Figure it out, I guess. I can probably fix the machine after the meeting. The other thing, I have no idea. Ask Lucas, maybe? I gotta go." Kellan ends the call and goes right back to unstacking the chairs. He exhales and pulls another chair off the stack.

His phone rings loudly, and something in me snaps. I can't take it anymore. I can make him feel better. I walk over and quickly take the phone out of his hand before he can answer it. I place it on the table and hold his face in my hands. "No more talking," I whisper. "You need something else. Am I right?" My eyes search his perfect face, while my cock throbs in my pants. I want to fuck him raw, bury my cock deep inside him, make all of this stress more manageable. I want to rip his clothes off and take him right here on the table, but I want him to tell me that he wants me. I need to know that this feeling of need is not one sided.

His gaze meets mine, and he nods silently, while I cradle his face in my hands.

"Now that won't do," I say softly. "Be a good boy and tell me you want my cock."

Holy shit—he grabs ahold of my bun, bringing his mouth near my ear. "I want you," he whispers. "I want your cock. Will you give it to me?" He kisses my earlobe softly, lightly licking it. "Please, Braden, I want you to fuck me."

"Oh fuck, Kellan." I lift him up, while he wraps his legs around me. He presses his lips tightly against mine, parting mine with his tongue. Our tongues collide, and our kiss is loud, wet and fucking hot.

"Nnn—mmm—"The softest moans escape Kellan's lips.

I kiss him harder, using my tongue to feel the entirety of his mouth, while teasing his hole with my middle finger on the outside of his jeans.

I carry him toward what I assume can only be a spare room, turning the doorknob, while keeping a tight grip on his ass. Once inside I realize this is not so much an extra room as it is a supply closet. I lock the door behind us and place Kellan down, rapidly pulling off that ridiculous sweater, exposing his hot, hard chest. I rub his nipples lightly with my thumbs, while Kellan grabs at my belt buckle, seemingly desperate for my cock. I tease one of his nipples with my tongue, while rubbing his cock on the outside of his jeans. "That's a good boy. Your cock already knows who it belongs to," I say, while slipping my hand down the back of his jeans. "How about your ass? Who does this belong to? Hmm?" I rub his entrance softly, teasing it with just the tip of my finger.

I don't quite know what the fuck is going on, but it doesn't matter because Braden is shoving his tongue deep inside my mouth. All the chaos and turmoil and headache of the day just melts away as he grips my biceps and pulls me in even tighter.

"You need that hole stuffed, don't you, boy?" Braden asks as we pull apart from the kiss. I've been doing an awful lot of kissing lately for a guy that swore it off twelve years ago. "It's the only thing that'll set you straight, isn't it?"

I whimper.

"Say it, boy."

"I need your cock, sir," I say. My cock is getting rock hard at this aggressive turn from Braden, though the hot body and the magical kiss are certainly enough to get me hard on their own. "I need you inside me."

"Good boy." Braden gives me one last kiss. "Now get down and suck it."

I obediently fall to my knees and rip open Braden's fly, then yank his jeans and underwear down to mid-thigh. His heavy, thick cock flops out. It's dark and warm and oh-so-suckable. I grip the base, open my mouth, and take Braden into me. I suck him deep and long, taking his lengthy shaft down to the base without so much as a cough.

Braden runs his fingers through my hair. "You're so pretty when you suck cock, you know that?"

I look up at him, making intense eye contact, but never once breaking the suction or rhythm. With my other hand, I massage his low-hanging balls. He throws his head back and lets out a deep sigh of pleasure.

When he brings his head forward again, he asks, "Are you ready to get fucked?"

I finally let his cock fall from my mouth. It makes a wet pop sound as it slips from my lips.

"I'm ready, sir," I say. "My hole is ready."

His face flickers with disappointment. "I don't have lube."

"I don't care. I don't need it; spit is enough."

Braden cups my chin and runs a thumb over my wet lips. "Good boy." Then he leans down to take my mouth in a kiss. The urgency and passion we'd felt mere moments ago with that first kiss had only intensified now. Braden is my whole world in this moment. Right here and right now, nothing matters except for us and the pleasure we're both experiencing.

Braden guides me upward with the hand cupping my chin, our lips and mouths never parting. His hands slip between us, tugging at the fly of my jeans and opening them.

"Turn around," Braden orders.

When I do so, he yanks the back of my pants and briefs down, exposing my round, smooth ass. I'm proud of my ass; as a bottom, a killer ass is a requirement. And when Braden lets out a moan of appreciation, I feel a surge of pride.

"Fuck me," I whisper. I lean forward, bracing my hands on the shelves in front of me. For the first time since this whole thing started, I take stock of where we are. It appears to be a large supply closet; in front of me is a shelf lined with half-used cans of paint.

My attention is instantly brought back to my body when I feel Braden's spit-slicked fingers probe at my hole. One slips inside, and then a second soon follows. He finger-fucks me a bit, teasing at my prostate, almost hinting at a repeat of last time's immense and overwhelming pleasure. I meet each finger-thrust with a push back of my hips, helping drive those fingers deeper.

"You like that, don't you, you little slut…"

"Mmhmm…" I moan. "I can't wait for the real thing."

Braden withdraws his fingers from my ass and a moment later, the warm, fat head of his cock nestles between my ass cheeks and gently probes forward. When the head finds my hole, he pushes his hips forward, sliding his cock inside with aching slowness.

I tighten my grip on the shelves as Braden's girth deliciously stretches me, and as his length plunges extra deep.

He places his hands on my hips, and his fingers dig in as he tightens his grip. It feels like Braden is claiming me, taking control of me, owning me, and all of these feelings only lead to me letting out a horny little moan.

And no more than a moment later, he's in to full depth, his smooth pelvis pressing hard against my ass cheeks.

"Fuck, you're so big," I moan.

He drags his cock out, the friction exciting all my nerve endings, and then he plunges back in. He does this over and over, picking up speed, landing with more force. Soon the *slap-slap-slap* of our bodies colliding repeats and echoes all around us.

"Oh, fuck…Braden…" I moan.

"Shh…" His hand grabs at my face and covers my mouth. "Don't say my name. You keep doing that. We don't want to draw attention."

I lick his fingers, which makes him yank his hand away. I smile with the small victory. I reassert my grip on the shelf in front of me and use this as leverage to push back and get Braden going extra-deep.

"Oh…" he groans with the renewed sexual charge. "Your ass is so good."

He leans forward and wraps his arms around my torso, hugging me from behind as he fucks me. I reach back, holding his head in my hand. Then I turn my face, and Braden leans in close, and we kiss. As he shoves his cock deep in my hole, he also shoves his tongue in my throat.

This has very quickly become a very intense fuck for me, rivalling if not surpassing the first time we'd fucked. The sexual energy between us and the deep intimate connection that glues us together is so fucking intense, more so than I have experienced with any other person.

I'm not aware of when Braden shoots his load. I'm just aware that he is now panting and his thrusts are now slowing. I was so lost in the rush and the intensity of it all that the moment hadn't stuck out. Because this whole thing is that good.

"You came?" I ask, just to be sure.

"So did you," Braden says.

I look down and see that my cum is pooled on the floor in front of me. This is the second time in a row that I experienced a hands-free orgasm while getting dicked by Braden.

That has to mean something.

I turn my head back once more, and he claims my mouth with a kiss. It's intense; nothing has died down in the afterglow of orgasm. We keep kissing, even as his softening cock slips from my hole.

Eventually, we pull our underwear and pants back up and do a quick clean-up of the floor.

I open my mouth to say something, but Braden holds up his hand. "Don't," he says. "Don't chance it. I enjoyed that. Immensely." He pauses to adjust his clothes. "Ready?"

I give him a smile. "Ready."

We walk out of the supply closet to find Mr. Barclay on the other side of the hall, carefully examining the poster for the women's book club. No doubt he'd been listening.

Braden's cheeks deeply redden, but I feel no corresponding heat coming from my own. I'm not as embarrassed as he seems to be.

"I'm gonna go grab a seat, Mister Princess," he says, then quickly hurries off.

When he's gone, I turn to Mr. Barclay and stare at his back. The man refuses to turn around.

"How much did you hear?" I finally ask.

Mr. Barclay turns around and has a mischievous grin under his white moustache. "Mrs. Barclay and I have had many a rendezvous in that supply closet. That might even be where Alice was conceived."

I grin broadly. Mr. Barclay is the former executive director of this community center and, now that he's retired, he volunteers here regularly, so I run into him often and have gotten to know him a little bit. This is a new piece of information, making me appreciate the older man a little more.

I head back to the meeting room with a new spring in my step and a new clarity in my mind. When Braden had first pulled me into the closet, he'd said something about how I *needed* this. And now that I had been thoroughly fucked and had blown my own wad, I'm heading into this upcoming meeting with newfound clarity and calm.

There are good fucks and then there are life-changing fucks. Braden is a life-changing fuck.

I enter the meeting room and turn on the coffee pot and get the last few pieces set up. Just as everything is ready and set to go, meeting attendees start filing in. Since most of the downtown core closes up at the same time, these business owners are all on time and eager. After several people come in, I spot Braden in the back row. He looks like he's just gotten off work, not that he's just gotten off in my ass.

I can be lowkey and discreet, but Braden's skill at that is impressive. He doesn't so much as glance at me with lust. No one in this room would ever know what we'd just been up to. Other than Mr. Barclay, of course, who takes a seat next to Braden and gives me a wink.

Given how the entire day has gone, it's a pleasant surprise that the meeting goes off without a hitch. Some of the craziness from earlier today is getting resolved in this meeting. The cinema owner now understands that I have no control over the weather, and cannot control if a snowstorm does, or does not, hit the town.

When the meeting is over, Braden lingers and, when everyone is gone, he helps me put away the chairs.

"Thanks," I say.

Braden puts the chairs he holds on top of the stack against the wall. "No problem. It's a lot for one person to clean up."

"That wasn't what I was thanking you for."

"Oh…" Braden says. A moment later, he adds, "I enjoyed that. A lot."

I bite my lip. There's something I've been wondering about—daydreaming about—during the meeting.

"Do you want to stay over tonight? We could do a repeat of the supply closet. I've got a little cubby where I keep my broom and mop. It's a tight fit, but we'd make it work. Or we could use the bed." I feel a nervousness I don't usually feel.

"I, uh, I shouldn't," Braden says. He avoids my eyes.

"That's okay. It was just a thought," I say, hoping I manage to successfully hide my disappointment.

"Nonna would ask questions," Braden says, "or leap to conclusions."

I chuckle. I hadn't considered the Leora factor. "That's cool," I say, feeling much less defeated. "But maybe we could hang out a bit more?"

"I do need to see that broom closet of yours," Braden says as he stacks the last of the chairs.

"Like I said, it's a tight fit."

Braden pats my ass as he walks past. "I like things that are a tight fit."

We shut off the lights in the meeting room and wave bye to the custodian as we leave the community center.

"It's a standing offer," I say. "Anytime you want to come spend the night, I'd love to have you."

"I'll keep that in mind," Braden says.

I want to do something—anything—right here and right now… hug him, bend over for him…but I find myself frozen in place, standing in the snowy parking lot, watching him. And he's watching me back, seeming just as expectant.

Why is this so hard? I'd hit up guys on Grindr too many times to count, I'd chatted up strangers in the bar, but telling my childhood friend that I like him and want to do more with him…? That suddenly feels impossible.

I wonder if he's feeling the same. He's giving me that look, after all, but he's also not making any moves.

"Well," Braden says after a silence that had gone on way too long. "I should go."

"It was great seeing you again," I say. God, I sound so stupid. He was balls deep in my hole just an hour ago and all I can muster up is *it was great seeing you again?*

Braden smirks. "Goodnight, Kellan."

"Goodnight, Braden."

I watch as he turns and walks over to his Jeep, gets in, and then drives away. When his vehicle turns the corner, and he's fully out of sight, I retreat to my car.

"Stupid, stupid, stupid!" I shout as I slam the steering wheel.

I turn on the car, pull out of the parking spot, and then take to the streets, quickly navigating my way home. When I enter, Senator Tunacan loudly proclaims how very hungry he is.

"I'm sorry, boy," I say, stooping down to scratch the top of his head, before then proceeding into the kitchen to live out my subservient human role. When I put the dish of food on the floor, I sit down and watch him eat.

"I think he likes me," I tell The Senator. He looks up at me as he chews on some chicken, then quickly lowers his head to gobble up more food. "But I can't seem to get through to him and say the right thing, and I think he can't seem to let his guard down and just have some fun."

The Senator finishes his meal shortly after and then turns and walks away, leaving the room. I roll onto my hands and knees and follow him through the condo. The cat has a routine; after a meal, he likes to go somewhere to sit and rest and let his food digest. He has a few favorite spots and with where he's headed now, I know he's headed to the bathroom to sit on the floor vent, one of the warmest spots in the place.

When I catch up to him, I flop on my side on the bathmat, looking up at my furry confidant.

"What do I do, Tuna?"

He blinks at me and then looks away.

Chapter Six
You Taste Like Mine

Phew, I wipe my brow, as I seal the last order of cookies into a festive red box. I've never been so happy to see stacks of pre-decorated gift boxes in my life. I can't imagine how difficult this would have been if my nonna hadn't placed the box order before she got hurt. Packing forty-five gift boxes before 7:00 am has to be some kind of a record. I was thankful for the work this morning, though. I barely slept a wink after my closet rendezvous with Kellan last night. It took all the willpower in me not to call him and take him up on his offer to sleep over. Since I knew I had all these orders to pack, I decided to start at 3:00 am.

I still have time to spare before my parents' flight gets in this morning.

I feel my phone vibrating in my pocket. I don't even have to look; I know it's my mother calling—no one else would call me this early.

I pull the phone out and answer it, "Hi, Mom."

"Hi, honey! Your father and I just landed, we should be there in another two hours or so. Gotta get the rental car, and the luggage is a mess over here." She sighs. "Hold on, sweetie. Mama Mia… Grab the big black one!" she shouts at my father.

"Sorry, honey, I'm back. Anyway, we'll be there soon. I'm hoping tonight we can all go out to dinner, maybe? Or we can stay up and watch movies? What do you think?"

"Oh, mom, it's seven am, it's a little too early for me to make dinner plans. I have no idea how the day is gonna go. I just packed, like, forty-five orders, all to be picked up today. I'm already exhausted."

"Bup, say no more, sweetie. When we get there, I'll leave your father with Nonna, and I'll come help you. I'll be the best helper you ever saw, and I'll be so quiet, it'll be like I'm not even there. Don't try to stop me. I'm gonna do it. I'll see you soon. Love you, bye."

"Mom, I don't—" And she hung up on me. She is so much like my nonna.

I hang my head backward. This is gonna be a long day. Even though I'm close with my mom, I'm really dreading the fact that my parents will be staying in the same apartment with me for the next two weeks. I could use the help at the shop, though. I still have no idea how my nonna was able to keep things running so smoothly.

I hear a knock at the door and realize I didn't unlock it yet. There are a few regular customers who come in for a cookie and coffee first thing in the morning. I haven't got all of their names memorized yet. The person knocking, however, isn't one of them. It's Lucas. He's standing outside, smiling and pointing at the handle.

I smile and unlock the door, holding it open for him. "Good morning, it's Lucas, right?" I extend my hand in greeting, once he's inside.

He smiles nervously and shakes my hand. "Uh yeah, Lucas. I feel weird shaking your hand because we've been around each other a few times. Feels like I'm introducing myself, which I probably should have done several times already."

I smile, walking back behind the counter. "No worries. It's nice to meet you. So, what can I get for you this morning?"

He points toward the espresso machine. "An espresso, but I can get it myself if you want. I'll still pay for it, but I'm used to running things here. Not sure if your grandma told you, but I was helping out here until a few months ago. I kind of miss it. It's so much nicer here than at the bar."

I smirk. "Mmm yeah, but the view at the bar is better, right?" I walk toward the espresso machine and grab a cup off the stack. "I can make it for you, you're a customer."

Lucas follows behind me and stands next to the espresso machine. I guess he feels like he can still walk back here.

"Alright, you know how to make it?" he asks. "This machine is pretty temperamental."

I don't really understand the vibe he's giving off. It's not flirty, but if he just wants an espresso, why didn't he order it and let me make it? Why bother coming around the counter and standing beside me. Still, I'm not really all that comfortable using the machine. I've only used it a handful of times, and one of those times was with Kellan. Most people order coffee or tea, those I'm more than capable of making.

"I can do it," I say.

"Alright. I'm gonna supervise, then," he says, leaning forward on his elbows.

I place the cup under the dispenser, hit a few buttons, and the machine starts up. I give him a smile. "See, I told you I could do it. I perform well when challenged."

He nods slowly. "Me too. Speaking of a challenge…" his voice trails off, as he rights his posture, while pulling his gray beanie over his ears.

I sigh, crossing my arms on my chest. "I knew you were here for something else. What challenge?"

He fidgets with his beanie a little more, then rubs his hands together, walking back over to the espresso machine. He picks up the finished cup and takes a sniff. "Ooh that smells great!" He blows on the coffee. "Yeah, so, what's the deal with you and Kellan?"

"Kellan? Why are you asking me about Kellan? Aren't you and Chad together? Or are you one of those 'no relationship' guys, too?"

Lucas scoffs. "No, I am not one of those guys…what about you? You and Kellan? Are you together?" He sips his espresso, raising his eyebrows at me.

I'm not sure that I want to talk to Lucas about the way I feel about Kellan, but I have a feeling that this is less about Kellan and more about Chad.

"Why are you asking? Are you interested in Kellan?"

Lucas's eyes go wide, and he almost spits his drink out. "Kellan? No. Never."

That's what I thought. I smile and straighten the cookie boxes on the back counter. "Then why are you asking me about Kellan if you're not interested in him?"

"He's in the way. Every time I want to do anything with Chad, he gets in the way. I know that he and Chad don't have feelings for each other, but damn—Kellan is just *always* in the way."

The bells on the door jingle, and we both look up. "Good morning," Kellan says, walking inside. His face beams brightly looking at me, he hasn't seemed to notice Lucas standing on the other side of the counter.

"See?" Lucas says. "Always in the way."

I drop an eyebrow at Lucas's remark, then walk toward Kellan. He looks so cute this morning. At least he doesn't look like he had trouble sleeping. I wonder if he was thinking about me last night. I'm not gonna even pretend to be anything other than ecstatic at the sight of seeing him here.

"Good morning, Kellan, it's nice to see your face bright and early. What can I get you?" I ask.

"Yeah, I wanted to—"

"Good morning, Kellan," Lucas interrupts, walking up beside me, while sipping his espresso.

Kellan is obviously confused as to why Lucas is here. "Oh, hi, Lucas…didn't see you there." He points at Lucas and me, with a concerned look on his face. "What uh…I didn't think you guys really knew each other. Are you helping out at the shop today?"

Lucas raises his eyebrows and playfully elbows me. "Nah, this guy wouldn't even let me make my own espresso. I was just here to talk about something that's been bothering me, but it's not important." He reaches into his pants and pulls his wallet out.

Kellan tilts his head looking at Lucas. "What's been bothering you? And why would you be talking to Braden about it?"

I correct him, "It's not *what's* been bothering Lucas, more like *who* has been bothering him." I lift my chin toward Kellan and mouth the word *you* to him.

Kellan points at himself, and Lucas laughs. "Ah you're so innocent, right, Kellan? No idea what you're doing, huh? Give me a break…"

I'm a bit uncomfortable with the tone that Lucas just used toward Kellan. Even though I hate whatever the relationship is between Kellan and Chad—I also have no right to hate it, not just because I have no idea what *it* is, but more so because Kellan hasn't agreed to be anything more than my friend. But in Lucas's case, he is in some kind of a relationship with Chad, they were even holding hands at the gym the other night. Still, I'm not going to let Lucas talk disrespectfully to him, I'm certain this is headed in that direction.

"Lucas, you're a bit younger than us, right?" I ask. He has a very cocky kind of demeanor about him. I'm curious if that's because he's only like twenty-two or something. I'm terrible with ages.

Kellan cuts in, "Wait, who cares how old he is? What are you so pissy about, Lucas?"

"Pissy?" Lucas asks, then finishes his drink, and tosses the cup into the trash bin. "And yeah, I'm younger than you guys, so what? What does my age have to do with anything?"

I laugh. "I was just curious about your age. Doesn't have anything to do with me telling you to take it down a few notches. If you have a problem with Kellan just talk it out, but don't be rude about it. I'm not a fan of the way you just talked to him."

Lucas nods at me and points at the two of us. "So, you guys *are* together."

"No, we're not," I say.

Kellan throws a hand up. "Wait, this is about you and me, Braden? I'm so confused."

"Oh enough!" Lucas says, pulling his beanie off his head, and ruffling his own sandy blond hair. "I thought that you were finally gonna get out of the way."

"Out of the way of what?" Kellan asks.

"My relationship with Chad. I'm not comfortable with you guys sleeping together whenever one of you is bored. I came here to see if Braden was into you, because I was hoping I wouldn't need to have this conversation with you."

Kellan looks at me, shaking his head in confusion. "You guys were talking about this before I got here?"

"That's apparently why he's here," I say.

Kellan sighs. "I haven't slept with Chad in a while, at least a few months, so I don't really understand how I'm getting in the way."

A tremendous wave of relief and excitement washes over me. Hearing that he hasn't slept with Chad in a while is the best thing I've heard all morning. I don't know much about Kellan as an adult, but I doubt that he suddenly turned into a liar at this point in his life.

"Really? You haven't?" I ask.

Lucas laughs a bit and puts his gray knitted beanie back on his head, smiling brightly. "If you're not sleeping with Chad, we don't have anything else to talk about." He knocks lightly on the counter and starts walking out of the kitchen area. "Just do me a favor, Kellan—the next time the ice machine needs to be fixed; tell him you can't do it. I can fix it for him."

He stops as he reaches the door and smiles at the two of us, waiting for confirmation that Kellan will do what he asked.

"Uh…yeah, sure. I'll tell him I can't fix it. I don't want to fix it anyway. That machine is a pain in the ass," Kellan says with a laugh.

"Ahhh, thank you. I appreciate that. Oh, and Braden, Kellan told Chad that you slept together, so I think that means he likes you. Chad also told me that Kellan kissed you, and he doesn't kiss anyone, it's like a well-known fact that he doesn't. Best to just be honest and talk about these things, right?" He pumps his eyebrows and pushes the door open. "Later," he says.

Kellan hangs his head down and exhales. "I can't believe he just said that."

I'm torn in between being ecstatic over the influx of information I just received, and the fact that Lucas is now the second person to tell me that Kellan doesn't ever kiss anyone. Because Kellan sure has no problem kissing me. In fact, I seem to recall that most times our mouths have met, Kellan was the one who initiated the kisses. I want to ask for some kind of an explanation or confirmation, but based on Kellan's body language, he's a little embarrassed. I don't want to make him feel bad, or pressure him into talking. Making him feel uncomfortable is the last thing I'd ever want to do. But I also can't just blow past what has been said—if there is any chance that Kellan has real feelings for me, I need to know.

"Kellan," I say, my voice is heavy with expectation.

He looks up at me and gives me a small half smile. "I did tell him we slept together; I didn't mean to—"

My phone rings loudly from inside my pocket, while the door to the cookie shop opens at the same time. The woman from the bakery walks in, while talking on her cell phone.

Kellan looks at the counter toward the decorated boxes. "Oh, Rachel is here, she always places an order this time of year. I'll get it for her," he says. He walks past me toward the back counter and grabs the box with her name on it.

My phone continues to ring in my pocket while Kellan hands Rachel her cookies. "Good morning, Rachel, here's your order," he says. "Did you pre-pay?"

I stand speechless watching Kellan handle the transaction. He's so comfortable here. I sometimes forget that he helped my nonna out for such a long time.

"Oh, hello, Kellan. Yes, I paid online. Is Braden here? I wanted to thank him for making sure these were ready. I was so worried that things may not be the same once he took over, but everything seems to be going well."

"Oh, he's in the back," Kellan says. "I'll let him know that you said that."

She nods slowly. "I see…are you helping out here until he gets used to things?"

Kellan glances over his shoulder at me. I'm still standing in the same spot like the dumbfounded idiot that I am, while my phone continues to ring in my pocket. I'm trying hard not to let my hopes get too high, but my heart is racing faster than I can control it.

I snap out of my momentary trance and answer my phone, "Hi, Mom."

"Honey, I'm almost there, just dropping the luggage off upstairs, your father had to use the bathroom, so we went straight upstairs to Nonna's. I'll be down in just a few after I get the scoop on everything that's been going on. She said she has some hot tea for me," she giggles. "She's so funny! The things she says. I think she gets half of them from Kellan."

I lift my gaze toward Kellan and shoot him a megawatt smile. "Oh yeah, Kellan has taught Nonna all kinds of things."

Kellan tilts his head at me, pointing at himself. "What did I do?"

I cover the speaker on the phone. "It's my mom: she's telling me what a bad influence you are on my nonna."

"What? No, I'm not! Your nonna is the bad influence! You have no idea what she's like, she's wild."

I don't doubt that my nonna is a different person around Kellan, after everything I've heard her say about him, I wouldn't be surprised to hear that she and Kellan have gone clubbing together at this point.

I return to my phone call. "Yeah, okay, Mom, I'll see you in a few minutes, then. Bye."

"Your mom is here? She didn't tell me she was coming in this week," Kellan says.

"You talk to my mom, too?"

Kellan shrugs his shoulders. "Yeah, of course, I do. I'm close with your nonna, I usually check in with your mom on things once a month, but we also see each other on holidays, when she comes to visit. I saw her at Thanksgiving. She loves the pumpkin spice candles, but I only order the oils for them in the fall, so I always pour a few extra for her after the season is over."

I haven't forgotten what had happened right before my mom

called. Lucas said Kellan doesn't kiss anyone…ever. That has to mean something. I need to talk to him about this.

The bells jingle on the door and another two customers walk in. I exhale, looking at Kellan. "Gonna be a long day, my mom should be down in a few minutes to help, though."

"Good morning," I say to the customers that entered. "I'll be right with you both."

Kellan smiles and walks toward the back counter. He points at two of the green boxes. "You'll need those two. That's Jared Rollins, and the other is Melanie Kwan, in case you forgot their names." I slide the two boxes from the middle of the pile out, like Jenga pieces.

"Thanks. I was really trying to remember their names and was drawing a blank."

"Do you want me to stay and help?" Kellan asks.

"Nah, thanks for asking." My mom will be down soon, and besides, your shop is probably going to be busier than mine today."

Kellan smiles, putting his hands in his pockets. "Yeah, you're probably right. Luckily my cousin, Riley, will be there today, so it shouldn't be too terrible. I should get back though."

I'm unsure of what to do. I want him to stay. I want to hug him or kiss him—any form of physical contact would do at this point, just some sign of affection, but the customers need their orders, so instead, I just smile. "Alright, well thanks again for your help." I feel so stupid not making plans to see him again, or even to call him, but how can I do anything with the customers so close by. I'm gonna call him on my next break and see if he wants to go out tonight.

KELLAN

The day had been busy, and I'd spent most of that time on my feet helping customers and running to the extra stock in the back. But now that it's mid-afternoon, and it's quieted down a bit, I can finally take a few moments to breathe, and I find myself looking out the window and across the very narrow street to Braden's shop.

It's been almost a week since he moved in and took over BJ's Cookies and in those few short days, I feel the man has gone from a baking disaster to, well, slightly less of a disaster. No longer am I finding Braden covered in flour or splattered with batter or with a smudge of melted chocolate across this face.

He's learned the ropes and learned how to keep everything together. He's even learned how to operate the temperamental mixer. And from what I've seen, the orders have not declined. It seems the people of Frosty Bottoms like the new cookie baker.

Today, though, is a different story. I can tell disaster is brewing across the street. Braden's mom had come into town. As far as I know, Braden and Belinda get along well—at least they did when we were teenagers—but working in the close confines of BJ's Cookies seems like a recipe for disaster.

When the shop quiets down mid-afternoon, I wander to the front of my store and look across the street at BJ's. Even from here, I can tell Braden is unhappy, though he's making a show of everything being fine. I can see it in the rigidity of his posture, and the way he's moving around the shop.

It looks like he needs a destressing fuck, just like he did for me. Maybe I should ask Mr. Barclay for more supply closet recommendations.

"How's Braden?" Riley asks.

I jump at her voice; I'd forgotten she was helping me this afternoon. I shouldn't stare moon-eyed out the window so much when she's here. "He's well. He's starting to adjust to life in Frosty Bottoms, I think."

The phone rings and Riley answers it, allowing me to continue watching across the street.

A customer enters BJ's and Belinda takes charge of the transaction, shooing Braden away. The look he shoots his mother makes it clear that if it were anyone else shooing him away, he'd tear them a new one, but since it's his mom, he'll let it slide.

Belinda comes up to Frosty Bottoms every few months to visit her mother and a lot of that time would be spent in the cookie shop, helping her out and easing the workload. So, it's to be expected that she would try to take control of things.

"I'm gonna pop across the street," I say to Riley. "You want anything?"

Still on the phone, Riley shakes her head no at me. I leave Dip Your Wick and hurry across the street—thankfully the brutal wind from the other day had died down, but the air is still frigid.

When I open the door to BJ's, a set of bells jingle to announce my arrival.

"Kellan," Belinda greets, hurrying around the counter. "It's so great to see you! Merry Christmas!" She pulls me into a hug.

"Merry Christmas, Belinda," I say. "It wouldn't be Christmas without seeing you in the shop."

When we break from the hug, she retreats to the other side of the counter. I notice Braden is nowhere to be found.

"What can I get for you? My Braden bear made some wonderful sugar cookies topped with crushed candy cane that are extravagant. He loves peppermint. And, of course, there's the traditional gingerbread men. Or if you want a coffee, I could fire up the espresso machine and whip up a special drink for you, too."

I lean down to look at the cookies in the display case. They all look absolutely amazing; I really had no idea Braden was so skilled as a cookie maker. I remember him baking a few batches when we were younger, but nothing on this level. I guess it became a hobby for him as an adult.

"Braden seems to be getting adventurous with cookies today," I say. There's a caramel crunch cookie in the center of the case that looks divine and is a step above what he normally has featured in his case.

Belinda *pffts* and waves her hand dismissively. "A little too adventurous, if you ask me. I've been trying to get him to focus more on traditional Christmas cookies. At this time of year people don't want something experimental, they want something comforting. You need to give them seasonal joy, not just sugar. You're selling good days, not just good cookies. He didn't even want to make these gingerbread men until I twisted his arm."

I'm starting to see why Braden's been looking a bit tense. Belinda means well and does have more experience in this shop than Braden does, but this well-intentioned advice, especially framed in a pushy manner, would likely rub Braden the wrong way.

"Can I get that caramel crunch?" I ask, pointing at the cookie in the center.

When I pull out my wallet, she waves me away. "You've taken such good care of my mother over the years; I'm not going to charge you for a cookie." She pulls out a pair of tongs and a wax paper bag, then grabs the cookie and slips it into the bag, handing it over the counter to me.

"Thank you," I say. I bite the bullet and ask the question I've been wanting to ask since coming in. "Where's Braden?"

Belinda looks behind her like she's just now realizing her son is nowhere to be found. "He must be in the office. You can head back if you want to say hi."

"Sure," I say. Then I hold up the cookie bag and add, "Thanks again."

I go around the corner and head to the back of the shop where Leora's office is. It's Braden's office now, I remind myself. The door is open a crack and through it I see Braden pacing back and forth, muttering to himself.

I knock gently. "Braden?"

The muttering stops suddenly and in its place is a deep inhale and exhale. A moment later, Braden pulls the door fully open, and there's a smile on the man's face, a smile that doesn't quite reach his eyes.

I hold up the cookie. "Want to share?"

He eyes the bag suspiciously. "Do you trust the baker?"

"Hmm…I think I do," I say.

Braden steps back and holds out his hand. "Come in and take a seat."

I sit on the battered loveseat and sink into it. The last time I'd been in this room, things had been very different. If I look hard enough at the front of the desk, I'm pretty sure I can see the outlines of my cum shot.

I pull the cookie out of the bag, snap off a piece, and shove it in my mouth. It's incredible. Even though it's a crispy, crunchy cookie, it still manages to be soft and gooey at the same time.

"My mom is here," Braden says. "As you saw."

"I've been watching from my shop," I say. "Looks like it's been going a bit rough."

Braden sighs and collapses on the couch beside me. "We generally get along great and she means well and she has a lot of experience in the shop…but I can't help but feel like she's taking over, you know? Like she's seeing what I'm doing and is disappointed."

I shove a second cookie piece into my mouth. "Well, if she told you to make these cookies, then listening to her is the right thing."

Braden smiles. "The gingerbread and snickerdoodles were her suggestion. The caramel crunch was mine, and it's a recipe I developed a couple years back. I've got a bunch of custom recipes to roll out over the next few months."

I shove the rest of the cookie in my mouth and say with my mouth full, "That's why you're the boss!"

Braden's gaze flicks to the door, like he's worried his mom will barge in and take over some more. I feel sorry for him; I know how much he loves his mom, so this friction between them can't feel good.

"Where's your mom staying?" I ask. Mentally, I have my fingers crossed that she's managed to book a room at the hotel so they'd at least get some space apart from each other overnight.

"With my nonna," Braden says. He stands up, clearly feeling antsy and restless.

I arch an eyebrow. "You, your mom, your dad, your nonna, and your cat, all in one tiny three bedroom unit? If it were me, I'd be pulling my hair out or something. I love my family, but I can't be in cramped quarters like that."

Braden rolls his eyes and sits on the edge of the desk. "Neither can I, especially if our daytimes are also in cramped quarters here. I called all the hotels to see if they have a room for me, but there's nothing."

I stand up and step closer, to the point our knees are touching. "My offer from last night still stands, you know…"

"Your offer?" Braden asks.

"To spend the night at my place. Or a few nights since your

parents are here in your nonna's apartment. It doesn't have to be sex; it can just be a hangout. We can pull out some old video games or something, relive our childhood."

Braden looks up at me and if I'm reading him right, there's heat in those eyes. "Or something…"

I step even closer, almost bringing my crotch in contact with his. I raise my arm and place my hand on the side of his face, cupping his cheek. I'm feeling feelings for Braden that I never thought I'd feel—not just for him, but for anyone. But a small part of me recalls I'd once had feelings for this man years ago that hadn't ended well. I'd learned to not give in with my heart. But now my heart wants to.

"Is it true what they say?" Braden asks. His voice is thick with lust, angsty with need.

"And what do they say?" I ask, leaning close.

"You don't kiss anyone."

"I don't," I say. "It's a general rule I live by. A hookup's a hookup. Kissing implies feelings."

Braden looks at my lips and then back up to my eyes. "You've kissed me a few times now."

I bite my lower lip. Braden is right; I kissed him more than once. Both times we fucked there had been lots of kissing, and then there was the incident in the bar where I claimed him as mine with a kiss. I've kissed this man more times in the past week than I could count.

"I did…"

Braden puts his hands on my hips, pulling me in closer. His hardness is crushed up against my own. "And what does that mean?"

Thoughts tumble over thoughts in my brain. What *does* it mean? Am I really so smitten? Or has Braden unlocked a new way of hooking up for me? What is it about this man that makes me want to kiss him so damn much?

"Braden bear!" Belinda shouts. Loud footsteps approach the office.

Wide-eyed, I take two big steps backward and shove my hands in my pockets to help hide my bulge. Braden adjusts the lay of his apron, but can't do anything to hide the blush on his cheeks.

Belinda bursts through the door. "There you are! Janice Greene is here for her order and I can't find it anywhere! You didn't mess this one up, did you?"

Braden rolls his eyes. "I didn't mess it up, Mom. Her cookies have jam in them, so her order is in the fridge." He shoves himself off the desk and to his feet, then charges past his mother to take care of business.

"We need to come up with a better system," Belinda says as she follows her son out of the office. I can hear them as they go around the corner and through the baking area of the store. "Maybe a workflow of some kind, a way to organize the orders so anyone can step in and do the job."

"Mom…" Braden warns. Then their voices are softer as they approach the front and deal with the customer.

I reach in my pants and adjust my positioning to make myself less obvious, then leave the office, following them. I linger at the side of the shop as Braden helps the customer with her order.

When the customer leaves, Belinda says, "Kellan, dear, we should have you over for dinner tonight. It would be great to catch up since we didn't have much time at Thanksgiving."

I smile and am about to accept the offer when Braden interrupts.

"Sorry, Mom, but Kellan and I have plans tonight already. I'm going to his place for dinner." He gives me pleading eyes, begging me to go along with this.

"Oh, surely, you can put that off till tomorrow, right?" Belinda says.

"Not really," I say. My mind goes a million miles a minute in a dozen different directions, trying to come up with an excuse. "The crockpot. It has food in it. I'm cooking it. With the crockpot. It's for dinner." I mentally kick myself for not using complete sentences. I have to learn to lie better.

"Ohhh," Belinda says, looking discouraged. "Well, we'll have to have you over very soon."

A customer comes in, pulling Belinda's attention away from us. *Thank you,* Braden mouths to me.

I wink and then head out the door to return to my shop. I pass a customer on her way out and find Riley recording the sale in our inventory logbook.

"Hi, Riley," I say as I burst in. "Can you take over for the afternoon?" Without waiting for a response, I grab my coat and keys. "Bye, Riley!"

"Wait!" she calls after me. "Where are you going?"

"To clean my condo!" When I get in my car and start it up, I do a mental run-through of what I have to do before Braden comes over. The bathroom has to be cleaned, as does the kitchen, and dinner has to be made…which means picking a recipe and getting some ingredients.

I hurry over to the grocery store and wander the aisles aimlessly until I land on the idea of a creamy pesto chicken pasta. I charge through the store to get all the ingredients I'll need. Just as I'm about to head to the self-checkout, I get a call. Braden.

"Hey…uh…hi," I say as I answer the call.

"Hey…thanks for covering for me with the dinner thing," Braden says. "Um…you don't have to, you know, actually cook dinner. I can find somewhere else to go tonight."

I suddenly feel a little heartbroken at the risk of not seeing him tonight. "It's good. It's cool. I'm excited to cook for you."

"Really?" Braden asks. He sounds pleased. "I'd love to still come for dinner."

"Awesome. Yeah, dinner will be at seven."

There's a very long pause. Then Braden says, "Were you serious about the houseguest invite?"

"Of course," I say. "I've got a second bedroom that's unused. I've got a bunch of streaming services and some retro gaming consoles; we can have a great time!"

Braden chuckles. It's a sexy sound that goes straight to my cock. Braden says, "Perfect. I love my mom, but we need just a little bit of space. If it goes well and you're up for having me, I'd like to stay for a couple days. But if one night is enough and you're ready to kick me out, no hard feelings."

"I'd never kick you out. My home is your home." I get a weird feeling in my chest when I say that. I'll figure out what it means later.

"Cool. Thanks, Kellan," Braden says.

"See you at seven."

With renewed purpose, I rush through the self-checkout and get back to my car. Speeding through town, I arrive home not more than five minutes later.

I'm a one-man cleaning crew, starting ten projects at once—vacuuming, sweeping, cleaning the toilet, wiping the counters, doing the dishes, and more. And when the cleaning projects come to an end, I switch to cooking. I eye the clock; it's already approaching five, and Braden is coming at seven, giving me just enough time to put dinner together.

As I chop up the basil and toast the pine nuts for the pesto sauce, I look at my gleamingly-clean condo and wonder for a moment what's gotten into me. I've never worked this hard for a hookup and certainly not for a friend…so what is it about Braden that makes him deserve special treatment? It's rare that I roll out the red carpet like this.

Well…it's because it's Braden. That's reason enough to do all this.

I hadn't really stopped to think *why* he deserves all this, nor had I thought too hard about Lucas's comment, or about how much I'd been kissing Braden when I normally avoid kissing like the plague. It's just…*different*. There's really no other explanation for it other than *it's Braden*.

I throw ingredients in the pan, making up the recipe as I go. I rarely follow a formal recipe and instead often go with the vibes I'm feeling for a dish. I've impressed more than a few people with my improvised cooking.

Just as dinner is ready to be plated, the clock ticks to seven, and the buzzer rings. My heart throbs in my throat as I go to let Braden in.

I knock on the door of Kellan's condo with my small travel suitcase in tow. The last time I was here, I yelled at him for taking Mister Fluffykins home. But now, things are different. I'm not truly sure if I'm more nervous, or excited—the one thing I do know is that something smells delicious. I have to focus, though. I absolutely cannot have sex with him tonight. I have to control myself. This is not the relationship I want with him. I want him, all of him, all to myself. If that's what I want, I need to let him know. But I can't force him to talk, just one step at a time. The first step is being sure that I keep my hands to myself.

The door opens wide. "Hey, I'm glad you decided to come," Kellan says. "Dinner is just about ready." He motions with his hand, gesturing inside. "Let me give you the tour."

I step inside the condo, following behind him. It's gorgeous in here. The décor is modern, and peaceful, nothing tacky, nothing extravagant.

"This is a nice place," I say. "And whatever you're cooking smells really good."

"*You* smell good," Kellan says, as he stops and turns toward me.

"Oh yeah?"

"Mmhmm, didn't mean to say that out loud, but yes, the cologne smells…really good."

"Funny you mention that, because you always smell good, but like clean. Just clean. Not like cologne. Do you wear cologne?"

Kellan laughs. "Well, I'm glad I smell clean. I don't wear cologne, too many guys I know have allergies, so I've just gotten used to not wearing it."

"I don't have allergies," I say.

"Good to know," Kellan says, opening the door in front of us. "This is the spare room. You can use this for as long as you need to. I've never had anyone stay over long term, feels kind of exciting. Kind of like the sleepovers we had when we were kids."

"Those were fun. They only became slightly uncomfortable in our teenage years." I give him a playful wink, while dragging my suitcase inside. It's so cozy in here. I wonder who taught him how to decorate. Every room looks like it's straight out of a magazine.

"Your room is right on the other side of this wall?" I ask, tapping the light gray wall with my finger.

Kellan sits on the edge of the bed. "Yep. Just a super thin wall in-between us."

Oof. I felt that in a way that Kellan likely hadn't intended it. I mean, there's a super thin wall in-between us, emotionally, too. If I could just get him to open up to me. But no, I can't push him.

He smiles looking up at me, and lightly tugs on the side of my jeans. "Hey, we have a few minutes before dinner. Sit with me, let's see if you like the bed. If not, you can always use mine."

I drop my head forward. I'm not gonna make it. I want nothing more than to strip Kellan down and feel the warmth of his body pressed underneath mine on this bed. Of the two times we've had sex, neither time has been in a bed, and I really can't wait for that.

But still, what I want more than that is to be with him—really be with him. I want to talk to him, just the two of us. We've barely scratched the surface on catching up. With the way things are now, I feel like sex before that, is pushing us closer to being hook-up buddies, and I can't be that for him. I exhale, long and loud, sounding like a balloon being deflated, and sit next to him.

"That was a lot of air you just let out. What did I say wrong?" he asks.

I look at him softly. "You didn't say anything wrong. I'm really grateful that you're letting me stay here for a few days."

"But what? There's definitely more to that." Kellan rubs his thumbs together, looking down at the floor, avoiding eye contact.

"Yeah, just a little." I have to be strong here. If I want him to see me as more than just a good fuck, I have to be honest. "If I'm going to stay here, I don't think we should have sex." I can barely keep a straight face, at my own suggestion. Even the thought of not having sex with Kellan sometime within the next thirty minutes feels impossible. "It's just that, we haven't really even talked, and I know you're not into relationships, but I am. And I'm not offering, or not offering one, I just—I think it's important that we separate the sex from our relationship while I'm here. Just to keep things from getting too complicated."

Kellan holds a hand on his forehead. "I'm not great at reading people, and I often say the wrong thing, as you've undoubtedly noticed over the past few days. But I want to try and understand what you mean, or at least try and understand *why* you're saying this. You're feeling like we're just fucking and nothing more? Is that what you mean?"

"Tch, I don't feel like that. I think that's what it *seems* like. I feel like you admitted that you never kiss anyone, and immediately pressed your dick against mine, when my brain was trying to make sense of everything. When you're that close to me, my body just takes over, and my brain doesn't have a chance to think. With us being in the same condo, only that wall separating us, I want to just take a breath and take sex off the table, until we can at least have a proper conversation. I've missed so much of your life; I just want to catch up."

Senator Tunacan appears from underneath the bed and hops onto Kellan's lap. Kellan pets him and kisses his head. "What were you doing under the bed? You were eavesdropping! Gonna tell all the cats at the spa about this, huh?"

"Did I make you upset?" I ask.

Senator Tunacan unexpectedly hops off Kellan's lap and onto mine.

"Oh, hello there, Senator." I rub the cat's head. "I'm gonna stay here for a few days; I hope you don't mind. You can come visit whenever you want. My boy is at my nonna's house. Since we just moved, I didn't want to bring him into another new place this soon. But I'm used to sleeping with him every night, so I might get kind of lonely in here."

"If you weren't making a dumb no sex rule, you could just sleep with me," Kellan says, sounding like a petulant child.

"Ahhh, I did make you upset. I didn't mean to." I feel like an asshole now. How do I make him understand what I mean without sounding pushy?

A timer buzzes loudly from another room. "Dinner's ready," Kellan says, standing up from the bed. Senator Tunacan jumps from my lap onto the floor. Kellan places his hand on my shoulder and smiles. "I'm not upset. I'm just pouting a little." He gives my shoulder two squeezes, then lets go.

I stand up, trying not to laugh. "Ahhh, you're pouting. Now that's something I'm quite familiar with from our younger days."

Kellan shakes his head. "I have no idea what you're talking about. If I was ever pouting, it was probably something you did."

"Oh, is that so?" I ask, following him into the kitchen. "Do you need some help with dinner?"

"Nope, I got it. Just take a seat," he says, gesturing toward the small white table in the dining room.

I sit down while Kellan quickly plates the food, then hands me a dish that smells absolutely amazing. I look around the kitchen and can't believe that this was made by his hands, those same hands that used to need help staying inside the lines when coloring. I used to tell him not to worry about it, but he would always have me put my hand on top of his and help him trace the darkened outline of the pictures. He thought it helped him color better.

"This looks and smells delicious," I say, placing the food in front of myself. "What kind of chicken is this?"

"It's creamy pesto chicken with pasta."

"Oh wow. So, you can cook, huh? When did you learn how to do that?"

Kellan sits across from me and starts to eat his chicken. "My mom taught me a lot once I graduated, but thanks to your nonna, the majority of the recipes in my arsenal are Italian. I'd have to say that I got most of my skills from her when it comes to cooking."

"I do love Italian food, since that's what I grew up with." I take a bite of the chicken and pasta. I can't believe how deliciously tender and flavorful the chicken is. "Oh my God, this is the best chicken I've ever had. Don't tell my mother," I say, stuffing another forkful into my mouth.

Kellan giggles. "Thank you, your mom said the same thing when I made it for her back in the spring. Told me I wasn't allowed to tell Leora that she said mine was better. But since your nonna taught me, I can't really take credit for it."

"Yes, you can. This is amazing chicken! I don't see my nonna here cooking it, and I don't think she hobbled her way over here to make it before I left, so you most certainly can take credit for it."

I look down at my plate, I've always been such a fast eater, I told myself before the meal started to try and consciously eat slower, but with how good this chicken is, I can't help myself. My food is almost finished already. I look at Kellan's plate which somehow has even less food on it than mine.

"Look at that," I say, eyeing Kellan's almost empty plate. "You're a fast eater like me! I've never seen anyone eat faster than me."

Kellan wipes his mouth with his napkin and smiles. "Yeah, I seem to always be rushing off to do whatever is next on my to-do list, especially these days. With all the planning for the festival, I think I've started eating even faster than before."

I stand up from my seat and pick my plate up. "Well, I don't blame you, because that was really delicious." I reach for Kellan's plate. "Can I take that? I'll do the dishes, since you cooked. I feel like I need to repay you somehow. Doing the dishes is the least I can do."

"Thanks, I'm glad you liked it. I love cooking, but I hate cleaning, so if you want to do the dishes, I'm not gonna stop you. You don't have to, though."

I laugh, because we've always balanced each other out like this.

"Well, this works out perfectly, because I love cleaning, but cooking? I'd rather not cook after a full day of baking cookies." I place the dishes inside the empty dishwasher and close it.

"Thanks for doing that. Don't worry about starting it, I run it before I go to bed, and I'll be up for a bit longer," he says.

"Yeah, no problem. I'm happy to help. I was hoping we could hang out a bit before bed. Are there any shows you like to watch?" I ask.

Shit, that was too pushy. He didn't offer to babysit me or hang out with me; he offered me a place to stay. I can't corner him into hanging out with me. I probably just made him feel awkward, judging by the way he's looking at the floor. "I don't want to mess up your routine," I say. "I should also get my clothes out of my suitcase, and hang them up, so don't feel pressured or anything."

"Oh, no I don't feel pressured. But I don't really have many favorite shows. My routine is normally just going to the bar at the end of the night. We should get your stuff put away, though. Come on," Kellan says, heading toward the guest bedroom.

I follow behind him, finding it really effing hard to stick to my own stupid rule at this moment. I can't touch him, I can't touch him. I'm a sucker for that ass, though, and being this close to it is driving me crazy. Wait, I *can* touch him; I just can't have sex with him.

Kellan walks inside the guest room and opens the double closet doors. "Here you go. I can move some of the stuff out of here if you need more room. I wasn't sure how much space you were going to need."

I stand beside him, and check out the closet, placing my hand on his lower back.

Once my hand touches him, he quickly turns to the side and sits on the bed.

That was weird. He basically jumped when I touched him.

"Thanks, this is more than enough space for me, but I have a question."

Kellan huffs. "I sat down because I really am finding it hard not to grab you, or flirt with you. I'm sure you're wondering why I moved once you touched me."

I chuckle and turn toward him, then plant a kiss on his forehead. "Flirting and grabbing are both acceptable. But that wasn't my question."

"Oh, what were you going to ask me?"

I turn back toward the open closet; and tap a large box. "Why is there a Christmas tree in this box?"

"You've never seen a fake Christmas tree before?" he chuckles.

"Of course, I have, I'm asking why the tree is still in the box, and not up and decorated already. It's so close to Christmas. Don't you want to decorate it?"

"No, not really," he says. "I've been so busy with the festival planning that I haven't even thought about it. I probably won't put it up this year."

I drop an eyebrow. "Won't put it up this year? Why not? I can help you put it up. Let me put my stuff away, then we can decorate it together. Ahh…I would've brought cookies with me, if I knew we were gonna decorate a tree."

Kellan stands and slides the box out of the closet. "I always forget how heavy this thing is. You sound like your nonna, you know that?"

"How? What did I say that sounded like her?"

"The cookie thing, well that and telling me I have to put my tree up. Both of those things sound like Leora."

"We don't have to if you don't want to. I don't want to be pushy." I unzip my suitcase and begin hanging my shirts in the closet.

"You're not pushy," he says. "Just hurry up and put your stuff away. I want to do it, too. I've never decorated a tree with anyone that I li—anyone besides family, which includes your family."

Kellan continues pushing the large box with his foot out of the door and down the hall.

I finish hanging the last few items that needed to be hung up and join him in the living room. Damn, he looks so cute staring at the sections of the tree with that confused face.

"I never know which piece is the middle and which one is the bottom," Kellan says, passing two sections to me.

"The biggest one always goes on the bottom."

"Not in Frosty Bottoms," Kellan jokes.

I stick the large artificial Douglas Fir piece into the base, and we work together to get the tree up and decorated. I remove one of the few remaining ornaments from the box of decorations. "This one looks familiar," I say.

"Of course it does, it's Leora's. She asked me to take care of it, because it's very special."

"Well, at my house, special ornaments go up high, so cats don't get them," I say, placing the ornament high up on the short branches.

"Yes, I abide by the same rule here," Kellan says. He takes the last remaining ornament out of the box and hangs it. "Done!"

I step back with my hands on my hips and admire the tree. "It's gorgeous! We make a great team. Thanks for letting me put it up with you."

"We always did make a great team," he says. "Now, let's see how it looks with the lights on!" He plugs the last set of lights into the surge protector, and the multicolored lights and star sparkle brightly. He claps his hands, clearly loving it, and I watch as he reaches for me, but I moved from that spot like thirty seconds ago.

I laugh seeing him reaching into the air. He looks like he's trying to feel for me. I flip the condo lights off, and the entire condo is quickly illuminated in dancing lights of all colors. "Look at that! Even prettier with the lights off!" I say from the other side of the room.

I walk behind Kellan and wrap my arms around him, embracing him from behind and interlocking our fingers, then perch my chin on his shoulder. "I saw you a few seconds ago, swatting at the air, seemed like you were feeling for me. It was very cute."

The smell of his skin and the warmth of his body drives me wild. I kiss him on his cheek and whisper, "This is going to be much harder than I thought. I can barely control myself right now."

Kellan turns his face toward mine and kisses me softly. He's pushing our clasped hands down toward the button of his pants.

Shit…I can't stop this…he's pushing my hands down. I don't even have to touch him to know how hard he is. I want him.

I press my cock against Kellan's ass, but keep my hands in the same place, refusing to let him bring me deeper into the danger zone. The kiss that started out so tenderly, quickly escalates into something primal and urgent, as Kellan turns his body around toward me. He grips the back of my long hair and kisses me with more force than before.

I squeeze his waist tightly, while he tugs on a section of my hair. I can't let him do that. Pulling my hair is so fucking hot. If he doesn't stop, I won't be able to control myself. I'm one dirty word away from taking him. "Mmm—" I moan. I pull back slightly from the kiss, and Kellan grips my hair tighter. "We can't," I whisper.

Kellan whines, "No—please don't pull back, we don't have to fuck. I just want to taste you. We don't have to do anything else. We'll go to bed right after a few more kisses. I promise."

I lick my lips. Damn, he's so sexy, and he isn't even trying. I hold him by the waist and stare into his eyes. "You said you wanted to taste me. That was very dirty. If I keep kissing you, I'm not going to be able to stop… I really should go to bed."

Kellan drops his head against my chest. His mouth is pressed against my shirt. "Braden, I—don't want to force you, so if you really don't want me, we can just go to bed. It's late anyway and we both have to be up early for work tomorrow."

The warmth of his breath combined with the hardness between us, is making this damn near impossible to walk away from.

I lift his chin and kiss him softly. "I do want you. That's why I can't do this. I promised myself that I wouldn't have sex with you tonight. Well, at least not until both of us can figure out how we're feeling. But don't think that I don't want you. I know you can feel how much I want you." I kiss him once more, barely touching my tongue to his before pulling back, then kiss him on the forehead.

Kellan's arms drop to his sides. "Okay. But if you can't sleep you can always just come in my room and sleep with me."

I quirk an eyebrow at him. "I said no sex. You are so naughty. I'll stay in my own bed. I want to be a good guest."

"Two things," Kellan says. "First, I meant that if you were missing your cat you could come into my room. Second, I should've made you sign a contract."

"What do you mean a contract?"

"Oh, I don't know some kind of a contract that makes you do what I want. Then I'd tell you that I need you to have sex with me tonight," he says.

He still thinks I don't want him. "I don't need a contract for that, I want to do it—just not tonight."

We both turn toward the hallway that leads to our rooms. "Alright, I'm heading to bed. Let me know if you need anything. If not, I'll see you in the morning," Kellan says.

"Goodnight. Thanks again for letting me stay here."

After I finish my nightly routine, I hop into bed, wearing a thin pair of blue boxers and a white shirt. I scroll through a few articles about the upcoming Snowflake Festival. I didn't forget about it, but I truly didn't realize everything that went into it. Kellan has to plan all this by himself, I should help him. I didn't realize how much he has to do.

Thinking of Kellan and the planning, reminds me of the sex we had in the closet at the community center. I slide my hand down the front of my boxers and begin to lightly stroke myself. Fuck, he gets so whimpery and needy when we have sex. I want him…and he's just on the other side of this wall. My cock responds quickly to thoughts of Kellan's ass bouncing against me, the feeling of coming deep inside of him fills me with so much hunger. I grip my cock tighter, and close my eyes, imagining Kellan's tight warm hole wrapped around it. I rub faster…why did I make this no sex rule? I want to fuck him. My fucking hand is not going to do it tonight. I want to come. I need to. I jerk my cock harder, imagining Kellan's mouth wrapped around it. I picture his pleading eyes looking up from his knees, while sticking his tongue out, begging for my cum. "Yes…Beg…Fuck…Kellan," I moan. My cock grows harder, while I stroke faster, and faster, ever so close to release.

What the fuck? My phone is ringing. Damn it. I was so fucking close. Who would even call me at this hour? Nobody ever calls me. I keep my right hand on my cock, and grab the phone with my left, squinting in the dark room at the bright light from the phone. I answer it, "Kellan? Is everything okay?"

There is only silence on the other end of the line.

Oh no—did he hear me? Was I being loud? Fuck, this is the worst possible thing that could've happened. Here I am telling him I can't have sex with him, and he just heard me jerking off and moaning his name. I am an idiot. I pull my right hand out of my boxers and close my eyes, waiting for Kellan to reply.

"Hey," he says in a sexy voice, barely above a whisper. "I um, can't sleep."

My chest is tighter than my balls right now. I feel completely constricted. All the blood that had rushed to my dick a minute ago has moved up to my brain. Do I apologize for the moaning? He must have heard it. Why else would he call me? Wait, I'll just play it cool. No reason to apologize for something if he didn't even hear it.

"What's wrong?" I ask. "Are you too stressed to sleep?"

"Yeah, kind of. I mean—I just want to…"

Definitely heard me.

Our voices overlap as we speak different things at the same time. "Kellan, I'm sorry. I shouldn't have made the no sex rule."

"I just want to talk, Braden. That's what I'm trying to say."

"What?" I ask.

"Huh?" Kellan says.

"You go first, you said you just want to talk."

"No, because if you want to have sex, we can do that. I don't really enjoy talking about my feelings, but you said you wanted to. I'd much rather have sex."

I can barely control my smile; the thought of Kellan offering to talk, even when it makes him uncomfortable, is a pretty good indicator of the way he must feel about me. My cock, which hasn't fully given up on sex for the night, responds instantly to the thought of Kellan committing to me. Do I think commitment is sexy? I've never thought about it before, but something about him wanting to do something just to please me, makes me want him even more. I stick my hand back down my boxers, deciding to switch tactics.

"Kellan, I want to talk, I really do. But I also really fucking want you. Knowing that you're on the other side of the wall is too much for me right now. My cock is going crazy."

"Well, you're the one that made the rule," he reminds me.

"I didn't say anything about phone sex. I said we couldn't have actual sex."

"Phone sex? I don't think I've ever actually done that. Why not just come in here and fuck me for real? My door is unlocked."

"Thirsty boy. No. I'm not gonna fuck you. But I'm gonna listen to you fuck yourself. If you're a good boy and follow directions, I'll make you come. Do you want that?"

I can hear him rustling around in his bed.

"What do I do? I just jerk off and you listen?"

"Tell me first, is your hand on your cock?"

"Y-yeah, but I'm not doing anything yet, he's barely hard. Interested, but not fully awake yet. It won't take lo—"

"Shh. You talk an awful lot for someone who doesn't like to talk. Take your hand off your cock. I haven't told you to touch it yet. Go get your favorite toy. I know you have some, don't even say you don't."

"I wasn't going to deny having toys. Hang on, I'll grab one. Unh—" Kellan grunts, sounding like he's reaching for something. "Got it. Now what? Can I use it? Wait, how does this work? What about you?"

"Talking again. Shhh—I'm already turned on. I was jerking off before you called. I was right on the edge and your call interrupted me. Stop asking questions. How big is your toy? Compared to me?"

"Not even close, it's a decent size, but the vibration is the best part. Can I turn it on?"

"Kellan, listen to me, if you don't stop asking questions. I'm not going to do this with you. I want you to take your finger and lick it. Pretend your finger is my cock. Lick the sides and underneath, let me hear you."

"Mmm—" Kellan moans softly. The sound of his saliva, mixed with his moans, makes my cock rock hard again.

"Good boy. I like how sloppy you get. Now I want you to rub your tight little rim for me. Don't go inside, just rub the outside, pretend it's my tongue. You like that—I know you do."

"I do like it; I love when you eat my ass…I want you to do it."

"Mmm—Kellan, I'm rubbing my cock, it's so hot and hard. So, fucking thick, perfect for that tight little ass. Fuck—your ass is so hot—how many fingers did it take to loosen you last time?"

"Th—ree," Kellan says, sounding breathless.

"Are you touching your cock?" I ask while I stroke myself faster.

"Yeah, just—just a little."

"Stop that. I didn't say you could. I want you to lick two fingers now. Get them wet for me. Let me hear you."

"Mmm—" Kellan moans.

The sounds from his wet tongue are really obscene. "Dirty fucking boy, can you taste your ass on your fingers? I bet you can. So sweet… Fuck." I pump myself faster. Precum drips from the tip, and I rub it down the sides, adding extra lubrication. "Listen," I say. I put the phone near my cock so he can hear. "Do you hear that?" I ask. "That's my wet cock, inside my hand. Do you like that sound? That's how it sounds when you suck it." I lick my lips remembering the sweet taste of Kellan's ass, and bring the phone back to my ear. "Mmm—unh—Kellan, push your fingers inside for me. Let me hear you. Loosen up for me."

"Okay—but I want your cock. It's not the same. Thinking of you jerking off is so fucking hot. I want to touch you—or touch myself. I'm so hard. Please, can I?"

"No. Don't touch your cock. Fuck yourself with your fingers, how many do you have in?"

"Unnhhh—" he grunts. "Three, but it's not—enough. I want you. Come in here and fuck me," he begs through moans.

"Finger yourself harder, do it faster. Close your eyes, imagine you're bent over, and I'm eating your ass, my tongue is rubbing all around your hole, mmm—and I'm lapping it all up like a fucking slave for you. I'm sticking my tongue inside, and I'm massaging your balls. Mmm—you taste so good, Kellan."

Kellan's breaths are heavy. "I—like that. Haah—mmm—I want you. Please—I want to come. I want to taste your cock so bad. Can I touch myself now?"

"Now that you're loose, you can use your toy. I want you to come. But you can't come until I say. Can you do that?"

Kellan's softly spoken agreement is accompanied by the sound of the vibrator, "Yes, I…think so."

"Good fucking boy. Tell me what you're doing, while I jerk my cock. I'm so fucking close already."

"I'm putting it inside. Mmm—nnn—mmm. I'm pushing it in as far as it can go, and I have it turned on high. Fuck, Braden. It feels so good. Come fuck me, please. I need you."

"No, baby, but keep begging me. You're so fucking sexy. I'm gonna come soon. Now you can jerk your cock while you take that toy."

"I—I'm jerking my cock. Fuck, Braden, mmm—nnn—more, please. I want more."

I feel my balls tighten. I'm right on the edge. "Mmm—my cock is so wet and I'm so close. Tell me you love cock, Kellan, beg for it. I'm gonna come—"

"I love cock, so fucking much—Braden. I want to—mmm—nnngh. I'm gonna—"

"Me too—fuck—do it. Come for me—haah—haah. Fuck, I'm

coming. Haah—" My abs are covered as my cum shoots out in long spurts. So. Much. Fucking. Cum.

"I'm—coming, Braden. Haah—haah—holy shit."

I need more. The amazing feeling of release is somewhat fleeting. He is the high that I want. I want him.

After a few moments of silence, I speak up, "Kellan, do you remember what you said to me earlier?"

"Right now? At this moment, I don't—phew—sorry. I'm still a few minutes away from post-nut clarity at this point. What did I say?"

"Come in here, and I'll remind you," I say, then hang up the phone.

I put the phone on the nightstand, then place my arms behind my head, and look down at my abs, still covered in cum. I close my eyes and wait for him. Fuck, that was so hot. But doing this with him will be even hotter.

Kellan opens the door, and I keep my eyes closed.

"I'm here…and you're still very naked," he says.

"You said you wanted to taste me earlier. There's a lot of *me* right here, if you're still thirsty. If not, I can go take a shower, and rinse off. No pressu—"

Within seconds I feel the bumps on Kellan's warm tongue slurping up my cum, rubbing across my muscles. "I'm still thirsty," he whispers, then presses his lips against the ridges of my lower abs.

My load is slowly being licked off, and it feels fucking amazing. I rub his head. "That's a good boy. Mmm—yeah. Listen to you, you really are so fucking thirsty." I keep a firm hold on the back of his head, while he diligently laps up all the cum that remains.

"Fuck," Kellan moans. "You taste so damn good."

I open my eyes and see him staring down from beside the bed. "I didn't know you were leaning down the whole time…my eyes were closed. Why didn't you get in bed?" I sit up slightly and lift him onto my lower half.

"What the? How are you so strong? No, how are you ready again?" Kellan asks, now straddled across my hardened cock.

"Ssshh." I pull his face toward mine, and stare into his eyes. "You're pretty. You know that?" I press my lips against his, then slowly move my tongue inside his mouth.

"Mmm—" Kellan moans, as he slowly starts to grind his dick against mine.

With only the thin layer of his underwear separating us and our tongues still deeply entwined, my no sex rule has quickly flown out of the window. I grip him by the waist and press him against myself forcefully. Encouraging him to grind harder while my fingers dig into the soft flesh on his hips.

"I love the way you taste," Kellan says, leaning down to lick across my mouth.

"What do I taste like?" I ask, while he slowly rocks back and forth.

He brings his mouth beside my ear and whispers, "Mine."

Did he just say what I think he said? I feel a slight change in Kellan's body, it's almost like he's questioning why he said that. Before he can lose himself in his thoughts, I grip his thighs and flip our positions. Now atop him, I lean down and devour his lips, nearly taking his entire mouth inside of mine. His legs wrap tightly around me, while he clutches at my hair through the kiss. Fuck, my hair. When he pulls my hair, electric waves surge through my dick. I grind against him, rubbing our cocks together.

I need to be inside of him. I break from the kiss, and move to the side of his neck, planting a small bite, then drag my tongue down to one of his nipples. I lightly flick it with my tongue, while teasing the other in between two fingers. He's writhing beneath me, alternating between pulling my hair and grabbing my arms. I circle his nipple with my tongue, and lightly graze it with my teeth.

"Oh, fuck—Braden. That feels—"

"You like that? You like when I play with your nipples?"

"I do—Fuck, I really do."

I nuzzle against his fully perked nipple, then lick a line down his stomach. I stop at his waistband and look up at him.

"Take it," Kellan says.

I pull his underwear down and toss them on the floor. Kellan's cock stands at full attention. "Braden—I—I want you. But I don't know if I can come again this soon."

I raise my eyebrows at him. "Challenge accepted." I press his legs open wider, encouraging him to lift his ass a bit. He's wide open for me, and I don't think I've ever seen anything so enticing. I move my tongue to his hole, and lick around the outside, making several circles around the rim before pressing my mouth against it. "Mmm—" I say, then slip a finger inside. Thankfully, he's still loose from earlier. He must have really worked himself with that toy.

"You're ready. I can't wait anymore."

I reach into the nightstand where I stashed a bottle of lube, then pass it to Kellan, and straddle him on my knees. Understanding the task at hand, he gratuitously lathers the lube on my cock, jerking me in the process. Fuck, that feels so good.

I press on his chest, urging him to lie back down. Then rub the head of my slippery cock around Kellan's entrance, sticking just the tip in, then pulling it out. In, then out, just the tip, I tell myself. I tease him, watching his mouth fall open and his chest rise every time I push inside, and he grips the sheets in frustration each time I pull out.

"Please…Braden. Give it to me," he whimpers, squeezing his legs tightly around my body.

I lean down and lick the side of his neck, then whisper beside his ear, "So needy."

I stuff my cock inside. No longer caring about taking my time, I begin forcefully pounding into him. "Fuck, you're so warm, so good." The desire to wreck this man's hole overtakes me, something about being inside of him, makes me unable to control myself. I pound harder and harder. "You like that? You like it—rough," I say, giving an extra deep push inside.

"Unnhh—yes—harder—more," Kellan pleads, rubbing his hands all over my body.

I grab ahold of his legs, tossing one over each shoulder.

His breath hitches as I push my cock into his needy asshole.

"I haven't hit your spot this way yet. Let's see how fast I can do it. You want to come?" I ask.

"Ye—yes, but I want—fuck it's so deep. I want—"

"Want what? What do you want?" I ask, while driving my cock deeper inside with each word he speaks.

"I—hah—I want to, but, I want yours—"

"That's a good boy. But you can go first. I'm already close."

I slowly shift my hips, grinding inside. "Mmm it's—right around here."

Kellan's eyes close, and he turns his head to the side. "Mmm—yes—yes—right there."

I reach down and turn his face forward. "Open your eyes and look at me. I want to see how pretty you look when you come from my cock."

He slowly turns his head forward, eyes half lidded, and nods.

He's fucking beautiful. "Right here, this is it," I say. I drive harder against Kellan's spot, watching him squirm underneath me. "You're close now, I can feel it."

Kellan's cock twitches against my abs, while I fuck him. I lock eyes with him, holding onto his legs. "Come, Kellan—do it. You want to, I know you do. Come for me…"

I press against his prostate harder, and feel the warm wet reward of his cum shooting against my abs.

"Fuck—mmmph—I'm coming," Kellan cries out.

I can't hold back any longer, and let go too. "Mmm—fuck—yes, take my cum," I say, releasing inside. Oh my God. Sex with this man—is absolutely mind-blowing. I swear I'm seeing stars right now.

My head drops on his chest, and he slides his legs down. After a few moments pass, once my dick has softened and we've both caught our breath, I slide out.

"Thank you," I whisper, rolling off of him.

"What are you thanking me for? That was so damn hot. Thank *you*."

"Now," I say. "Let's shower, and I'll take that conversation you were going to give me earlier." I kiss him on the cheek and get up from the bed.

Kellan sits up and offers a half smile. "I said I would talk because I wanted you to have sex with me. You've already given me what I want, so I don't see any reason why I should talk at this point."

"Is that so?" I giggle, walking around to Kellan's side of the bed. "I could throw you over my shoulder, if I wanted to. So, I'm gonna give you a choice. Get up and take a shower with me, and we talk, or I lift you like the other day and carry you in there."

He puts his hands up. "I'm getting up, don't pick me up right now," he says through laughter.

He leads me into the shower, and we rinse off, starting in complete silence. "This doesn't have to be awkward," I say while lathering my hair.

"I know, it's not awkward. I just have so much to say that I don't know where to start. I want to know things, but I also feel kind of embarrassed by some of the things."

"What's there to be embarrassed of? I mean, I've fucked you—three times now. What do you mean? Just ask me whatever questions come to mind. If anything makes me uncomfortable, I'll let you know."

"Same goes for you," Kellan says.

"There's nothing you could ask me that I wouldn't want to answer. If you're curious about something I'm gonna tell you."

Kellan blurts out, "Why are you still single?"

Oof. This is such a complicated question every time anyone asks it. "Starting with the big questions. Alright. Well, I suppose it would be great if I could say something really romantic, but the truth is that no one has been able to make me want them, in a way that I feel you should want a partner. There was a time I felt like marriage and relationships just weren't in the future for me. Lots of very quick relationships, I get bored pretty easily. There was someone who crept into my mind every once in a while, but he seemed to be unattainable. I also didn't know much about him as an adult, so whenever I thought of him, I felt like it was just a part of me holding onto something that never really had a proper shot. Besides him, there hasn't been anyone I've really been interested in claiming."

I watch for any type of reaction to what I said. Trying to see if he's really willing to get into this conversation with me.

"I see. Similar story for me," he says.

He's not gonna dive into this right now. His body language tells me that he's clamming up already. I need to shift to something lighter. I don't want him to feel uncomfortable.

"Tell me about the candles. What made you decide to go into candle making?"

"Oh, the candles. You know, I just really love creating things.

Making things with my own hands. When I make a candle, there's tangible proof that I created something. Something that makes people happy. Candles bring all kinds of emotions to people, which is something I've never been good at. I mean my sister still calls me an emotionless robot to this day—says I don't understand emotions, because I don't have any." He laughs. "But when someone comes in looking for a candle for their new house, that scent is something they are going to remember. It's something that means something to them. I don't know why, but I really like that feeling. It just feels good. Same goes for holidays, people associate their favorite time of the year with scents that I created. It's just a good feeling."

"That makes me happy. The shop is really something. Wait, Charlie calls you an emotionless robot?" I ask, while turning the water off.

He sighs. "Ah, yeah. She's just Charlie. Always wants me to open up. Protective and yet also pushy. I don't know how her husband puts up with her."

Kellan shivers as he steps outside of the shower, then grabs his towel and wraps it around his waist, while I do the same.

"Get dressed and come into my room," he says, hurrying out of the bathroom.

I exhale. There we go, he's opening up a bit more. This is good. Gosh, I could listen to him talk for hours. Pretty stupid of me to think I could spend the night in the same space as him without having sex. Couldn't even make it a measly three hours.

After a quick stop in the guest room, I brush my teeth and walk into Kellan's room.

"Come on, hop in," he says, lifting the covers for me.

"This is a nice bed," I say as I lie beside him.

"Yeah, I spent a fortune on it. Since I'm on my feet all day; I sprung for something fancy."

I want to try and talk to him, pick up where we left off in the shower, without pushing him. I'm not quite sure how to do that. Senator Tunacan jumps onto the bed and snuggles up beside him.

"Oh, there you are!" Kellan says, petting his cat. "Braden is gonna sleep in here with us tonight. But I think we should make him tell us things before we go to sleep. What do you think?" he asks the cat.

"Tell you things? Oh, like in the shower? I'm happy to. I am a little tired, but never too tired for conversations with cats—or you, of course."

"Nice save," he says. So, what I'm curious about is just one thing—okay, a lot of things, but right now I'm just wondering something."

I take a deep breath and try to mentally prepare myself for whatever he's going to ask. If he wants to get into everything from high school, it's gonna be a long night—but I'd welcome it. These feelings that I have, they've weighed on me for so long. He says things that make me feel like he feels the same—like he still needs answers, which I honestly still do. Even if that may sound silly.

"I'm an open book," I say. "What have you been wondering?"

"When did you first realize that you had feelings for me?" he asks. "Before you think I'm expecting a big dramatic answer with some elaborate storybook moment—I'm not. I'm just curious to know when it started for you."

"It started when we were ten. Everyone was playing dodgeball, and you were just dancing along the line, daring people to hit you with the ball. I remember thinking that I'd stop the ball from hitting you no matter what. Then that prick Aaron tossed the ball at you, and I dove in front of it. Do you remember that?"

Kellan laughs. "Of course I do! It knocked you right off your feet! But you were always protecting me from something. I knew you wouldn't let anyone hit me, that's why I was so brave. But you were my best friend, of course you'd protect me."

"Yes, and you were right to believe that. I saw you as mine, and it was not in a best friend way, it was in a very different way that I wasn't familiar with. Sometimes you made my stomach hurt, just from being around. I'd get so nervous that you were gonna be able to tell how I felt. It was just weird thinking that I liked you. But we were so little then. As we grew, those feelings changed, they got stronger. I'd usually imagine what it would be like if we lived together when we grew up. Then I started to imagine us getting married. When I'd hear about some girl that had a crush on you, I'd be terrified that you were gonna one day marry someone else. But yeah, ten years old is when it started."

"Oh," he says, petting his cat. "Did you hear that, Senator?"

I look at his cat, who seems to be eyeing me suspiciously after what I just said. Kind of feels like he's judging me if I'm being honest.

"So," I say, looking at the cat. "When did your dad realize he felt something for me? Was it when we were twelve and he hurt his knee at the lake?"

The cat tucks against Kellan's arm. "Ah, Senator, the man says he wants to know if I was twelve when I realized I liked him." He kisses the cat's head. "Hmm, The Senator said to tell you it was long before then."

"How long?" I ask.

"Mmm, hard to say."

"Kellan, look at me. Since when? Don't say you don't know, because I told you exactly when it was for me, and I know you haven't suddenly developed a condition that makes you forget everything."

"Actually, I am pretty forgetful. Just not when it comes to certain things, or people." The cat wriggles out of his arms and hops off the bed.

I lie flat on my back, and Kellan does the same. He looks upset, and I want to ask him why, but I shouldn't. He's probably so spent from the sex. I lean over and kiss him on his forehead.

"Let's rest, now," I say. "It was a long day, and we have to work in the morning."

Chapter Seven
Otters Mate for Life

 **Kellan**

I wake up with a smile on my face.

Things are almost *too good*, like it's not real, like I might still be dreaming. And, for a brief moment, I wonder if that's the case. But, no, Braden is in bed beside me, fast asleep and snoring softly. It's *very real*. He's in my bed, the bedsheets smell like him, and he's got a hand on my chest. There's no way this is a dream.

And this is the first time I've slept through the whole night solidly. I'm usually a light sleeper, and I get up for bathroom breaks or to check out noises or I'm lying awake because of insomnia. It usually takes heavy medication for me to sleep through the whole night. But last night was perfect. Maybe it was because I had Braden at my side.

And it's more than just the sleep that has me feeling amazing. Last night's sex was so intense and made me feel so good that I am still riding that high now. I never knew it could be like this.

I glance at the clock and see it's a half hour before the alarm is set to go off, so I slowly get out of bed, being careful not to wake him. When I'm out, I gently tug the blankets up to cover his chest.

As I make my way to the kitchen, Senator Tunacan barrels past me and starts meowing next to the cupboard where I keep the cans of cat food.

"Don't get used to early breakfast," I tell him as I scoop food out of the can and onto his dish. "This is one time only." To make the day extra-special, I add a few treats to his dish. If I'm going to have an amazing day, then he should have an amazing day, too.

"So," I say to him as he eats, "what do you think our houseguest would like for breakfast?"

The Senator looks up at me, then shoves his face back in his salmon pate.

"I don't think he wants that," I tell him. "But he might want pancakes."

I start making a fresh pot of coffee and then set about making pancakes. I don't use a recipe, at least not one written out, and go by memory and intuition. I'd helped my mom make pancakes every Saturday when I was a kid, so the recipe is burned in my brain, but now that I know how to cook as an adult, I make little tweaks along the way—like adding dashes of cocoa and cinnamon to the batter to give it a warm and spicy chocolate taste.

Just as the first few pancakes are coming off the griddle, Braden walks in, looking bleary eyed and adorable with his bed hair and the old shirt and boxers he wears as pajamas.

"Morning, sleepyhead," I say.

"Morning," Braden mumbles. He opens a few cabinets until he finds the mugs and then serves himself a cup of coffee. "Creamer?" He pulls the fridge open and looks into it. I point at the container in the door. "Thank you."

"Hungry?" I ask.

Braden steps closer, close enough that I can feel the heat emanating from him. "It was the smell of pancakes that woke me up and actually got me out of bed."

I smile. "Perfect." I put the last of the pancakes on the plate and carry it over to the table where I've set out plates, cutlery, butter, and syrup.

Braden seems to wake up a bit more and smiles; he seems impressed. "Do you do this every morning?"

"Only when I have someone to cook for," I say. Braden gives me a strange disapproving look, and I realize he thinks I have hookups that sleep over, and likely on a regular basis. I need to fix this. "Which isn't that often. It's really just when family visits me. Sometimes your nonna comes over for breakfast, too."

Braden's face seems to relax as he sits down and puts a few pancakes on his plate. "Thank you again for taking care of her, by the way. I really appreciate that you kept her company. I worried about her often with the family being in different cities."

"Leora is a special lady and it's been an honor and a privilege to help her out. I just hope I get to still see her regularly in retirement."

Braden rolls his eyes. "I think you know my nonna well enough to know she won't fully retire. Once her foot is healed, she'll likely be in the shop often. It's her love of cookies that's kept her working all these years; I can't see her just giving it up like that," he says with a snap of his fingers.

"That's very true," I say with a laugh. I shove a piece of pancake in my mouth. It tastes better than usual, but that might be the effect of the company I'm eating with.

We pass through breakfast with a bit of small talk. He tells me some of his favorite stories as a vet, and I tell him some of the stories of the life he missed in Frosty Bottoms. Soon we're talking about our cherished memories from school—the funny moments mostly, but also just about what it's like growing up in a small town like this. When Braden reminds me of the time we were responsible for cleaning out the hamster cage in third grade and how the hamster—named Potato Chip—escaped, and we had to chase him down, we're both laughing uproariously.

Senator Tunacan meows and jumps on the table. He stands in front of me and starts meowing loudly and aggressively.

"I swear he's been fed and he's well taken care of," I tell Braden. "Don't listen to him."

Braden scratches The Senator behind the ears. "Does your daddy treat you well? Yeah? Does he treat you like the special little prince that you are?" The cat meows back in a way that almost sounds affirmative. "Well, that's good to hear. Being nice to animals is number one on the list of qualities for guys I like."

Before I can prod a little deeper on that to see what other qualities he looks for, The Senator steals a pancake off the pile in the middle of the table and runs off with it. I chase after him and by the time I catch up to him, he's behind the couch and gnawing away at the pancake.

"Give it here, buddy," I say. He growls at me and then goes back to eating. "I said, give it here." I stretch all the way and manage to grab the end of the pancake, dragging it out. When I sit back with my prize, I realize I only have half the pancake. Senator Tunacan picks up the remaining half and runs off into the spare bedroom.

When I manage to retrieve most of the rest of the pancake and return to the kitchen, Braden is already washing dishes. I toss the mangled pancake in the trash and then shovel the final two pancakes into my mouth and bring the rest of the dishes to the sink.

"I'll wash them," Braden says, taking the dishes from me and adding them to his sink of soapy water.

"You're a guest, you don't have to."

"I told you last night; I like cleaning. Besides, *as a guest*, it's how I can show gratitude for letting me stay here."

I put my hand on Braden's back and say, "You are *always* welcome here and don't have to show gratitude." I want to take my hand back, but it feels so good to be touching him, even if there's a layer of cotton between us.

After a few moments, he seems to realize my hand is still there. He looks at me and gives me a smile. "We should, uh, get to work." He puts the last plate on the drying rack.

I can tell he wants something different. But we're both responsible adults.

I finally remove my hand. "Yes. Right. Work."

We drive in our separate cars downtown—three streets away. I enter the candle shop and just sit at the counter, looking out the window and across the street. This is the earliest I've ever been at work; there isn't really a need to get to a candle shop by seven in the morning for a nine o'clock opening, but Braden needs to be at work early. Being here at this time allows me to watch my handsome friend as he works away in the kitchen.

Friend? We were friends once, but we're something more now. You don't shove your cock in your friend's ass. And you certainly don't kiss him.

Braden seems to have grown even more comfortable with running a cookie shop. He looks confident and professional, and if I'm seeing clearly enough, he's also singing while baking.

After about an hour, Braden's mom comes down from his nonna's apartment and gives him a hand packing orders. The two of them seem to get along well, laughing together and even dancing to what must be a song from the radio. The tensions of day one together appear to be long forgotten.

When the candle shop opens at nine, my day becomes a whirlwind of sales. With it being the final Sunday before Christmas, the locals and tourists are getting some Christmas shopping in. And with Riley taking the day off, I'm nearly run off my feet at times with the surge of customers. Thankfully, I'd budgeted my time for today to be all sales; I'll make new batches of popular candles early next week when the shop is slower.

In the early afternoon, there are a few moments of quiet for both my store and Braden's, and when I look through the window, I see Braden with his phone in hand, typing something out. A moment later, my phone dings with a text message.

Looking forward to tonight. It should be fun!

I had nearly forgotten about tonight's plans with how busy the day was turning out to be. It's the annual Christmas masquerade at Bottoms Up, and it's *the* gay event of the Christmas season. It's probably the one event I most look forward to each year. I usually go alone…but this year will be different. I'll be showing off my guy.

Leora had texted me yesterday to say that my mask was ready and that she'd made one for Braden, too, in case he wanted to check out the party.

Your nonna made you a mask, I text him back.

Braden replies with a wide-eyed surprised emoji.

That puts a smile on my face, right as a customer comes in, and that smile carries me through to the end of the work day. When it's time to lock up, I cross the street to BJ's, and Braden lets me in before locking up and shutting off the lights. His mom has already returned to his nonna's suite.

"Good day?" I ask.

Braden nods. "Super busy, but it was fun."

I take his hands and lean in for a kiss. Braden's lips are soft, and his mouth is warm—just the mere contact of the kiss sends a thrill through me that thickens my cock. But I back away from the kiss before I get *too* into it. Don't want to get extra hard right now…we don't need a repeat of our first fuck, as hot as that would be…

"We should go get our masks now," I say. "I haven't seen them yet; I don't know what Leora put together for us."

His gaze shifts up to the ceiling of the cookie shop, then falls back to meet mine. "My parents are up there," he says.

I smile. "I haven't seen your dad in ages. And it looks like you and your mom had a great day today."

He smiles, too. "We did. But…they're…well, they're a bit much."

My smile broadens. "You think I don't know that? Besides, I've got a sex therapist for a mom, being embarrassed by family is part of the package."

"Oh, I remember your mom," he says with a smirk. "My parents will be a bit…overexcited if they get the hint we're, uh, having a bit of fun."

"Ah…no worries. We can play it cool. I can be discreet." I wink at Braden.

He rolls his eyes. "Kellan, you are anything but discreet." He exhales loudly. "Alright, let's go."

He leads me to the back stairwell and up to the suite on the second floor. We separate our hands and keep at least a foot of distance between us at all times. When he lets us in, we're greeted with chaos.

From what I can take in at first glance, Leora—who should still be resting with her foot raised—is baking Christmas cookies, Belinda is wrapping gifts, his father, Andrew, is watching a football game with the volume on full, and Mister Fluffykins is chasing a small mouse toy around the place at frantic speed.

And they all stop when we enter. His dad even puts the game on mute. Fluffykins comes rushing over to brush against Braden's legs.

"Hi," Braden says. "Dad, you remember Kellan."

The silent stares from all of them continue. The cat is even looking at us curiously.

"What?" Braden asks.

"You brought a boy home," his mother says.

I put my hand over my mouth to hide my struggle to hold back laughter already.

"I didn't *bring a boy home*, I brought Kellan home," Braden says, while rolling his eyes.

"After spending the night at his place," Belinda says.

"Because this place is too crowded," he counters.

"We're here to pick up our masks," I say, trying to divert the back-and-forth and save some potential embarrassment for Braden.

At that, Leora says, "Oh, right!" and hobbles out of the room. She comes back with two masks covered in sequins and feathers and glitter. They are mostly brown. "I made you matching masks. It'll be very cute! Very couple-y."

"Um…thank you, Nonna," Braden says, taking them from her. "Not a couple. But thank you."

"Put them on," Leora urges.

Braden hands one of the masks to me. It looks cute, and I'm pretty sure it's an otter…though I don't know of any otters with feathers on their faces. I put it on and watch as Braden puts his on. We face each other; it *does look* ridiculously cute on him.

"What are we?" Braden asks.

"Otters, obviously," I say, hoping my hunch is right. "Though I don't have enough body hair to make the mask convincing."

Leora claps excitedly. "I'm so glad you like them! You make quite the pair!"

"Fun fact," Andrew says, speaking for the first time since we entered the suite, "otters mate for life. Once a couple, always a couple."

I can almost *hear* Braden rolling his eyes as he says, "Wow. Fun fact. We're not a couple. But thanks for playing."

"Also, a fun fact, otters hold hands when they sleep," Belinda says. "You two should hold hands."

"Not holding hands. Not a couple." He turns to me and says, "Come with me," then leads me to the spare bedroom he'd claimed as his. The bed has clearly become a nest for Mister Fluffykins, with the messy blankets and the heavy dusting of cat hair. Opening the closet, he pulls out a few things. "This shirt? Or this one?"

My eyes flare wide. "Which one shows off your pecs the best? We want to make all the gay boys jealous."

Braden gives me a stellar smile. "Blue shirt it is." He yanks it off the hanger. "Let's go." He leads me quickly out of the bedroom and to the door of the unit. "Goodbye. I'll be back tomorrow. I'll see you in the shop, mom." Before anyone can respond, we are out of the apartment and in the short hallway.

I giggle as we come to a stop halfway down the hall. "You're ridiculous."

Braden rolls his eyes, but has a winning smile. "They're ridiculous."

I kiss him, which is awkward since we both still have our otter masks on. "Come on. Let's go get ready."

BRADEN

I tighten my half bun in the mirror, and tug at my navy-blue turtleneck, feeling that it may be too tight on my biceps. Never a bad thing to have something tight on my arms, unless I need to lift something, I guess. Kellan did say he wanted to show off my muscles.

"We're late," Kellan reminds me. "The party started forty

minutes ago. I like to make an entrance, but I don't want to be an hour late."

I grab my wallet off the dresser and extend a hand toward him. "Let's go."

Following an uneventful, and chilly walk, we arrive at Bottoms Up Bar, just a few minutes later.

The place is packed wall to wall with men in masks of all kinds. I'm finding it somewhat difficult to see through the otter mask, but I know how much he likes them, so I'm not about to complain. Besides, wearing matching masks with him is something I never thought would be possible. Being here with Kellan, being the one standing next to him—I would have worn a mask that looked like a garbage truck if he asked me to.

"Let's hit the bar," Kellan says, tugging my hand. "There are two seats right at the end. Come on!" He hurriedly pulls me across the room, toward the stools, and we both sit down.

The music is extremely loud, and the many smells of cologne and men permeate the air around me. Some smells are better than others. I'm pretty sure the person next to me is wearing the same cologne, but far more than any human should.

Lucas stands in front of us, he's wearing a little bunny mask. He flips the gray mask up. "Hey, you two, what can I get you?"

"Hi, Lucas," I say, removing my mask and placing it on the bar in front of me. "Kellan, do you want a gin and Coke?"

"Yep, that sounds good. Thanks," he says.

Lucas grabs a glass from beneath the bar and quickly starts making Kellan's drink. "And for you, Braden?"

"I'll have a rum and Coke, please."

Lucas slides Kellan's drink to him and starts making mine. "Hey, what uh—what are you guys supposed to be?" he asks.

Kellan pulls his mask over his face. "We're otters, obviously."

A loud rhythmic clapping comes from the dance floor. Kellan turns his stool around to watch. "Oooh, a dance battle, my favorite," he says.

I swivel around slightly to check out the competition. "Oh, I think the guy in the peacock mask is going to win," I say.

"No way," Kellan says. "That's Eddie, he's not going to win, no matter what."

I turn around and sip the drink that Lucas placed in front of me. It's good. I don't feel like drinking too much tonight, though. I'll probably just have this one drink.

"What are you supposed to be?" Chad asks, leaning on the bar in front of me.

He's shirtless in December, for crying out loud. And isn't there some kind of health code that says bartenders should be clothed? I shake my head at him and ask, "Where is your shirt, man? It's freezing outside!"

Lucas walks over and stands beside Chad. "He's a wolf, he doesn't need a shirt," he says, rubbing Chad's hairy chest, earning a smile from the wolf himself.

Chad lets out a loud howl, prompting Kellan to swivel his seat around.

"A wolf and a bunny! That's cute!" Kellan says.

"*You're* cute," I say, wrapping my arm around Kellan's waist.

Chad and Lucas exchange a questioning look, then whisper in each other's ears. Chad wraps Lucas up in a tender embrace. "I think he likes me," Lucas says with a smile.

"Of course I like you, you're a bunny. I'm gonna eat you up," Chad says. He playfully bites Lucas's shoulder.

I sip my drink and laugh. "You're a biter, huh? Somehow, I'm not surprised," I say.

"He's also a squealer," Lucas adds.

Chad wraps his arms around his bunny tighter. "Shhh, don't tell people that. Keep it up and I won't let you top tonight."

Lucas shoves him backward. "Oh, don't try to threaten me with that," he says playfully. "I could use a good nap after work, I'll let you top tonight, baby."

Chad tickles Lucas's stomach, as Lucas backs away, waving a bar towel.

"Oh, you're so bored you fall asleep when I'm top, huh?" Chad pokes him a few times for good measure and follows him toward the other end of the bar.

I just assumed Chad was the top—Lucas is the top? I don't—I normally don't think about these things, but now I'm confused.

I swivel around in my chair and tilt my head quizzically at Kellan.

"They're vers," Kellan says. "Lucas is top-vers, but Chad is just— vers, he's cool with either. That's what you were wondering, right?"

I give Kellan a quick kiss. "Sadly, I *was* wondering that."

The music blares over the speakers, and the dance battle comes to an end. The peacock drops to the floor in dramatic fashion at his loss. The pink swan gives the peacock a few friendly pats on the ass and helps him up. The two hug and laugh, then head toward the bar where Kellan and I are sitting.

"No, thank you," Kellan says, quickly standing, and pulling my hand away from the bar. "Come this way, quick! Don't look at them, pretend you don't see them coming."

"Okay, but watch where you're going—"

Kellan's body comes to a halt, as he bumps face first into a shirtless penguin. A very large shirtless penguin. "Hey, Kellan. Contest is starting soon, where are you off to? Who is your friend?" The penguin extends a hand toward me.

"Don't shake his hand," Kellan warns me, blocking the

handshake. "He probably just finished jerking someone off in the bathroom."

The penguin lets out a hearty laugh, then says in a serious tone, "Sadly, I only arrived a few minutes ago, haven't had the chance to do that yet."

Kellan rolls his eyes and pulls me by the hand toward the bathroom. "Yeah, bye, Eric!" he says loudly over his shoulder. "So annoying," he mumbles.

I'm a little confused by Kellan's back-to-back escapes. I squeeze his hand as we slip through the crowd. "I thought these guys were all your friends, why do you keep pulling me away?" I ask.

"Acquaintances. Not all friends. Besides, you were surprised by Chad and Lucas being vers, you have no idea what these other guys are like. They would all be willing to blow you in the bathroom if you'd let them."

Kellan opens the bathroom door, and we both walk inside. "I was not expecting a nice bathroom. I was expecting something…I don't know, dirtier?" I say.

"Chad would never allow this bathroom to get dirty. He's really particular about making sure everything is clean in here. He knows the things that go down in these stalls." Kellan lifts his chin toward a stall on the far side of the expansive restroom.

Chad's voice sounds through the speakers, "Costume contest starts in ten minutes. Last call for entries. I don't see the two beavers that were at the bar earlier. Anyone know where Kellan and Braden ran off to?"

"Beavers? How do we look like beavers? This is so clearly an otter," Kellan says, pulling his mask off and examining it.

"Eric said they went in the bathroom," Lucas's voice says, as the bathroom door opens.

Kellan quickly pulls me into the closest stall and shuts the door. "Pick me up," he says, draping his arms around my neck.

I have no idea why he wants me to do this, but I do it anyway. I lift him up, and he kisses my cheek.

"The shoes," Kellan whispers. "I don't want him to see two sets of shoes under the door."

"What could possibly happen if he knows we're in here? It's not like we'd get in trouble."

"I have no idea, sssh." Kellan tucks his face against my neck.

Holding Kellan tight makes my dick begin to stir. I kind of like hiding with him. Feels a little bit exciting.

"Mmm, you taste as good as you smell," Kellan says, licking the side of my neck.

"Fuck, don't do that," I plead.

Lucas's shoes pass by the stall we're in. "Guys, are you in here? Chad is looking for you, in case you didn't hear him. People are all talking about your groundhog masks!"

"We're otters!" Kellan shouts, then covers his own mouth.

"Very discreet. I doubt he knows we're in here now," I say, shaking my head. "You're lucky you're cute."

"What are you guys doing in there?" Lucas asks. "Actually, don't answer that. Are you entering the contest? That's all I need to know."

"No, we're good. You don't need to wait for us," Kellan answers.

"Alright, you two have fun!" Lucas replies, leaving the bathroom.

I give Kellan a quick kiss and massage his ass. "I like this position," I say. "I should fuck you right here, but I can't get past the thought of being in the bathroom."

"That's not the real problem. The bigger problem is that Lucas knows we're in here now. Who knows which person will come in next?"

"Good point. Maybe one more drink, then we head back to your place?"

"That sounds good. Also, as much as I hate dancing, I wouldn't mind dancing with you before the night is over." He unlocks the stall door as I place him down. "One drink, one dance, then back to my place."

"Perfect," I say, giving him a quick kiss before leaving the bathroom.

"Oooh, I love this song, it's sexy," Kellan says, hanging his arms around my neck, and moving in close.

"Mmmm—this is dangerous," I say, while moving my hands to Kellan's juicy ass cheeks. Giving them a squeeze, I whisper, "You're even sexy with the otter mask on."

"What did you say?" Kellan asks, tilting his ear closer.

"I said you're even sexy with the otter mask on. I'm having a hell of a time keeping my hands out of your pants," I say, squeezing Kellan's ass again.

Kellan tilts his head at me, then lifts his mask, prompting me to lift mine, too.

"What did you—?"

I pull him closer and kiss him, using my tongue to make quick work of the space inside his mouth.

He leans into the kiss, and grabs a fistful of my hair, pressing our mouths even harder together. "Mmm—mmm," he moans through the kiss while grinding on me.

This is so hot—we really did waste so much time. I can't believe I'm here. I'm kissing Kellan…and he's kissing me back. What a stupid thought, after all we've done, but still, this feeling of his mouth entwined with mine is more than I could have ever hoped for. Damn, I need this man.

The song ends, while our lascivious kissing continues. I feel a tug on the mask in my hand and open my eyes, pulling back from the warmth of Kellan's mouth.

"What the hell is this mask?" Geoff asks.

Kellan, ever the goof, remains in place, pretending to kiss the air. "I can't hear you, Geoff. We're busy."

"Hell yeah you're busy, and you're kissing Braden? When did this happen? Your mouth is a no entry zone. I mean, tis the season for kisses, but I don't see any mistletoe around. Unless my boy Braden here has some inside his mouth," Geoff jokes.

I laugh and shake his hand. "You coming to the park tomorrow?"

"Nuh uh—no changing the subject. Same as when you were in college. Reporters would corner you, and you'd shift topics every time. Unbelievable. But not this time. What's going on?"

I quirk an eyebrow at Kellan. "I don't know how to answer that."

Kellan sighs. "What's going on here, is that I was being kissed, and then an asshole showed up and interrupted it, asking all kinds of stupid questions."

"We're otters," I add.

"You're kissing because you're otters?" he asks.

"Gah, we're kissing because—because—well look at him! Who wouldn't kiss him?" Kellan gestures wildly to all of my body.

"Oh, I don't blame you, Bray has always been a fine piece of ass," Geoff says. "I'm not surprised that someone is kissing him, just that *you're* kissing him. If this isn't going to continue into the night, I'm down to pick up where you two just left off."

"Get out of here, Geoff!" I say, swatting at him. "About tomorrow…you look like you can still play. You up for it?" I ask.

"Yeah, I'll be there. So, no threesome tonight, either? Or is that still on the table?"

"That was never on the table!" Kellan says, dragging me toward the exit. "Calling you Bray, he's so annoying," he mumbles.

KELLAN

I'm a little tipsy, but I still have my wits about me. I'm clear-headed, though not entirely sure-footed. Braden is in better shape than me, walking with the confidence of a sober man. We've left the bar and we're headed back to my place.

"You're an amazing dancer," I say. I take his hand in mine and snuggle in close. We still have our otter masks on.

Even under the mask and in the semi-darkness, I can see Braden's blush. "I don't know if you'd call that dancing, but sure."

I wave my arms around to a beat that no one hears, including me. "Dancing isn't so much about looking great, it's about finding the beat and leaning into it."

"If anyone's a good dancer," Braden says, "it's you."

I grab his arm and snuggle in close to his shoulder, stealing warmth from him. "What's important is we had a good time. Right?"

He looks down at me. "I had a wonderful time. I think I'm liking Chad and Lucas a bit more now that I know they're not after you."

I roll my eyes. "They're a match I didn't see coming, but they're a match that seems to work."

He sounds almost hesitant when he asks, "Can I ask what's the deal with you and Chad? I thought you were together when I first came back here, but clearly you're not."

I feel a bit uncertain of how to answer. But I can't just not answer, so I dive in. "We're good friends," I say. "You're right that we're close and we, uh, we *have* had fun together a handful of times, but it's never been more than just getting our rocks off. There was never any emotion to it. It was fun, but mechanical." I feel like I'm babbling, so I quickly bring this to an end. "With you, though…everything is different and everything is mind-blowingly better." When he's silent for a long moment, I ask, "Are you mad?"

He shakes his head. "I can't hold your history against you, but it just feels a bit odd for him to still always be around and for you to be so close to him. But if you swear nothing is going on…"

"Nothing at all. That's in the past now."

"Then I'll be okay with it. It helps that I know Chad is with Lucas now and Lucas seems to want that boundary drawn, too." He takes a deep inhale and then lets it out, and it feels like he's letting out more than just a breath. He puts his arm around my shoulder, and I slip one around his waist. "You're mine now." He kisses the top of my head.

"I wouldn't have it any other way."

As we turn the last corner before my condo, Braden squeezes my shoulders, pulling me in tight. "I don't want tonight's fun to end. I don't want to go to bed."

I look up at him. "The fun doesn't have to end. We can have a little afterparty." As we step up to my front door, I say, "I'm sure you've seen the hot tub in the back. We can pop open some wine and relax under the stars."

When I open the door and lead us in, Braden grabs my arm and spins me around, pinning me to the wall. "No drinks. Just you and me. Naked."

I swallow. "Yes, sir."

We proceed through the condo to the back door, where a little enclosed patio sits with an open and clear view of the night sky above us. While the water is already warm to prevent freezing, I turn up the heat and activate the jets. Then I retreat inside for a few moments to let it warm up.

Braden is looking at me with eyes dark with lust.

"That no sex rule…" I say, "we broke that last night. We're not trying that again…right?"

He steps forward, pinning me to the wall and kissing me deeply, shoving his tongue far into my mouth. "I couldn't even make it four hours last night. You think I'm going to try again? I've been fucking horny all day."

I'm already achingly hard. My heart thuds rapidly against my ribs. I want to be closer to Braden, to be one with him. "I think the hot tub is ready."

Never breaking eye contact, he quickly strips. He's all muscle and perfection, with just a smattering of hair across his chest, just enough to drive my horny imagination wild. I also strip off my clothing, and he finally breaks eye contact so he can look down at my body. There's lust in those eyes. And desire.

"Get in the hot tub," he says, his voice barely above a growl.

I open the door and lead us outside. The air feels colder now that we're naked, but I'm so hot with horniness that I barely notice. I step into the hot tub, the water instantly warming my wind-chilled legs. When I'm in, I sink down to neck-depth so only my head is above the surface.

Braden steps in and similarly submerges himself to his neck.

Without words, I wrap a wet hand around the back of his head and pull him close for a kiss. His five o'clock shadow scratches against my cheek as our lips and tongues wrestle for dominance. I can taste the rum he downed earlier and the mint he'd used on the way home. But beyond that, I can taste Braden—earthy, salty, delicious—a taste I'm already hopelessly addicted to.

Under the water, I reach out with my other hand, quickly finding his thick cock and wrapping my fingers around it, cupping it, stroking it, pleasuring it. Even in the heat of the hot tub, I feel the warmth of his flesh searing into my hand.

"I need that sweet ass of yours," Braden mumbles into my mouth.

I thrust my hips forward, bringing my hard cock in contact with his thigh, but more importantly bringing my ass within reach of his hands. Those muscled arms circle around me, and those gentle veterinarian hands grab my ass, a cheek in each hand. Braden massages my ass cheeks—squeezing, squishing, pulling, stretching—which is slowly loosening my hole.

I'm horny—so fucking horny—and I'm certain he's just as desperate. I've never needed a man as badly as I need Braden. Only he can satisfy my needs.

He moves his hands, probing more at the center of my ass, gently pushing at the hole. That finger then slips in, and I let out a slutty little moan. I break from the kiss and nestle my face in the crook of his neck, my arms now wrapped around him.

Braden shifts back until his ass is seated on one of the hot tub benches, and I'm now in his lap. With this new position, he has easier access to my hole, and he's taking advantage of it. I ride the sensation of one finger after another slipping in and out of me. Then it's two fingers, and then three.

"Fuck me," I moan into the hot skin of his neck. "Claim me."

Braden flicks his tongue over my ear. "Gladly."

He reaches between us and with a shift of his fist lines his dick up directly under my hole. I lower myself, sitting on his cock and impaling myself with it.

I put my hands on his cheeks, holding his face, and resting my forehead against his. I close my eyes and sink into the pure bliss of the moment, of Braden's thick cock entering me and stretching me wide as I sink down as far as I can, until my ass meets his pelvis. I rest there for a moment, breathing, letting it all sink in. He tilts his head up, and I meet his mouth with a kiss. This one is slower, more sensuous, more intimate. More loving.

"You like that, don't you, boy?" he murmurs between kisses.

I whimper in response.

"You're so tight," he says, "so warm. I could fuck you all night long."

I ease my hips up and then back down. Up and down. Up and down. Everything feels so right about this, so perfect. Our bodies are in tune. Our souls are aligned. And we fit together like we were made for each other.

He grasps my hips and helps guide the up and down, picking up the speed a bit and raising the height of the up. The friction and heat are just too much for me—in a good way. I've never been fucked this good. But, really, it isn't *just* the physical sensations that make this sex so mind blowing. It's the connection. It's Braden.

With him taking more and more control, I relax and sink into the whole experience. He hugs me tighter, pulling my body closer to his, crushing me against him.

"Fuck…" I moan. "Fuck, Braden…"

"Moan my name some more," he orders, whispering into my ear. Then his tongue flicks across my earlobe. "I want my name in your mouth when we both come."

When we both come…I haven't even touched myself, haven't needed to. I'm absolutely fucking rock hard and just the anal stimulation alone likely would get me off, but with Braden hugging our bodies close together, my cock is trapped between us, rubbed on both sides by our stomachs.

"Braden…I'm so close…"

"I'm close, too, baby," he says, his voice tight and his words clipped. "Keep doing that thing you're doing with your hole."

I flex my ass, clamping down on him, earning a whimper from

him. His fingers dig into my back, the strength of his grip signifying just how close the man is to orgasm, and just how intense that orgasm is building up to be.

"Bray…" I moan, raising my mouth to his ear so I can moan barely above the sound of a breath. "You're so amazing, Bray. So incredible…"

"My name…moan my name…" He sounds so fucking close.

"Bray…"

He suddenly jerks his pelvis up several degrees, digging his cock in deeper, and his hug tightens, squeezing the air out of me. I can feel his thick cock pulsing as it floods my insides with cum. And his breath comes in short, sharp gasps.

All of this, but particularly that final deep thrust, shoves me over the edge myself. My arms tighten around his neck, and I bury my face in the hair at his temple. My cock pulses as shot after shot after shot after shot of cum rockets from my dick, still caught between our bodies.

When the headiness of my orgasm starts to dissipate, my grip on him loosens, and I whimper, face buried in his hair. "I didn't want it to end."

"Neither did I," Braden says. He, too, loosens his grip. His arms now lay lower, wrapped around my waist, his finger resting over the crack of my ass. "But I wouldn't have been able to last much longer, no matter how hard I tried. Especially not with you calling me Bray, you haven't done that since we were kids. It was hot."

I glance away, kind of embarrassed that I'd done that. "Sorry…"

He kisses my ear. "Don't be. It's hot. Everything you say and do is hot. Your body is enticing. I look at it and I get horny. I touch it and I get hard. We get close and I can't control myself."

I lean against him. "You drive me wild, Braden, like no man has ever done before."

I can feel him relax a little more and then he kisses my collarbone. I said something right for once.

Eventually, his cock softens and slips from my ass, then I roll off and sit beside him, holding his hand under the water and sinking down so the water comes to just below my nose. I try to ignore the cum floating past me in the water's current.

Steam rises off the water, disappearing into the cold night. I lean my head against the padded headrest and look up at the night sky, at the stars that stare back down at us.

The jets choose that moment to shut off; the timer has run out. "We should head in," I say. "We've been in the hot tub long enough."

The rush back inside is frigid with our naked and soaked bodies. A polar-like gust of wind chooses that moment to go barreling through the area. Once we're back inside, I grab some towels from a stack I keep by the door for this very purpose and hand one to Braden. We dry ourselves off, then move down the hall toward the bedrooms.

"You're, uh, sleeping with me tonight…right?" I ask.

He chuckles—it's low and rough and goes straight to my now-revived cock. Down, I urge my dick. This is the wrong time for another boner.

"Of course," he says. "Unless you want to do a phone call again."

Dropping our towels, we go to bed naked and snuggle close, spooning, with me as the little spoon.

"Tell me about the Snowflake Festival," Braden says, murmuring into my ear.

"There's not much to say," I say, brushing off the topic.

"I want to hear," he says. "It's a big project for you and I want to support you, even if all the support you need is someone to vent all your frustrations to."

I exhale as I try to sort through the roiling thoughts in my head.

"It's going better," I say. "Now that everyone is getting into the festival mood and events are happening, they're all falling back into their routines. The Snowflake Festival happens every year, so everyone knows how it goes, they've all done it before." I pause as I scrunch my forehead and parse through the rest of my thoughts. "But there's a part of me, a pretty big part, that worries that it's all going to collapse at any moment and I'll be to blame."

Braden hugs me harder and kisses the back of my neck. "Everything will work out perfectly," he says. "What event are you doing? I'm sure yours will be fun."

I feel my mood shift as I think about his question; I have to give him credit for so swiftly and expertly handling my emotional letting-out. "I do a dip-your-own-candle event. You can make it any color you want and you get a small candleholder for free to display your creation."

"That sounds cute," he says.

There's a meow and then the bed shakes as Senator Tunacan joins us.

"He said my idea sounds cute," I tell the cat, "not that *you're* cute."

"Don't be so mean to Senator Tunacan," Braden scolds me. When he comes close to Braden, he pets the cat's head and scratches behind his ears. "I miss sleeping with my cat. I'm sure he's doing just fine at Nonna's, but going to bed isn't the same without him."

"Well," I say as my cat leans against him, seeking more attention, "what do you think, Mister Tunacan? Would you like an extra houseguest maybe? Possibly a new friend?"

Braden looks up at me. "You mean that? I can bring him here?"

"Technically, he's already been here once when the spa mixed our boys up," I remind him.

"I'd love it if Fluffykins could join us. Thank you, Kellan, that means a lot."

I kiss him gently. "I want you to be happy and at home here, and if Mister Fluffykins is part of that, then he should be here."

Senator Tunacan rolls onto his back between us and meows for attention.

Chapter Eight
Put Your Dick Away

 BRADEN

I tighten the string on my black track pants and flop backward onto Kellan's bed. I really don't know what it's gonna be like to be around all those guys. I haven't ever played on the same team as any of them as adults, and they're all used to one another. I just want to stay here with Kellan.

"Are you about ready to go?" Kellan asks, standing in between my legs. He's wearing gray sweatpants, freaking gray sweatpants. I can see the imprint of his dick; I'm only a man, what am I supposed to do in this situation? I already don't want to go. Now that he's standing in front of me like this, I don't think I can do it. I sit up and grab him by the ass, pulling him toward me. I can't think about rugby right now. "I'm ready to go, but I'm starting to wonder why we agreed to do this." I nuzzle his dick with my face and kiss it through the fabric.

He grips my topknot, and pulls it backward, moving my open mouth away from his crotch. I stare up at him with my mouth wide open. He jerks my bun playfully. "We agreed to this, because we are stupid. I haven't played competitively in years, we usually just toss the ball around. I'll be lucky if I don't pass out, or break my ankle," he jokes. "How about you? When was the last time you played?"

I'm still being held by my hair. I don't know if he realizes how much this turns me on. He could be genuinely mad at me, or saying

I was the ugliest man in the world; if he was pulling my hair like this, I'd still be turned on. But he seems ready to go, so I shouldn't push.

"I play more than you would think. A bunch of guys from my old team get together and do it. So, my not wanting to do it is because I already play enough."

He finally lets go of my bun. "Well, it looks like it's starting to snow, so you might not get to play today anyway. Half the guys that are supposed to be there are all talk, we'll see who shows up. Come on, let's head out," Kellan says, pulling me into a standing position.

I follow him outside, and we hop into his car. He said he wanted to drive, made a big deal out of it this morning. He's too cute to say no to. That could be a problem for me. It's another holdover from our younger days. I don't think I actually know *how* to say no to him.

"This is a nice car," I say. "I'm not used to being a passenger, so it feels weird sitting on this side."

Kellan laughs from the driver's seat and presses the start button. "Thanks. It's new-ish. I like it, I don't have to drive too much because everything is so close-by. That's why I wanted you to be the passenger princess today." He gives my thigh a little squeeze. "Although, I don't know of any passenger princesses with muscles like these." He pats my leg, and I place my hand atop his, moving it to the steering wheel.

"I don't think you should touch me while driving, seems dangerous," I say.

Kellan reverses out of the lot and heads toward the field. "What could be dangerous about it? I'm just a sweet, innocent Snowflake Princess, driving an incredibly sexy man to the park. Nothing dangerous about that."

"If you keep your hands to yourself there's nothing dangerous about it. Then again, I haven't seen you drive yet, that could be an entirely different type of danger."

"I'm a great driver," he says. "Never had a ticket and never caused an accident. How about you?"

"Wait, clarify please—you've never caused an accident, or you've never been in an accident? There is a difference."

"That doesn't matter, none of them were my fault. Besides, Passenger Princesses can't be picky. They're supposed to just sit there and look cute. So be quiet."

I sit up straight and check my seatbelt. "Ah, see I didn't know the rules. I can't be held liable for that."

"I'll forgive it this time," he says, pulling into a parking space. "See, if it wasn't kind of snowing, we could have just walked. I love how close everything is. Look, the town tree is right there! Isn't it so pretty?"

I glance over at the tree. "It's pretty, but you're prettier," I say, pulling his face in for a quick kiss. "I'm having serious second thoughts about getting out of this car. I want to go back to your place and do other things…"

"We can do those things after. Besides, the snow is starting to come down a bit more, so I doubt these guys will want to play for very long. He points outside the window. "Look at Chad, he's jogging in place, must be freezing. He's not going to want to play, and Lucas will do whatever Chad wants. Come on," he says, opening the door and stepping out of the car.

"Ugh—fine." I begrudgingly get out and walk around toward Kellan. It's freezing outside. I extend my hand toward him, which earns a loud shout from Geoff across the field.

"See! I told you!" Geoff points excitedly while hanging an arm around Lucas's neck. "They're not just fucking, they're together!"

Lucas smiles and gives Geoff a shove to the side.

Oh God. This is gonna be hideous. We didn't talk about what

we are, or what we aren't—should we have done that? Do people do that? Seems stupid to even ask.

Damn it…now I'm questioning things. Should I not have held my hand out for him to hold? Just as I'm about to stick my hand in my pocket, Kellan's fingers interlock with mine. And instantly my entire body feels warm.

"Who said we were just fucking?" Kellan asks as we approach the small group of four.

Three of our friends turn to look at Geoff, which is not surprising. I'm sure after last night, he called everyone gossiping about the way we were making out at the party. It probably wouldn't be a big deal if it were anyone else, but Geoff, like everyone else, seemed particularly fixated on the fact that Kellan never kisses anyone.

"Who do you think said it?" Chad asks.

Geoff shrugs at us and bumps our fists. "Are you saying you're not?"

"Why do you care so much?" Kellan asks. "Braden's not gonna sleep with you anyway, and we're not looking for a third. You tried that last night, remember?"

"Damn right," Lucas says. "Because if you were looking for a third, that spot would be mine!"

Chad's eyes look like they may fall out of his head. I don't blame him; I'm finding it hard to keep mine in their sockets after that comment.

"Excuse me? What did you just say, Lucas?" Chad asks.

Lucas is just laughing, while stretching his legs out. "Just kidding," he says. "I figured that was what you were gonna say, so I beat you to it. I don't want anyone getting any ideas. *You're* not going to be anyone's third," he says to Chad. "Not anymore."

I extend my hand to Danny for a handshake. I haven't spoken to him since we played against each other in college. "Hey, Danny, how's it going?"

He shakes my hand and pulls me in for a half hug, firmly patting my back. "Damn. You're bigger than you were in college. I thought the same thing at the gym the other night." He steps back with his hands on his hips, looking me over. "You know, my wife really wanted to come watch this. She didn't think we should be playing today because of the snow, but once I told her you were gonna be here, I had instant permission. Full disclosure, I'm supposed to take pictures of you, quote"—he makes quotations with his fingers in the air—"'looking hot'. She went to the same college as you, told me she had a big crush on you."

"Thanks…I guess?" I say as Kellan's fingers tighten. I don't know what he's squeezing my hand for? I tilt my head at him, trying to read his expression. I whisper in his ear, "Do you not like his wife?"

He doesn't answer me. Instead, he gives Danny a forced smile, and speaks through gritted teeth to him, "What exactly do you want him to do with that information?"

Geoff laughs and wags his finger at Kellan. "Oooh, Kellan. You know what you sound like?"

I guess Kellan is not in the mood right now. Not for Geoff nor Danny. I have no idea what he's mad about, but he definitely seems a bit jealous. Still, I've learned that he really doesn't like it when people point that out.

He lifts his chin at Geoff. "What do I sound like?"

"Who cares what he sounds like?" Chad asks, bouncing in place. "The snow is really starting to come down, and I'm freezing. I thought we came here to play, not to talk about Kellan's obvious jealousy."

"I am not jealous!" Kellan shouts. "Where's the ball?"

Everyone in the group looks at one another. "I don't have it, don't look at me," Lucas says.

"Whose idea was this anyway?" I ask. "We couldn't play even if we had a ball. I thought there were gonna be enough guys here for two teams."

"Ahh, I think Dylan was supposed to bring it," Geoff says. "But he and the others bailed at the last minute this morning. They didn't want to play in the snow."

"Uh, I don't want to play in the snow either," I say.

Lucas raises his hand. "Same here."

"Why didn't you tell us that they canceled?" Kellan asks. "This is so annoying; we would have just stayed in bed."

"Wait, in bed? He slept over, too?" Danny asks. "How serious *is* this thing you two have going on? I seem to remember you saying you don't let friends sleep over."

"I don't let friends who are fighting with their wives stay the night," Kellan clarifies. "Braden is staying with me because his parents came in to visit Leora for Christmas. It's a big condo, but I thought he'd be more comfortable with me."

"Are you here for good?" Danny asks.

"I'm here for good," I say. "I'm having a house built in Sticky Pines. It will be ready by the first of the year, at least that's what the builders said. I need to drive by this week and check on the progress."

"That's a nice subdivision, what are you rich?" Danny asks. "I know your family has money, but you must be loaded to have a house built there."

Before I can answer, Lucas lets out a loud groan. He's rubbing Chad's arms up and down in a bear hug from behind. "We're cold, if we're not gonna play, do you guys want to head to the café, or somewhere warmer?"

"Do you want to go somewhere else and warm up?" I ask Kellan.

Kellan whispers in my ear, "I want to feel you inside of me. That will warm me up." He lightly licks my earlobe and pulls back. He's giving me the naughtiest smile I've ever seen.

"Yeah, sure, we'll go hang out at the cafe," Kellan says, pulling his phone from his pocket, giving me a playful wink.

I am speechless. What the hell did he do that for? What a little tease. He whispers in my ear, then pretends he didn't just lick my damn earlobe. Well, two can play this game.

"Yeah, we'd love to do that," I say, pulling Kellan's body tightly beside mine. Since the other guys are standing on the opposite side, they can't see my hand behind Kellan, much like they couldn't see Kellan lick my earlobe a few seconds ago. I slip one finger into the waistband of his sweatpants, then trace the inside of his ass. His ass is so warm, and my fingers are so cold. I can't believe he hasn't screamed or jumped. I lightly rub down the center, purposely avoiding touching his asshole. I'm only trying to tease him just a little.

This ass is so perfect. At this moment, I wish we were playing rugby. I was looking forward to lifting him and shoving my face in his ass. I've always wanted to do that. Not that I could have done it with all these guys here, anyway. I continue tracing my index finger down Kellan's crack. I gotta give him credit. He's not reacting at all. I can feel goosebumps on his ass every once in a while, but besides that, he is cool and collected.

"Nice, let's hit up the diner, like old times," Chad says, leading Lucas by the hand toward the parking lot. "Does that work for everyone?"

"I'm good with that," Geoff says, pulling his keys from his pants.

"Same," Danny says. "Let's go! We can call the others and see if they want to meet up."

"Yeah, we'll see you guys in a—" Kellan's words are cut off, when

I finally press on his hole, and lightly pet it. The two of us are still standing in the same spot, while the other guys are already headed for their cars.

"They can't hear you now," I whisper. "They're too far away. You want to finish that sentence, or do you want to skip the diner, and I can finish what you started when you licked my ear a few minutes ago?"

Kellan turns toward me as the snow really starts to come down. I grab his face and press our mouths together. The heat from our kiss can be seen in the air around us.

He pulls back from me, while little pieces of snow land on top of his beanie. "Let's bail," he says. "I want you to fuck me. Don't make me wait."

"That's a good boy," I say, while squeezing his ass with both hands.

I pull my car to a stop in front of my condo. Finally, we're here. I'd kept my hand on his thigh the whole drive back. I'd wanted to grab his cock, bite his nipples, and give him my ass…but that would make me a distracted driver, and I could almost hear my mom scolding me in the back of my head. Especially, if it was sex that was distracting me—she'd tell me to at least pull over and find some bushes to take a tumble in.

To try and get my mind off sex, I brought up an old childhood memory, and it still has us laughing.

"I had forgotten all about that," Braden says, wiping a tear from his eye. But through the humor and happiness, I can see absolute horniness simmering in his eyes. We might be talking casually now, but any moment now we'll be fucking like wild animals. "It had felt so traumatic at the time and now I can just laugh it off."

"I want to say everything felt so dramatic when we were thirteen," I say, "but I feel like if I accidentally wet my pants while standing in front of the classroom at this age, I'd be just as mortified." I break into more laughter as a new memory hits me. "At least we have better haircuts now than we did at thirteen."

Braden points at me. "The mullet with the rat's tail!"

"I was always a paragon of style!" I vogue to emphasize my point.

"Am I a paragon of style?" he asks. He tries to vogue too. It's a cute attempt.

"You're a paragon of topping," I say. I lean over and finally grasp the bulge in his track pants. It quickly thickens under my touch and starts hardening. "You perform miracles with this thing."

He slips a hand behind me and then down into the back of my sweatpants. "I think it's you that does the miracle with this. I'm willing to share my title as paragon with you if we call ourselves the paragon of sex."

I lean forward and kiss him. "Sounds nerdy. Makes me horny."

As I'm leaning, he slips his hand deeper down the back of my pants, and I soon feel his fingertips brushing against my hole. "If you tease me, I'm going to make sure you follow through."

Braden presses a finger at the center of my knotted flesh. "That sounds like a threat."

"It might be," I challenge.

"I spank boys who threaten me," he says.

"Then it's definitely absolutely one hundred percent a threat."

He suddenly pulls his hand out of my pants and sits up straight in his seat. I follow his gaze to see Mrs. Parker walking her toy poodle down the sidewalk toward us. She gives us a dirty look as she passes.

I slowly take my hand off Braden's bulge, never breaking eye contact with Mrs. Parker.

"Geez," Braden says. "She certainly doesn't approve."

I blink a few times, trying to figure out what he means. "Ohh…that's not what that was about. I discontinued the cranberry sage candle because my scent distributor no longer has what I need. She took it personally."

Braden looks over his shoulder at where Mrs. Parker had gone. "She takes her candles seriously."

"Most people do," I say, chuckling. "You'd be surprised how many people come in frequently to restock on their favorite scents. I also regularly sell out of the low-temperature candles meant for wax play in the bedroom."

Braden's eyes go wide, and his brows raise with a question.

I chuckle and say, "Not into it, sorry. I just supply the candles. Harvey, the older librarian downtown, though, buys at least a candle a week. But you have to keep that between us."

"Kinky," Braden says.

"Besides," I say, leaning over the console and gripping Braden's bulge again, "who needs candle wax when just kissing you is mind-blowingly erotic?" I kiss him again, caressing the man's tongue with my own.

"You're such a horny slut, aren't you?" Braden says. He slips his hand down the back of my pants again, stroking my crack with his fingertips. "You just never get enough."

"I can't help it if you make me desperate for you. Besides, it's your fault for wearing these slutty track pants that show off your thighs, your bulge, and your muscular ass. What's a gay to do when you strut around like that?"

With a quick glance to assure no one is around, I tug down the front of Braden's track pants and briefs and wrench his hard dick out.

I give him another kiss and then sink my face down to his lap, taking his cock in my mouth. It's as delicious and warm and thick and velvety as always. I can never get enough of it.

"Ohhh…fuck…Kellan…" he moans. He puts his hand on the back of my neck and guides the up and down. "God, you're good at this."

I whimper around Braden's dick. I need it deep inside me and as often as possible. As I suck, I pull out his balls too and massage them in time with my sucking tempo.

I eventually come up for air, and he captures my face in his hands, pulling me close for a kiss, much more passionate and romantic than before.

"Let's go inside," Braden says, "and see about exploring the holes on both ends of your body."

"Mmm…fuck yes," I say. "But pack your dick away so we don't get arrested."

He kisses me again. "I wouldn't mind being in a jail cell with you."

"Could be a hot scenario," I say, "but I wouldn't look good in prisoner orange."

He puts his dick and balls back in his underwear and pulls up his pants. "God, I need you so badly."

"My hole was made for you. You satisfy me in ways no man could ever hope to do."

"Race you to the door? Loser has to bottom?" Braden says.

"I'll give you a ten-minute head start, in that case."

Braden laughs. "You goofball. Come on, I need to get my dick somewhere warm and I bet you know the perfect place."

"Alright, but regardless of who gets to the door first or second, I'm bottoming."

Braden rolls his eyes. "Yes, we get it. Now, let's get naked and sweaty."

We get out of the car and hurry up to the door of the condo, and I quickly let us in. As soon as the door is closed, I throw Braden against the wall and kiss him with all the passion I have in my body and soul. My hands explore his muscular body and the fuzz on his chest. My hands go south and grab the waist band of his track pants and briefs, shoving them down to his knees. I lower myself to the floor in front of him.

"Kellan?" a feminine voice calls from the kitchen. "Kellan, is that you?"

"Oh fuck," I say, shooting back to my feet. "Put your dick away before she sees you," I whisper urgently.

"Who the fuck is that?" Braden whispers back. He tugs at his track pants, but can't pull them up. When I'd shoved them down, the pants and underwear had apparently rolled over on itself and gotten tangled.

"My sister," I whisper. Then I call out, "It's me, Charlie! Just getting in from a morning out!" And to Braden I whisper, "Put your fucking dick away. Now!"

"It's tangled. I can't!"

"I hope you don't mind, I let myself in," Charlie says. She comes around the corner a mere fraction of a second after Braden finally untangles his clothes and covers up. She gasps when she sees who I'm with. "Braden?" She rushes forward to give him a big hug.

"Hi, Charlie," he says. "It's been a long time. Good to see you."

When the hug ends, she asks, "Is that your stuff I saw in the guest room?"

Braden glances at me. "Uh…yeah. Kellan didn't mention you were coming over."

Charlie rolls her eyes. "I'm not surprised Kellan forgot. He also forgot to pick me up at the airport. Thankfully, I had the key he gave me last time, or else I would have had to sit on the front step until he got home. I would have frozen my ass off by now."

"Sorry," I say. "I had it in my planner to pick you up, but the last week or so has been unusually, uh…busy."

Her gaze moves from me to Braden and back again. I can tell she's thinking something; there's a light in her eyes. "So, who *actually* gets the guest room? I think it should be me since I'm the big sister."

"Age before beauty," I say.

She slaps me on the shoulder. "I have always been and will always be the better looking of the two of us." She turns to Braden. "You agree of course, right?"

Braden looks at us both, wide-eyed. "Uh, no comment."

"Besides," she says, raking her gaze up and down Braden again, "something tells me the two of you wouldn't mind bunking together."

"Uh, it's not like that," I say.

"Mmhmm," she says. She turns and heads back to the kitchen. "I've opened a bottle of wine if you boys would like a glass? Or do you want to shower first?"

"We're fine," Braden says, right as I say, "We'll shower."

"Uh, I guess we'll shower," Braden says. "But not together."

"Definitely not together," I say.

She pokes her head around the corner. "You're really not convincing me of anything other than the fact that you two are boning." She disappears into the kitchen. "Go shower, the wine can wait till you're done!"

I lead Braden down the hall to my bedroom and its en suite bathroom. "You can shower first," I say.

He crosses his arms. "You're showering with me.".

"But my sister—"

"Shush," he says. "Get naked."

We both doff our clothes. I turn the shower up nice and hot, and the bathroom gets steamy. "I enjoyed our morning together," I say.

Braden puts his hands on my upper arms and pulls me closer for a gentle kiss. "I enjoyed it too. I think I would've liked to play rugby with you, since it's been so long since we've done that, but I still had a wonderful morning."

I grab his cock and give it a few strokes, picking up where we left off. It quickly stiffens in my hand. "We can make this a wonderful afternoon, too."

"Get in the shower," he orders.

I enter, and Braden follows, sliding the shower door closed behind us. He watches as I soap up and rinse off, then we switch places, and I watch as he does the same. There's something incredibly sexy about watching him get soaking wet from the shower.

He gives me a very horny look. "How quiet can you be?"

My cock instantly starts stiffening. "No one caught us when we fucked in the closet at the community center. Well…except maybe Mr. Barclay…but he knew what he was looking for." I shake my head. "I can be super quiet, is what I mean to say."

One corner of his mouth quirks up in a half-smile. "Good. Turn around."

When I do so, Braden comes up close behind me, hugging me from behind and kissing my neck. Then with a wet finger, he probes at my entrance.

"Mmm…" I say. "Don't tease me. Just go in."

He obliges, sliding his finger in until there's some resistance. Then he finger-fucks me, pushing deeper each time, until his finger slides into full depth with each stroke.

"Think you can fit a second one, boy?" he asks in a low and growly voice. He nibbles on my earlobe.

I whimper. "Yes, sir, but I really want your dick instead of your fingers."

"Fingers first," he says.

He eases a second finger into me, working up a good rhythm and a nice depth. I'm like putty in his embrace, like my bones are made of jelly, like I could at any instant just melt and flow down the drain. But, instead, Braden keeps me upright with his strong embrace.

"Are you ready for my cock?" he asks.

I'm in such a sexual high that my brain is like mush and thoughts are hard to form. But I manage to say, "Yes, sir."

"Beg for it."

"Please, sir," I say. Words are still difficult to form with how much he's fucking my whole body and soul. "Please let me have your cock. Please fill me with you, sir. Please, I'm begging you to fill me up."

"Good boy," he says. "Now you get your good boy reward." He spits into his hand and slicks up his cock.

I brace myself against the shower wall, preparing for Braden's thick, manly cock. In the half dozen or so times we've had sex, I've always found that the fingers—no matter how many he stuffs inside me—never quite prepare me for the real thing. Braden's cock isn't overly long, but it's impressively thick. But more important than size, it seems to fit me perfectly, hitting all the right spots, giving me all the right sensations, and just straight up rocking my world.

I inhale sharply when he pushes his fat cock head against my tight hole, slowly breaching the entrance and sinking in. The fingering makes this *easier*, but it's still not *easy*. When he reaches a certain depth, I exhale, trying to release all the discomfort, and instead sink into the pure pleasure of the moment. He makes me feel so full and puts me in such a state of bliss. I ease my hips back, meeting his cock halfway.

He groans in pleasure and then whispers in my ear, "You feel so fucking good on my dick."

"Pound me, Bray. Pound me."

He grips my hips and fucks me good and hard, slamming into me over and over again. I reach down and stroke my dick in time with the ass-slamming, working myself up in a frenzy of erotic energy.

"I'm gonna come," Braden growls in my ear.

"Fill me," I beg.

He slams into me several more times, each thrust forward an incredible burst of pleasure that brings me careening toward the edge. Then he suddenly falls forward against me, wrapping his arms around me and hugging me tightly, our bodies leaning against the shower wall. His body trembles as his orgasm overtakes him, and his heart beats so hard, I can feel it against my back.

"Fuck, you're amazing," I say when it seems like his orgasm subsides.

"Come for me," he says.

I turn around, still trapped by his thick arms. "Kiss me," I plead.

He puts a hand behind my head and pulls me in for a kiss. I jerk my cock; the kiss turns me on more than I ever thought a kiss could do. It takes no more than a few tugs—and Braden's tongue down my throat—to have me shuddering into an orgasm of my own. My cum splatters against his thigh, and he moans into the kiss when my cum hits his skin.

When the heat of sex subsides and our kiss recedes, I open my eyes and look at Braden, who is looking back at me. It's a curious look, one that certainly contains lust, but might contain something else, too.

"We should clean up and get to the kitchen. Charlie will get suspicious with how long we're taking," I say.

He kisses along my jaw and then along my earlobe. "I'm sure she already knows," he whispers.

We quickly wash, dry, dress, and return to the kitchen. Charlie had already poured glasses of wine for us.

"So…" she says, "this is new."

"This? This is none of your business," I say to her, giving her the kind of sass only siblings can give each other.

"Next time you're supposed to pick me up at the airport, can you let me know if you're falling head over heels for someone? I can make better back-up plans then," she says. There's no anger in her voice, just teasing.

"Sorry about that," I say. "Things have been wild lately. I just got elected Snowflake Princess."

"Wait, what?" Charlie says. "I know you're changing the subject, but *you're the Snowflake Princess*? What happened to Leora?"

I glance at Braden before answering. "She hurt her ankle and she's out of commission for a bit, so I'm stepping in."

"Have you had to deal with crazy old Morris at the movie theater yet? Has he asked you to cancel a blizzard?" Charlie asks. She laughs and tosses back the last of her glass of wine. To Braden, she says, "I worked there when I was a teenager. He's…something."

"Wait…" I say, realization dawning on me. "If you're here, that means tonight…"

"You forgot dinner with our parents, didn't you?" Charlie says. She rolls her eyes at me. "Braden, you should come." She snickers. "Though I think you did that already. I mean you should join us for dinner."

Panic rises in my chest, and my mind is flooded with a dozen scenarios of how this could go horribly, mortifyingly wrong. "Braden doesn't need to come."

"Oh, he most definitely does," Charlie says.

"I'd love to see your parents again," Braden says.

"No. Absolutely not." I cross my arms.

Twenty minutes later, Braden pulls his Jeep to a stop in front of a Mexican restaurant, with both Charlie and I as his passengers.

"This is worse than torture," I say, burying my face in my hands.

"Oh, shush. You endured this with my boyfriends over the years. It's about time I get to enjoy it happening to you," Charlie says. "Oh, and just a heads up, I'm meeting my friend Rin at the bar afterward for a couple drinks and might spend the night on their couch. So, if you two boys need some privacy…" She opens the door and gets out before I can toss a retort her way.

"This'll be fun," Braden says, after we get out of the Jeep.

"Braden, you *do* remember our mom is a *sex therapist*, right?"

"Oh, I remember," he says. "Her office had a dildo collection."

"A dildo collection that set unrealistic expectations for what flesh and blood men might be packing, I might add," I say.

"Amen," Charlie says.

My heart thunders against my ribs as we approach the door. I pause just in front of it, take a deep breath, push it out, and then grab the handle. "Alright, let's go."

We find our parents at a table in the back. They give me a hug, but give Charlie an extra big hug since they haven't seen her for several months.

"Braden," my mom says, "Merry Christmas." She pulls him into a hug, while my dad offers him a handshake.

We sit and order a cheesy appetizer and a round of beers. Conversation inevitably shifts over to Braden.

"Tell me," my mom says, pulling out the sex therapist voice that I always hated, "are you a top or bottom or vers? Or are you a side?"

"*Mom*," I scold. To Braden, I say, "You don't have to answer that."

"Oh, shush," Mom says, "we all know you're a bottom. It's good to talk about these things; it takes the taboo veneer away from it all. Besides, if you two are shacking up—"

"*Mom!*"

"—then I want to be sure you're compatible."

Braden gives a smile that I don't like. He might be uncomfortable, but he's enjoying my extreme discomfort too much to care about his own. "I'm a top," he says to my mom.

She looks at me. "Good to hear, though I've been told tops aren't all that difficult to come by."

I bury my face in my hands. "Why me? Why am I part of this family?"

"That's a bit regional," Braden says, fully engaging my mom's outrageous behavior. "Some areas are more bottoms than tops. Other places it seems to be pretty evenly split."

"Interesting…" Mom says. "But we can talk more about sex a little later. Any long-term relationships going on? Anything of note in the recent past?"

"Mom…" I say, my words muffled by my hands still covering my face. "You don't need to do this."

"Shush, dear, I'm not *doing* anything. So, Braden, relationships?"

Braden chuckles. "Nothing new and nothing for quite some time."

"Thirty and perpetually single," Mom says. "It does make one wonder why…"

"I've been waiting for the right guy, I guess. I'm definitely looking for something long term, but he has to be worth putting in the effort, and he needs to put that effort in, too."

I spread my fingers a bit and peek between them. Charlie is bright red and nearly bursting with laughter. Dad is giving me a sympathetic, apologetic look. And Mom and Braden are just carrying on with the same intensity as if they were talking about the weather.

My mom shoots me a smile before launching into her next invasive question. "Then what are you doing with Kellan? From what I hear he's more into hookups and not so much into relationships. He tried the boyfriend thing a couple times, but he has this odd aversion to kissing, so, naturally, those relationships didn't last more than a week. Casual is more his style. He's probably been around town twice by now."

Charlie finally bursts out laughing. I just want the floor to cave in beneath me and for me to fall through and disappear forever.

"Mom, please…"

"Oh, shush, everyone knows you're the village bicycle."

"Village bicycle?" Braden asks.

"Everyone gets a ride."

I peek through my fingers at Braden to see if he's upset by that comment about my…promiscuity…but he seems to be enjoying everything about this dinner conversation.

"Well…" Braden says, "everyone's got a past. What matters is the present and where you plan to go in the future."

"That's a smart way of putting it," she says, seeking an approving nod from my father. "I've always hoped Kellan would grow out of his little hedonistic phase and settle down, you know?"

The cheesy appetizer arrives, along with a big bowl of chips.

"Mom, please stop," I mumble, still hiding my face. "Can we talk about anything else? Like, *literally anything else?*"

"You know I'm a doctor, right?" she says to Braden. When he

nods, she continues, "This is what I do, I talk about the things that people find uncomfortable. And my son thinks this is embarrassing. You know, if everyone would just talk openly and honestly about sex, we'd lose the taboo that surrounds it and everyone could just have a good time smashing body parts together."

"Good God, Mother!" I say, finally pulling my hands from my face. When I realize I'd raised my voice, I whisper-shout, "How much wine did you drink this afternoon?"

"Oh, hush, dear. I'm stone cold sober and you know it. I'm just making conversation."

When the waiter comes with our dinners, I'm immensely grateful for the interruption to my mother's one-track conversation. My father tries shifting the conversation to weather and sports. But when dessert comes, Mom changes the topic again.

"So," Mom says to me, "now knowing what we all know, it does beg the question of if this is long-term or a weekend fling. I think you two are good together; could this be the magic one that changes everything?"

I scoff and roll my eyes. "We'll see." I really don't want to get into this here at the restaurant and potentially open up another line of invasive sex questions.

Besides, given how many times I've said the wrong thing to Braden, I know it's only a matter of time before I do it again. I seem to have a habit of screwing this up, but so far Braden keeps wanting me back.

"Well," Mom says, "it certainly looks long-term to me. As long as you two fuck regularly and thoroughly."

BRADEN

We step out of the warm restaurant and into the frigid air. "I don't know why I assumed it would still be light outside," Kellan says.

I give him a silent nod. I'm still stuck on what he said earlier. Sure, the entire evening was filled with more good moments than bad ones, but those two words, "we'll see" made all the good moments seem less important. I walk with my hands in my pockets toward my Jeep beside Kellan. Before he reaches the passenger door handle, I pull it open for him.

"Thank you," he says. He places a hand on my chest and gives me a quick kiss on the lips, then I close the door once he sits inside.

The short time it takes me to walk around to the driver's side feels like an eternity. I'm being immature. I need to talk to him about what he said. He's obviously not good at reading people, probably has no idea that what he said sounded like he had no faith in me…or in us. Ah…but if I ask him, does that make me seem even less mature? Damn it, I sound like such a child either way. I know that communication is important, but this is so new, and he's not used to relationships. I don't want to make him uncomfortable.

I sit inside the car, press the start button, and quickly turn the heater on. "Ah, sorry, I should have come out before you and warmed the car up," I say. "I got so caught up in the conversation, that I forgot to do that."

"You're always so considerate," he says. "Always worried about me. It's the same as when we were kids."

Yep, he's completely oblivious…maybe I shouldn't say anything. I place my hand on the headrest of Kellan's seat and reverse out of the spot.

"Damn…" he says, adjusting his pants. "That's fucking hot, the way you turn the wheel with just the heel of your hand. Making me feel things."

"Don't know if anyone has ever said that to me before." I put the car in drive and head toward Kellan's place.

"That's good. I like being the first one to say it. Did you have fun tonight? Sorry about my parents, they're a bit much sometimes."

I'm still not sure if I want to try and dive into Kellan's feelings, or just leave it alone. But for me, relationships require 100% honesty. I don't want to lie to him, but I also don't want to pretend to be unaffected.

I decide to change the subject at least for now. "I forgot to put the Christmas lights up. I need to do that. I feel bad driving through and seeing everyone else's shop lit up all pretty. Especially because I love Christmas lights."

"I didn't know you liked Christmas lights that much," he says. "We should go look at some tomorrow night, if you're up for it. There are a few other neighborhoods that have massive displays. It would be fun. I could also help you decorate the outside of BJ's after work, if you want."

I shake my head while pulling into Kellan's parking lot. "No, you have enough stuff going on. I can't be asking the Snowflake Princess to help me put Christmas lights up."

"You're not asking, I'm offering," he says. "So, do you want to?"

"We'll see," I reply, parking in the spot, and quickly stepping out. I am such a child. I can't believe I just said that. Actually, I wonder how many times I can say "we'll see" before he realizes something is wrong. Especially since I always say yes to whatever he wants.

I walk toward Kellan's door to open it for him, but he's already getting out.

"I would have opened the door for you. You didn't need to do that. You're impatient."

"Yep, that's me. I hate waiting for things, or people. That doesn't apply to *our* situation, though. I don't mind waiting for you. I just want to get inside where it's warm," Kellan says rubbing his arms.

"Lead the way," I say.

He grabs my hand and turns to quickly kiss me. Before our lips meet, he says, "I want to go inside where it's warm…do you want to come inside where it's warm, too?"

Even though I'm half mad at him, I'm not about to turn down sex. I waited far too long for him. "We'll see," I say.

He places a hand on my chest. "What do you mean, 'we'll see'?"

"Oh, nothing. I thought that's what we say when we really want something."

He tugs my hand pulling me inside the condo. "I'm sorry again about my parents. They have no filter."

"Oh, *they* were fine. I had a good time with them," I say, slipping my shoes off inside the door.

Kellan brings his mouth in front of mine and kisses me. He pulls the elastic from my hair and drops it on the floor. Both his hands are gripping thick sections on either side of my head. I can barely keep up with his tongue as he moves it wildly inside of my mouth, kissing me at an almost frantic pace. I move my hands to his ass and give it a little squeeze.

"Mmm, more, please. I want you," he whimpers, gripping my hair tighter.

"I know you do, but I'm kind of mad at you."

"Me?" He releases my hair and pulls back from the kiss. "Why would you be mad at me? I didn't even do anything."

"Ahhh, you didn't *do* anything, that's true," I say.

"Okay, if I didn't do anything then what could it be?" He looks more than confused right now.

"I probably just need sleep." I pat his ass lightly and turn toward his bedroom.

"No, you said you were mad at me. So, what is it? What made you upset?"

"It's nothing," I say, walking into Kellan's room. I sit on the edge of the bed, while trying to decide what to say. I really don't want to make him feel bad. I should just drop it. But still, he means so much to me, and I really do want to know what he meant by that.

He quickly straddles my lap and kisses my neck. "Are you really mad at me?" he asks, after planting a few kisses. His big blue eyes stare helplessly at me, almost pleading for an answer—while what he's doing with his bottom half is sending a different message.

I grab ahold of his waist. "What are you doing? Giving me puppy dog eyes, and grinding on me…which one are you, remorseful or horny?"

Kellan grinds his cock against me slowly, while kissing the other side of my neck.

"Fuuuck," I groan. "That feels so good."

He nuzzles against my neck. "Why were you mad at me?"

Shit, I can't give in to him yet. "No talking," I say, abruptly lifting him off my lap and onto the bed. I climb on top of him and look down. "And I'm *still* mad at you." I kiss his chest through his shirt, then begin unbuttoning it. I feel like I need to show him I'm not replaceable, I'm not something that can be used and discarded.

With his shirt now unbuttoned, I move my fingers to his nipples, massaging them between my fingers. He loves it, his nipples are so sensitive. His breath hitches as I capture one with my mouth and squeeze the other. Working my way down, I rub his chest, then remove his belt and unbutton his pants. "You want me to suck your cock?" I ask, placing kisses on the soft trail of hair below his navel.

Kellan runs his hands through my hair, and he spreads his legs wider, nodding. "Yes—please—I really want it."

I kiss the outline of his hard cock through his pants. "Mmm—I really want to." He pulls his pants and underwear down, and kicks them off. The inside of his thighs are so smooth, there's muscles here, but the skin itself is so soft, I can't help but to kiss them. I hover my face above his cock, lightly flicking it with my tongue.

"Mmm—you're so hard for me already. But I don't let boys who upset me, come. So, I don't think I can help you out," I whisper, while rubbing his balls.

"What?!" Kellan props himself up on his elbows. "Why are you mad? Just tell me. Braden, come on, please?" He grabs at my shirt, unbuttoning the top button. "I want you so fucking bad."

"Lick," I say, holding my open palm to his mouth.

He pulls my hand toward his mouth and licks each finger, then does the same to the inside of my palm. Fuck.

Leaning back down, I grip his cock tightly, and kiss the tip, popping just the head into my mouth. Using my wet palm, I rub up and down his shaft, maintaining eye contact with him.

"Ahh, fuck, yes," Kellan moans.

"Mmm—you like that? You want more?"

"Yes—please."

I lean back down and slowly take the rest of him into my mouth, moving up and down, while massaging his balls.

He holds onto my hair, gripping it tightly, while closing his eyes. "You don't feel mad anymore…"

I pull his cock out of my mouth and look up at him. "Mmm—no, you're a good boy," I say, while rubbing his cock against my cheek. "But you weren't good earlier, so I'm not gonna make this easy for you."

"Wh—what—did I do?" he asks through broken breaths.

I slip my tongue in between his ass cheeks, feathering it against his hole. "So tight—so warm—this is mine—" I press the tip of my tongue inside and suck.

Kellan grasps my hair with both hands. "Mmm—Braden, it's so fucking hot—don't stop."

He's falling apart already, and I love it. "Such a slut for me, look how much you need me." I grip the base of his cock and slowly run my tongue along his slit, lapping up the precum that has begun to leak.

"Braden, please—fuck me. I need it so bad."

"No—I'm not gonna do that yet. You said something tonight that I did not like…" I push my index finger inside of him and begin to stretch him out.

"What did I say? I can't—focus. Not—when you're fingering me—"

"Focus on this feeling," I say, teasing his prostate.

Kellan's head leans further back into the pillow, his back arching from the sensation.

"Yeah, like that, baby. You're loosening up so nice for me," I say, slipping another finger in.

I don't know how long I can hold back for, he's ready, and I want him. But I'm gonna teach him a lesson. I can't have him thinking he doesn't need me. I want him to want *me*, not just my dick.

He reaches down for his cock, but I stop him before he can reach it. "No," I say, grabbing his hand.

"Please, I'm so fucking hard. I can't take it. I need it," he whines.

"You need what? My cock?"

"Yes—I need your cock," he begs. "Please give it to me."

I keep pumping my fingers deep inside, my own cock is begging to be let loose. I'm so hard that it hurts.

I need to be inside of him.

I remove my fingers and stand beside the bed. Slipping out of my pants under Kellan's gaze.

"The lube is in here, right?" I point toward the nightstand.

He nods his head, eyes half-lidded, then reaches for his own cock.

I quickly pounce, grabbing both of his hands and pinning them over his head. "I said no. You don't listen." Holding Kellan's hands over his head with one hand, I grab the lube from beside us, squeeze some on, and line my cock up with his entrance.

I push myself inside, inch by inch. Needing to drive in further, I let go of his hands, and toss one leg over each shoulder, bending him in half. "Fuck yeah, that's it—mmm—" I moan, now fully inside of him. "So fucking good." I pump harder and harder, as Kellan whimpers in pleasure, his head hitting the top of the headboard every few thrusts.

I am going to fuck the doubt out of him…he needs to know who he belongs to.

I lick his open mouth, then kiss him forcefully.

"Mmm—mmm…" Kellan moans.

I continue pounding into him. Moving my mouth to his neck, licking the skin, kissing it softly.

Fuck, he drives me crazy, I want to wreck his hole, and at the same time treat him like a princess. His skin tastes so fucki—

My thoughts are interrupted by the feeling of his hand hitting me in the abdomen.

He's jerking off…he's so impatient.

I bite down into the side of his neck. Then whisper in his ear. "I. Said. No."

I remove his legs from my shoulders and pull my cock out.

"Noooo—don't take it away. Fuck—Braden. Put it back."

"You want your hand so bad? I'm not gonna stop you." I slide two fingers inside of him, pressing hard on his spot. "You're impatient. I know where to touch you. I can make you come whenever I want."

His breath hitches with every swipe of his prostate.

"Hahh—please—do it—fuck me. I need you back inside."

"Of course, you do. You're ready, you're ready to come. I can feel it…" I slide a third finger in, pumping slowly. I bring my mouth near his ear, and whisper, "My cock wants to be inside, but if you think you can do it by yourself…I can just watch."

He grabs my hair forcefully and kisses me. He's riding the high of my fingers, moaning, while raking his hand through my hair. I slide my fingers in and out, only brushing against Kellan's spot, purposely trying to bring him close to the edge. "You want that? You want to jerk off and I'll watch you? Or do you want to bend over, and I can show you who this greedy hole belongs to?"

"That—I want that. Fuck—please," Kellan begs.

"Good boy," I say, pulling my fingers out. "Now bend over." He quickly flips over on all fours and raises his ass.

I slap both cheeks, then squeeze, spreading him even wider. "Fuck, that's pretty—"

Kellan giggles, while burying his face into his pillow.

I press my lips against Kellan's entrance, slipping my tongue inside, while massaging his balls.

"Yes, fffuck me with your tongue. Don't stop—"

I reach past his balls to rub his dick, and feel his hand. I pull my tongue out and slap his ass, making a loud crack.

"How many times must you be told? I asked you if you wanted to do it yourself." I slap his ass again. "So fucking impatient."

Now he's gonna get it. I shove my cock in without warning, watching his body jerk forward, while his hands grip the sheets.

"Haah—haah—please—I just want to come. Make me come. I need you," he begs.

I ram my cock into him, over and over, pounding deep inside.

"That's right, you need me to make you come. You need me, you want me—"

My balls are so fucking tight. I'm gonna explode. I can't hold back anymore. I need to fucking come…

"Ungh—I do—need you—I need you, Bray—"

I dig my fingers deep into the sides of Kellan's juicy ass, while tormenting his spot. "There it is—right—fucking—there—now come for me."

Kellan rocks his hips back further; his ass is clinging to my cock. His mouth falls open, "Aaa—unh—Bray—I—I'm coming."

I fuck him through his release. His moaning drives me fucking wild. "Holy shit—take my cum—ungh—ahhh—"

I relax onto his back, panting from one of the most intense orgasms I've ever had.

"Thank you," I say, lightly kissing Kellan's back. I slowly pull out, as he collapses onto the bed.

"Whoo. Thank you…wow…" he says, rubbing his face into his pillow.

I stand up from the bed and ruffle his hair.

"Come on, let's go clean-up. I really want to go get Mister Fluffykins so he can stay the night—well, that is, if my nonna lets me."

"Okay, I'm coming"—Kellan stands up and holds his hand out—"Stop—no, I already came. Not asking to come again," he jokes.

I walk into the bathroom first with Kellan close behind. Before we step inside, I turn the shower temperature to hot, letting it warm up.

"Your cheeks are all red after sex," he says, looking at me. "That's cute."

I check my ass out in the mirror, looking over my shoulder. "If my ass is red, it's because of you—but I don't remember you really groping me back there."

Kellan pinches both of my cheeks. "Not your ass; I'm talking about your cheeks, these cheeks."

I laugh. "Ohhh that makes way more sense." I slide the shower door open, and we both step inside.

"I'm gonna wash really fast. I know my nonna will be asleep in probably another hour or so," I say, scrubbing myself down. "Do you want to come with me to get my cat?"

"Of course, that will be fun," he says. "Seeing your parents is always entertaining."

"Mmm—I don't know, there's not much that could top the conversation from earlier tonight."

"Pretty embarrassing having a mom that's a sex therapist. She says the craziest stuff sometimes."

I wipe the water from my face and pull him in for a hug. "Hey," I say, kissing the top of his wet head. "I want to be honest with you, even when it may be uncomfortable or seem stupid."

He wipes the water from his face and nods. "Honesty is the best policy. Are you gonna finally tell me what I did wrong?"

I squeeze him tightly. "Mmm, let's save it for later. We don't have time for a huge conversation."

Kellan's mouth drops open. "What? Come on, I can't take it. Just tell me. If you're mad you have to tell me. That's honesty."

I ruffle his hair and turn the water off. "Nope. What I said *was* honest. You hurt my feelings, and it was probably dumb, but I do want to talk about it. I just respect what we have too much to rush through a conversation. Especially not when you're naked in the shower with me and we have to get my cat. We seriously have to get him before everyone is asleep. Come on." I step outside of the shower and smile.

"Well, how am I supposed to feel until we talk about it?" he asks. "I don't want you to be mad at me."

I hold his chin with my hand and lift it slightly, giving him a quick kiss. "I'm not mad at you. You didn't do anything wrong. Having a discussion about feelings doesn't mean someone did something wrong. We gotta hurry."

We arrive at my nonna's place just a few minutes later. I unlock the door, as Kellan giggles behind me.

"What are you laughing about?" I ask, as we walk inside.

"Oh, just thinking about the accidental motorboat situation we had last week. Definitely did not expect to run into you like that. Literally. And your chest was…so hard."

"What's hard?" my mom asks from the kitchen.

"Mom!" I shout. "I didn't know you were in there. Were you just listening the whole time?"

She dries her hands on a dish towel and places it on the counter. "Oh, don't be so dramatic. You've been here for less than three minutes. Now, what was hard?"

"I ran into Braden's chest the night that he came into town, it was like running into a brick wall," Kellan answers.

She laughs. "Oh wow, that's hilarious. Especially because I heard you were a busy little bee before Braden got here. Cooking and cleaning up a storm. So, you just ran right into him, that's some luck." She turns toward me. "And what did you do?" she asks.

"He did *him*!" my father interjects from the living room couch.

My father normally keeps quiet, unless there's something

scandalous going on. He loves celebrity news, scandals, town gossip, all that stuff. So, of course, he would chime in at this moment. If we were talking about cooking, or cars, even candles, he wouldn't say a word.

I place my hands on my hips and exhale. "We had dinner with Kellan's parents tonight, that was embarrassing for him—this, this is worse. Far worse."

My nonna is laughing from inside her bedroom. I walk toward her room while Kellan follows behind. "Not you, too," I say.

She wiggles her foot with a huge grin. "Bet you're glad I hurt my ankle."

"No, I'm not happy that you hurt yourself," I say.

"I second that," Kellan adds. "I'm definitely not happy that you hurt yourself. Now I'm stuck as the Snowflake Princess, well that, and you're hurt, so both are bad."

Mister Fluffykins has made his way to my feet. "There you are! I was wondering where you were," I say, while picking him up. I kiss the top of his head. "You wanna have a sleepover tonight?"

My mom enters the room from behind. "Are you staying at Kellan's again?" she asks. My mom and Nonna exchange a "told you so" kind of glance.

"Yeah, I am. Don't want to wear out my welcome, but he said it was fine." I elbow Kellan playfully.

"More than fine," he says twisting his back a bit.

I was probably a little too rough with him earlier. I think having him bent in half like that probably did a number on his back, judging by the way he's twisting.

"Hurt your back?" my father asks Kellan from behind us.

"Where the hell did you come from?" I ask. "You were just on the couch."

"Yeah, so? And now I'm here," he replies, then places a hand on

Kellan's shoulder. "What are you twisting like that for, and what's that mark on your neck?" He leans in closer, like he's inspecting something.

My nonna picks her glasses up from her nightstand and puts them on. "What's wrong with your neck, Kellan?" she asks.

My mom walks closer toward him. "Oh, don't tell me that's a hickey!" she squeals. "You can't give hickeys in your thirties, Braden! Look at poor Kellan's neck!"

Kellan's eyes go wide, and he reflexively covers his neck with his hand.

There's no way I gave him a hickey. She's probably just trying to get me to react. I'm not even going to look at it. "Oh, come on, stop," I say. "Look you're making Kellan cover his neck. There's nothing there, because we didn't *do* anything." I rub Kellan's back lightly.

He leans in toward my ear and whispers, "Did you give me a hickey? I felt you bite me earlier. Is there a mark there?" He lifts his hand off his neck and tilts his head to the side.

"There's nothing, they're just trying to—" Whoops. There is a mark, a very large purplish mark. There is definitely a hickey there. "We gotta go," I say. "It's getting late and we need to let Fluffykins check the place out a bit before sleeping for the night. Besides, Senator Tunacan may not be very excited about another cat sleeping over."

My nonna laughs heartily from the bed. "Look at you! The kings of evasiveness. You two don't have to leave just because you're embarrassed," she says.

"Pftt…he might be embarrassed, but I'm not," Kellan says. "I just wanna get a good look at it. Don't think I've ever had a hickey."

Holding Fluffy in my left arm, I pull Kellan out of the room with my free hand. "Alright, everyone, we're leaving," I announce. "I think we're putting up Christmas lights after work tomorrow, so you'll have to come and check them out."

Fluffykins hops in his crate, while I grab a few of his favorite things from the guest room, and place them inside a bag

"Oh, The Senator has one of those!" Kellan says, seeing the small gray mouse toy. "I wonder if they'll play with them together?"

The idea of our cats playing together sounds cute, but Fluffykins can be a bit of a snob when it comes to other cats. It's probably because I always had the scent of other animals on me from the office, but he usually doesn't play well with others.

"Maybe? It would be adorable if they were best friends," I say. "But I should tell you, my cat usually doesn't like play dates. He's not mean to other cats or anything, he's just kind of snobbish."

Kellan laughs. "Well, this should be interesting then, because The Senator is quite territorial. I had to cat sit for Riley once, and, within twenty minutes, my cousin had to come back and get her cat."

I pause in the midst of picking up Fluffy's bag. "Well, maybe this is a bad idea? I don't have to bring him."

Kellan waves me off. "No, it will be fine. You'll be there anyway. Don't worry."

"Alright, if you're sure, then let's head out."

"Super sure. And I'll carry this," he says, slinging the tote bag of my cat's things over his shoulder.

"You boys want to stay for some coffee?" my mom asks from the other room.

"Come on, let's get out of here," I urge. We head quickly for the door. "No thanks, Mom. We're already out the door. Bye!"

Kellan waves goodbye, too, and follows me downstairs toward my Jeep.

"It's freezing tonight. Even my ass feels cold," Kellan says.

"I'll warm it up," I say, pumping my eyebrows at him, while opening the passenger door. "Get your cute little butt in there."

He gives me a quick kiss on the cheek and sits inside the passenger seat, holding his arms out for Fluffykins's crate.

I pass him the crate, and watch for a reaction from my cat.

"Hi there, Mister Fluffykins, do you remember me?" he asks. "I'm the idiot that brought you home by accident. You liked my place the other day. My kitty will be there today. I bet you'll like him. He's handsome like you."

"I'm sure he remembers you. You're the only catnapper he's ever met," I tease, shutting the door.

I quickly jog around the front of the car and join him inside.

Kellan's mouth is wide open. "I am not a catnapper!" He playfully pushes my arm.

"Uhhhh, you kind of are," I say, starting the car and backing out of the space.

"You're lucky you're so damn sexy, you know that?" Kellan says, squeezing my thigh.

"Shhh! Don't talk about sex in front of my kid!"

"Well, you better hope he and The Senator don't get along, or my cat is gonna tell him about all of the dirty things you've been doing to me."

I place my hand atop Kellan's and hold it. "Oh, you're raising a little gossip, huh?"

"Like father like son," Kellan retorts, with a cheeky grin.

When we get back to Kellan's place with Fluffykins, Kellan opens the door to let us in. "Do you think your sister is back?" I ask.

It's completely dark inside. Kellan flips the Christmas tree lights on. "Mmm, nope she isn't here. We did such a good job with this tree," he says, admiring it. We both stare at the tree, as The Senator prances his way over. Kellan picks him up and kisses him. He turns toward me. "Alright, what do we have to do? How do we introduce them?"

I walk inside his bedroom and close the door. Me and Fluffykins are inside the room; Kellan and Tunacan are in the hall. "Well, it should take a few days, but for this case, we'll just keep them apart until we think they're ready…or 11:00 pm, whichever comes first. I'm gonna keep the door closed until we're sure they won't murder each other."

I open the gate for Mister Fluffykins, who springs out of his crate. "Woah, calm down, buddy. We just got here; you can't act like that. Chill." He darts for the closed door and begins sniffing and pawing at it.

"Braden, The Senator is sniffing the door, seems like he wants to get in there. Oh, I see paws! Hi, Fluffykins!" Kellan says, under the door.

I change my voice into a high-pitched squeak, and reply as Fluffykins, "Hello, mister catnapper."

"Stop calling me a cat napper!" Kellan says through laughter.

"Hey, you can't correct other people's cats," I joke. "He's just a baby, and besides, he's calling you a cat napper because you are one."

"How long until we can open the door?"

"Mmm, is your cat trying to get in? What's he doing out there?"

"Yep," Kellan says. "He's trying to get me to open the door. He's purring really loudly for some reason. Should we just open the door and see what happens?"

"I uh—yeah, I guess so. It usually takes longer. But let's open the door and see where it goes."

Kellan opens the door, while I sit on the floor beside my cat.

Our two orange furballs sniff and rub their faces against each other, they both seem extremely interested in the other one. It's so cute.

Kellan laughs, watching them. "Well, it looks like we were both wrong. I think they're in love," he says pointing at the two.

"They are not in love. It does look like they like each other, though." I stand up and look down at them.

"What do you mean they aren't in love?" he asks. "They're rubbing their cheeks against each other. This is the cutest thing I've ever seen!"

"It is pretty cute, but I've had the pleasure of seeing your ass, which is in fact, the cutest thing I've ever seen." I give his ass a firm squeeze.

Kellan leans against my body, resting his head against my shoulder.

I love when he kind of falls into me like this. I kiss the top of his head. "Your hair is still cold from being outside," I say, hugging him tightly.

The cats follow one another outside of the room, and Kellan giggles. "Those two are in love, I don't care what you say. Look how they just stuck to each other like glue, the second they got together."

"Hmm…love. Maybe they are, then?" I told him we'd talk about what bothered me earlier, but I also don't want to upset him. Still, I refuse to be intimate again when this is still bothering me. Sex is the most raw, pure, unfiltered form of intimacy there is, and if I'm going to be inside Kellan, I need to clear the air between us first.

I give him a kiss on the top of his head, placing my hands on his shoulders. "I want to talk about earlier."

"Now? You want to talk now?"

"Yes, now, it's important to me that we talk about this. You're the first person that I've ever had trouble reading, you know that? I look at you, and I think I know what you're thinking, but I don't."

"Where is this coming from?" Kellan asks softly, placing a hand on my chest. "What's making you feel like that?"

I exhale, taking his hand in mine and kissing it. "Before I do, I want to say that I know this is immature and what I'm saying is stupid, but I still want to talk about it."

He gives me a quick kiss on the cheek. "Whatever you're feeling is not stupid. Just tell me what it is."

I sit on the edge of the bed, while he sits beside me. "Earlier your mom was saying—"

"The craziest stuff," Kellan interjects.

"Yes, that's true, but that's not what bothered me. She said she thought we seemed like we were destined to be together forever…or something like that, and you said, 'We'll see.' You said it so flippantly, like you were planning on this ending already—I don't know, or you didn't have faith in us, or maybe you didn't want it. I know that when this started you weren't looking for a relationship, and I guess we didn't really talk about it, because I think I didn't want to give you the chance to reject me. But we've been hanging out for a few days, and I like where this is going. The problem for me is that I can't force what I want on you. So, if you aren't looking for a relationship, I can't make you want one. You had this whole lifestyle until a few days ago, and now I'm starting to feel like maybe I just inserted myself into your life. I'm not asking you to decide now, I just—I don't know. Sex is very special to me and, for me, it's something we've done a few times now and I want to keep doing it, but not if it's going to lead to nothing. I can't be that for you…I know other guys would say that's stupid. But for me, I just need to know that you want this, too—and not necessarily in a forever way, but not in a temporary way. I don't know. I'm not even making sense anymore."

Kellan leans his head against my shoulder, placing a hand on my lap. "I'm sorry. I didn't mean that the way you took it. I meant that I would probably screw it up somehow, because I—well you've known me my whole life, I say the wrong thing all the time. It happened the first time we had sex, remember?"

My head drops. Definitely haven't forgotten that happened, of course, but I certainly don't want to remember the way I felt when it did. "I remember. I don't think I'll forget that."

"See? I do it all the time," he says. "I tried to compliment you, and I ended up hurting your feelings. I'm just not great at explaining the way I feel. It doesn't mean I don't feel the things that you're feeling, I just don't know the right things to say…especially when it comes to you. But I *do* like you, and you didn't insert yourself in my life. I'm a big boy, I know what I want, I just might not always say it." He moves his hand to my inner thigh, lightly massaging it. The warmth of Kellan's fingers, combined with the look in his eyes tells me all I need to know in this moment. He wants to be with me…I wrap an arm around him and pull him in tighter. "Maybe we just don't let you talk then?"

"I agree, that seems like the safest thing for all parties involved," he says.

I bring my lips in front of his and press our foreheads together. "I like you, too," I say. Our lips meet in a soft sweet kiss. I rub the back of my hand over the hickey on his neck. "I'm sorry about this, I didn't mean to leave a mark."

Kellan laughs. "Nothing to be sorry about." He lets out a yawn and twists his back.

"You were twisting earlier, though, was I too rough?"

"Nah, definitely not. I am completely exhausted in the best way. Let's get ready for bed and see what the cats are up to."

"Oh, the cats! Yes, let's do that," I say.

After we change our clothes and brush our teeth, Kellan flops onto the bed.

"You stay here and relax," I tell him. "I'll go check on the cats."

He gives me a barely audible "mmhmm." His eyes are already closed, he really is completely spent.

Entering the living room, I'm greeted with the sight of Mister Fluffykins and The Senator, lying beside one another under the brightly lit Christmas tree.

Wow—they really do look like they're in love. Aww…I should just leave Fluffy out here, but I want to talk to him, we haven't talked in days.

"Psst—Fluffy," I whisper, squatting down. I kiss his head, and he nuzzles his face against mine. "It's time for bed." I lift him, and he cuddles up into a ball in my arms. "There you go," I say, kissing him, and rubbing his chin. The Senator decides to follow closely behind into Kellan's bedroom.

Kellan is asleep on his side. I carefully climb into bed, placing Fluffykins beside me.

The jostling of the bed startles Kellan, who quickly turns onto his back. "Wha—what time is it? How long was I asleep for?" He rubs his eyes and reaches for his phone from the nightstand.

"I don't know how long it's been, because you were half asleep when I came out. I didn't want to wake you."

My cat settles against my chest, and Senator Tunacan jumps onto the bed, placing himself right beside Kellan.

I kiss my cat's head. "No, we can't talk about Kellan now, because he's awake. How was your night?" I ask Fluffykins. He purrs loudly and rubs his face against my hand. "Oh, you like him? Well, that's good, because I don't think I'm going back to Nonna's for a few days."

"What do you think about that, Senator?" Kellan asks. "Do you like having Braden here?" His cat gives him an affectionate headbutt. "I know you like Fluffykins, you don't have to tell me that. I could tell as soon as you laid eyes on him."

Senator Tunacan stretches and steps across the bed to where

Fluffykins is. The two cats rub against one another and settle in a cuddle position at the foot of the bed.

"You leave me just like that?" I ask Fluffy. "Well, Kellan, I knew he'd grow up and meet someone someday, but geez, we were in the middle of a conversation."

Kellan laughs. "Yeah, what about you, Senator? Just leaving me like that. I didn't even get to finish my thought."

"Aww, but they are cute," I say. "Look at them all cuddled up. It's adorable."

Kellan leans in toward me. "You're adorable," he says, rubbing his nose against mine, then kisses me softly.

"Oof. I'm tired, you completely drained me," I say, kissing his forehead.

I can feel myself falling asleep. Kellan lets out another yawn and turns onto his side. His feet find mine under the sheet. "Ahh your feet are so warm, they feel amazing," he says, rubbing his ice-cold feet against mine.

"Mmmhmm—you can use my feet, just come closer. I want to hold you."

Kellan backs up against my body, and I pull him close, wrapping my arms around him. I kiss his cheek, holding tightly onto him. "Ahh, you make a perfect little spoon."

"And your feet make the perfect feet warmer," Kellan says.

Chapter Nine
Whose Ass Is This?

Waking up the next morning, neither of us has moved from the spot we fell asleep in. Our feet remain touching, and Kellan is still tucked tightly against my body. How is that even possible? I'm such a restless sleeper. Either way, now that I'm awake I can feel how numb my arm is from the weight of his body all night. I would think we had to have moved a few times, but the fact that my arm feels completely useless tells me we didn't.

I nuzzle into the back of his neck, giving him soft kisses. "Good morning."

"Good morning," he says, rolling onto his back.

Man, my arm feels awful, but seeing his face smiling over at me, makes it all worth it.

"I don't know if I'll ever get used to seeing you in my bed when I wake up," Kellan says.

"I could get used to it," I say, rubbing his cheek with the back of my hand.

He's kissing the back of my hand. Looks like he has something weighing on him, even though we just woke up. He lets out an over-exaggerated sigh, as the alarm beeps loudly from his phone.

"Not this day, let's go back to sleep," Kellan says, tucking back beside me and pulling my arm around his body. "Just go back to sleep, Braden. I don't want to work today. I have like a million problems and the day hasn't even started. Who knows what fresh sort of hell I'll be expected to deal with today."

I embrace him from the side and squeeze him tightly. "How can I help?"

"That's very sweet," he says, scooting closer against me. "But right now, it's morning and I can feel all of *you* pressed against me, which is only furthering my want to play hooky from work. But before you get any ideas, don't, because I absolutely have to get out of this bed right now."

I lift my arm up and smile. "I won't force you to stay in bed. We both have responsibilities. It sucks being adults. I want to help you, though. What can I do to make things better?"

"I just have to deal with a million things, and no one is prepared for anything because everything keeps going wrong. I have no idea how Leora did this for so many years. I can barely track everything."

"Alright. Let's get up. I'm gonna help you," I say standing up from the bed.

He's still lying in bed with his hands behind his head. He's shirtless, and his body is so freaking hot. He knows it, too. I tilt my head at him. "Yes, I see your sexy body, but I'm not gonna pay attention to that right now. Let's go try to get a handle on everything before our stores open. We'll grab some coffee before our run, and we can sort it out."

He's giggling at me. "How about if I do this?" he says, sliding the sheet down, and placing a hand on his cock inside his black underwear.

"Kellan!" I say through laughter. "No, come on. I want to help you."

"Alright, fine," he huffs. "Let's go in the kitchen and I'll show you my list." He stands up from the bed and walks toward his dresser. Pulling out a pair of sweatpants, he slides them on, giving me a disappointed sort of scowl. He turns around, making sure I can see his ass. Damn, his butt really is the cutest.

"Alright, come on," he says, walking toward the kitchen. He grabs two coffee pods and two mugs from the cabinet. "So today, I'm expecting a few deliveries, Riley is leaving early for the next few days, and I have to be sure everything is ready for my candle making day tomorrow." He starts the coffee maker up and gives me a smile.

"That's not too bad. Can I help with any of that?"

The first cup of coffee is done, he opens the fridge and pulls out the creamer adding some to the mug, then stirs it. He places the mug in front of me and kisses my cheek.

"You made me coffee?" I ask. Obviously, he did, because he gave it to me, but it was just so sweet, and he didn't even ask if I wanted it. He just made it, like it was commonplace for him to care for me. Not only that, but he made mine first. I can't explain how incredibly happy this makes me.

"No and yes," he says, walking back to the coffee maker.

"No, you didn't make this coffee for me?"

He laughs and shakes his head starting the next cup. "No, there's nothing you can help me with, but thank you. Yes, I made the coffee for you. Hopefully, it was the right amount of creamer."

I take a sip, even if this was the worst cup of coffee I'd ever had, I would be hard pressed to say anything. But it's not—it's perfect. "This is delicious. Thanks. That's a newer model, right? Seems faster than the one I have. Ahh, my coffee maker. I can't wait to get all of my stuff out of storage. Movers crammed everything in a tiny unit. But it was either that or leave everything behind."

He's tilting his head at me as he sips his piping hot coffee. "You could've just got new stuff, left everything behind. It would be easy, just replace everything with new."

"Nah…that's not as easy as it sounds. There are some things that can't be replaced." I'm sure that neither of us are talking about material things at this point. Our eyes are locked in a desperate kind of stare.

"Was it easy when you did it before? When you left me?"

And there it is. I've been waiting for this, some acknowledgement that what we had wasn't one sided when we were younger, some kind of insight into why he didn't call me.

"When I left you? I didn't leave *you*, I left for college. You didn't want anything to do with me…that's what happened. What are you talking about?"

"Then why didn't you call me? If you left for college, why didn't you call me the very next day to talk about the dorm, the roommate, your classes, any of it?"

Our voices are calm, this is just a conversation, it doesn't need to escalate. I need to respond calmly, despite the way he's putting this all on me. "Do you actually remember what happened? We kissed and you left me standing outside in the dark all alone. You said it was a mistake or something, and said you didn't want to talk. Why would I call you? I was the one waiting for you to call me. So why didn't you?"

He places his mug down and folds his arms across his chest. "Because I didn't do anything wrong. You should've called me."

I hold my face in my hands, rubbing it. "Kellan. Listen to me. Do you have any idea what you're saying? You're saying that for the past twelve years, you've thought that I did something wrong, and you've been waiting for me to call you?"

He's shaking his head no at me. "I don't—I don't know, I—maybe, yeah. Actually, yes. I do and I did. Well, not so much right now, but it's, just, I waited for you to call me, I assumed you were going to and then you just didn't."

Now I'm shaking my head. "Why didn't you call me? You never

waited for me to call you before our kiss. Before you told me it was a mistake."

"I was used to you fixing everything—just like you're trying to do right now. It's—I was waiting for you to fix me. To make everything better. And when you didn't, I just—decided that I wouldn't care about, I don't know—anything—anymore."

His words are killing me, and I want to cut him off and make him feel better. But he needs to get it out, and I need to listen, so that we can move past this.

"I just don't understand, Braden. Didn't you need me like I needed you? How did you do it? How come you didn't fall apart like me? I didn't want to do anything, or be around anyone and you—you were fine. You just…didn't you care? I was so used to you taking care of me. Of course, I'd wait for you."

I take a deep breath in and exhale. "There wasn't a day that went by in those first few months that I didn't think about you. That I didn't look at my phone and think about calling. But, Kellan, I was hurt, too. I had no idea how you felt. I kissed you and you ran away. Of course, I wanted to talk to you and make it better, but how could I make it better when I thought that I was the problem? I thought that the kiss was the problem. It doesn't even"—I rub my temples—"I can't take back what happened, but, Kellan, if I knew that you were waiting for me, I would have called. If I knew that you wanted me, I would have been there. I would have given everything up to be with you. Instead, I just buried myself in my classes, and blocked everything out. How do you think I felt? My life revolved around you, too. I had no idea if you were taking care of yourself or if you were okay. I just wanted to hear your voice."

"You know…that first year…I came to see you at Christmas," Kellan says.

"What? What do you mean?"

"It was Christmas Eve and the entire month before I told myself that I'd go to your dorm and just show up. Maybe tell you off"—he raises an eyebrow at me—"just kidding. I really wanted to see you and to talk to you. I knew that if I came to see you on Christmas, you wouldn't turn me away. I thought we could have some sort of romantic reunion or something. But when I got to your dorm, which was not easy to find, I heard the sounds of girls inside, and loud music. I should have knocked but I didn't. I ended up finding a cheap hotel just outside of your campus and stayed the night. Then I cried for the last time about you. I drove for four hours to see you and was greeted by the sounds of you screwing around with girls. I felt like such an idiot."

I am shaking my head at him, because I had completely blocked out the memory of that night. "I hate to break it to you, but I was not screwing around with girls. And although I'm just now remembering this, because my brain had locked it away, I can promise you that you didn't hear me."

"How can you promise that? You don't know what I heard. It was awful."

What a little dummy. I stand and walk toward him, then take his hands in mine. "True that I don't know exactly what you heard, but the reason I know you didn't hear me, was because I wasn't there."

"Really? I could've sworn I heard—"

I'm shaking my head softly at him and holding his face in my hands. "I was at your place. I got your apartment address from my mom."

"You were at my place?"

"Yes, because I just wanted to talk to you. We'd spent every Christmas together since we were kids. I was dying to kiss you again, but you weren't there. I knocked, and there was no answer. I waited in my car for a few hours, then I drove by your parents' place, and didn't see your car. I figured you were out with someone. I was devastated, because at that point I felt like things were really over, and I couldn't do anything about it. I stayed the night at my nonna's, she was thrilled of course, and my parents were here, so they were happy, too. The thing is that I've never been good at fully giving up on you. Because even on Christmas morning I drove past your place one more time, no car there. By then I had no tears left to cry. I don't think there's any worse feeling than imagining your person, spending the night with someone else."

His eyes widened when I said that.

"I said what I said. You were my person, and you belonged with me."

I press my lips against his, kissing him softly. Holding his face in my hands, he feels so fragile. I can't believe he went to my place. He was all alone, too…

He's nuzzling against the side of my neck. "Don't think about it anymore," I say. "It's over now. I'm here now and so are you. For what it's worth—I never tried to replace you. When my nonna called me and asked me to take over, the first thing that came to my mind, was you."

"I never tried to replace you either. I hated being apart from you—I hated feeling like we never had a chance. That's why I didn't kiss anyone else. I felt like if you were the only person I kissed then that would be something that kept us together, I didn't want to lose the memory of it, the feeling—I needed some piece of you with me, something that still felt like something. So, every time I made the decision not to kiss anyone, it was because that was special to me— our kiss was special to me and I didn't want that with anyone else. It must sound so stup—"

I capture his lips with mine, kissing him deeply. He pulls my face in by the back of my head. Damn, he's got a good grip on my hair. I pull my mouth back and whisper, "We were supposed to go for a run this morning." I kiss him again as I walk him backward toward the bedroom.

He rubs his nose against mine. "Snowing out, can't go for a run in the snow…we could exercise in other ways."

Fuck. His hand is sliding down my sweatpants as we step into his room. He's holding my cock firmly and staring into my eyes.

"I need you," he whispers.

"You need me? Or you need him?" He's stroking me softly.

"Can't I have both?" he asks, now petting my fully hard cock. Fuck he's petting me; his hands are so soft. He's circling the head of my cock with his finger. I can't resist him.

I pull him by his waistband against myself, reaching down and pulling his cock out. He does the same to mine. I lick the inside of my palm and press his dick against mine, side-by-side. I stroke them together; his head falls back. "Fuck—that feels good."

"Yeah? You like that. You like it when I rub your dick against mine?"

"I do—I really fucking do."

My hand rubs harder and faster, the sound of it drives me crazy. But I want to be inside of him. I can't go to work without fucking him.

I place my mouth beside his ear, licking his earlobe, then lightly sucking it. "I want you to ride me. I want to watch you bounce on my cock. Will you do that for me?"

"I thought you'd never ask," he says, pushing me onto the bed.

I pull my sweatpants down and sit up against the headboard. He drops his sweats to the floor, then straddles atop me.

I grab his ass in my hands, squeezing it. "I want you, Kellan. I need to be inside of this juicy fucking ass," I say slapping both cheeks.

I reach around and rub his rim with my finger, then press inside.

He lowers himself onto it, lining it up perfectly with his prostate, and drops his head back. Fuck that's hot. "You want more? You're extra tight today, I don't want to rush," I say while teasing his prostate.

"I want more," he whines.

He's so fucking sexy. I pull him close to me and kiss him, pressing a second finger inside. It's so warm and tight. He's riding my fingers, as I kiss him ravenously. I want to fucking eat this man. I pump my fingers in and out, while my tongue swirls around the inside of his mouth.

He's grabbing a fist full of my hair. "Fuck, Braden, let me ride it."

I move my mouth to his neck and plant a small bite on the hickey I left on him. I pull my fingers out slowly, and he grabs my dick, lining his ass up, slowly taking it inside. "Tsss—fuck, you're so big."

This feels fucking amazing, and the view is incredible, watching him lower himself inch by inch on me has my cock leaking already. I'm halfway inside, and Kellan's cock is dripping on my abs. He lowers himself the rest of the way, my cock buried deep inside. "Good boy, look how good you take me. Now bounce for me." His fingers are raking my chest as he slowly rises and falls, up and down my shaft.

"Fuuuuck—" he says, grinding up and down on my dick, his head leaning back. "Unghhh that's—"

I grab his ass tighter, bouncing him up and down. "Fuck, look at you riding my cock so good. You're fucking gorgeous, Kellan."

"Unghh—mmmph—Braden. It's so deep…I'm gonna come soon."

The headboard is really thumping against the wall, and I'm worried that his neighbors are gonna hear that. I lift him off my cock.

"Wha—why?" he whimpers.

"Bend over," I say.

I get on my knees behind him. His ass is in the air, and he's on all fours as I line up.

His ass is open wide for me, and I smack his reddened cheeks.

"Look at that greedy hole, it's begging for me to come back inside. You want this?" I ask reaching underneath him to play with his wet cock for a moment.

His breath hitches. "Haaah—yes, ffffuck. Braden put it back inside. Give me your big fucking cock. Call me your slut."

He shivers when I place a kiss on his entrance, and his knees weaken for just a moment. I smack his ass. "Lift up higher for me, if you want me inside."

He does as he's told. "Good boy, look what a little slut you are for my cock." I drive myself inside, placing one hand on his back. "I wish you could see this. You're taking my cock so good. It's so fucking hot, Kellan."

I pound into him from behind, thrusting as deep as I can. "Whose ass is this?"

"Yyyours—yours—haah—Braden."

"I'm gonna come soon. Where do you want it?"

"My ass—ungh—please—come inside my ass, fucking fill me. I want to feel it."

I'm ramming full force against his ass. "Unghh—fuuuck—what a dirty little boy, begging for my cum." I thrust deep inside him and slap him on the ass, while he grinds against me harder.

"Haah—oh my God—right there—I'm gonna fucking come, Braden."

"Come for me, you dirty little slut. You love this big cock in your ass. You love it when I fuck you."

"Oh fuuuck—haah—haah—I'm coming. Bray, I'm fucking coming." Kellan's cum explodes from his cock, shooting out all over the navy-blue sheets. His ass is sucking on my cock as he rides his orgasm out.

Just the sound of him calling me Bray is enough to finish me off.

I open my shop, enter, close the door, and finally groan from the pain I'm feeling. After a thorough—and *hard*—pounding last night, followed by another this morning, I'm walking a little funny. But the stiff legs are a more than an acceptable compromise for getting railed by Braden.

And we had that heart to heart this morning. That was the conversation we'd both been dancing around since we first laid eyes on each other in Leora's apartment. Or, rather, since I first face-planted in his chest in Leora's apartment. I kind of knew that conversation would go fine, but I hadn't expected it to go where it did. I'm still blown by the fact that we missed out on twelve years because we had the kind of "just missed each other" scenario you'd see in a TV show.

I groan again as I sit down on my stool. I'd hidden the pain and stiffness from Braden; I don't want him to be apologetic or make a big deal of it. This is the good kind of pain, the kind that reminds me why I love bottoming so much. I'd topped a few times over the years, but the sensation of sex always ended as soon as I blew my load, but when I bottom, I have the morning after stiffness that turns twenty minutes of sex into, sometimes, two days of sensation. I love every moment of it.

Thus, I'd managed to hold it together as we got dressed and

walked to work. It took everything in me not to limp or walk bow-legged. I only allowed myself to relax and act naturally once I was in the privacy of my shop.

I pull out my phone, but put it on the counter and take a few deep breaths to relax before diving in. I'd seen a ton of notifications pop up earlier, and I'd ignored them all, putting them off till I was at work. And now that I'm here? I need a minute more.

Inevitably, my gaze travels upward and across the street. Braden is already working some cookie dough he'd whipped up yesterday and had chilling in the fridge. He rolls it out on the counter and digs out Leora's cookie cutters. His mom enters through the back, and the two of them look like they're getting along well still. It helps that Braden's mom is *not* a sex therapist.

I rub my hands over my face, trying to scrub away the memories of last night and the conversations with my mother. While she always was a bit embarrassing to bring around my friends, that was truly out of this world embarrassing. I don't think any of Charlie's boyfriends got that kind of treatment.

"Ugh, whatever…" I mumble to myself when the embarrassing images and memories won't fade.

I finally pick up my phone and dig into the text messages and emails. "What the ever-loving fudge?"

Apparently, some high school students—or so everyone assumes—had gotten into the sex education supplies from the local high school and stolen all the dildos used for condom demonstrations…and hung them all over the town Christmas tree. The focal point for the Snowflake Festival. It was now a dick tree. "An XXX-mas tree," I say out loud, laughing at my own joke.

Scrolling through the texts, I see message after message from business owners begging for someone to do something about the dick tree and including pictures of it. Yet, from what I can discern, no one has actually walked over and taken the dicks down.

"You have got to be kidding me…"

I stand and hobble to the front window of the shop. I press the side of my face against the glass, trying to look all the way down the street to the town square. I can see the tree, but I can't make out if the dicks are still there.

I put my coat back on and leave my shop, tromping through the snow toward the town square. "Seven people texting me about these fucking dicks and not a single person thinks to take them down."

Indeed, as I approach the Christmas tree, I can clearly see flesh-colored ornaments from a distance. Several of them. At least a dozen. And all very big.

When I get close, I get a better sense of it. There are massive schlongs all over the place. I grab one and yank but it stays stuck to the tree. "What…?" I look closer; the kids have used zip ties to strap the balls to the branches. "God fucking damn it," I mutter as I yank hard enough to snap the tie. I stumble backward and fall on my ass, and the rubbery dick bounces all over my face, laying to rest across my eyes.

I swear to myself and get up. I then rip every dick off the tree—and there are fourteen of them—without falling to the ground. Gathering all fourteen rubber dicks in my arms, I stomp back toward Dip Your Wick.

As I pass Pump 'n' Go, I see Geoff unlocking the gym. "That seems more like a Saturday night thing, doesn't it?" he asks. "Seems a bit adventurous for a Tuesday morning."

I grumble at him and continue on.

As luck would have it, as I'm stomping back toward my store with fourteen rubber dicks in my arms, I have a couple customers waiting to get into the shop. "Aw, fuck," I mutter when I realize it's my mom and Charlie.

"Didn't think you need those anymore," Charlie says, "now that you've got your cookie stud."

"Ha-ha, very funny," I say. "Some teen vandals hung these on the Christmas tree."

Mom grabs one of the dicks—the biggest one—from my arms and examines it. "Where on Earth did those kids get a Max Girth 4000 model? These are hard to come by."

"Max Girth?" I say. "Why do you know the model names of these dildos?"

She points out a ridge to me. "Max Girth is a well-known porn star with a very distinctive vein on the top side of his dick. I'm surprised you don't recognize it, dear, given your penchant for porn."

I close my eyes and refrain from releasing a biting comeback. Instead, I say, "What brings you two to my humble shop this morning?"

Mom flops the Max Girth 4000 around as she talks, like she's using the massive dick to emphasize every word she says. "Charlie hasn't seen your quaint little hobby for a few years now, so we thought we'd stop by before we go for coffee."

"It's a business, Mom," Charlie says, defending me for once, "not a hobby."

"Of course, of course." She holds the base of the Max Girth in one hand and uses the other to stroke along its length. "This is too wide; how would anyone have a good time with it? Well, I guess that's why he chose Max Girth as his stage name. I'll have to tell him about this next time I talk to him."

"Mom…" Charlie says, "you *know* Max Girth?"

A smile lights up her face. "Of course, I do! Oh, but I shouldn't tell you since he's a client. Keep that between us three." She wiggles the dildo a bit more. "Is Braden hung like this?"

"Mom!" I shout. I dig in my pocket for my key, and in doing so, lose balance of all the dicks, and they tumble from my arms and bounce around the snowy pavement. "Fucking hell."

"Whoa, calm down, Kellan," Mom says. "When's the last time you had sex? It really sounds like you need some. Is Braden not able to, uh, rise to the occasion?"

"Things are *fine*, Mom," I say. I find my key and open the shop, then scramble to pick up all the dicks. "Come on in." I dump the dicks in a bin in the back room, then come and sit on my usual stool. I find Charlie perusing candles on the far side of the room, and Mom standing right in front of me. My shoulders sag a bit—Mom wants to talk to me about something.

"So…Braden is nice. He seems to have developed into quite the man since I last saw him."

I cross my arms. "Yeah, I like him. I wasn't sure how well we'd get on given the twelve-year gap since we last seriously talked, but it seems to be running smoothly."

Mom puts her hands down on the counter. I know her tells; she's about to unload the question that drove her to come here this morning. "Last night when I asked about this being long term, you said 'we'll see'. Your answer seemed to catch Braden by surprise, if his death stare was any indication. It's fine to have different feelings than Braden and different expectations as long as they overlap a bit, but it gets difficult when your feelings and expectations don't align at all. I want to check in with you to see where you are on all of this and if that aligns with Braden. I want you to have a good time, but not at Braden's expense if he wants something different."

I hang my head. "Mom, I'm thirty. I don't need dating advice."

"It would seem you do, given how that question was answered."

I sigh and pinch the bridge of my nose. "I said something stupid, yes, but I cleared it up with Braden last night and we're good again. But for the record, the 'we'll see' was a bit of a joke because I always end up saying the wrong thing and having him mad at me…which is exactly what that joke did. So, case in point."

Mom smiles tightly. "You *do* like Braden, don't you? You like him a lot. I can see it. A mother always knows."

"I do," I say. I start relaxing a bit because I know my mom's patterns; she's slipping out of sex therapist mode and into supportive mom mode. She would, of course, argue that both modes are one and the same. "I wasn't expecting it to happen, but it's definitely happening."

"If you want this to work long term and be able to ride through those verbal snafus so they have less of an impact, then you should put more work into this than you think you need to. The difference between a casual affair and a relationship is the trust that you build between you. From that trust comes a shared sense of purpose, which gives rise to shared fun as you take on the adventure of life together. To build that, you need to put in that extra work by doing couple things. Little dates, appreciating each other, gestures of affection, things like that. Make him feel special. Once you do that and a solid foundation of trust is built, then when you inevitably misspeak, it won't cause seismic chaos."

"Yes, Doctor Mom."

"So, you and Braden are…good?"

I nod. "We're good, Mom."

She smiles, broader and more genuine this time. "I'm so pleased to hear that. Your dad and I have been hoping for a long time that you'd find the right man for you and settle down. I know you love the life you're living, but at a certain point you need stability. There's a comfort that comes with it, and after a while an easiness to the relationship. For what it's worth, I'm really getting the sense this is long term, too. He *clearly* likes you."

"Thank you, Mom," I say. I look past her to the window and BJ's Cookies beyond. Braden is busy with a line of customers, but he's smiling and laughing as he's helping people through their orders.

"You've got it bad, brother," Charlie says as she comes to stand at the counter, too. "I haven't seen you smile like that since you were in high school."

"Come on," Mom says to Charlie, "let's go and let Kellan get to work, or leave him to moon over Braden. Both are good options."

Charlie blows me a kiss. "See you later, lover boy."

After they leave, I set to the task of wiping down the display shelves to make them dust free and sparkling. A few customers come in and buy candles, and the day starts to pass nicely.

Around lunch, Chad hurries in, wide-eyed with panic. "What do you get a boyfriend for Christmas?"

"Whoa, slow down," I say. "Boyfriend?"

"Uh…yeah. You know how you did that kiss in front of me at the bar last week? Someone was hitting on Lucas and I did the same thing and then I called him my boyfriend. It was all out of instinct and felt right, but now Lucas is over the moon with it all and I want to cap it off with the perfect Christmas gift," Chad says. "I've never bought a boyfriend a gift. I've never had a boyfriend."

"That's a huge change, Chad. I'm happy for you," I say. "I like seeing you and Lucas together."

"Thanks," he says. "So, Christmas gift. What do I get him?"

"Well, you're in a candle shop right now, so…candles?"

He looks around like he's considering it, but then he says, "Maybe not. He didn't like you so much at the start when he thought you were competition for me. Candles from your shop might not help with that…"

I hold up my hands. "I get it, no worries. Not offended in the slightest." I still remember Lucas confronting me in BJ's Cookies the other day. I certainly don't need a repeat of that. "What about a couples massage at the day spa? What's it called? Rub One Out? That cements the idea that you're a couple and turns it into a fun date night for the two of you."

Chad's eyes light up. "That's perfect! Thanks, buddy!" And like a shot of lightning, Chad is out the door.

I wander up to the window and look across at Braden's shop. Mom's words come back to me. *You should put more work into this than you think you need to.*

I pull out my phone and send Braden a text. *Let's put those Christmas lights up on your shop today. Just you and me.* Hopefully, that will earn me some boyfriend points.

I watch Braden through the windows as he picks up his phone, and his face lights up, then he glances across to me with a big smile. He replies with, *That would be lovely.* Then he follows up with, *How has your day been?*

I send an eye rolling emoji, and text, *Did you hear about the dildo tree?* I attach a photo of the dicks piled in my back room.

I did! Brings new meaning to "make the yuletide gay"!

The rest of the afternoon seems to crawl by, but eventually it's closing time. I hurry through the shop and shut off all the lights and lock up. When I exit and cross the street, I find Braden with his coat on, just inside the shop.

"Hey," I say. Acting before I can think about it, I lean forward and give him a kiss. That feels very boyfriend like, the greeting with a kiss without a second thought about it.

"Hey, yourself," he says, after the kiss ends. We look at each other for a long moment, and I feel a rush of heat at having Braden's eyes on me. Then he points at the boxes at his feet. "I found the Christmas lights my nonna had in the attic." He'd also pulled out the ladder and has it leaning against the wall next to the door.

"Perfect," I say. "We installed some nice hooks last Christmas, so it should be easy to set these up." I pick up the ladder and carry it outside, and Braden does the same with the lights. "Do you want to go up on the ladder or should I?"

"Uh, I'm a little afraid of heights. So…you?"

I chuckle. "If you want to just stare at my ass while you hold the ladder, you can just say so."

"Okay," Braden says, "I'd much rather stare at your ass while you hang the lights."

"Fair enough," I say, leaning in for another quick kiss. "Better hold that ladder tight, though."

"Yes, sir," Braden says with a smirk. He helps me untangle the strands of lights and then does as assigned—holds the ladder securely while I climb it and hang the lights.

Ten minutes later, all the lights are hung, and Braden flips them on so we can admire our work.

"They look nice," he says. "Thank you."

"Of course," I say. "Hey, do you want to drive around and check out some of the light displays in town? There's one neighborhood where they go all out and everything."

"That sounds nice," Braden says.

After putting the ladder away and locking up BJ's Cookies, we walk back to my condo to get his Jeep. I direct him through the streets, but it seems the more he drives, the more the layout of the city comes back to him.

Eventually, we make it to the neighborhood where they go all out. Lit-up sculptures dot front lawns, houses are decked out in lights, and there is even a house where they've created a skating rink in their front yard. The street is clogged with cars and pedestrians.

Braden pulls into what looks like the last parking spot on the street. "Do you want to just go on foot? There's no driving through that mess of cars and people."

"Sure," I say. We get out of the Jeep and walk side by side through the snowy street. Braden puts his arm over my shoulders, pulling me closer. The touch, such a public display of affection, sends a burst of warmth through my chest. I lean my head to the side, letting it rest on his thick shoulder.

"Everything alright?" he asks me.

"Everything's perfect," I say.

We stroll casually down the street, stopping briefly in front of each property to admire the displays. One house has kids selling hot chocolate at the curb. I buy two cups to help keep us warm.

After reaching the end of the street, we turn around and take in the other side on our way back to the Jeep. We stop in front of a cute bungalow.

"Have you ever thought of getting a house?" Braden asks.

I shrug. "I've come to like the condo. I don't have to worry about maintenance or yard work or anything. I can just enjoy living there."

Braden takes a sip of his hot chocolate. "My house should be ready in a few weeks or so."

"That's coming up soon," I say. "It sounds fancy."

He smiles at me. "It will be. I'll have to worry about maintenance and yard work and stuff." He chuckles. "Luckily, I like those things. So, if I were to live with someone, he wouldn't have to do those things. He could just enjoy the house. I might ask him to take out the garbage, though."

"And it'll be just you and Mister Fluffykins alone in that big house?" I stare ahead at the lit-up house in front of us.

"Just me. Might get lonely." He, too, looks ahead at the house.

"Maybe I can spend some time there," I say. My heart thunders like I'm asking my teenage crush out. In a way, I am.

"I think I'd like that," he says. "I'll have a guest room done up and everything. You can phone me when you get horny."

"You mean when *you* get horny," I say.

Braden put his arm around my shoulders. "I have a feeling we'd get horny together."

When we get back to the Jeep, the hot chocolate is long drunk, and the cold is starting to seep into me. I shiver as I settle into the passenger seat. When Braden turns on the Jeep, he cranks the heat to high, and I place my hands against the vent, letting the heat soak in and bring them back to life.

"That was nice," I say. I bring my now-warm-ish hands back to my mouth and blow into them, warming them a bit more.

"Yeah, but the company was nicer," Braden says. He leans across the console and gives me a kiss.

It hasn't escaped my notice that the kisses we share are becoming more frequent, but that doesn't make them any less special. Every kiss is a moment of intimacy and a reminder of the feelings we have for each other. This comfort developing between us feels secure and warm, feelings I didn't know I was missing from life. And that only makes me want to kiss him more…and to make love to him. I never want these feelings to end.

Before he can shift into gear and drive off, I grab his coat and pull him close for one more kiss, and I moan into his mouth. He gets the hint; he sags in his seat, giving in to the kiss. While our kiss moments ago had been of affection and comfort, this one is of lust and need. I *need* Braden like I never needed a man before, and I'm certain he feels the same about me.

"Is your sister at your place?" he asks in a rush between kisses.

"Fuck," I say, pulling back from the kiss and trying to force up the memory of what Charlie had said she was going to do today. "I think she is; she said something about a video call with her husband."

Braden groans. "So, we can't fuck?" He grips his bulge, drawing my attention there.

"We can't fuck *there*," I say. "I'm sure we can fuck *somewhere*."

After a moment, he says, "My place?"

"You mean your nonna's?"

Braden shakes his head. "Not *her* place. *My* place."

"Huh?"

He winks at me. "Buckle up."

Braden backs out of the overpacked neighborhood and does a U-turn, taking us away from the lit-up houses. It takes me a few moments to realize he's taking us to Sticky Pines, the new housing development on the other side of town, where his under-construction house is located.

The streets here are darker with the streetlights sporadically installed and mostly not turned on.

"Nice area," I say. I'd driven past this new development several times, but never actually gone into it.

Braden chuckles. "It'll look nicer once there's people living here and it's not a constant construction zone."

"So, which house is yours?"

"This one here," Braden says, pointing down the street. Of the houses I can see up and down the street, Braden's is the most put-together. He pulls up in the driveway. "We can fuck here without worrying about anyone seeing."

"Here?" I say, looking all around us. "Not inside your house?"

He shakes his head. "I don't have keys yet; it's still a construction zone." He leans his chair back and undoes his fly, wrenching his fat cock from his briefs. "You'd need a hard hat to go in."

I take Braden's cock in my hand. "You're hard enough already, baby."

"Suck me."

I undo my seatbelt and lean over, taking him in my mouth. He's so big; he's always a mouthful and more for me. I bob my head up and down, taking him all the way to the base. I dig in his fly and pull out his meaty balls, massaging them in time with my sucking.

He puts his hand on the back of my head, guiding me to take it deeper, until my nose is pressed hard against his fuzzy pelvis. I manage to hold off from gagging, giving in to the pleasure of having a cock stuffed deep in my face.

Braden's other hand slides down my back and then under the bottom of my coat and into the rear of my pants. I feel those fingers explore my crack, soon finding their way to my hole, circling the rim and testing the tightness at the center.

"Fuck, you're good at this," Braden says with a heady exhale.

I want to say I've had lots of practice, but a bit of personal growth helps me understand this isn't the right thing to say with Braden in this moment.

"I love your cock so much," I say when I came up for air. "It gets better every time." That's the right thing to say.

"Suck the balls," Braden says breathlessly.

I lay my head on his thick thighs and take those balls in my mouth, sucking in one, then the other, then both. He strokes his cock and then slaps it across my face, leaving sticky precum on my cheek.

"You got somewhere else I can stick this?" he asks.

"Mmhmm," I say, balls still in my mouth.

"Show me what you got, baby."

I lift my ass in the air and shove my pants and briefs down over my butt. Braden rubs his hands over the curve of my ass and then spanks a cheek. I whimper with pleasure; the shock of impact very quickly feels good and makes my cock stiffen. He spanks me again, and I whimper again.

"You like that, don't you?"

"Yes, sir," I say, mumbling because of the balls in the way.

"Maybe I should warm your ass up a bit before I fuck it. What do you think, boy?"

I raise my ass higher in the air and twist my hips a bit so it's angled more toward him, hoping that would be answer enough. Braden's eyes widen with hunger as he reaches over and spanks me a little more, this time alternating between cheeks. I continue sucking on his balls, sinking into the pleasure-pain of the spanking. It's making me horny—so fucking horny—and I ache to have him inside of me again.

"Fuck me," I beg as I let Braden's balls slip from my mouth, "please."

"Then turn that ass around," he says. "And put that seatback down."

I turn around in my seat and push my pants and briefs further down to just above my knees. Pulling the lever, I push the seatback down as far it will go, then I prop myself up on it, ready to take him doggy-style.

He clambers across the console until he's finally behind me, and our bodies are pressed tightly against each other. This is the way we are meant to be and what I love most about being with Braden—our bodies just feel so amazingly good together.

He spits in his hand, then slicks himself up and shoves a wet finger in my asshole. "God, you're so tight," he murmurs.

"Fuck me," I say. "Fuck me, please."

He presses his fat cockhead against my knotted flesh, and my body slowly lets him inside. Inch by glorious inch, he enters me. It feels just as amazing now as it did the first time. Braden's cock truly is perfect.

"And warm," he says, "you're so warm."

All I can do is let out a grunt of pleasure. The way he makes me feel is just so fucking overwhelming.

"Yeah," Braden says, placing a hand at the small of my back and another on my shoulder, "just like that, baby. Yeah, push your hips back like that. Oh…fuck…fuck, you're good at that. God, you're so fucking amazing, Kellan."

"Bra…Braden…" I gasp out. "Oh, fuck, Bray."

"Yeah, say my name, baby, say my name."

"Bray," I say, the name sounding like a dirty word coming from my lips. "Braden. Fuck me, Braden, fill me."

"God, you're gonna make me come, baby." He grunts as he shoves in deep. "You want my cum in your ass, baby?"

I grunt. "I do, Braden. I want your cum."

He slows his pace a little, making me whine.

"You gotta come first," he says. "I want you to come for me."

I take my rock hard and leaking dick in my hand, stroking it furiously. "But I'll come on your seats," I say between gasping breaths.

"It's okay, I don't care. Come for me. Come for me, Kellan."

White hot heat builds up in my taint, and my balls pull tight to my body. "Ungh…fuck…I'm gonna come, Braden, I'm gonna come."

"Yes," he says, picking up his pace, slamming into my ass harder than ever before. "Come for me, baby. Come. Come for me."

I roar as the most intense orgasm of my life overtakes me. My cock throbs in my hand as cum jets from it, pelting the seatback, and in my orgasm my asshole clenches down hard on Braden's cock, making it feel impossibly large, like it's grown three times the size.

"Oh, God," he shouts. "God, fuck, I'm coming!"

He slams into me once more, going deeper than before, and

holds me tight, his fingers digging into my hips. I can feel his whole body going stiff, and with how tight my hole has become, I can feel Braden's cock throbbing with orgasm as it pulses and floods my insides.

When his orgasm finishes, he collapses onto my back, and I collapse onto the seat. Braden's cock still plugs my ass, softening, but staying in place. He struggles to catch his breath, warmly panting against my ear. I struggle with my breath, too, but slowly it comes back to me.

"That," I say, pausing to inhale deeply and exhale slowly, "was fucking incredible."

Braden kisses my ear. "*You* are incredible."

There's a sharp tap on the fogged-up driver's window.

"Fuck," Braden says, quickly clambering back to his side of the Jeep while struggling to do up his pants. I roll over and yank my pants up. Looking down, I realize I have my cum load smeared all over the front of my coat—and with me turning around it was likely on the back of my coat, too. I pull the seatback up, right as Braden turns on the Jeep to lower the window.

A flashlight shines into the car. Fuck, it's Justin. I turn in my seat to look out the passenger side fogged-up window. Justin had gone through a curious phase several years ago and once came over for a late-night hookup. I think I convinced him he's straight.

"Good evening, officer," Braden says. "What can I help you with?"

The flashlight flickers to my side of the Jeep, casting a shadow onto the window, but Justin doesn't seem to recognize me or even let the light linger on me for more than a fraction of a second.

"Just making sure everything's alright," the officer—Justin—says. "No one lives in this neighborhood yet." From what I can tell, he hasn't realized I'm the passenger yet.

"I was just, uh, showing my, uh, partner where our new house will be." Braden sounds nervous as hell. As far as I can tell, he doesn't know Justin; Justin is newer to town, having moved here from Maine.

"Windows are a little foggy for sightseeing," Justin says.

"It's, uh, it's been a long time since I've seen my partner. Things got a little carried away," Braden says. "I'm sorry, officer. We'll be on our way."

"Don't worry," Justin says. There's a hint of humor in his voice. "My girlfriend lives back in Maine, so when we see each other, well, we make windows foggy, too."

"Yeah, my girlfriend gets a little crazy for me when she sees me again," Braden says. I can hear the delight in his voice at calling me his *girlfriend.*

"Just don't do anything that I have to follow-up with you over, got it?" Justin says.

"Got it, officer. Thank you."

As Justin walks away, Braden closes the window, and I slap him across the chest with the back of my hand. "Girlfriend?"

"It was a bro bonding moment," Braden says. "Just two macho men talking about our girls."

I roll my eyes. "Whatever. I give head better than any girl could do."

"No argument there," Braden says. He turns his Jeep on and hits the heat to defrost the windows.

As we wait for the view to clear, I say, "I really enjoyed today."

"I did too." Braden leans over for a kiss—soft and intimate. "Other than, you know, that just now."

"Well…" I examine my nails, giving my best nonchalant appearance, "if you get us home, I could give you a demonstration of my skills at giving head."

Braden quickly shifts his Jeep into reverse and backs out of his driveway. When he shifts back into drive, he peels out of the development and through town. I clutch the door handle as he speeds back to my condo.

"That was fast," I say as he skids to a stop in front of my building.

"I'm motivated by blowjobs," he says.

When we enter the condo, I hear my sister washing dishes in the kitchen. "We're home!" I shout.

"About time!" Charlie shouts back. "Both your boys have been desperate for cuddles this evening and I've been their surrogate parent. I'm *covered* in cat hair."

"Thank you for babysitting," Braden says.

Charlie pops around the corner. "It was my pleasure, especially since you two were clearly out on a date." She wasn't kidding about the cat hair. Her T-shirt looks like an angora sweater. "But, as I don't want to hear about my little brother's sex life, I'm going to take a shower and go to bed. Goodnight, boys."

We both wish her goodnight, and she quickly heads away. Senator Tunacan and Mister Fluffykins come up to us, and each of us pick up our cat, and together we walk to the bedroom, and we all four pile on the bed. When the cats feel they've had enough cuddling and attention, they start wrestling and quickly chase each other out of the room.

"We're alone…" Braden says.

"We are…"

"I believe I was promised a blowjob."

I climb across the bed and gently push him back so he lays down with his head on the pillow, then I get between his legs and undo his pants. I pull out that fat cock I love so much. It isn't fully hard, but it is almost there. I take it in my mouth and give it a few strokes with my lips and tongue, bringing it to full hardness.

Braden groans softly and sinks into the mattress and pillows, letting me take over completely to savor this man's cock and just fully enjoy this experience. I make love to his cock, giving the man pleasure that, from what I can tell, is damn near overwhelming. Even though he'd already come like an hour ago, my talents have the man close to coming again in just a matter of minutes.

"Fuck...Kellan..." Braden moans. His hands find their way to my head, and his fingers run through my hair.

I keep up the steady rhythm and tight suction, and not too long later, those fingers in my hair are gripping tightly as orgasm tears through Braden, and his hips buck, and his cock floods my mouth with warm, salty cum. I swallow it all down and lick him clean.

When everything is lapped up and I'm done, I pull his underwear up, but then pull his pants off. Braden is already half asleep, and the after-effects of that orgasm will surely knock him out the rest of the way. I snuggle up next to him and pull the blanket up over us and turn off the bedside lamp.

Braden murmurs something in his half-asleep state; it isn't clear, but I'm pretty sure I hear the word "love" in there. I softly kiss his forehead. When I'm sure he's fully asleep, I slip out of bed and go to the en suite to brush my teeth.

I find Senator Tunacan chilling on the bathmat. After rinsing, I then get down on the floor with him.

"How are you doing, boy?" You enjoying your new roommate?" He rolls onto his side, and I pet him along the length of his body. "I'm certainly enjoying my new roommate. I think they make a good package, don't you?" He stretches his paws out and flexes his toes as he starts purring. "Good kitty, I'm glad you like them so much." I push myself to my feet. "You going to join us in bed?"

Senator Tunacan gets up and follows me back into the bedroom. Braden is fast asleep, and Mister Fluffykins is curled up by his feet.

My cat jumps up and quickly settles against Fluffykins, and the two start grooming each other.

With a gigantic smile on my face, I slip into bed. I give Braden a soft kiss on the temple, then soon fall asleep myself.

Chapter Ten
Horny Reindeer

 **BRADEN**

"Nooo, turn it off," Kellan whimpers beside me. The alarm from his phone continues to blare loudly. His feet rub against mine, he really loves to try and steal the warmth from me. I kiss his cheek. "You can stay in bed if you want. I have to go for a run, snow or no snow. You want to come, or you want to stay?"

He giggles in my arms.

"Oh, I wasn't asking if you wanted to come, like actually come. I meant, do you want to come with me on my run?"

He turns onto his back. "Hmm…I really want to stay here, but if you want me to go with you, I won't say no."

"Good. Let's get up, and head out. It's probably freezing, though. So definitely bundle up."

We both get up from bed, then dress in warm sweats, long sleeve performance shirts, and sweatshirts. I take his hand in mine. "Ready?"

"Ready," he says, interlocking our fingers.

It's still quite dark outside as we start our jog down Main Street. It's also freezing, but it's quiet outside. Normally, I like to run while listening to music, but with Kellan beside me, I'm happy to be here in the moment. I feel so much better since we got all that stuff off our chests yesterday…I feel stupid of course, for wasting so much time, but I feel better. Being with Kellan just feels good, that much is obvious. I give him a little smile, when we pass by my shop. He looks so freaking cute in his black beanie. I just want to make him happy.

"What are you smiling about?" he asks.

"What do you mean? I'm with you. That's why I'm smiling."

"*I'm* not smiling. Do you want to know why?"

Kellan is definitely smiling; I have no idea what he's talking about. "If I ignore the fact that you *are* smiling, and ask why, will that make you feel better?"

"Of course it will. I'm not smiling because it is freezing outside, and we have to be back"—he points over his shoulder—"at work in, like, ninety minutes."

"We have enough time. Are you maybe a little sore from last night? Is that why you're feeling grumpy?"

"I'm not grumpy. I'm just—I don't know what I am, but I'm not grumpy."

"Ohhhh, I see what's happening. I know this guy. I haven't seen him since we were younger. Hello, hangry Kellan, how are you? Why don't we stop at the café, and grab you something to eat? That'll make you happy again."

"Hangry? I don't get hangry."

I elbow him while we jog. "Come on, let's just stop in really quick."

We pass the giant Christmas tree in town square. "Still can't believe that was covered in dildos," I say with a laugh.

"Me neither. I don't even know what to do with all of them."

I nudge him into the entranceway for Sticky Bunz café. We stop just outside of the door. Wow. I'm not even sweating; we were jogging at a pretty leisurely pace. Meanwhile, Kellan looks like he may keel over. He's stretching his arms behind his head. Damn, he looks good. I don't think I'll ever get tired of looking at him.

"Let's go inside," I say, extending my hand for him to hold. He takes my hand and squeezes it tightly.

"How come you're not sweating?" he asks, looking me over.

"I'm not hot…I guess?"

He looks side to side and steps toward me. "You are very hot," he whispers in my ear, then kisses my earlobe.

"Don't start something you can't finish," I warn him.

The door swings open, and the owner, Manuel, greets us. "Hello, welcome, guys. How are you this morning? Come in! No need to wait outside."

"Oh shit," Kellan mumbles.

I smile and greet Manuel, briefly ignoring Kellan until I can find out what he's upset about.

"You boys are here for pancake making, right? So, we have a few pancake shapes for you to choose from; Christmas trees, Christmas ornaments, or Santa shaped ones. Which do you want to make?"

The pancake making station is set up right in the middle of the restaurant. This must have been what he remembered a minute ago. We don't really have time for this, but I'm sure we can do it quickly.

"Ah, Manuel, we really gotta get back to my place. We still need to shower before work," Kellan says.

"This is quick. Pancakes are done fast. Just pick your shape, step up to the bowl, mix it up, then pop them on the griddle. Couldn't be easier, and besides, the Snowflake Princess is supposed to attend all events. I thought that's why you were here? Did you stop by for another reason?"

"The Snowflake Princess is a bit hangry," I say.

Kellan gives me a playful whack in the stomach. "I am not hangry. I planned to stop by around brunch, but since I'm here now, and not hangry, let's do it."

I place my hand on the small of his back, rubbing it, while we approach the cooking station. We stand in front of the bowls, and use the pre-measured ingredients. Kellan grabs the cinnamon and sprinkles a dash into my bowl. "Trust me, it makes them better," he says. "You liked the pancakes I made the other day, right? Those had cinnamon in them."

"Of course I liked them! They were delicious! What kind are you making? Are you using any other mix-ins?" I grab the bowl of milk chocolate chips and spoon some into my batter, along with a few drops of green food coloring.

Kellan drops an eyebrow looking at my bowl. "What are you doing? Chocolate chips go on when they're on the griddle."

"No, now it's your turn to trust me—mix them in, and don't use semi-sweet. Milk chocolate all the way." I pass him the bowl, and he spoons some into his batter, then mixes in some green coloring, too.

"I'm gonna make Christmas trees," he says.

"I'm going to make Christmas ornament shaped ones," I say, picking up the silicone cookie cutter.

Christmas songs play loudly over the café speaker. I can't remember what this song is called. There are only usually ten to fifteen songs on Christmas radio rotation—it's one of those.

The griddles are hot, and our pancakes start to bubble quickly. We flip them over at nearly the same time, smiling at one another. I have no idea why, but there's something so cozy and warm about this moment. I feel warmed from the inside out standing beside Kellan. He's permeated every inch of my soul—like pure dopamine circulating in my veins, and I am hopelessly addicted to the feeling.

We flip our pancakes onto our plates and smile at our creations. "The only thing missing from mine is…" He looks around the table, then grabs the can of whipped cream. "This," he says, squeezing the whipped cream onto his pancakes. He holds it above my plate. "You want some, too?"

He presses the nozzle, and the cream sputters out; a little fleck finds the tip of his nose. "Ah, this one is empty," he says, shaking it. He grabs another one and covers the pancakes with it.

I have no idea why, but I can only think of using that whipped cream in other places right now. "Ooh, that looks delicious," I say. "But it looks even better on your nose." I kiss the tip of his nose where the whipped cream landed. I look down at my plate, then raise my eyebrows at him. "Would you be down for some food play?" I ask.

"Now?" he asks, looking side-to-side, while taking a bite of a pancake.

"Not right now, but maybe soon? I can think of a few things that could be fun, if you're up for it."

"Mmm—intrigued," he says, taking a bite of my pancakes from my plate.

"I haven't even tried them yet! We're not even sitting down and you're stealing my food!" I say with a laugh.

"Sorry. If you don't want a hangry princess, then I'm gonna need to confiscate your pancakes."

"I'd give you far more than pancakes." I cut a piece of the pancake and feed it to him. He looks too sexy opening his mouth and taking a bite from my fork. I really don't want to jog back to his place with a boner. I push the plate toward him. "You can have them. I'm not really hungry."

He takes a few more bites and smiles. "This was the best breakfast I've had in a long time. This day is gonna be amazing, nothing is going to get on my nerves today."

"Are you kidding me?! What else is going to go wrong today?" Kellan asks, taking a giant box of oversized peppermint sticks from Rachel.

The line of complaining townspeople hasn't stopped since before

I walked in. Everyone has some kind of a problem. From my shop window, I could see things looked stressful over here, so I came over to invite Kellan to the movies. It's been twenty minutes, and I haven't been able to get a word in.

I take the box of giant peppermint sticks from him, picking one up and examining it. "This is wild. I don't think I've seen one this big before," I say.

Rachel holds one in her hand and waves it wildly. "What would anyone even use these for? This is a ten-inch peppermint stick. I can't use this in hot cocoa!"

"Whoa, you're at like a ten and I need you to come down to, like, at least a five," Kellan says. "I get it, you don't have mini candy canes for the hot cocoa, but you can still have the event. Can't you just buy some from the store? A few boxes of mini candy canes…seems like you could."

"Seems reasonable," I chime in. I tap one of the sticks against the counter. "This thing is rock hard. Solid."

"Yes, exactly, who would even eat this?" Rachel asks, placing the stick back in the box. "Anyway, I can go to the store, I just prefer the ones from the company I ordered from."

"I understand," Kellan says. "You can't cancel the event, and I don't think you can get the company to deliver to you within the next three hours, so I think you're only left with one option."

"I might have another option," I say.

Kellan tilts his head at me. He's giving me a disbelieving look. I really do love that this man says he doesn't get jealous. The look on his face right now. I haven't even said anything. Honestly with the way he's looking at me, I should just backpedal out of this conversation. He's in one of those "I'm mad and someone is gonna get the brunt of it" kind of moods.

"Oooh! What's your idea, Braden?" Rachel asks, slightly bouncing on her toes and grabbing my bicep.

"Yeah, what's your idea, Braden?" Kellan asks, facetiously, exaggerating every word and widening his eyes.

Yeah, I don't want any part of this. Backpedal it is. "Oh, I was thinking that Kellan could, um, donate these to someone. That's all."

Kellan is giving me an indiscernible look. "No, you said you had another option. Did you have a good idea…something to help Rachel?" he asks, fluttering his lashes.

"Nope. Definitely not. I've probably never had a good idea, ever. I have nothing else to say."

Kellan smiles at me, then turns to Rachel. "Alright, so are you gonna go grab the candy canes from the store? I have about twenty other problems to deal with."

"Yeah, I guess so," she says. "Do whatever you want with those. I don't want any part of them. That's a lawsuit waiting to happen. I can just see someone getting hurt with one of those things. No, thank you. But you know, Kellan, you are supposed to attend the event, what time will you be stopping by?"

"I have no idea right now, but, yeah, I will definitely stop by at some point."

"Okay…you could always send Braden in your place; I won't tell anyone. Or just bring him along when you come." She turns to me and says, "Braden, you have got to try my hot cocoa. It's the best in town."

Kellan rolls his eyes at her.

I shake my head and take the box from Kellan's hands. "I have to get back to my shop. My mom is holding down the fort, but I really should get back. You want these in your office?"

"Fine, fine, I'll see you later, Kellan. Bye, Braden," Rachel says, as she heads for the exit.

"Come on," Kellan says, walking with me toward his office.

"Whoa, what is all of this stuff in here? I haven't seen your office this messy before." There are boxes everywhere of what appears to be the most random things.

"This is everything that has gone wrong today," he says. "You can just put the peppermint sticks anywhere there's space." He lifts a large box that says *Slick n Lick Oils* onto his desk.

"What's that?" I ask.

"This one is my problem. The rest belong to everyone else. These should be oils for my candles, but what they are is—"

He passes me a medium sized red plastic bottle. "Ah," I say, reading the label aloud, "Peppermint Paradise, Massage Oil. You didn't order this? Seems fun. Can I smell it?"

"Be my guest, I'm probably stuck with them. My supplier has never made a mistake like this before. He should be able to get me a small batch of oils within the next two days, but I need more for tomorrow."

I twist the cap off and bring the bottle to my nose. "Oooh, that does smell like Peppermint Paradise. It smells so good, I kind of want to taste it."

"It's edible. You can try it."

I spin the bottle around, reading the label. Hmm, it is edible. I dab some onto my finger and taste it. "Oh my God, Kellan, this is delicious."

"Yeah, I've tried that before, it's pretty amazing that it's massage oil."

I screw the cap back on and place the oil back into the box.

"Your mom is probably waiting for you to get back," he says, closing the box and moving it to the floor. "I don't know how I'm gonna deal with all of this."

I place my hands on his waist and pull him into an embrace. "I have an idea. Why don't we go to the all-night movie marathon tonight? They're showing classic Christmas movies. We could go on a little date to escape the stress."

"Oooh, a date? That sounds fun. I'm supposed to go check it out anyway since I'm the Snowflake Princess, but I was going to skip it. Now that it's a date, I'm excited to check it out." He kisses me softly, hanging his arms around my neck. His entire body relaxes in my embrace.

I squeeze him once more. I really have to go, but damn I am so obsessed with the feeling of him in my arms. "Now, I really have to get back. My mom probably wasn't expecting me to be gone for this long." I pat his bottom lightly and give him a quick kiss. "I'll see you after work."

KELLAN

Braden comes out of the bedroom with a cute Christmas sweater on, and it makes me smile. He doesn't strike me as the kind to get into the kitschy side of Christmas, yet he has this knitted sweater with reindeer all over it.

"Wait…" I say. I pull him closer and tug at the sides of his sweater to flatten it out and get a better view of it. "Are these reindeer…"

"Fucking? Yes. Exuberantly, too," Braden says. "My nonna made it for me a few years back."

"Well, let's hope Morris at the movie theater doesn't notice it," I say. "He can be a bit old-fashioned."

"The old-fashioned ones are usually the kinkiest," Braden says.

Before I can reply with a question as to exactly how he knows this to be a fact, he grabs his keys and leads us out of the condo.

We take his Jeep across downtown to the movie theater. The weather has turned in the last half hour, going from clear and breezy to heavy with snow. The flakes come down in fat clusters and obscure the surface of the road. Braden drives slowly since he isn't sure how much grip he has if he has to stop.

I suddenly burst out in laughter, and Braden looks at me quizzically. "Morris," I explain. "He wanted me to change the weather so it doesn't snow on the movie marathon day…and which day is it snowing…?" Braden laughs with me.

We soon reach the movie theater. It's an older-style building and carefully maintained, with a row of incandescent bulbs lining the entryway overhang, and the old white and black marquee announces the movies for the all day and night marathon.

"*Rudolph the Red-Nosed Reindeer* and *It's a Wonderful Life*," I say, reading the marquee for the evening movies. "Should be a good double-header."

As we walk up to the ticket booth, Braden says, "It was *Rudolph* that inspired me to be a vet. Did I ever tell you that?"

"What? How?"

"When Hermey pulls out the Abominable's teeth, and the grumpy beast feels better, I knew I wanted to work with animals," Braden says. He buys two sets of tickets from Morris.

Morris eyes Braden's sweater and for a moment I expect Braden to be admonished for such vulgar reindeer, but instead Morris says, "Your nonna made me one of those, too! I wear it when I want some Christmas loving from my wife. Gets her in a randy mood."

My eyes go wide as I desperately try not to think of Linda getting randy with Morris. "Thank you," I say, then take Braden by the arm and quickly lead him away. To Braden, I ask, "How come seeing that scene didn't make you want to be a dentist? That would be the more obvious connection, wouldn't it?"

Braden shivers. "Sticking my fingers in a person's mouth? No, thank you." Then he leans in and whispers, "Unless it's your mouth, you little slut."

I instantly go hard. Achingly so. "Let's get some popcorn," I say, trying to pull my mind away from images of Braden using my mouth for things.

There's no line at the snack bar, so we get our popcorn and a drink pretty quickly. In fact, the place looks pretty empty. When I remark on this, Braden says, "I bet the snowstorm kept most people away."

We go in and find our seats for the showing of *Rudolph the Red Nosed Reindeer*. There are a few other folks in the theater, mostly millennials looking to relive their childhood and introduce their kids to it.

"Are you going to miss working with animals?" I ask as the previews start.

He takes my hand and gives it a squeeze. "I will. I think I made the right choice because the hard parts of being a vet were too hard, but I'll miss the good times." After pausing for a moment, he says, "I'm thinking of expanding into cookies for dogs and cats, maybe bring some happiness to small animals. I could even make seed crackers for birds and rodents."

I squeeze his hand back. "I love that idea. You should definitely do it."

The previews end, and the lights dim. I settle into my seat and then lean my head to the side, resting it on Braden's muscular shoulder. It's comfortable, and I feel completely at peace here with him.

When the scene where Hermey removes the Abominable's

painful teeth comes up, I try watching it from a young Braden's point of view, and I can see where that connection comes from. The Abominable was simply acting the only way it knew how since it couldn't communicate with language, and Hermey was able to see past the pain and see the Abominable for who he was and then help him feel better. I can easily see that inspiring a young Braden to go to veterinary school.

Eventually, the closing credits roll, and the lights come up. Everyone in the theater gets up and heads out, leaving only Braden and I. There's a ten-minute intermission between movies, but no one seems to come back and no new guests have arrived.

"Looks like we have the place to ourselves," I say as the lights darken, and the trailers before *It's a Wonderful Life* begin.

Braden leans in close and in a very low and dangerous whisper, he says, "Good, because I don't think I can keep my hands off you any longer."

My eyes go wide. "Here?" I say incredulously, even though I'm already hard. I look up at the projection booth above our heads; we're in the last row.

"Relax," he says, "they can't see us. Besides, Morris is probably up there playing naughty reindeer with his wife anyway."

"Please…that is a mental image I don't need, thank you."

He reaches over and undoes my fly, wrenching my dick out.

"*Braden*," I say, looking frantically around, but we're still alone.

"I want to suck you," he says. "I want to make you feel good."

"Braden, we can't. We'll get caught and then Morris will—" My pleas are cut off as soon as his warm mouth is wrapped around my cock, and his velvety tongue is giving me intense pleasure. "Mmmf… Braden…"

I lean back as much as the seat allows and rest a hand on the back of his head, fiddling with his hair as he bobs up and down on me.

"God…Braden…"

Braden pauses and backs off my dick for a moment, just to pull the armrest up and out of the way. Before he dives back down to my cock, I cup his face in my hands and lean forward, bringing our lips together in a crushing kiss.

"Are you the good boy this time, Bray?" I ask, with a wicked grin on my face.

He smirks at me. "Yes, sir. May I suck your cock, sir?"

I grab the base of my cock and wave it around, smacking him in the face with it. He sticks his tongue out, trying to catch a taste of it.

"This cock, boy?" I ask.

"Yes, sir. May I suck it, sir?" Braden asks.

I angle my cock straight toward Braden's face. "Suck it."

"Thank you, sir," Braden says. He takes me in his mouth again, sliding down until his nose is pressed hard against my pelvis, and my cock is halfway down his throat. It's tight and warm and wet, and it feels amazing.

Braden continues up and down, sometimes swirling his tongue around the head of my cock, sometimes playing with my balls, and each movement pushes me a little closer to orgasm, until it finally overtakes me.

"I'm gonna come," I whisper urgently.

In response, Braden just clamps his lips tighter around my cock, determined to not let even a single drop go to waste. Electricity surges through me, culminating at a tight spot behind my balls and then exploding outward as my load shoots out and into Braden's mouth, who then promptly swallows it all down. I jerk with each spasm and then shudder as I roll into the after-orgasm.

He loosens his oral grip and gently, softly cleans my cock, licking up any remaining cum and saliva—I jerk when his tongue touches a particularly sensitive spot—until I'm completely clean again. When he determines he's finished, he tugs my briefs and jeans up, zipping the fly closed. Then he sits back in his seat, and we look at the film playing out on the huge screen in front of us.

I try to catch my breath; I'm still panting from the intensity of it all. Eventually, I turn to Braden and say, "That was fucking hot. I've never done a blowjob that risky. Morris could have walked in at any moment, or even a late ticket holder."

He kisses the side of my face. "You worry too much. No one walked in, so maybe it's the Christmas magic in the air," he says with a smirk.

"If that was Christmas magic then I guess I believe in magic again."

As we settle in to watch the rest of the movie—which I have some difficulty following since we missed the first twenty minutes—I cuddle up next to Braden. I hug his arm and rest my head on his shoulder. His hand ends up in my lap, and he wraps it around one of my thighs, holding me in place, laying claim to my body. At least, that's what it feels like. And it's a feeling I like.

By the time the movie reaches its conclusion, I had mostly caught up with the plot and the characters. When the end credits roll, we get up and hold hands as we walk out of the theater. It's completely empty now, with Morris waiting for us at the door, wishing us a goodnight as we leave.

"Holy moley, it snowed a lot," Braden says. A good six inches had come down in the few hours we were in there. The streets are quiet since everyone is likely at home right now. We let go of each other's hands as we take in how the snow has transformed downtown Frosty Bottoms. "It's so peaceful."

"Do you have winter tires on your Jeep?" I ask. I leave Braden's side and walk up to the car. Snow blankets the windows and the hood; I brush some of it away with my coat sleeve.

"I do. Got them swapped in a week ago—and good thing! But…Kellan…" Braden says, from somewhere behind me.

"Yeah?" I say, brushing off more snow. When he doesn't respond, I turn—and get a snowball to the face. "Bastard!" I shout between laughs.

I brush the snow off my face, then scoop up a handful of my own, forming a ball and throwing it at him. It hits him on the top of his head, cascading snow all down his face and body as the snowball explodes.

Braden laughs and then charges at me, and I turn and run, circling the Jeep. In only a matter of moments, he catches up with me and grabs my jacket, and we both lose our balance and tumble into a snowbank on the side of the street. I land on my back, and he lands on his chest on top of me. Our faces are only an inch or two apart.

There's a slight hesitance in this moment, a sense of words unsaid that we both want to say. We look into each other's eyes with the weight of this closeness and what it truly means to both of us. At least, that's what it feels like to me, but I'm sure I'm reading the same in Braden's expression.

I know him well enough to read him like that. I've always been able to read my man like that. Wait…*my man?*

"Braden," I say. I don't know what I want to say next. My heart is thundering in my chest, and I'm pretty sure I feel the vibration of Braden's heart doing the same thing.

"Shut up and kiss me," he says. He crushes his lips against mine, and I kiss him back just as hard. It's a kiss with more passion and intimacy than we'd shared before. It's taking us to a new level…or maybe the kiss is catching up to the level we're already on.

After a very long and very intense kiss, we part our lips and get up and into the Jeep. We ride back to the condo in silence, but it's a comfortable silence.

When we enter the condo, we find Charlie fast asleep on the couch with a trashy reality show blaring on the TV. Both cats are curled up with her—Senator Tunacan and Mister Fluffykins both wake up and look at us, but they soon settle back down to continue their group nap.

"Let's leave them be," I say. I take Braden's hand in mine and lead him to the master bedroom at the end of the hall. I nudge the door closed as we enter, but this isn't time for sex—not yet, anyway. This is time for closeness and intimacy. There was something that passed between us in the snowbank that makes me just want to be held by him.

I strip down to my underwear, and Braden does the same, then we climb into bed and snuggle under the covers.

"Spoon me," I say, rolling on my side.

He snuggles up close, pulling my smaller twinky frame tight against his bulkier, broader body. He tightens his arms around me and then nestles his face against my neck. This closeness feels good. It feels perfect.

"Braden?" I say.

"Yeah?"

"I'm really glad you're back."

He nuzzles against my neck and plants a kiss there. "So am I." He kisses my neck a few more times. "This move back has been about re-centering myself, new beginnings, and figuring out what I really want in life."

"And what have you figured out so far?"

He hugs me a little tighter. "That I want this. You. Us."

I feel a flush of heat in my chest. This talk would normally get me squirmy and have me rushing out of the room. But with Braden? With Braden it feels right. It's something I know I want, too.

I roll onto my back, and Braden is half lying on top of me. His delicious mouth is close to mine. His body is hot against me. And his cock is engorged and still thickening against my thigh.

"I love you," I whisper. These are the words I've been wanting to say since that moment in the snowbank. These are the words I've been waiting my whole life to say.

"I love you, too," Braden says.

"Kiss me," I whisper.

He closes his eyes and opens his mouth, and I do the same, meeting him halfway in a collision of our tongues. His mouth is warm and wet and inviting, and I kiss him deep and hard. He pushes himself more fully onto me, resting his bulky weight on me, melding our bodies into one. Hastily, we both tear off our underwear.

He interlaces his fingers with mine, pushing my hands back above my head. Then he starts thrusting his hips, sliding his thick cock, wet with precum, alongside mine, giving us both pleasure. I gasp as electricity surges through my body. He lights every nerve ending on fire. He makes me feel this with every inch of my body. He isn't making love to my body; he's making love to my soul.

I gasp with pleasure as he kisses down my neck and to my chest, teasing my nipples a bit. Then he shifts his legs, putting them between mine and spreading mine apart. He slides in closer. I feel his shaft along my crack; it's warm and reassuring.

He finally lets go of one of my hands so he can spit in his and reach between us. He slicks up his cock, then spits in his hand again and massages my entrance. And then slowly, intimately, he presses his cock against me, and I open to let him in. He slides in, locking our bodies together.

Fully inside, he falls forward, lying on top of me. I wrap my arms and legs around him, holding him tight, wanting to never let go. He slips his arms under me, hugging me, too.

We move as one—in movement, in breath, in spirit. Time seems to slow, and I freeze in this moment. I'm in complete bliss. In complete love. And I want this to last forever. And in that moment, I feel my cock throb and pulse and shoot. I hadn't even touched myself. It was all him. He does this to me.

His pace picks up, and his breathing comes faster, heavier. He suddenly goes stiff, every muscle in his body rigid and his heart racing hard against his ribs, so hard I can feel it and almost hear it. He lets out a little sound of pleasure, and then collapses on me, gasping and panting and struggling to catch his breath.

I lower my legs, and his cock slips from me, and he rolls on his side. We're still entangled, but he's not on top of me anymore. I hold his face and kiss his forehead. We say no words because nothing needs to be said. We're in this moment. We're here. We're together. That's all that matters.

We linger there, enjoying each other's company, wanting to be nowhere else.

Eventually, we hear a pair of meows, and Senator Tunacan and Mister Fluffykins jump onto the bed and clamber over our bodies, and the covers to sit on top of us.

"Our boys want to be part of cuddle time," I say.

"I think they're happy for us," he says.

"Probably because they love us so much and they want us to be happy." I scratch The Senator behind his ears.

"That they do," Braden says.

CHAPTER ELEVEN
TEN INCHES OF PEPPERMINT

 KELLAN

Okay, so it isn't just the old fogies that are getting all panicked and worked up about little inconveniences related to the Snowflake Festival. It's also me. I am now in full-on panic mode.

Somehow, I had made it to today—mere hours from hosting a make-your-own-candle event here at Dip Your Wick—without doing a full inventory check for the event and being sure I had everything. Like the custom Snowflake Festival candle boxes, I had designed by a college kid. I paid that kid a nice chunk of change for the artwork and had it printed, so I'd have these lovely little boxes for people to take their souvenir candle home in.

Or at least I thought I did.

I definitely paid the kid to design something because I had the design files, and the money for the design was missing from my bank account. But that was where the paper trail stopped. I seemed to have no record of ordering a print run of these boxes, and I had no corresponding charge on my credit card.

"Fuck me," I mutter.

"Again?" a too-familiar voice asks.

I spin around. "Braden, I hadn't heard you come in." Seeing him always puts a smile on my face.

"So, it wasn't *me* you wanted to fuck you?" Braden says with a teasing grin. He approaches the counter and puts his hands down on it, leaning over it. "You got another top tucked away back there somewhere?"

I roll my eyes. "Not a flesh and blood one, anyway."

At his quizzical expression, I remind him of the dildo tree and the Max Girth dildo that had provoked more awkward conversations with my mother.

"Can I see it?" Braden asks.

I blink tiredly. "See what?"

"Max Girth."

I roll my eyes, but also push myself off my stool to grant his request. "Come to the back room," I say, "I don't wanna be waving that thing around out here in case a customer comes in."

He follows me through the door to the back room. This space functions as partly warehouse and partly shop floor. While I do order in the occasional gourmet candle by someone else—like those pine candles for the woman that reads lumberjack porn—I make most of the candles myself.

"They're right over here," I say, taking him around a corner to where a box filled with dildos sits on a shelf. I grab the monstrous one on the top. "And this is Max Girth." It flops around in my hand.

Braden's eyes widen. "That is…massive." He takes it from my hands and props it against his crotch as if comparing his dick to Max's.

"I don't know if my hole would ever recover if you were that big," I say. Part of me had been tempted to take it home, sanitize it, throw a condom on it just in case, and try riding it. But I know my limits and Max Girth is past those limits.

"I dunno…" he says. He grabs my bicep and spins me around, crushing me against the shelves. He thrusts his pelvis against mine, the dildo sliding up my ass crack and riding up into the back of my shirt. "Something tells me you could take it." He leans in close and bites my earlobe. "You're a little slut, aren't you? And little sluts can take big dicks."

I whimper with need as my cock quickly hardens. "I'm a little slut, sir."

He nibbles along the back of my neck and then follows it with a line of kisses, which make me shudder in pleasure. But my blood goes instantly cold when I hear the jingle of bells when someone opens my door.

I spin around and now Max Girth is pressed alongside my own erection, putting it to shame. I kiss Braden quickly. "Customers." I squeeze out from under him and hurry around the corner and into the shop, subtly adjusting the front of my pants before finally coming in view of the customers.

An older couple is standing in the middle of my shop, looking kind of lost. I don't recognize them, so they must be tourists here for the Snowflake Festival.

"How can I help you find the perfect candle?" I say, doling out my well-rehearsed opening line.

"We're here for the thing," says the woman. The man, who I assume is her husband, just rolls his eyes. Clearly one of them was dragged here.

"The thing?" I ask.

"The candle making is today, right?" she asks.

Oh shit. With Braden distracting me, I hadn't set a single thing up and had somehow totally blanked on it in the last five minutes. "Ah, yes," I say, managing, I think, to hide my skyrocketing anxiety. "You're our first candlemakers today and I was just in the process of setting up."

Braden comes wandering out of the back room; I hope he left Max Girth behind. The last thing these two need to see is a giant dildo flopping around in Braden's pocket.

"Braden, can I borrow you for a few minutes?" I ask.

He looks at me with hunger. "You can have more than a few minutes."

If looks could kill, he'd be dead on the floor right now.

"I have a couple tables and a handful of chairs in the back; can you help me bring them out?"

Together we bring out two tables and four chairs. I cover them in festive tablecloths. The couple sets themselves up at one of the tables; the wife is looking patient and interested, but the husband is already watching YouTube videos on his phone. It sounds like a hunting podcast. I hurry into the storefront area with an armful of containers of beeswax—but then trip over my own feet and drop everything. Dried beeswax pellets burst from the containers and roll across the entire floor.

"Sh—" I start, but then catch myself when I remember I have customers. The wife looks at the mess wide-eyed, and the husband finally has a smile on his face, laughing at my misfortune.

"Here," Braden says. He hands me one container that has mostly survived intact. "I'll sweep. You get them started."

"You don't have to, it's my mess, I should—"

"We're not negotiating this," Braden says. "Get them started and I'll sweep."

I try to give him a look that both says thank you and I'll punish you later for giving me orders in my own shop in front of customers. With the way he smirks at me, I think he understands it but is determined to remind me who's the boss, especially in the bedroom. I have to turn away from him before his smirky glower gives me a hard on.

I put the container of beeswax beads on the table in front of them. "Have you made candles before?"

The husband scoffs like he wants to tell me he'd never be caught doing something so millennial, but the wife shakes her head. "I've been watching YouTube tutorials, but haven't done it yet."

"Well, you're in for a treat," I say. "Let me get a couple burners to melt the wax."

I retrieve two portable burners from the back and manage to not trip over my feet this time. They basically look like little crockpots that warm up and melt the wax so they can dip their wicks in and build their candles. But when I plug them in, the one I'd put in front of the husband isn't turning on. What else could fucking go wrong today?

"I got this," the husband says. There's actual interest in his voice. "I like fixing things," he says, as he gingerly picks it up and rotates it in his hands, looking for external damage and obvious points where problems could happen.

"He'll be busy for a while," the wife says. "Walk me through this?"

I pull up a chair and sit across from her. Together we work through the process of setting up the wax melter and all the steps of preparing the wick and then dipping it. I rarely do dipped candles in the shop—hand-poured candles are the popular item—but wick dipped candles are such a great hands-on activity.

About ten minutes into the project, Braden pulls a chair up beside me and sits across from the husband. Together they work on fixing the melter, with Braden walking into the back room in search of screwdrivers. As they work, they talk about old Christmas traditions and eventually get onto the topic of animals; the husband had grown up on a farm, and he and Braden bond over tending for sick animals. The wife and I have a great time talking about candle scents and the memories they trigger. When the wife and I are finished her candle, the husband and Braden are putting the panel back on the melter and testing it to ensure it works properly now.

"Success!" the husband exclaims.

They leave a few minutes later, both content with how they'd spent the last hour. The husband even buys his wife an expensive candle before they head out the door.

Braden comes up beside me and puts an arm over my shoulders. "That was fun," he says. "I knew you'd do great."

I look up at him. "Thank you for everything."

He kisses my forehead. "You got it."

The door opens and a crowd of nearly a dozen people come in; I recognize them from the bank down the street. They're likely taking the activity in on their lunch break.

I look up at Braden again and whimper. "Stay and help?"

He chuckles, low and warm. "I need to get back to BJ's. I promised my mom I wouldn't leave her alone over there too long and now it's been more than an hour. Besides, you'll have Riley here soon." He squeezes my shoulders once more. "But you got this." Then he leans in close to my ear. "And tonight, I'll fuck you good and hard as a reward for getting through the day."

"Ugh," I say, "*I am* reward motivated."

He pats me on the butt. "You can do it; I believe in you."

With a kiss, Braden turns to head back to BJ's, but as he puts his hand on the door, he says, "I love you."

I give him a warm smile. "I love you too."

When he's gone, I turn to the group that watched that whole exchange. Half of them are giving me goo-goo eyes.

"Welcome to Dip Your Wick, are you ready to—wait for it—dip your wick?"

It's a cheesy line, but it always earns a couple chuckles from a crowd. And this one certainly seems to enjoy it.

I quickly set up an extra table with a few chairs and everyone finds their seats. After a very rough start, things seem to be going alright now, including seeing that the wax melter Braden and the husband fixed is indeed fixed.

After the work lunch crowd filters out, a bunch of retired folks come mid-afternoon, and when they leave, the after-school crowd comes, and my shop is filled with teenagers making Christmas gifts for each other.

When the day is over and I finally close my shop, I turn around from locking the door to take in the mess the day left behind. Truthfully, it isn't too bad considering I had like fifty people come through to make candles, but I'm pretty sure wax has been ground into the tight-weave industrial carpet, and that will be a bitch to get out. I set to the task of cleaning, and a whole hour later, I have the place looking semi-decent again.

I knock on the door of Kellan's shop. He smiles and quickly lets me inside. "Man, it's freezing outside. It's so warm in here."

He rubs my cheeks with his hands and presses our noses together. "I am so glad you're here. This day is finally over. Now we can just relax for the rest of the night," he says. "Oooh, do you want to get Chinese and bake cookies?"

"Chinese sounds delicious. We can do whatever you want. My event is tomorrow, so I'd love to make some cookies with just the two of us tonight. Maybe try out some new frosting colors."

"Food play?" he asks.

"Hmm…not with cookie dough, but frosting could be fun," I say. Damn, the thought of licking frosting off his body has already got my cock tingling.

His eyes widen, and he pats my chest. "Oh, that reminds me. Do you want to use these peppermint sticks for anything at the shop?" Kellan takes one of the sealed sticks out of the box and examines it.

Seeing his hands on that thick long stick is only furthering the dirty thoughts that were already swirling around.

"Paul's Peppermint Stick," he says reading the label. "Damn, Paul; ten inches is a big boy. Phew," he says, stroking his hand up and down it.

The stroking is not helping. God, Kellan, don't do that. My dick is fully invested in this filthy idea that I'm having. What is it about this man that turns me into such a beast? I think the dirtiest things. I've never thought things as dirty as I do with Kellan.

I take the candy from his hand and look at him, while I run a finger up and down the massive sealed stick. "Kellan…baby. I want to try something. Will you let me?"

He tilts his head at me, looking rather oblivious. "Yeah, of course. What is it?" he asks, rubbing my arms.

I rub the stick lengthwise down his ass, on the outside of his pants. "I want to fuck you with this. Can I?"

His head nods against my chest. "Yes."

I lift his chin using my finger. "Dirty little boy." I lick his lips and slip my tongue in between them. He doesn't even feel nervous, his body completely melts into mine when we kiss like this. I unbutton his pants, placing the stick on his desk beside the box of oils.

Our mouths remain entwined as he pulls his pants down. I'm so hard right now. He's so obedient, so willing to please me. It's such a turn on for me. I grip his cock and give it a few tugs, as we lick each other's tongues.

Fuck, every flick of his tongue on mine makes me harder. Part of me wants to just fuck him over his desk right now, but the other part of me wants to see what happens here. I pull back and reach my hand into the box of oils. "You said I could use the stick—can we use this, too?"

He nods, eyes half-lidded. "Mmm, yes. Definitely."

I take my pants off and stand in my underwear behind him, then quickly remove the wrapper from the candy cane and place it on his desk. I unscrew the top of the massage oil, and let the cap fall to the floor, then dab some on my pointer finger and press his back down, urging him to use the desk for support. He leans on his elbows bent over the desk, while I rub my oil-slickened finger down his back.

"Ahhh, that feels good and the oil is so warm, too," he says.

I kiss the small of his back, then stick my tongue out, slowly licking all the way up the center toward his neck. "Ah, I gave you goosebumps, that's cute," I say, beside his ear. I massage his ass like dough in my hands, kneading it while spreading him at the same time. I love the way he whimpers a bit under my touch. "I want you to touch yourself. Stroke it for me." His hand quickly finds his length, and he starts jerking off, leaning on one elbow, legs still spread wide for me.

I release his ass and pour the massage oil on the peppermint stick, then rub some on my fingers, sliding them around his rim, gently petting his entrance with two fingers. I swirl my fingers in circles around it, while his body jerks from the ferocity of his own hand. When I press one finger into the warmth, it sends fucking pure electric waves to my cock. My long index finger moves in and out of him, while he continues pumping himself. "Look at you, with your hand on your dick. Tell me, Kellan, how many times did you jerk off thinking about me over the years?" I ask, while stretching him out, and adding a second finger to the mix.

"I—used to jerk off all the time thinking about you," he says.

"That's hot." My two fingers stretch his ass wide, swirling and pumping, matching the speed of his hand. I feel his prostate hard against my fingertips, and his breath hitches. I move my mouth to his asshole, flicking my tongue around while I continue fingering him. He presses back, seemingly trying to get more of me inside. "You want me inside?" I ask, feathering his entrance with my tongue, then slipping it inside, beside my fingers.

"Yes, more. Give me more, fuck me with your tongue."

I slap him on the ass, while I continue pressing my tongue deeper. I love the taste of this man.

"*Mmmore*—I want more," he begs, riding my tongue.

I slip my tongue out and grab the stick, and rub the oil around the top of it then along its entirety. "Tell me if it feels good, okay, baby?" I say, gripping the cane tightly in my hand.

No longer jerking his cock, he braces himself on the desk and nods his head.

I spread him open wider using my thumb and press the stick against his entrance. I slide it in with almost no resistance, watching his hole swallow it, inch by inch. It looks so fucking hot, seeing him wrapped around it.

"Oh fuck, that feels amazing. Fuck me with it, Bray."

"No calling me Bray, yet. The sight of your hole greedily slurping on this stick is already making my cock wet." I have the stick about eighty percent in, and start fucking him with it. "Yeah—take that stick, you dirty fucking boy." I fuck him with it harder, pressing it almost all the way inside, and his breathing turns ragged. His moans are broken, and I can't understand him...but I can tell he's loving it. Precum drips from his cock to the floor, as he presses back harder. He's so sexy right now. "That's nearly all ten inches, should I push you further?"

His head drops, and he lifts his ass higher, arching his back. "Yyyes—ffuck—more."

I slide my hand into the back of his sweat drenched hair, grasping a fist full of it, pulling it back tightly. "Your sweet hole is really turning me on." I pull his hair tighter, and shove the rest of the stick inside, leaving just enough out for me to control him with. I push and pull it in and out, squeezing his hair tightly. My dick may revolt against me if I don't get inside him soon. "Bray, fff—hah—fuck me, with your cock, please…I want to feel you."

I slide the stick out slowly, wondering how it would taste. Kellan's ass is already sweet enough, this sugary peppermint probably tastes amazing now. I have the stick in my right hand and keep pressure against his entrance with my thumb. I lick the peppermint stick. Holy fuck—this tastes amazing.

"Bray—fuck me, please," he begs.

"Mmm, I'm licking the taste of you off this candy first." I press my thumb inside him, knowing it's not enough.

"You're what?" he asks looking over his shoulder.

I pull my thumb out and grip him by the waist, turning his body to face mine. His dick is so hard pressed against me, and mine is fucking screaming for me to take it out of my underwear. "Taste this," I say, bringing the stick to his lips. He licks it shyly at first, then wraps his lips around it. The most carnal impulse I've ever felt overwhelms me. I slide the things off his desk, shoving them to the ground, then quickly lift him onto his desk. I spread his legs open wide on the edge, and dive face first in between his ass cheeks. Fuck, he tastes like fucking peppermint. I rub my tongue wildly around his rim, while sucking his asshole, my tongue swirling inside as he trembles underneath me. I've never tasted anything so fucking sweet. "Baby, your ass is dripping, it tastes like peppermint. Mmm." I moan in his hole, shoving my tongue in and out.

"Fuck yes, Braden." He pulls my hair tightly, clearly loving the feeling of my tongue inside of him. Keeping my tongue inside I pull my dick out, quickly jerking it, smearing my precum around my tip, then down the sides. I stand upright and line my cock up with his perfect asshole and plunge my fat cock in without hesitation. His desk rocks backward from the forceful entry. I lift one of his legs over my shoulder and thrust hard inside of him. His eyes are closed as I ride him rougher than ever before. His moans are so loud, and I'm not sure if the shop next door is still open. "Shhh, baby, you're being too loud," I say.

"I can't help it; your cock is so fuucking deep."

"Yeah, it is, and you fucking love it."

"I do, I do, fuck—yes. I love getting fucked by you."

I'm gonna make him come, because I want to watch his gorgeous cock shoot for me, while I fuck him like this. I grind my hips deeper, thrusting slowly and purposefully, absolutely ravaging his spot, until I feel him clamp down.

The most guttural grunt escapes him as he comes, and the sight of his beautiful cock coming for me is absolutely fucking gorgeous. His body shudders, as he rides his orgasm out. "Bray—fuck, you're so good. I fucking lo—"

His words are cut off as my hot cum fills him, and he begins to moan loudly again. "Shhh, baby," I say, tilting my head back, until my cock is completely drained.

I pull my cock out and place my hand on his abs that are covered in his cum. "Stay," I say, pressing my mouth against his dripping hole. I lick across the outside, then suck, my mouth is filled quickly with my cum and the taste of peppermint, mixed with Kellan. The taste of us. I savor the taste, not swallowing, then bring my mouth to his, and feed him my cum, he holds my face, eagerly lapping from my mouth and swallowing. We swirl our tongues around and share the taste, both moaning into one another's mouths, until the taste of peppermint subsides. I kiss him once more softly, then drop my head on his shoulder.

"You're trouble," I say.

"The best kind of trouble," he says.

The doorbell rings loudly inside of Kellan's condo. "Oooh! That should be the delivery driver with our Chinese food," Kellan says. He's holding a glass of eggnog in his hand, and he opens the door with his other. "Good evening and the most festive greetings to you," he says, inexplicably bowing, holding his glass up high. I tilt my head in confusion. He is a bit more drunk than I realized. But he's so cute, I just want to see where this goes. The delivery driver is just staring at him, while Kellan is telling him about the cookies that we just made.

He hasn't even passed him the bag of food yet. The driver is just staring into the condo. I shout from behind the kitchen counter, "Hey, babe, maybe you should just take the food and let the driver go. It's time to put the frosting on the dicks." Yes, we made dick shaped Christmas cookies and, also, little Christmas sweater shaped ones.

The delivery driver raises his eyebrows at me. I don't really care what he thinks, he was looking a bit too interested in Kellan until he realized I was standing here. I can't blame the guy, but still, I'm not gonna stand here quietly and wait to see if some young guy tries to make a move on him.

"You guys made dick shaped cookies?" the delivery driver asks Kellan.

Kellan hiccups loudly and takes a sip of his eggnog. "Yep, we sure did. You want one? They don't have any cum on them yet," he says with a laugh.

"Oh, I don't think I want—" the driver says.

He stops talking mid-sentence, as I walk over and kiss Kellan on the cheek, then extend my hand for the brown paper bag. "Thanks," I say as he passes it to me.

"When did you get over here?" Kellan asks me, looking confused.

"Shhh," I whisper in his ear. "We're all set. Thanks again. You have a good night," I tell the driver, while closing the door. "And you," I start. "You don't answer the door when you've had probably four glasses of eggnog." I give his cheek a playful pinch.

He giggles then takes the bag of food from me, walking toward the kitchen table. "There's barely any alcohol in that eggnog," he says, placing the bag onto the table. "Besides, if I was drunk, I wouldn't have noticed what just happened." He pulls the plastic trays and utensils out and places them on the table.

"What did you notice?" I ask him.

"Sit first," he says, pulling out my chair.

"You too, " I say pointing with my chin at the seat across from me.

"You were jealous!" he says, laughing loudly. "You were so, so jealous!"

"Uhh, why are you saying that like it's new to you? I've always been jealous, that didn't change because we grew up. Of course, I was jealous. I want to keep you all to myself, I won't apologize for that." I take the lid off my container, damn, this chicken smells delicious.

"Were we both jealous?" Kellan asks.

"Well, you were jealous all the time, for me it's always been there, but it's definitely kicked up a notch these past few days." I try to take another bite of my food, but my cheeks are being smooshed together in Kellan's hand.

"I like you being jealous," he says, kissing my mouth.

"Mmm, that's good because I don't see that changing. The rest of the world has had you for the past twelve years, I don't want to share you anymore."

He smiles and kisses me on the cheek. "No one else ever had me. Who would have wanted me?" he asks.

Oh, he is definitely drunk.

"What are you talking about? Lots of guys wanted you from what I saw. Don't make me think about it," I say, taking a few more bites of my food.

"I only cared that *you* didn't want me. I didn't really care about any other guys. I was so desperate to find someone to take care of, just to prove that I could do it." He lies his head on his arms on the table.

I don't really understand what he's talking about, but I don't think he does either. "You're tired, baby, you're not making sense," I say, ruffling his soft hair.

He picks his head up and stands quickly from his seat. "The dicks are done!" he says. He doesn't seem too steady on his feet, walking around the back of the counter.

"You didn't eat any of your food, Kellan. We can put the cum on the cookies later, bring your cute butt over here and sit down."

He's staring at me. He looks so freaking cute. "I want a cookie, though," he says, pouting. "I just want to put frosting on it, then I'll sit down." He grabs the white frosting that we made and a spare spreading knife out of the drawer. "Come make one with me," he says, holding a dick shaped cookie up. I reluctantly join him, standing beside him at the counter.

"Let's see what you got, show me how you decorate the cookie," I say. He picks up one of the cookies and brings it to his lips, licking it the way that he licks me. "Naughty! Kellan, you know I love your filthy little tongue, but please, you gotta stop," I say, giggling.

He's licking the cookie up and down, while giving me the sexiest look I've ever seen. How can someone look sexy when they're licking a freaking dick shaped cookie? I have no idea but it's happening right in front of me. I can't have sex with him tonight though, he may be horny, but there's no way he isn't tired from that peppermint sex we had earlier. I walk over toward him and bite the cookie that he's holding. "No more sexy stuff," I say, with a mouthful of cookie.

He's staring at the cookie, and his mouth is wide open. "When did you become such a tick in the mud?" he asks me with a pout.

"A tick in the mud? What's a tick in the mud?" I laugh, because he's had way too much eggnog, and his words are slurring together at this point. I slide a vanilla bowl of frosting toward him. "Here, decorate this for me. I want to see your skills."

He pulls his mouth to the side and reaches for the eggnog glass that he set down just a moment ago. "I'm gonna fish this first—" he says, followed by a hiccup.

Oh man, drunk Kellan is too cute. I can't help but to tease him a bit. "Now, you don't like fish, you told me so. You want to add fish to your eggnog? Sounds kind of gross," I say.

"I hate fish, I don't want fish," he says with a scowl. He downs the rest of his eggnog then wipes his mouth. "Alright, let's decorate some dicks," he says, reaching for the white frosting.

I smile at him and grab a sweater shaped cookie. I paint the green frosting on it, then add some red details. His eyes are wide looking at my cookie. "Is there actually anything you aren't good at? No matter what we do, it's always easy for you." He smears a giant glob of vanilla frosting on the head of the cookie and laughs.

I put the frosting down and stand behind him, I kiss his cheek from the side, leaning around him. "You are good at everything. I just pretend, so it looks like I know what I'm doing."

"Hah! No, no, you've always been this way." He turns around to face me. "Just naturally talented. Even with that," he says, pointing at my crotch. "You probably didn't even have awkward sex once in your life. It's probably always been good."

"Um, not accurate. But I'd rather not talk about that." I squeeze him tightly.

He mumbles something against my chest. I can't understand him, honestly, he feels half asleep in my embrace.

"What did you say?" I ask lifting his chin.

"Huh?" he asks. "I didn't say anything, did I?"

He doesn't even remember.

"Oh, cookies, we were decorating cookies! Tomorrow is BJ's cookie decorating! Are you excited?" he asks me.

"As excited as I can be," I say. I reach for the cookie he decorated. These cookies really look so dirty and with the white frosting globbed on the tip, they feel especially X-rated.

"Look at this cookie you made, it's perfect!" I hold the cookie to his mouth, and he takes a bite.

"Mmm, this is delicious," he says.

Earlier, we'd turned the TV on to the Christmas channel that played non-stop movies in between Thanksgiving and Christmas. A loud "Ho ho ho" blares loudly from the living room.

"Ahhh, should we finish watching the movie?" he asks.

"We can watch, if you don't feel like decorating any more cookies," I say. "You also didn't even touch your dinner."

He shakes his head no. "Not really hungry."

He's so tired, his eyes are half closed. "Okay, how about I put this stuff away and you go lie down? We can watch the movie or just call it a night. How about that?"

"Okay," he says, heading for his bedroom.

A few minutes later, the door opens, and his sister Charlie enters the condo. "Hey, Braden," she whispers.

"Hi, Charlie, why are you whispering?"

"Oh, it's after ten and I don't see my brother, I assume he's slee—" She looks around the kitchen, noticing the eggnog. "I assume he's passed out."

"He's tired, he just went to lie down; did you need him for something?"

She waves me off. "No, no…oh my God, are these dick cookies?" She takes a few pics with her phone, laughing. "Only you two would make these," she says.

"Yeah, we didn't get to decorate all of them, but that's alright." I finish putting the cookies in a container and start heading for the bedroom. Charlie is nice, but we don't really have anything to talk about. Besides, I should check on Kellan to make sure he isn't passed out in the bathroom.

"Oooh, whose Chinese is this? It's not even opened!" she says, pulling the container from the fridge.

"That's Kellan's, he didn't eat it. He had a bunch of eggnog and didn't seem to want to eat that. Which is funny since he was the one that wanted to order it."

"Yeah, that sounds right," she says, placing the container in the microwave and heating it up. "Kellan has four modes when he's drunk: super tired, super flirty, super loud, or super melodramatic. Which one did you hang out with?"

I laugh. "Well, I think Kellan was pretty much all of those tonight. His alcohol tolerance is lower than I thought, even though he drank almost the entire bottle of eggnog, it shouldn't have been enough to make him that drunk."

"Oh wow! Where did you guys get this eggnog from? The liquor store is nearly always sold out! Did you have some of this?" she asks me.

"Yeah, a little, we stopped and grabbed it on the way back. Kellan seemed to think it was a big deal, too. Tasted like regular eggnog to me." I shrug my shoulders, standing in the hallway near the bedroom.

She laughs loudly. "What type of eggnog have you tried that has this much alcohol in it?" She walks around the counter and passes me the near empty bottle, and I spin the bottle around examining the label. *Cousin Eddy's Eggnog, 30% alcohol by vol.*

"What the hell?" I ask. "Why is there so much alcohol in this? No wonder he's passed out. Well, I assume he's passed out, I haven't gone in to check on him yet." I place the bottle back on the counter and turn back toward Kellan's room.

"He's definitely asleep," she says. "He would've come out here if he wasn't. He likes to be involved in every conversation. He's too insecure to leave me out here with you."

I somehow doubt that he would be worried about the two of us talking in the kitchen. "What do you mean by that?" I ask.

She's digging into the Chinese food, well, Kellan's Chinese food, that is. She's not even sitting down, she's just hunched over the counter, piling the lo mein in. She slurps a noodle and holds a finger up to me, asking me to wait a moment.

"I really should go check on him," I say, while taking a few steps in the opposite direction.

"Wait, sit." She snaps her fingers at the barstool. "Come on, he's passed out, you're not gonna get any conversation out of him tonight. Besides, I want to talk to you about what you've been doing for the past twelve years."

"Ah, well, I was a veterinarian, then left the practice to run the cookie shop. That's really it. Not much more than that." I shrug and take a few more steps toward the bedroom. I really don't want to talk to Charlie. For no real reason other than I have to get up early tomorrow and set up for the cookie decorating event.

"Do you want to know what Kellan was doing for the past twelve years?" she asks, pouring the remaining eggnog into a glass.

"No, that's okay, he's filled me in on everything. He's told me everything he wants me to know." I wave her off and continue toward Kellan's room.

"Braden, I think there are some things we should talk about. I'm not really asking at this point. I want to talk to you about my brother. If it makes you feel better, I'll fill him in tomorrow morning. Come sit on the couch with me."

I don't even know what I'm supposed to do in this situation, but I peek my head inside the room, and Kellan is indeed passed out on the bed.

"Alright, what do you want to talk about?" I ask. Charlie walks toward the couch and sits, pointing to the loveseat across from the couch she's sitting on.

"How did this happen? How did you end up back in his life?" She grabs the gray fuzzy pillow beside her, and Senator Tunacan, followed by Fluffykins, trots over from one of the other rooms.

As soon as I sit on the loveseat, my cat jumps onto my lap. "And where have you been for the past few minutes?" I ask him. He headbutts me affectionately as I give him a few snuggles.

I look over at Charlie. "For your question, I moved back into town, and we started hanging out once I got back, now here we are. Are you…upset? Is there something wrong with me being with him?"

"Not exactly," she says. "Then again, kind of, because you just up and left everything behind. I don't want to get into whatever happened between you guys when you were younger, but I mean, you are kind of what broke him."

I'm gonna take a deep breath before I react to this. "Charlie, we've already talked about everything. Honestly, I never wanted to leave him when we were younger. He was my best friend."

"Then why did you? Why didn't you call him? Do you know how withdrawn he was? How sad he was? His self-esteem just plummeted. It was awful. For probably the whole first year, he just shut down, then he decided he was going to just—I don't know, bang any guy he could. Wouldn't let anyone get close to him. As time went on, he kind of evened out, but now I'm seeing him here, and you're like in his kitchen taking care of stuff—which I'm happy about, but he worked so hard for everything he has, and there are still times that he doesn't feel like things are permanent, like everything he's worked for will just poof away one day. That trauma, that insecurity, stems from you."

"Ignoring the fact that I left for college, and nothing else, you're acting like I did something horrible to him. We were eighteen years old. Wait, are these things he's said to you? Or things that you just think are true?"

She takes a big sip of her eggnog. "Don't worry about it. I really just wanted you to know that he was hurt, because I'm sure that knowing him, he didn't talk to you about his life after you left."

"He did, actually. We talked about everything. Charlie—I love him. I wouldn't do anything to hurt him, and the only way I'm ever leaving him, is if he tells me to."

"Alright," she says, standing up with her glass. "My job here is done. Or one could say, I didn't even have any business talking about this, and my brother is going to screech impossibly loud at me tomorrow. The latter is definitely true." She shakes her head at herself, then leans in for a hug. I offer a half hug and pat her back lightly.

Her phone rings from inside her purse, and she quickly sprints over to grab it.

I give her a playful salute and finally head into the bedroom with the cats following close behind. "Are you guys ready for bed, too?" I ask, looking down. Both cats quickly jump onto the bed, making themselves comfortable beside Kellan, who's on his side clutching a pillow. He's so freaking cute. I want to wake him up and talk to him about what Charlie said, but he looks so peaceful, I should let him rest.

I head into the bathroom and get ready for bed. Even though I know Charlie meant well, I'm slightly bothered by the things she said. It was in the past, but it still upsets me. To think that there was a time when I made him upset and hurt him, it's not a comfortable feeling. It's over though, and we cleared the air, that's what matters.

I climb into bed beside Kellan, spooning him, then plant a kiss on his cheek. He scoots back closer into my arms. "Mmm—you're so warm," he whispers. "Where are your feet?" he asks, as his socked feet move around the bottom of the bed.

I move my feet near his, rubbing them together. "Right here. See?"

His eyes are closed but he's pouting, full on pouting. Even has a little scowl about him.

I squeeze him tightly. "What's wrong? What are you pouting about?"

"Nnnn…I can't feel your feet. I just want to feel your feet near mine."

"Your feet are touching mine; can't you feel this?" I ask, rubbing my feet against his.

"Nooooo, I can't," he whines. I couldn't love this man any more than I do. This pouty version reminds me so much of our younger days. I pull my arm out from under his body and duck underneath the blanket and sheet, moving my head down by his feet. If I pull his socks off, he'll be able to feel my feet beside his. I grab the top of his sock, and his foot jerks upward.

"Ahhh!" he screams.

"Shh! It's just me, stay still, baby, you almost kicked me in the face." I gently tug his sock down.

He's mumbling, but the sound is muffled since I'm underneath this thick blanket. "I don't want to do feet stuff...no feet stuff. Okay, if you want to, Bray...I'll do whatever you want. Just don't leave me again."

I pull the other sock off quickly and move back up beside him, embracing him with every ounce of love I can. I place my feet in between his and rub them together.

"Kellan." His eyes open when I say his name, but he can't seem to focus, so he closes them again.

"Hmm?" he asks.

"I am never going to leave you." He's not saying anything, but he could just be asleep again. How am I supposed to feel hearing him say that? I don't want him to ever think I would leave him. He needs to know that I won't. When he wakes up tomorrow, I need to talk to him about what Charlie said. The last thing I want is for him to feel any insecurity when it comes to us. I squeeze him tighter and close my eyes.

His body trembles a bit, and a tiny sniffle breaks the silence. "Pinky promise?" his sleepy voice asks.

A pinky promise...something so small, somehow means everything to me in this moment. I link my pinky with his, while keeping him tightly pressed against me, rubbing our feet together. "I promise." At my words, his body completely relaxes. He's definitely fallen asleep again. I kiss the back of his neck, and close my eyes, while our cats snuggle up against each other by our feet.

Chapter Twelve
Judgy Eyes & Shameful Things

Why did I think this cookie decorating event was a good idea? There are so many people here, and I didn't make nearly enough frosting when we came in early this morning—so I'm currently mixing more by hand, while the mixer works alongside of me. Kellan demanded that I let him help me after we talked about what happened with Charlie. He felt the need to apologize, which only made me feel worse. I certainly wasn't upset with Charlie for doing that, I was upset with the version of myself that ever thought I could live without this man. Kellan, on the other hand, was not happy with his sister. Luckily for her, she was asleep when we left this morning. He'll have cooled off by the time we see her later at my nonna's Christmas party. I'm really looking forward to this day being over, and finally getting to the party, and not just going there, but having Kellan with me—holding his hand and introducing him as my boyfriend. This may sound cheesy, but I can't wait to do every couple-y thing with him, including kissing under the mistletoe. I want everyone to know that he's mine.

"We need more vanilla frosting for this table," Kellan shouts over to me. He wipes his brow with the back of his hand. He's working so hard, and he really needs to go back to his own shop.

"I got it, it's almost done, just a few more strokes!"

His eyes widen, and he comes toward me quickly. He covers his mouth with his hand, it looks like he's trying to stifle a laugh.

Oh yeah, he's definitely holding in a laugh. "What? I said I was almost done with it."

He shakes his head at me. "Please don't shout the word 'strokes' across the store." He places his hands on his hips, sucking his lips in.

"What else do you want me to say?" I ask through laughter. "I could say I just have to beat it a little more, or I'm beating it as fast as I can. Would either of those be better?"

"Stop, stop, stop," he says, holding his stomach, laughing loudly.

I love that after all these years, his laugh still sounds the same. It's adorable.

"No, Braden! Don't say beat or stroke! My mind instantly thinks dirty things!"

I shrug my shoulders. "That sounds like a *you* problem." I give the frosting one more mix and scoop with the spoon to check the consistency. "Oooh, look at all the thick, white, delicious—"

He places his hand on my mouth. "Shush! Stop! I can't take it. You're gonna make me hard and my jeans are too fucking tight for that. You said no sex until after the party, so don't tease me and get this started," he says pointing at his crotch.

"I make the stupidest rules, you really shouldn't listen to me." I really want to kiss him, but there are about twelve people waiting for frosting, and I need to go help them.

"Boys, we need that frosting!" my mom shouts from the register.

I pick the finished bowl of frosting up and quickly kiss his cheek. "Thank you. Now, you need to go back to your shop—you've done enough. Really, you helped me so much. I couldn't have done this without you."

"I can stay a bit longer—"

"No, I mean it. Now that the frosting is mixed, the rest of the day will be easy!"

"Okayyy…" he says, looking around the baking space then back to me. He's standing in the same spot. He agreed to leave, but hasn't moved an inch.

A loud beep sounds from the mixer, signaling that the red frosting is done.

He quickly turns toward the storage cabinets, pulling four bowls out, then removes the large bowl from the mixer. "Let me just separate this, then I'll go. I want to do this for you. Please?"

"Ah, giving me puppy dog eyes when you're wearing a cute Christmas sweater seems like a dirty move. You don't play fair."

"Rarely," he says, already scooping the frosting into the bowls. "I'm going to fill these extra fast, then I'm out the door, and I'll see you on our lunch break. We can grab something light from the cafe, maybe? Your nonna always makes so much food for her parties, we don't want to fill up, but we can't wait to eat until then."

My mom comes around the corner, pulling her glasses off the top of her head, and throws her hands up in frustration. She shakes her glasses at me. "What is taking you so long?!" she shouts. She glances at Kellan, then back to me. "And you stole my helper too! Kellan, come on, chop chop. You boys are back here swooning over each other, when people are waiting. We need that frosting," she says, turning on her heel. She spins back around and takes the bowl from me. "Why didn't you separate this? Look at Kellan—he knows it needs to be put in bowls. Who owns the store, you or him?"

She flings open a cabinet pulling out a few smaller bowls and aggressively slaps the frosting into each one. Kellan is trying hard not to laugh. I don't know what he's thinking about, but this certainly reminds me of my tenth birthday when Kellan and I were helping in the kitchen. My mom was making chocolate pudding "dirt cups".

She tasked us with one job each—Kellan was supposed to place two gummy worms in the bottom of each cup, then I was supposed to scoop pudding into each one. We made a huge mess. It was mostly my fault, because Kellan loved the red and clear gummy worms the best, so I told him we'd try to avoid using those, so he could eat them. We decided to hide those in his pockets and ran out of gummy worms. My mom grabbed the cups from us, of course she was laughing, but she was just rapidly stuffing extra cookie crumbs into the cups to make up for the lack of gummy worms, then adding spoonfuls of pudding on top of each one.

Kellan shakes his head at me, while giggling. He grabs a tray out from underneath the counter and places his bowls on it. My mom adds her bowls to the tray and gives him a smile. "Thank you, Kellan," she says, then gives me a look on her way back toward the front of the store.

"You're in trouble," he says, hanging his arms around my neck and pulling me in for a hug.

I kiss his forehead and pull him in by the waist. "If I'm in trouble, then why are you laughing? It's not very nice to laugh at your boyfriend."

He nuzzles his head into my chest. "I was just remembering something funny, from one of your birthdays."

He remembered. I lift his chin up by two fingers. "I think me helping you stuff your pockets full of worms was a pretty brazen declaration of love."

"Oh my God, I can't believe you were thinking of it, too," he says. "That was your tenth birthday party."

"Twenty years ago…weird that I can remember that day, but not what I had for lunch yesterday."

"Well, I definitely remember it," he says. "You asked the other day when I knew—when I knew I had feelings for you; I'd say it was then. Although some people would argue those were just kid feelings, I can remember thinking as you shoved the worms in my pockets that I wanted to share the worms with you. I wanted to make you happy, too. Something about that moment changed the way I felt about you. So, yep, we were ten when I realized I liked you."

I hold his face in my hands and plant a quick kiss on his lips, rubbing my thumbs on his cheeks. I can't find the right words to say. I think that's the cutest thing I've ever heard. I really had no idea he was feeling that way back then. How could I ever have doubted him? How was I so oblivious?

"Ahh, now I'm kind of embarrassed," he says, tucking against my chest. "That probably sounded so stupid. Saying I fell in love with you at ten years old, all because of gummy worms. You know, I haven't eaten them since we were kids. Whenever I saw them at the store it was always kind of a mixture of really complicated feelings that I just didn't want to deal with. I really am a ridiculous person."

"No, baby, you're perfect. I'm sorry I made you hate gummy worms."

He laughs and shakes his head. "I don't hate them. Sometimes I loved seeing them, because they reminded me of you, other times I would shove the bags behind the other candies at the store. Kind of rude of me, now that I think about it."

"Braden Anthony Jaeger!" my mom shouts around the corner.

"Oh, I am actually in trouble now," I say, patting his ass. "You gotta go, and lunch sounds great. I'll come by around twelve and we can head over to the cafe together. I love you."

"I love you, too. See you in a bit. If your mom gets to be too much, or if you need hel—"

"Shush, no more offering to help. If you stay here any longer, I'm gonna get grounded, and we won't be able to go to the party," I joke.

"Alright, I'm going," he says, finally separating from the hug and heading out the door.

"It's about time," my mother says. She whacks me with a towel behind the counter. I watch Kellan walking back to his shop, he has the biggest smile on his face.

"After you," I say, holding the door open to Sticky Bunz Cafe. Kellan walks inside and looks around at the extremely packed cafe. He has to be thinking the same thing as me, there are no empty tables in sight. This is going to take much longer than an hour. It smells like freshly baked cinnamon buns in here, and I'm really hungry. The cafe serves breakfast and lunch, but most people seem to order breakfast from what I can see. There are two people standing in front of us, waiting to be seated. I nudge Kellan with my elbow lightly, and whisper, "Do you want to stay and wait? I don't know how soon a table is going to open up."

He stands on his tippy toes scanning the restaurant. "I just need to find Manuel; he knows down to the minute how long it will take. He's like a machine, *literally* down to the minute, knows how much time it will take someone to finish eating."

I drop an eyebrow at him. "Come on, I seriously doubt that. How could he possibly know that?"

Kellan shrugs at me. "I have no idea, but I think it's because, aside from the tourists, he knows everyone's patterns. He's been running this place for thirty years, I guess he just picked up on things."

I feel a hand on my shoulder and turn to see Manuel, smiling brightly. "Excuse me, boss, I gotta slide past you to get to these people," he says to me. I step to the side allowing him to pass. He walks around to the host stand, and pulls out two menus, then greets the pair in front of us. "Hello, welcome! You two aren't from around here. I'm Manuel, welcome to Sticky Bunz. Is it just the two of you this afternoon?"

"Yes, hi, I'm Trista and this is my brother Trent. We're here for the Snowflake Festival. Just got into town this morning."

"And, yeah, it's just the two of us," her brother chimes in.

Manuel smiles and points to Kellan. "That man behind you is the Snowflake Princess," he tells them.

Kellan's eyes are wide, seemingly in shock that he was brought into the conversation, but he's forcing a smile. "Hello, I'm Kellan, Snowflake Princess by default," he says, extending his hand to the pair.

"I wouldn't say by default," Manuel says. "The town's usual Snowflake Princess; that guy's grandmother"—he points to me—"was injured, so the local business owners voted for Kellan to take her place. He's done a great job."

"It's nice to meet you, I'm Trista, and this is my brother, Trent." She shakes Kellan's hand, then mine. "I'm sure you both overheard our names a minute ago, but it would be rude not to properly introduce ourselves. I just love your sweater, that little Christmas kitty is so cute," she says to Kellan.

Her brother smiles and shakes our hands. "Good to meet you both."

"These guys also run two of our most successful businesses in town!" Manuel adds.

"Oooh! Which businesses are they?" Trista asks Kellan.

Kellan answers with a smile. "He runs BJ's cookies, it's our most popular business. Most people come into town just to get an order of their famous made-from-scratch cookies."

My heart is so full, watching Kellan brag about me. But I can't take credit for anything at the shop. I only just started there. The legacy, the recipes, and all the history belong to my great grandparents. Kellan is the one that's impressive.

"Oh, I'm looking forward to trying those," Trent says. "Do you make them by hand? I mean with your hands?" he asks me.

"Yeah, I do. But it was my great grandparents' shop, long ago, so I just got lucky. Kellan, actually, owns the most impressive business in town."

"Ooh, which one is it?" Trista asks. She places her hand on Kellan's shoulder and turns her body in between the two of us. Seemingly trying to block me from their conversation. With that gesture, she basically told me that my input is not needed.

Her brother rolls his eyes and looks at me. "Which shop is it?"

Kellan shakes his head at the sister and steps backward. "It's just a little candle shop," he says, being far too modest. He really has no idea how accomplished he is. I am so proud of what he's built. I'm not sure if he realizes how amazing he is.

"Oh, that's the shop I most want to see! Ah, I love the name," she says, taking a step closer to him again. "It's Dip Your Stick, no— it's, uh…" She snaps her fingers like she's trying to remember the name, then giggles.

I grab Kellan's hand and pull him close to me. Once his body is beside mine, I hang my arm around his neck and kiss his cheek. "It's called Dip Your Wick. He built the business all by himself, pours all the candles, everything. He had a candle making day yesterday, that was a lot of fun, people loved it."

She smiles at the two of us, and her brother laughs a bit. "Ha! They're together, I knew it! You were being so flirty, too, how embarrassing for you!"

"I was not flirting! You know I wanted to see that candle shop! I told you that was the first place I wanted to go after lunch! Ugh, why did Emma have to get sick? I hate having you here instead of her," she whines.

The brother rolls his eyes. "Emma is her best friend, she got sick right before the trip, so like the good little brother that I am, I stepped in so she wouldn't have to make the trip by herself. Well, that, and she said she'd pay for everything."

Manuel gives a whistle. "I don't want to break this up, but there's a line forming and I have two open tables, so let's go. Kellan, you and Braden take the table over there by the window." He passes us two menus, and then shifts his attention to the siblings. "And for you two, let's head this way."

"Nice to meet you," Trista says. We smile and wave at her, while her brother gives us a nod.

Kellan and I quickly seat ourselves near the large window. It looks cold outside today, and just sitting near the window chills me to the bone, although the heat is definitely on inside the cafe.

"That was fun," he says. He shakes his head and rubs his thumbs together.

I reach across the table and cover his hands with mine. "Kellan, do you know how impressive you are? Do you realize what you've built? What you've done? The Snowflake Festival is tomorrow and you've worked so hard…everything is running perfectly because of you. People are here, in this town right now, visiting from states far away to see your shop, to get one of your candles. They're here for the Snowflake Festival that you put together. I could not be any prouder of you, you've done so much, baby." He covers his face with his hands and shakes his head.

"Thank you," he says, with his face in his palms.

"Alright, I won't embarrass you anymore. You can take your hands off your face." He gives me a big smile, while wiping the corners of his eyes. "Now, tell me what to expect from my nonna's party—besides our mistletoe kiss that is definitely happening, and sex afterward—also happening, what else should I expect?"

"Ooh, lots of games! A bunch of our friends will be there, too!"

"Our friends? Like the high school crew? Or the guys we hung out with at the—"

My phone vibrates in my pocket, and I pull it out, only to silence it. As I press the button on the side, I see that it's Molly, my old business partner at the vet clinic. Shit. This can't be good. As I decide whether to answer the call inside or wait until after lunch, the phone call goes to voicemail.

"What's wrong?" Kellan asks, reaching across the table.

"It's Molly, she wouldn't call unless it was an issue with one of the animals."

"Did you tell her to call you if there was a problem?"

"Mmmhmm. She usually takes the Christmas holidays off and with me leaving at the last minute, she wasn't able to change her plans, so I agreed to be on call for emergencies if something came up."

"Oh, okay. Should you go call her?"

"Nah, she'll leave a voicemail. Actually, she just left one, give me a sec." I listen as Molly explains the current situation in a detailed voice message, then sigh heavily and look at Kellan. "You're not gonna be happy."

"What is it?" he asks. He shuffles in his seat, looking quite concerned.

"Ms. Finch, the one person that I really did not want this to be about—her cat, Walter, is not feeling well. I'm like 99.9% sure this is pancreatitis; in which case he just needs a shot."

"Awww, poor Walter. Why would that make me upset?" he asks, looking over the menu.

"I have to leave, like within the next hour. If I head out now, since it's a four-hour drive, I can be back here by probably 9:00 or 9:30 at the latest. I just won't get to walk into the party with you, and I'll need to miss a bit of it. But the quicker I leave, the quicker I can get back. I'll have to get my mom and dad to fill in for me at BJ's."

Kellan is just staring at me silently.

"You can't come with me, or you'll break my nonna's heart. She's used to having you here every year. Besides, you're the Snowflake Princess, everyone will be expecting you."

KELLAN

I don't want to go, I text Braden. *It's no fun without you.*

Go, Braden texts back. *My nonna is expecting you.*

I let out a groan of defeat.

Braden had planned to come home tonight, and we were supposed to meet at the party, but a bad snowstorm meant the roads were too treacherous to travel. They'll probably plow overnight, and he can come back tomorrow. But for Leora's party, that means either going alone or staying home and sulking.

Well, not really alone, I remind myself. I know everyone who will be there.

I sigh, impatient with myself, and get up off the couch and head toward my bedroom to change.

"Getting ready for Leora's party?" Charlie asks as I pass her bedroom.

"Yeah, I picked out a nice outfit like three months ago. Her parties are like the who's who of Frosty Bottoms; it's an exclusive invite list."

"And she invited you? Me, I can understand, but you?" Charlie jokes, rolling her eyes.

I stick my tongue out at her. "Is Claude still coming in tonight?" Her husband was due to arrive earlier today.

She indicates the window with the thickly-falling snow. "It's still a bit weather-dependent, but yes. He's finally on a flight and should land within the hour. We'll make it to Leora's, too, but we might be a little late."

"I'll save you a drink or two or twelve," I say with a laugh.

"Hey, uh, I wanted to say," Charlie says with a suddenly serious face, "I had a nice chat with Braden last night when you were passed out."

I give her a soft smile. "Yeah, he told me."

"I think he really likes you," she says.

"Well, that's a coincidence, because I really like him, too."

"You're a goofball," she says.

"Oh, I know—thankfully, Braden likes that quality in men!" I laugh with my words as I turn and head down the hall.

I close the bedroom door and pull out the secret box from the back of the closet. The one with the raunchy items of clothing that I only wear to certain engagements. It's where I keep my stuff for the kink parties at the bar—leather jockstrap, neoprene harnesses, chains of all sizes…and that one specific Christmas sweater. Tonight is the night to break that one out.

Of course, the sweater seems to be in the very bottom of the box, but I soon have it pulled out and proceed to unfold it in my arms. *Deck the balls!* the sweater reads. As its central image, there's a nearly-naked man tied up in ropes and straps and suspended from above…upside down. His body somewhat resembles the generic shape of a Christmas tree and a Christmas star—complete with gold sequins—has been placed over the man's crotch, hiding all the goods from prying eyes. Along the straps encasing his body are a series of strings of Christmas lights, which are actual mini strands of lights that hang from the knitted yarn. There's a battery pack under the hem of the sweater and, if the battery still holds a charge…the lights flicker to life, blinking at random intervals.

"Perfect," I say to myself. I chuckle as I think of how Braden might respond to such a sweater, especially when he learns that Leora had found it online and sent me the link in case I was interested. "Doubly perfect," I add.

I quickly change, throwing on a comfy tee and then the sweater on top, pairing it all with a nice pair of dark corduroys. I snap a pic and send it over to Braden with the text: *You're missing all this hotness.* Then I pull down the back of my pants and turn around, taking a pic of my ass in the mirror. I send it over to him with: *You're also missing all this.*

*Mmm…fuck…*comes the reply text. And a dick pic. A big, hard, thick dick pic.

Things going well with your animal client, I see? I tease.

I'm in the bathroom, staring at the pic of your ass. Cats don't get me hard, but your ass does.

I squat in front of the mirror and with the way my ass cheeks spread, the barest glimpse of my hole is visible. It takes some contorting, but I get a pic of it and send it over to him. *One final shot for you. Now I'm gonna hang out with your grandma.*

There's a silence of a few minutes, and then he sends me one final pic of his cock with a thick load drooling down the sides of it. *I'm gonna fuck you so hard when I get back. Tell my nonna I said hi.*

I pull my pants back up and adjust so my boner isn't as visible, then open my door and exit from my bedroom. The place is quiet— Charlie seems to have left. I find a note on the kitchen island. *Took your car to go pick up Claude. See you at the party!*

While I see my sister infrequently, I see Claude even less than that. I'm looking forward to seeing him again; he's one of the few straight men that can hold my interest. Of course, I'll never repeat that compliment in the presence of my sister. Brothers don't roll that way.

I throw on my nicest boots and my dressy winter coat, then set out in the night to walk over to Leora's. The night is quiet and cold…and lonely without Braden. I had been so upbeat back at home, but now… Maybe it's because I was sexting with Braden, so in a way it was like he was here, but now my phone is put away, and Braden is likely taking a nap or watching a movie or something, and the distance between us feels vast.

I plaster the brightest smile I can muster onto my face as I climb the stairs at the back of Leora's building. The coded door has been left unlocked, and the door to her unit is wide open. Even from here at the top of the stairs and still outside, I can hear the cacophony of her party. For eighty-something, she really does throw parties that rival those of frat boys.

Passing through the doorway, I shuck my boots in the hallway, letting them pile on the floor next to dozens of others, and hang my coat on one of the many coat racks Leora had set up in the little hallway.

Big band renditions of Christmas classics come thumping from the open doorway, along with the clamor of dozens of voices and plenty of red and green lights and the smell of Christmas baking and mulled wine. I step into the apartment—the air is overly warm from what appears to be thirty-plus bodies—and I immediately want to go home. Normally, this is my scene, the place I let my social butterfly flutter freely. But tonight, I just want to cuddle with Braden. I imagine him in a hotel room watching a Christmas movie and falling asleep with a bag of chips in his lap. I want to be tucked under his arm, falling asleep with him.

"Kellan!" a friendly voice calls. I turn to my right and find Leora seated on a high-legged barstool that looks suspiciously like something borrowed from Bottoms Up. I give her a big smile—much more genuine than the one I'd attempted upon entering—and walk up to her.

"Great party!" I say, having to almost shout to be heard over it all. "That's quite the throne you've got."

She laughs and pats the barstool. "Lucas brought it over. This way I can stay off my foot, but still be up nice and high—like the Snowflake Princess I am."

I tut at her and wag my finger. "Excuse me, miss, but *I* am the Snowflake Princess. I even have the sweater to prove it."

"Well," she says, adopting her best British accent, "if you're the new Snowflake Princess, that must make me the Snowflake Queen." She gives a royal wave.

I pull her in for a hug. "Merry Christmas, Queen Leora."

"Merry Christmas, twink." When we break from the hug, she says, "I'm sorry Braden couldn't be here. I know he wanted to spend the evening with you."

"I'm disappointed, but I get it. I'd much rather have him a day late and completely safe, than having him try to rush home in this storm and risk those roads. We'll just have to stop by on Christmas Day and have a follow-up celebration and drink with you."

"I'd like that, Kellan," she says. Someone new comes in the door, and she shouts to them in greeting.

I shuffle away from Leora to let her do her hostess duties. Circling the room until I find the food and drink table. I scoop a mug of mulled wine from the crockpot and fill a little plastic bowl with some Christmas themed Chex Mix. And I stand there.

A few people come by and congratulate me on being Snowflake Princess, but those conversations quickly end, and they move on, leaving me standing by myself again. When I spot Chad and Lucas come in, my mood lifts considerably.

Chad leads them over to talk with Leora, but before they do, Lucas and I make eye contact. For a moment I'm a bit nervous; Lucas and I haven't really cleared the air over the things that had been said, though nothing too terrible was said, so I don't know if air-clearing is really necessary. But my fears of awkwardness and uncomfortableness quickly dissipate when Lucas gives me a genuine smile. And after they do their greeting with Leora, Lucas points me out to Chad, and the two of them beeline through the party to me.

Lucas gives me a hug. "Merry Christmas, Mister Snowflake Princess."

"Merry Christmas," I say back. Chad and I then exchange hugs and Lucas doesn't seem to give us any side-eye over that. When their hands find each other's again, I point at their clasped hands and say, "Things seem to be going well with you two?"

Chad smiles and looks at Lucas. "This was unexpected, to say the least, but Lucas is the best thing that's ever happened to me."

Lucas stands on his tip-toes and gives Chad a kiss. "I love you, boo."

"I love you, too," Chad says. "Where's your boy?" Chad asks me, his head swiveling around in search.

"He had to go back to Sandy Butte for an emergency vet thing, and the storm stopped him from coming back today. He should be back tomorrow." I pour more mulled wine into my mug. "So, it's a bachelor night for me."

"Strippers and gambling?" Chad asks.

"If you mean stripping to my underwear when I get home and

gambling if I can stay up till midnight, yes," I say, laughing. Chad and Lucas laugh, too.

"Still," Lucas says, "I'm sorry he couldn't be here tonight."

"Thanks. He should be back in time for the Snowflake Festival tomorrow. Definitely in time for Christmas."

"Gentlemen," says a new voice. Geoff slips an arm around my shoulders. I can smell the mulled wine on his breath; he's had too much. "Merry Christmas to you all. Where's Braden?"

I explain the whole thing over again to him.

"Well," Geoff says, "if you get lonely tonight, you know how to reach me. I can keep you company all night long." He's joking, I think, though he does pull me closer with those words and whisper them in my ear. I think his tongue touches my earlobe. Joke or not, I need to respond.

"Thanks, but in the absence of Braden, I've got dildos to keep me company. They provide more stimulating conversation than some guys I know."

"Eh, whatever," Geoff says, finally sliding his arm off my shoulder. "I'm just here for the mulled wine anyway." He quickly fills up a mug and saunters through the place, seeming to look for someone.

"He's on the hunt," Chad says when he sees my concerned gaze. "He's horny and having no luck on the apps, or so he said earlier today."

I roll my eyes. "I can be as horny as the rest of them, but even I know not to proposition a guy in a relationship."

Chad's eyes flare wide. "So, it *is* a relationship? Confirmed, signed, sealed, delivered, all that jazz?"

I give him a sly smile. "You're not the only one who found his perfect match in the past two weeks. Braden becoming my boyfriend is all kinds of right."

Chad scoffs. "I'd hardly call Braden someone you found in the last two weeks! You were so fucking head over heels for him back in high school, and he was all into you, too. The fact that it took twelve years for you two to get over that shit and get together is nothing short of astounding and also really long overdue."

I can feel my cheeks warm with a blush. "Were we really that obvious? I tried to bury it so hard. Braden buried it hard, too, since I didn't even know until we—" I cut myself off.

Chad leans in. "Until you what?"

"We, uh," I take a sip of mulled wine, "kissed at eighteen."

"What?!" The party silences down for a moment and everyone looks at us. Chad doesn't seem to care or even notice. "You kissed Braden at age eighteen and I'm only finding out now, twelve years later?"

"I don't kiss and tell."

Chad rolls his eyes. "Kellan…"

"That's bottoming and telling. This is kissing and telling. It's different."

"You're moving away from the point. You kissed Braden twelve years ago. This isn't a new *finally-they're-together* thing, this is a reuniting. This is a second chance romance," Chad says. "This is the stuff they write romance books about."

It's my turn to roll my eyes. "No one wants to read a romance book about me and Braden."

"You and Braden?" says a new voice. I turn to find Charlie and Claude here; he looks a little tired from the nearly-day-long commute thanks to the storm. Claude points at me, "You and Braden are shacking up?" He turns to Charlie. "Your brother finally found someone and you didn't tell me?"

Charlie pats his arm. "I was going to fill you in later."

Someone behind me gasps. I turn to see Belinda and Andrew,

and she has her hands over her mouth. "Really?" she says. "For real real? The otter masks worked?"

"They mate for life," Andrew says.

I turn back around and roll my eyes. "Is my love life really the talk of the town?"

"Yes, it is!" Leora shouts from across the room, throwing me two thumbs up at the same time. How she'd heard me through all the chaos of the room, I don't know.

Thankfully, my time being scrutinized by family and friends and interrogated about my relationship status soon comes to an end—or at least a pause—when Leora declares it's time for the Christmas games. She launches into a series of *Minute to Win It* style games, with the first being the Cookie Drop.

Chad shoves me forward, volunteering me to compete. I decide to play along and sit in a chair, as do several other people. Leora hands out beautifully decorated Christmas cookies that I recognize as Braden's handiwork, giving me a momentary pang over him not being here with me.

When Leora declares the game is on, I lean my head back and place the cookie on my forehead. By shifting our face muscles—and in the process making facial expressions that have the crowd laughing uproariously—we have to get the cookie from our foreheads into our mouths, without the use of our hands.

When the cookie lands in my mouth, I throw my hands up in victory. I'd won!

For the next game—for which I step far away from Chad so he can't volunteer me to play—Leora fills her sink with water. She then pulls out a box of shrink-wrapped peppermint sticks. The same kind that Braden shoved up my ass the other day. Was this the same box of them? How the hell did it get here? God, I hope we threw *that one* out.

This time, Chad steps forward to compete, and I see Lucas's hand at his back, pushing him forward. Leora dumps the sticks in the sink and gives Chad thirty seconds to pull out as many as he can with his mouth. He gets an impressive seventeen. Three other people compete, with Chad's seventeen being the victorious number.

And on the games continue into the night. And when the games stop, everyone mingles. With Chad and Lucas and Charlie and Claude and Belinda and Andrew, I don't feel as alone as I was feeling at the start, but I'm still really missing Braden.

When the party starts winding down—at a respectable hour since the host is eighty-plus and likes to go to bed early—I stumble through the streets back to my condo. I've had more than my share of mulled wine.

Both Senator Tunacan and Mister Fluffykins rush to the door to greet me when I enter. I sit on the floor and give them both lots of attention. I snap a pic of the three of us and send it to Braden. He replies with a pic of himself in his underwear on the hotel bed with takeout packaging scattered beside him.

I know I should control my cock better, but seeing those thick thighs of his has me stiffening.

What are you doing? I text him.

Just lounging. Missing you. And your ass.

I smirk at that. I get up and pour myself a glass of eggnog. Then I text him back.

If you were here, you could manhandle my ass.

Don't put thoughts in my head. You'll get me in a naughty mood.

My sister's not here. I wouldn't mind a naughty mood. Charlie and Claude are apparently going out for a late-night date with appetizers and drinks and will likely be out for at least another couple hours.

How slutty are you feeling?

I take a pic of my hand holding the eggnog. *I've had mulled wine and now I'm into eggnog. Sober-ish but feeling loose.*

We can make you loose, alright...

My cock hardens, and my heart thuds with anticipation. *What do I need to do...sir?*

Go to your room. Get naked. Prop up your phone. And then video call me.

I just about fucking run down the hall to my room. I put the eggnog on the dresser and quickly strip everything off.

Senator Tunacan comes wandering in. "Oh no. No. You can't stay in here," I tell him. "I don't want your judgy stares as I do shameful things."

He blinks slowly at me with what I can only interpret as disgust. Thankfully, he turns around and struts out of the room. I close the door to keep him and his step-brother out and to also give me a bit of privacy if Charlie and Claude come home early.

I prop my phone up on a chair next to my dresser and video call Braden. He answers on the first ring.

"Good boy," he says when the video feed kicks in, and he sees my fully naked body. Then he smiles. "I miss you, Kellan. I wish I was there with you."

"I miss you, too," I say.

Then the smile fades and what I now recognize as his assertive sex face appears. "Turn around, let me see that glorious ass of yours." I do, then he says, "Spank it for me. Ten times."

I spank myself. I put full effort into it because I know it will turn Braden on. I'm gasping in pain at the sharpness of the spanks I'm giving myself. "It feels good, sir."

"Good boy. I love that you're so obedient."

I turn back around and see that the video feed on his end is shaking a lot; he's taking off his underwear and tossing it aside. "I'm naked now, Kellan. And I'm so hard for you."

"Show me," I beg.

He taps his phone, and the feed switches to his other camera. In his hand, he has his thick, hard, veiny cock. Precum gathers at the tip and then rolls down the head. The feed switches back to the one focused on his face.

"Touch yourself, baby," he says. "Play with that cock of yours."

I take my cock in my hand and stroke it slowly. I'm so achingly hard and just looking at Braden is turning me on immensely. "I miss you," I say. "I want you to fuck me so bad."

"Suck on a finger," he orders. I stick a finger in my mouth and suck it. "Now slide it in your ass."

I turn around to give him a good view as I take my spit-slicked finger and rub at my hole, softening it, relaxing it, and then press at the center until it relents and lets me in. Slowly, my finger sinks to full-depth. I gasp in pleasure.

"Finger-fuck yourself."

I do as ordered, jamming my finger back and forth, shoving it in deep, hitting my prostate.

"Two fingers now."

I pull my finger out completely and spit on my hand, slicking up that finger and an additional one, then work on getting them in. Now that my ass is loosened a bit, it seems eager to accommodate more, because it takes little effort to get a second finger in. Soon, Braden has me stick a third finger in.

"You're so fucking hot," Braden says, his words coming through as an urgent whisper over the phone. "I want you so fucking bad."

"Show me your cock," I beg.

He switches cameras, and I watch as he jerks his cock furiously.

The head is dark and thick, and his breath comes in shuddering waves.

"I'm close," he whispers.

"Me too," I say with a whimper. My balls are already tightening against my body.

"Let me come first. You don't come until I tell you," he says.

I whimper again. "Yes, sir."

"Call me Bray," he begs.

"I want your cock, Bray. I need your cum. Give it to me, Bray."

"Ohh…*fuck*…" Hot, white cum jets from his dick, splattering on his stomach and pelvis. Spurt after spurt paints his skin white. He lets out several shuddering breaths. "Fuck, that was intense. Somehow you do that to me. Even when we're not in the same city, you do that to me."

Seeing his load shoot out almost has me shooting my own. It's only with all my self-restraint that I'd loosened my grip a bit and slowed my stroking so I don't go careening over the edge like he had done. I don't have permission yet.

The camera switches back to focus on him. "Are you ready to come?"

"Yes, sir," I say, my words tumbling out with urgency. "May I come, sir?"

"Not yet. I want you to come in something. What do you have?"

I pick up my half-drunk eggnog glass. "I have this. Would this do?"

A dark look crosses his face, followed by a smile I'm not sure I should trust. "That'll do. Come for me, Kellan. Come."

I hold the glass down in front of my dick and stroke furiously. I've been so close to losing it for several minutes now; holding off till now has been near torture. The pressure in my balls has built to unbearable levels and when I allow my body to do what it wants to do, it's like fireworks are going off behind my eyes. My whole body spasms as pure erotic bliss overtakes me and cum rockets from my dick and into the eggnog glass. My orgasm hits me with wave after wave of electricity and with each surge a new blast of cum shoots into the glass.

When it all eventually subsides, I'm struggling to catch my breath and blinking furiously to try and clear the stars. When sight fully returns, I find Braden giving me the hottest stare I've ever seen from him.

"Impressive," he says. "Good boy."

"Thank you, sir," I say.

"Now…drink it."

My eyes go wide, and I look at the glass and then at him. "Bray?"

The camera jostles as he rolls over onto his stomach, and he hovers over it like he's on top of me in bed. "If you want to be a good boy, you'll drink your eggnog. You want to be a good boy, don't you?"

Every time he calls me a good boy, it makes the butterflies in my stomach go wild. I look at the glass in my hand; cum has splattered on the inside of it, but the rest of my load is presumably in the eggnog and indistinguishable—visually, at least. I shrug; I'd eaten more than my share of cum over the years and certainly drank eggnog.

"Bottoms up," I say, putting the glass to my lips and tilting my head backward. The last of the eggnog—and my load—pours into my mouth and then I swallow it down. It's only slightly noticeable, and it isn't bad. I hold up the empty glass for the camera. "All done."

"Good boy," Braden says. Then he rolls onto his back and holds the camera above him, so I'm looking down on him. "Let's get in bed now. I want to cuddle and this is the best we can do."

I pull my underwear on, then grab the phone and head into bed, slipping in under the covers. We talk for over an hour, with most of our conversation being about how much we miss each other. When he struggles to keep his eyes open, we say our goodnights and end the call.

I get out of bed and brush my teeth. Throwing on a robe, I go and tidy the house to end off the night. As I'm headed back to my room to go to bed, Charlie and Claude come in. I bid them goodnight, then retreat to my bed.

Senator Tunacan and Mister Fluffykins are both there, waiting for me. They're laying against each other, with my boy on top of Fluffykins. I climb onto the bed and lay on my side next to them, my feet resting on my pillows.

"Hi, boys," I say. "How are you two?" I stroke one cat's back, then the other, going back and forth. Pretty soon they're both purring loudly. "Do you two like being brothers?"

As if they understand what I'm asking, Fluffykins starts grooming the back of Tunacan's head. Between the attention from me and from his step-brother, my cat seems to be in total and complete bliss.

"Do you maybe want this to be permanent?" I ask. Fluffykins continues grooming Tunacan. I kiss both of them on the head. "Goodnight, boys."

I snuggle under the covers, and my feet instinctively go in search of the warmth of Braden's feet. But, of course, his feet aren't there. I sigh and roll over.

Chapter Thirteen
Mistletoe & Gummy Worms

 **Kellan**

It's the day of the Snowflake Festival—the culmination of two weeks of activities, but also the end of my duties of dealing with every tiny detail that fully grown adults seem incapable of handling on their own. All I have to do is get through today.

It doesn't help that I didn't sleep the best. When my alarm goes off, I reach for Braden, only to hit empty space and the cold remembrance that he's out of town and will likely be back sometime today.

When I roll onto my back and sigh, it catches the attention of a cat. Mister Fluffykins hops onto the bed and gracefully walks across the mattress to me and then onto my chest.

"Your daddy will be home soon," I tell him, petting him on the head as I do so.

The past two weeks have been a whirlwind of life-changing emotions. Pre-Braden, I felt relationships were not for me, and all I needed was Grindr and an active social life. But now with Braden in my life, I feel like everything I've ever thought to be true about me and my life has been turned upside down.

I'm feeling things for Braden I've never felt for anyone before. Well, that isn't quite true. I've felt them before…*for Braden*…when we were eighteen. That kiss we'd shared hadn't just rocked my world because it was my first kiss with a boy, it was because it was with

Braden, someone I'd come to really be attracted to. He was my first and only crush. Yes, in the years since then, I'd felt all sorts of sexual feelings for all sorts of men, but none of them measured up to Braden. And none of them made me feel what I felt for him back then…and what I feel for him now.

Fluffykins settles in on Braden's pillow, and I pick up my phone from the nightstand. Time to see what chaos awaits me the moment I get out of bed.

"Starting off strong with some good news," I mumble. Santa is feeling better—turned out to be mild food poisoning and not something contagious or something that would knock him out for a week. So, he was back in to lead the parade.

"And with more good news," I say. The next message is from the church choir. They were supposed to do the caroling at the festival, but due to some internal politics that I just don't get, they'd almost backed out. Thankfully, they were fully in for today.

And that…seems to be it. Other than a few emails and texts confirming events and vendors and rentals—all of which seem to be proceeding exactly as planned—there's nothing. No crises. No bickering. No petty fights. No pleas for me to alter weather patterns.

I decide to finally get out of bed and face the day. I give both cats kisses on the head before heading into the en suite and taking my morning shower. Afterward, I quickly dress. I hesitate before donning the Snowflake Princess sweater. I really don't want to wear it, but it's tradition. I manage to squeeze it on, though it feels tighter. Surely, the sweater has shrunk, and it has nothing to do with all the Christmas treats I'd been eating this week.

I look up to find the cats staring at me, entranced by the sweater. The overhead light is hitting the rhinestones, and they're sparkling and glittering, drawing the rapt attention of the cats. When I step closer to them and the light shifts against my sweater, it sends glimmers of light across the wall and both cats leap at them, trying to catch the light.

"Boys, boys, boys," I say. "You need hobbies."

I head to the kitchen and grab a cold bagel and make a quick cup of coffee.

"Good morning, lover boy," Charlie says, as she comes out of the spare bedroom and into the kitchen.

"Good morning, dull married sister."

She sticks her tongue out at me and then says, "Last night was fun at Leora's. Shame Braden couldn't be there."

I smear some cream cheese on the bagel. "I had a great time, but, yeah, would have had a better time with him there.

She pauses in that way that our mother does when she wants to shift the topic to something more serious. Then she says, "This thing with Braden…it's *serious*-serious, isn't it?"

My heart swells at that. "Yeah, it is. Like, declare my love for him and live happily ever after kind of serious."

"I saw you…" she says.

"Saw me…what?"

She glances at the island and then back up at me. "When you were eighteen. I saw the kiss."

I stop chewing. My mind can't seem to process that I'm in the middle of breakfast. Instead, all it can focus on is that the biggest secret of my life wasn't exactly so secret.

"I came to find you and, well, I found you deep in the throes of a kiss with Braden. I didn't want you to know I saw you guys, so I quietly went back to the house and then called out like I was looking for you."

"So, you knew…everything. The kiss, the feelings…hell, even the fact that I was gay. I definitely wasn't out by then." I feel a blush warm my cheeks, but I'm not sure if it's shame, embarrassment, or something else.

"I saw, yeah. But I wasn't about to spill my little brother's secret. You had to come out when you were good and ready. And with Braden…well, I definitely wasn't going to gossip about that either." She comes around the island and puts her hands on my arms. "I'm so glad you found your way back to each other. You two would have made a wonderful match back then, but now as adults I feel you're even more of a perfect match than before."

I look down at the floor between us; I can't look in her eyes right now. "Thank you." I don't know if I'm thanking her for the compliment or for keeping my secret, or both. Maybe it doesn't matter.

She pulls me in for a hug. "I'm so happy for you, little brother. I hope you and Braden make each other happy for the rest of your lives."

I hug her back. "Thank you, Charlie."

She pats me on the shoulder as we break from the hug. "Now, go do your princess duties and get Frosty Bottoms in the mood for Christmas."

I give her a salute. "When duty calls, I must answer." I end it with a curtsy, since I'm a princess.

Shoving the remainder of the bagel in my mouth and pouring my coffee into a thermal travel mug, I head out the door, opting to walk downtown. It's a brisk morning, perhaps a touch too chilly for a walk, but the exercise will help me work out the last bits of anxiety and nervousness that remains.

As I walk, I text Braden, *Good morning, cutie.*

The reply is almost immediate. *Good morning, baby.*

I missed you, I text. *My feet got cold.*

I can't wait to warm up your feet tonight.

I hesitate before texting more. There are things I want to say to him, but I feel they're better said in person and not through the cold medium of text messages. Instead, I opt for: *I'm on my way to the Snowflake Festival.* And I attach a selfie of me with my coat open and my glittery sweater sparkling in the sunlight.

He sends me a kissing emoji and says, *You'll be the prettiest princess in the history of the festival!*

As I turn one last corner before entering into downtown, I can suddenly hear the noise of an excited town, eager for the festival. And when I enter into the town square, I can see the crowds of early festival goers. It's still a couple hours before the arrival of Santa, the caroling, and the reindeer petting zoo, but there have to be more than a hundred people here already.

Food trucks with everything from hot chocolate to fried mini donuts to tacos, line one side of the town square. In the center stands the town Christmas tree—which I hope is dildo-free. In front of the tree is the stage for Santa and Mrs. Claus with a pair of grand chairs and a photographer currently setting up his equipment. And to the right are the stands for the choir.

For me, the festival was never about wowing anybody, it's about bringing the town together, to celebrate this special time with our friends, our family, and our neighbors.

As I approach the festival crowds, a familiar face comes through the crowd to me. A face I don't particularly want to see. Geoff. While it wasn't unusual for him to be overly flirty, he'd gone a little too far last night, and it made me uncomfortable.

I try to pretend I don't see him and veer away, but then he calls my name and comes running up to me. "Kellan, wait."

I close my eyes briefly and let out a small sigh. When I open them, he's in front of me, and he looks embarrassed.

"Listen, about last night…" he says. He looks away from me, searching for words.

"Let's just forget it," I say.

"No, I owe you an apology. I'm sorry, Kellan. I'm really not trying to get between you and Braden. I was just a little tipsy from Leora's eggnog and blue-balling it a bit…" His ramble dies down. He shakes his head. "I'm probably making a bigger deal of it than is necessary, but I just don't want you or Braden to feel uncomfortable around me. He's a great guy and I'm so glad you two have finally gotten together."

"Thank you," I say. That apology seems to help, because I can feel the tension in my gut relaxing.

"Can I make it up to you by buying you a hot chocolate or something?"

I smile at him. "I'm okay, but thank you." I'm about to walk away but then stop and turn back to him. "Actually, if you want to help with something…"

"Yes?"

"Could you keep an eye on Morris from the movie theater? Apparently, reindeer get him and his wife in the mood and we don't need to see any of that here. This is a family event."

His eyes are wide. "Oh my God. Uh, sure."

I wink at him. "Thanks, bud."

When I pass through the crowd to Santa's stage in front of the Christmas tree, I find Leora sitting on the edge of the stage.

"How did you get here?" I ask.

She rolls her eyes and points at her crutches propped up against the stage. "I keep telling you I'm not an invalid."

I decide to drop the scolding stare because, really, when I'm eighty-plus, I want to have the attitude that nothing's going to stop me from doing what I want to do. "I'm glad you're here."

She points at my glittering sweater. "I didn't realize you were *that* twinky to fit in my sweater. You do know it's not a mandatory part of the job."

I sigh. "Try telling that to the Chamber of Commerce. They handed me the sweater and everyone wanted me to put it on. It's as much a tradition for the Snowflake Festival as some random kid getting nervous and puking on Santa."

"Kids will be kids," she says. "If I remember right, Braden did that when he was four." After chuckling at the memory, she says, "Braden's not back yet?"

I shake my head. "No, but he should hit the road soon. He wanted to be sure the plows had scraped the highway."

Leora scoffs. "Sometimes he drives like an old lady. He's in a Jeep for God's sake."

I step closer so I can lower my voice. "Anyone bitching and complaining about anything yet today? Any fires that need putting out?"

She shakes her head. "I haven't heard a thing, at least not about *that*."

I squeeze my eyes shut in frustration. "And *what* did you hear about?" I squint an eye open, looking at her like she's the sun.

"Just that the new Snowflake Princess did an impressive job on his first year in the role."

I open my eyes wide. "What? But...everyone complained. About everything. All the time."

She laughs. "You read too much into it. The people in this town like to complain because they like to know someone cares and that they'll be listened to. You did just that—and more. Even Morris was happy when that snowstorm happened on his night, after he explicitly asked you to change the weather. He had nothing but praise for you."

"Really?" To say I'm stunned would probably be an understatement. "I thought everyone was angry and that I didn't measure up to your legacy."

"Now, hold on there," she says, "I didn't say you were *as good as me*. I'm the *original* Princess, after all." She smiles broadly, and it makes her eyes twinkle. "But you're more than adequate."

"Woohoo!" I throw an arm up in the air. "Adequate!"

I'm pulled aside from my convo with Leora by a couple event planners who want to go over the last few details of the morning's festivities. And when we confirm everything—and still nothing seems to be falling apart—it's about time for me to give the welcoming address.

I climb the stairs to the Santa stage, and I can see just how large the crowd has grown. It looks like almost everyone in Frosty Bottoms is here today, along with loads of tourists. Chad and Lucas give me an excited wave from over near the food trucks. I see Geoff standing with his arms crossed and scowling—he's watching Morris and Linda over by the reindeer petting zoo and if I'm seeing things right, Morris's hand is inside some of Linda's clothing. Everyone is here. Except Braden. But he'll be here soon.

"Good morning and Merry Christmas, Frosty Bottoms," I say into the microphone, immediately earning a wave of cheers and applause. The crowd has doubled, if not tripled, since I got here earlier. "Welcome to the annual Snowflake Festival. I know you were expecting Leora up here"—a surge of cheers sounds at her name—"but I hope I make an adequate princess." An almost as large surge of cheers ring out in support. It warms my heart and makes me wonder if Leora wasn't exaggerating, that people were indeed appreciative of the work I did. "To start off the fun for today, I present to you the Frosty Bottoms Community Church Choir!"

The choir, consisting of singers from teenagers to seniors, file onto the risers, and the choir director leads them—and the crowd—into a series of carols. A large screen had been set up next to the choir with the lyrics projected onto them. I feel a flush of panic when I realize there'd apparently been no coordination between the choir director and the IT person, because the verses to the carol were in a different order on the screen…meaning everyone was singing the same song but the choir was singing different verses than the crowd. But when I realize everyone is just having a wonderful time and no one seems to even notice, I crawl back from the edge of panic and just enjoy the moment.

After going through half a dozen carols, the choir breaks into a rendition of *Here Comes Santa Claus*. Everyone knows what that song means. Young children and their families look down Main Street with wide-eyed wonder.

A short procession consisting of the high school marching band playing in accompaniment to the choir, the high school drama club dressed as elves, and a horse drawn carriage bringing Santa, Mrs. Claus, and an enormous bag of prop presents, comes into town square. They do a circle around the festival grounds and then volunteers from the high school football team help part the crowd to allow the band, elves, and carriage carrying Santa and Mrs. Claus to come down through the center of the space and right up to the stage. The band and elves march onto the stage and Santa and Mrs. Claus climb down from the carriage and up the stairs.

"People of Frosty Bottoms!" I shout into the microphone, barely loud enough to be heard over the noise. "I give you the one…the only…Santa Claus!" The cheering from the crowd only increases in volume.

I discreetly leave the stage, letting the experienced team of volunteers take over and corral the crowd. One by one, children come onto the stage to sit on Santa's lap and tell him what they want most for Christmas. Each child has a photo taken that will be then emailed to their parents.

After about fifty children, Santa is looking a little worse for wear, though no kids have puked on him yet. I order a tray of hot chocolates and take them up onto the stage, asking the volunteers to let us give Santa and Mrs. Claus a ten-minute break.

"Thank you," Santa says, after I lead him and Mrs. Claus around the backdrop and away from the crowd. I give both of them hot chocolates and keep the third for myself.

"I don't know how you do it," I say. "There are a couple hundred kids here today."

He smiles, and his eyes twinkle, almost like in that poem. "It's something we do together." He grabs Mrs. Claus's hand and gives it a squeeze. "Looking forward to the Christmas season has always been something that brought us joy, and when the opportunity to play Santa came up…what was that…twenty-eight years ago? Twenty-nine?"

"Twenty-nine, I think," Mrs. Claus says.

"Twenty-nine years. I leapt at the chance and loved it and have done it ever since."

"Wait…" I say, feeling a little mind blown. "You've been Santa for twenty-nine years?"

He nods. "In fact, I remember a little toddler named Kellan who came and sat on my lap every year."

"Oh, yes," Mrs. Claus says. "He was a real cutie. He was always so polite, too. And you always had that other boy with you—Braden."

My cheeks warm with a blush. Braden and I were inseparable for our whole lives. Well, till eighteen anyway. But it seems we're inseparable again. And that gives me warm, fuzzy feelings. I don't want to be separated from him ever again; I want to be his forever, and for him to be mine.

"You've got a look," Mrs. Claus says. "We noticed Braden is back in town…"

"We, uh, we've reconnected," I say. "Perhaps a little closer than we were before."

There's a storybook twinkle in Santa's eye. "If I can make a suggestion, young man…don't let opportunities slip past you. Seize them while you can."

I wonder for a moment just how old this Santa is. My memory of him from years ago was that he looked exactly as he does now. His Santa look is timeless and for a moment I wonder if this is indeed the actual Santa and Christmas magic is real…even if the logical part of my mind reminds me that this is in fact Peter and his wife, Melissa. He's a custodian at the church, and she's an office admin at the high school. Even though they're not really Mr. and Mrs. Claus, I can't help but talk to them as if they are.

"How do I…how do I know if I'm ready for a big change? Like…*big*-big?"

Mrs. Claus looks at Santa, and they share a secret smile. Then she says, "Like my husband said, seize the moment. Don't let it pass you by. If you want it, then you're ready for it."

My heart thunders in my chest as I ponder just what exactly I'm thinking. Do I want to *marry* Braden? Be husbands with him? While I love my single life, I love my coupled life so much more. There's something that being with Braden brings to me and my life that I've simply never found anywhere else. Something I'll never find ever again.

Suddenly, a great cheer goes up in the crowd. I turn and peek around the curtain and Mr. and Mrs. Claus peek, too. Justin, the cop who had come knocking on Braden's Jeep window, is down on one knee in front of his girlfriend. She holds her hands to her heart, gives a tearful and gleeful nod, and then he slips a ring on her finger. He jumps to his feet, and they embrace to even louder cheers.

The sudden longing I feel to do that with Braden becomes overwhelming. Not the doing it in the middle of a crowd for cheers—there's nothing wrong with that, but that's not what has me longing for Braden and suddenly anxious to replicate that—but rather the declaration of love and the commitment to make it lifelong.

It's too soon, I tell myself. It's way too soon to seriously consider something like a proposal. But then I remember what Chad said— this isn't a two-week fling where we're in over our heads. No, this is a lifelong romance that's finally come to fruition. It's years— decades—of closeness, of intimacy in its many forms, and connection. And now, finally, it also means sex and romance.

And that romance never had the "new" feeling to me. It had the comfort of familiarity and security. I love Braden for who he is and how he makes me feel. I love him with every fiber of my being. He's my everything, and I want him to be my forever.

When I eventually pull my head back around the edge of the curtain, I find Mr. and Mrs. Claus watching me, now with a twinkle in both of their eyes. They clearly know what I'm thinking.

"How's it going back here?" a voice says, interrupting my train of thought. I turn to see Alex, the stage coordinator. "Just about ready to go back on?"

Santa nods. "Lead the way, son." He and Mrs. Claus follow Alex, leaving me alone backstage.

What would I even need to propose to a man? Are engagement rings a thing for men? Then I conclude it doesn't really matter what other men do in this situation; this is about me and Braden and no one else. All that matters is that Braden and I love each other.

"Kellan?" a voice intrudes. I realize it's Alex again. "The kids are nearly done." That means I've been here backstage thinking about Braden and how much I want a forever with him for quite some time.

I nod at him. I need to go out and give our concluding remarks. I can sort out this Braden thing later.

Just as I come around the curtain and forward onto the stage, a voice speaks into the microphone, and I stop in my tracks.

"Before I hand the microphone over to Kellan…" Leora says. She's standing on the stage, crutches under her arms, speaking into the mic. "I wanted to take a moment to say how much I absolutely loved working with all of you over the years with the Snowflake Festival. When I hurt my ankle and had to give up being Snowflake Princess for the year, I was devastated. But then Kellan was nominated to be the new Snowflake Princess"—a cheer erupts from the crowd—"and I have to say I have been *so impressed* with him and I know you have, too. I've also discovered this year that I absolutely love being part of the crowd here, just enjoying the magic of the day. And, so, I wanted to take a moment to say that I am officially retiring from being Snowflake Princess and I hope that Kellan will accept the honor of being Snowflake Princess going forward." A *huge* cheer erupts.

Then I see him. He's at the back of the crowd. He's come back. I knew he would. We made a pinky promise.

"And, Kellan," Leora continues, angling to look back at me, "I hope you'll accept this gift."

I keep my eyes locked on Braden; I don't want to look at anything else. I suddenly realize I'm not ready for my plans with him—not *not ready* as in emotionally, but *not ready* as in I still haven't figured out the ring thing, I don't know when I want to ask him or how. Plus, I know he wants a forever with me, but what if he thinks this is too soon?

"Kellan?" Leora says.

I finally snap my gaze over to her and give her my winningest smile. Then I see what she's holding in her hands—her gift.

It's a princess tiara, the one she always wore at the Snowflake Festival. It might be made entirely of plastic, but it glitters in the sunshine like crystalline snowflakes, and it matches the sweater. It's gorgeous. And it's meaningful. She's officially handing me the crown to the queendom.

I walk forward and get down on one knee so she can place the tiara on my head. The crowd cheers even louder when she does. And when I stand back up and my eyes find Braden, I see he's cheering louder than anyone else. I can even hear him over the rest of the crowd.

I love him. I want him. Forever.

BRADEN

"Whoo!" I shout, then whistle loudly, watching as Kellan takes a bow. I am so overcome with emotion at the sight of him, that my eyes tear up a little. Maybe it's because in this moment, I think he can finally feel how much he means to this town, and how much the people here truly depend on him. He is nothing short of perfection standing up there in that ridiculous bedazzled sweater, it's so old and yet somehow it looks adorable on him. Then again, he looks good in anything. Man, I've only been gone for a little over twenty-four hours, and I feel like I haven't seen him in months. Every moment away from him feels like an eternity. I never want to be apart from him. Never again. I want to hold him, but this moment needs to be about him, and all of the work that he put in. He deserves to be celebrated. I stay toward the back of the crowd, and his eyes meet mine, he gives me the most precious smile, one that speaks to my soul. He takes a few more bows, then our eyes meet again, and I give him a come-hither gesture with my finger, along with a smile that simply cannot be controlled. The surge of happiness I feel as he begins to walk toward me is almost inexplicable, it's like my entire body is tingling from head to toe, my heart feels like it may burst out of my chest.

He stands in front of me, looking me up and down, "Mmm you look good, do you have a request for the Snowflake Princess, handsome stranger?"

"Indeed, I do," I say, pulling him into an embrace by his tight little waist. Our foreheads touch, and our eyes lock. Man, direct eye contact with Kellan is so intense. His eyes reflect so much love and trust, and I know that mine must do the same, because in this moment there is only love between us. I kiss him softly, knowing there are far too many people around for any type of intense make out session. I pull back from the kiss and wrap my arms tightly around him. He tucks his head against my neck, and his sparkly tiara bumps my face. I take in the sight with my entire world wrapped in my arms, and I am just overcome with so much pride. I don't think I've ever been proud of another person in my entire life. I've admired people's work before, sure—but pride? No, I haven't. Only him. Kellan is the only one that I've ever felt proud of. "Look at what you did, baby! I am so proud of you! Everyone is having such a great time! This is amazing, Kellan."

"Thank you," he says. "I am so glad you made it. I wanted so desperately for you to be here. I feel like I can finally exhale, like I've been holding in a breath all day, just hoping to see your face in the crowd. Oh, wait," he says, springing back from my arms looking around.

There are so many people here, I couldn't even estimate how many there are. He's just looking around; I have no idea what he's searching for.

"Come on," he says. He pulls me by the hand toward the group of food trucks. "Let's get something to eat, then I wanna show you something at home."

"You were looking for a certain food truck?" I ask. He was looking so intently, I was sure it was something else.

"Oh no, I wanted you to go see Santa, but I think he might be on a break. You'll just have to settle for sitting on my lap later." He gives me a playful wink.

"Real talk, did you sit on Santa's lap?"

"No, definitely not, but I had a nice time with him and Mrs. Claus earlier. They got me thinking about a lot of things. The kind of things that I thought wouldn't ever be possible. Things that I never thought I'd want." He turns toward the window of a brightly painted red food truck. "I love these burgers, is this okay? Or do you want something else?" he asks.

"Oh, a burger would be good. I don't often eat from food trucks. Are these all local people you know?"

"You know them, too. Look closer," he says, pointing with his chin toward the window of Professor Pickles food truck.

It's our old high school science teacher, Mr. Pickles. He looks almost the same as when I last saw him. "Braden! Look at you! I haven't seen you in years!" He yells inside the food truck, "Barry come over here, look who's with the Snowflake Princess."

"I swear, Chris, if you called me out to see some daddy bear, that we know Kellan isn't going to end up with, I swear I'll throw a tomato at you."

Our old gym teacher, Mr. Lewis, appears standing beside Mr. Pickles. "Oh, my goodness. That's not Braden, can't be?"

"Hi, Mr. Pickles, Mr. Lewis, It's really nice to see you both." The music from the DJ is blaring loudly, and they both appear to be struggling to hear me.

"Are you two dating?" Mr. Lewis asks.

Mr. Pickles elbows him. "Of course they're dating, you dolt, they're holding hands, aren't they? Don't think we've ever seen that from the little Snowflake Princess."

Kellan laughs at the two, then turns to me. "They are so ridiculous together. Seems like they're fighting but it's just the way they are."

"I heard you were coming back to take over your grandmother's cookie shop," Mr. Lewis says. "Since we don't live here anymore, we haven't had a chance to see you in action. How are things? Are you here permanently?"

Mr. Pickles pulls a notepad out and looks at Mr. Lewis. "How many questions are you going to ask him? We haven't even got their order yet."

"Ugh, heaven forbid I try to"—he lifts the ketchup—"*ketch up*, with anyone." He laughs at his own terrible pun, while Mr. Pickles appears to try not to laugh.

"Yes, honey, you're very funny. Always the funny teacher. Thank goodness you aren't funny looking—or all of this would never have happened."

Mr. Lewis's mouth is wide open as he picks up a tomato, and tosses it back and forth in his own hands. "You married me for my looks, is that what you're saying?"

"No, honey, I married you for your amazingly fast puns. That was what did it for me all those years ago in the teacher's lounge."

"Anyway, don't worry about him, he has to do the laundry, so if he pelts me with that tomato, he'll have to clean the stain out."

"Oh, that is true," Mr. Lewis says, placing the tomato down.

"It's really nice to see you both," I say. "I'm here permanently; I'm having a house built in the new Sticky Pines development." I lift our clasped hands to my mouth and kiss the back of Kellan's hand. "And yes, we're together." I want to say that we're together permanently, too, but since I haven't asked Kellan to marry me yet, I shouldn't speak for him.

"Ah, that's wonderful! You two always were a great little pair," Mr. Lewis says.

Mr. Pickles gives us a big smile. "Yes, now, what can we get you to eat? Wait, before my husband interrupts your order, he would like to invite you over for dinner sometime soon. I know this because, we've been together for twenty years, and I know him better than anyone else. Now, before you accept, just know that we are going on a trip to Mexico in two months, if you wait until after that, the entire visit will be spent looking at pictures from our trip to Mexico. So, if you don't want to hear about Javier, our pool guy, and his speedo, call us sooner rather than later." He turns toward Mr. Lewis. "Is that about right?"

Mr. Lewis laughs, kissing him on the cheek. "Yes, that's exactly right, but who wouldn't want to hear about Javier and his banana hammock?"

Mr. Pickles holds a hand up. "Bup, bup, no more, Barry. Now, what kind of burgers do you guys want?"

I feel Kellan's hand inside my back pocket, he's squeezing my cheek firmly. His touch sends a direct message to my dick, one that I need to cut off until we head back to his place. "I'm that kind of hungry too, let's just order quickly," I tell him.

We place our order and finish up our conversation with our former teachers. "Do you want to sit down over there and eat?" I ask him.

He's shaking his head no at me, while his eyes are scanning the parking areas. "Where did you park?" he asks.

"Over that way, near the shop," I say, pointing.

"Let's just eat while we walk. I really want to show you the surprise," he says, giving my ass another squeeze. I'm so curious what the surprise is. Is it sexual? He's giving me bedroom eyes, and feeling my ass up, so odds are that it is, but maybe it's not? Either way, I need to get *my* surprises into the condo without him seeing.

We take our burgers and head for the parking area. "Wow, this is the best burger I've ever had. This was a good choice," I say.

"Mmmmm," Kellan answers, his burger is nearly gone already. He must have been starving. He looks lost in thought. He gets this far off look in his eyes when he's really weighing some kind of a decision, he did that when we were younger, too.

I can't say I'm really all that hungry right now, because all I can think about is hiding Kellan's surprises from him, and worrying that he might see them before I can do what I want to. I mean I also want to go to sleep, because I'm really tired, and there's another part of me that wants to bring him inside and completely ravage him. I'm not sure which feeling is the strongest right now. I guess we'll see when we get there.

Kellan opens the door to his condo, and I follow behind. Both my front pockets contain a surprise for him, and the one on the left is crinkling a bit, so hopefully he doesn't try and feel me up, or ask why there's a noise coming from my pants. I stretch and let out a yawn. I'm so tired. Mister Fluffykins runs over to greet me. Shit, I can't bend down without my pocket making noise, and the other thing is going to make a noticeable bulge if I squat down.

"Okay, stay here," Kellan says, walking toward the bedroom.

"Oooh, mysterious, I like it." I wait until he's out of earshot and quickly empty my pockets, sticking the surprises inside the couch cushions. Then I bend down and pick Fluffykins up. "There you are! Did you miss me? I'm sorry I didn't pick you up as soon as I saw you. I have a surprise that I need to talk to you about, it's inside the couch. Do you like it here with Senator Tunacan? Do you want to have another daddy?"

I hear Kellan's footsteps coming around the corner. I kiss Fluffykins on the head and place him down. He's heading straight for the couch. I should stop him from going over there, but Kellan is standing in the hallway smiling at me. "Are you ready for your surprise?" he asks.

He's not naked, which is admittedly a slight relief, because as soon as I got in my Jeep, I realized exactly how tired I actually am.

"I'm ready! What's the surprise?" I ask, walking toward him. If I can get him into the bedroom, it won't matter what Fluffy does, because I can just move the stuff in a few minutes.

He stands under the door frame of his bedroom, and I walk toward him. "You smell like peppermint; I can smell you from over here. Did you bring a peppermint stick home? Is that the surprise?" I ask.

He laughs. "No, it's not a peppermint stick. I just brushed my teeth. I had cheeseburger breath."

"Wait, if you brushed your teeth, I'm going to do that, too. Should I wait until after the surprise? Or brush them now?"

"That's up to you. I don't mind your cheeseburger breath, I just didn't want you to taste mine."

"Oh, forget that. If you're even thinking this surprise is going to lead to my mouth against yours, I'm gonna go brush. I need to use the bathroom anyway. I'll be right back." He steps outside of the doorway, and I walk quickly into the bathroom.

"Keep walking," he says, "no peeking."

I brush my teeth, wondering if I should abandon what I had planned for tonight, but catch a glimpse of myself in the mirror. I scold myself for even thinking of chickening out. I love Kellan, and I know that he loves me. He's going to love it; I have nothing to be afraid of. Oh my God, I forgot about the couch! I finish brushing and gargle with mouthwash. I really hope the cats don't ruin the surprise.

As I open the bathroom door, I see Kellan standing in the doorway. His eyes are closed, and he's holding a small bundle of mistletoe over his head. "It's time for our Christmas kiss," he says.

"Aww you got real mistletoe?! For us?"

I walk toward him and pull him into a hug, pressing my lips against his. Our tongues touch gently, meeting in the softest, most tender kiss we've ever shared. I love this man so wholly and completely.

"I love this surprise," I say, breaking from the kiss.

"I know you were disappointed that we didn't get to—"

The sound of a wrapper crinkling interrupts whatever he was going to say. Shit, I didn't think they'd be able to pull the bag out. The other thing is safe, they can't pull that out.

"What's that sound?" Kellan asks. He walks into the living room, and I follow behind, wincing.

Mister Fluffykins and Senator Tunacan are on the couch cushion pawing at the bag.

"Gummy worms!" Kellan shouts. "You got me gummy worms? They're all red and clear ones! Where did you get these?" he asks, taking the bag away, to the cat's dismay.

This moment was entirely worth the extra thirty-minute drive to the candy shop. His face is lit up brighter than the Christmas tree, which is shining brightly, thanks to the timer. The blue lights reflect in his eyes, and I want nothing more than to pull that box out from inside the cushions, and do this thing, right now.

You know what? Screw the plan. I sit on the couch beside him, while he opens the bag of gummy worms.

"Kellan," I say. I hold his free hand in mine. "The past two weeks have been the best two weeks of my life. I always knew something was missing, and had no idea what it was until the day that my nonna called me. On that day, every single feeling that I felt for you came rushing back to me. I should have been worried about money, or housing, or running a cookie shop, but I wasn't. The only thing I was thinking about was coming home to you. I couldn't make sense of it at the time, but in that initial moment when she asked if I wanted to take over—I thought of you. I knew that I'd be coming back home—coming back for you. You have always been my solace, my comfort and the thing that I want to protect the most in this world. I never want to be without you again. I want to spend the rest of my life making you happy.

I slide my hand inside the cushion and pull out the small box. A few tears build in the corner of my eyes. I don't usually cry, but I can't help it. I shift to the floor onto one knee, opening the box to reveal a gold ring. "I promise to keep your feet warm for the rest of our lives. I'll clean, and bake you cookies, and treat you like the princess that you are. Will you marry me?"

Epilogue
Everything is Perfect

 Kellan

"Can you put the cookies on a plate?" my husband asks me.

Husband. I love that word. I love it so much.

When he proposed to me last year, we were ready to get married on the spot, but we knew we wanted to do it right and make it extra special, so we held off. Until two days ago at this year's Snowflake Festival. Now it's Christmas Day and we're newlyweds.

It often felt like the whole town was invested in our romance, so we made our wedding public, happening just before this year's festival started. It was optional and people could come if they wanted.

Everyone came. Literally everyone.

I wore a glittery Snowflake Princess sweater—a new one that fits me better but is just as gaudy as the original—and Braden wore a Snowflake Prince sweater, equally gaudy. The minister from the community church performed the ceremony. And in a surprise to us, the choir sang all the wedding songs for us.

The Snowflake Festival was more magical than it had ever been. It's a place where magic happens, and what is love if not magic?

I open the cupboard and pull down the gold serving platter we bought for events like this. I line it with a variety of carefully decorated cookies that Braden spent all day yesterday making. I cross the kitchen—*our kitchen*—and give my husband a kiss.

"I love you," I say, giving him a little pat on the butt.

"I love you, too. I'll be right out." He's stirring a big pot of mulled wine, and it's filling the house—*our house*—with a heavenly aroma.

I take the platter and pass through the doorway into the living room where I find our families and friends having a wonderful time. My parents, his parents, Charlie and Claude, Chad and Lucas (who are showing off their engagement rings), and Geoff and his new boyfriend Zach, fill our cozy, festive space.

The only person missing is Leora. She attended our wedding—we had to flip a coin for who got to claim her as best woman and, in the end, we decided she would be best woman for both of us. She's really enjoying retirement—both from BJ's Cookies and from being Snowflake Princess. She still helps out at the shop regularly, but she has more freedom now. Yesterday, after giving us all Christmas hugs, she hopped on a plane with her new boyfriend, Rupert, and they flew to Aruba for a month.

"I have cookies!" I announce. I place the large platter in the middle of the glass coffee table in the center of the room and everyone oohs and ahhs over them before promptly grabbing a cookie and munching down.

"And I have mulled wine!" Braden announces as he comes up behind me. He puts a silicone mat down first and then the hot pot on top of it. He dishes out mugs of wine and starts passing them around.

After hours of conversation, laughs, and hugs, our friends and family cajole us into standing in front of the tree for a photo. We're wearing matching sweaters with HUSBAND spelled out in rhinestones. As if on cue, Senator Tunacan and Mister Fluffykins come barreling into the room, and we scoop them up—The Senator in my hands and Fluffykins in his.

We pose in front of the tree, our little family of four.

Our loved ones take photos and promise to text them to us so we have them for our memory book. But before everyone can wander off back into their conversations, I corral them all in front of the tree for a group photo.

"What's this?" Chad says, poking a dick-shaped ornament.

"It's to remember the dildo tree," I tell him, earning a laugh from everyone.

"Definitely not a Max Girth 4000," my mom says, a little private joke between us.

We've got the tree decked out with a number of ornaments that have meaning to us—ones shaped like cookies, others like candles, little dicks, glittery princesses, and orange cats. But the best memory we have for ourselves and our love—other than being married—is our house. I moved in as soon as Braden did, and we quickly made this place *ours*. Nothing brings me more peace than coming home with Braden, cuddling with our cats, and enjoying our time together. And occasionally we go in the bedroom and close the door, so the cats give us privacy while their dads get up to things they're not meant to see.

"Now, group photo," I say, bringing everyone's attention back to the task at hand. "I want everyone we care about in this picture."

"But Leora's not here," Charlie says.

"Oh, shoot, I forgot!" Braden says. He hurries out of the room, to everyone's confusion. A moment later, he re-enters with a life-size cardboard cut-out of Leora. "She sent this along so we wouldn't miss her this Christmas. She glued the rhinestones on to make it more lifelike."

"It's perfect," Belinda says.

Braden sets the cut-out up at the back of the group where it can still be seen, as if she's here in the room with us. I get on my knees in front of the group, Tunacan in my hands, and Braden gets on his knees next to me, Fluffykins in his. Behind us are our parents, and surrounding them are some of our dearest family and friends.

"Ready?" I say. "The counter is going! Five…four…three…smile like you just got railed…"

The phone flashes at us as it snaps a photo. Everyone's face is breaking out in laughter. Just the way I want it.

Perfect.

Everything is perfect.

I lean over and kiss Braden. Between us, our cats boop noses with each other.

"I love you," I say, "forever and always."

"Always and forever," he says. "I love you, too."

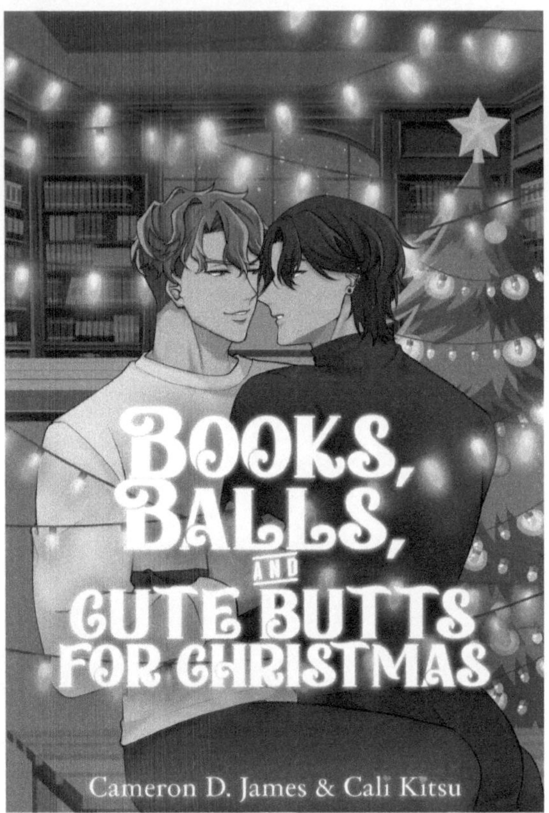

Books, Balls, and Cute Butts for Christmas
Cameron D. James & Cali Kitsu

Frosty Bottoms, Vermont, is home of the largest Christmas festival on the east coast and the state's hottest gay bar, Bottoms Up.

Two months ago, at the bar's Halloween party, a wolf with abs like Adonis had a scorching hot hookup in the men's room with a sexy, tattooed mouse. Now that Christmas is almost here, the burning embers of that night come roaring back to life.

International soccer superstar Jacob Rizzo is hiding out in

Frosty Bottoms after being suspended for punching a referee. Laying low during his suspension, he starts up a contracting business, doing odd jobs for the locals, who've agreed to keep his whereabouts a secret.

Twilight-obsessed bookseller Edward Kane is moving to Frosty Bottoms to open Hot for Plot, a new romance bookstore. With the help of his bartender brother, he hires a contractor to bring his dream shop to life. Between the contractor's sexy voice on their daily calls and his brother's teasing about how hot he is, Edward can't wait to meet him.

Despite wanting to make a good first impression, when the two finally meet, Edward ends up face first against Jacob's bulge. Jacob instantly recognizes the top of that head: it's the mouse from Halloween. But Edward has no idea they've met before.

Jacob is everything Edward is not—athletic, confident, and soccer-obsessed—while Edward is quiet, dresses in emo blacks, and hopelessly romantic. They couldn't be more opposite. While Jacob is certain he can't ever have a relationship, Edward carries around a personal Book Boyfriend List.

Playful teasing soon ignites into a secret holiday romance amid the town's glittering Snowflake Festival. But if the media discovers Jacob's hiding place it will mean the end of his privacy and the quiet life he's built in Frosty Bottoms.

Books, Balls, and Cute Butts for Christmas **is a high-heat MM romance filled with potent pineapple juice, a book boyfriend auction, and a foul-mouthed parrot.**

More from Cameron D. James

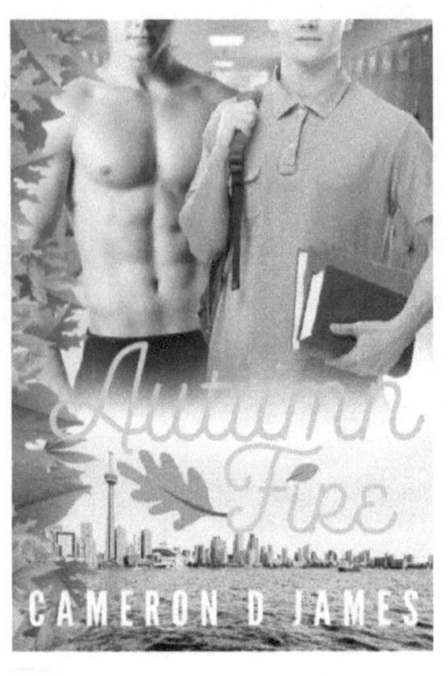

Autumn Fire
Cameron D. James

True gay love is a fairy tale. No matter what everyone says, that's what Dustin firmly believes. As he starts his first year of university, Dustin is happy in the closet, where he can meet his gay needs secretly through anonymous hookups.

But when Dustin has his first hookup of the university term, with a muscular dark-eyed jock in the library men's room, he can't help notice the deep and immediate connection he feels, one that seems almost like love. It's over as quickly as it begins and, as all anonymous hookups go, Dustin never expects to see him again.

The term gets difficult, especially when his math class begins. Dustin destresses with more hookups, but they don't sate him the way they used to, and he finds he cannot stop thinking about his start-of-term encounter. Soon, his academic needs outweigh the sexual, and Dustin caves in and gets a tutor.

Attractive, well-built, dark-eyed…and a jock, his new tutor, Kyle, is none other than his anonymous hookup from the men's room. Fate seems to have connected him to the man of his dreams.

Or maybe not, since Kyle is even more in the closet than Dustin is.

MORE FROM CALI KITSU

Vincent & Sivan: Book 1: Rum-Soaked Awakenings
Cali Kitsu

Vincent & Sivan is an explicit, best-friends-to-lovers, dual gay awakening, adult MM romance novel.

Vincent and Sivan, sons of the world's most powerful pirates, are to be named captains this year, an honor for when they turn twenty-one. Under their fathers, they will rule in the modern age of pirates where the seas are at peace and long gone are the days of pillaging and plundering.

Best friends since childhood, they couldn't have more opposite views on love. Vincent wants to settle down with the right person, despite pressure from his father to marry once he's named captain. Sivan, however, finds the idea of love and marriage laughable.

Reunited after months apart as their fathers' ships patrolled opposite ends of the seas, Vincent and Sivan share a bottle of rum in the ship's storage room. A moment of curiosity steeped in hidden desire, filthy with lust, leads to a very hot and heavy night of rum-soaked awakenings…

But no one can know about this, no one can find out, or their promotions as captains, and the trust of their fathers, may be altogether shattered.

Vincent and Sivan are thrust into a world of secrets and betrayal, as their crews now face a long-buried threat when those determined to bring back the old ways of pirates emerge from the shadows.

About the Authors

Cameron D. James and Cali Kitsu are besties who couldn't wait to team up to bring you the smuttiest Christmas book ever.

Cameron is the spicy gay romance pen name for Craig, who is publisher at Deep Desires Press. He also writes queer young adult romance as Dylan James.

Cali is executive assistant at Deep Desires Press, and an author of both spicy gay romance and steamy gay young adult romance.

You can listen to both of them on the Cali & Craig Talk… podcast, where they talk about books, butts, and everything in between.

When they're not writing or podcasting, these besties can often be found baking, playing Stardew Valley, or just chatting over some coffee.

Also By The Authors

Cameron D. James

Cookies, Candles, and Cute Butts for Christmas
Books, Balls, and Cute Butts for Christmas
New York Heat
Silent Hearts
Autumn Fire

Cali Kitsu

Cookies, Candles, and Cute Butts for Christmas
Books, Balls, and Cute Butts for Christmas
Froderick, Gay Son of Dracula
You Can Call Me Cooper
You Can Call Me Cooper: Author's Cut
Only My Husband Calls Me Cooper
Vincent & Sivan: Book 1: Rum-Soaked Awakenings